Katherine Dyson studied Crea[...] Leeds and worked as a mark[...] card verse writer for over fift[...] back to fiction. These days she works as a teaching assistant in a reception class by day, and by night she writes uplifting stories about love, everyday heartbreak, and the common joys and fragilities which make us human.

Katherine lives on the outskirts of Barnsley with her husband, two children and two belligerent cats. When she's not writing you'll find her merrily eating cake, swearing at her sewing machine or taking eight million photos of a really good sky out of her bathroom window.

Also by Katherine Dyson

Lily Bennett's Bucket List

EVA MALLORY'S HUSBAND HUNT

KATHERINE DYSON

One More Chapter
a division of HarperCollins*Publishers*
1 London Bridge Street
London SE1 9GF
www.harpercollins.co.uk

HarperCollins*Publishers*
Macken House, 39/40 Mayor Street Upper,
Dublin 1, D01 C9W8
This paperback edition 2023
1
First published in Great Britain in ebook format
by HarperCollins*Publishers* 2023

A catalogue record of this book is available from the British Library

ISBN: 978-0-00-853200-0

This novel is entirely a work of fiction. The names, characters and incidents portrayed in it are the work of the author's imagination. Any resemblance to actual persons, living or dead, events or localities is entirely coincidental.

Printed and bound in the UK using 100% Renewable Electricity
by CPI Group (UK) Ltd

For all teachers, but particularly mine.
Mrs Bateman, Mrs Frobisher, Mrs Hegarty, Mr Todd.
Mrs Newns, the first person who made me believe I could be a writer.
And Mr Brown and LJL, for everything.

Mr B, you told me to dedicate something to you one day. Here it is.

Chapter One

There were a few ways that Eva had imagined she might mess up her twin sister's anniversary party. Something like calling her sister's husband by Hanna's ex-girlfriend's name, or a poorly timed sneezing fit, perhaps. Unavoidable lateness, that was an old favourite, though it didn't seem nearly grand enough for the occasion.

She didn't imagine, not even for a second, that there was a chance she would have ruined the day with a bit of casual arson. That hadn't been on her list at all.

And yet here she was, standing in the car park of a beautiful four-star hotel with her equally bewildered family, each wrapped in a foil blanket, as a paramedic nodded sagely at Ciocia Irenka's bilingual ranting and held an oxygen mask firmly to her face. In the background, small licks of flame fought the flow of the firefighters' hoses as smoke spiralled up the old stone walls and spat small flecks of ash at the assembled crowds from high up in the sky.

It would probably have been fair to say that Eva was

shocked at how the day's events had unfolded, but she wasn't *surprised*. Not one bit.

Because she, Eva Mallory, was the unluckiest woman in the world.

It had all started with her great-grandfather, Jozef Mallory. He'd been Jozef Malinowski in those days, but, exiled from his home country in a post-war resettlement camp and still reeling from the years of horror he'd endured, he'd set about the process of changing his surname.

He'd told his family that it was because he wanted them to fit into the land they'd unexpectedly found themselves permanent citizens of. And maybe that was the reason, in part. It was a good enough reason as any. Certainly as good as trying to escape from a past that he could never have made his peace with.

He'd seen it on a street sign on the bus ride to the registry office.

Mallory Avenue.

It had seemed like fate, like a sign from God or something like that, that his eyes had darted towards the sign at just the right time to see it, and how he'd noticed the similarity between Mallory and Malinowski quickly enough to scribble it down in the small leather-bound journal that he always carried.

'Jozef Mallory,' he'd repeated to himself in a strongly accented whisper, a huge smile spreading across his face as his mind whirled with the possibilities of this bold new beginning.

Two weeks later he was dead.

How could he have known, with barely enough English to get by, that he had chosen to saddle his family with a name which literally meant *unlucky*?

How could he have known, on that crisp winter morning, that decades later his great-granddaughter would not be a bit surprised that she'd accidentally burned down a hotel because she had become so accustomed to a life of back-to-back misfortunes?

'It was me,' Eva blurted, trying her hardest to maintain eye contact with the dark-haired police officer who was taking her statement. 'I did it. There was a candle on our table, and I think my necklace or maybe my handbag might have caught on the tablecloth, because when I stood up to leave, everything was fine, and then I looked back two minutes later and the whole table was in flames.' The smallest of sobs crept up her throat. 'Are you going to arrest me?'

'Don't worry, Miss Mallory,' the officer replied, his brows nipping into a frown. 'You're not under suspicion.' He scribbled in his notebook for a few more moments before shoving it, along with his pen, into a pocket. 'There'll be an investigation, of course, but from the other witness statements it's clear to me that this was an accident.' A small smile softened the hard lines of his face. 'Just a bit of bad luck.'

Try an entire lifetime of bad luck, Eva wanted to say, but she didn't. She didn't think it wise, not with how she'd just escaped a criminal record. Instead she returned the officer's smile and thanked him, noticing how her words made his smile widen, just a little, and how that seemed to transform his entire face.

He was handsome, she thought to herself, but she didn't voice that either, just nodded once and turned back to her family, now huddling like foil-wrapped potatoes on a fire.

'How long do we have to stay?' her sister was asking as Eva re-joined the group. At that, their mother's eyes darted towards Ciocia Irenka, still giving the paramedic an entirely misdirected piece of her mind. 'Can we leave her here?'

Eva couldn't help but smile at her tone. Hanna had always been the outspoken twin.

Their mother found no such amusement. 'Hanna!'

'Can we though?' Hanna's voice was strained, as if she were fighting a tut, and there was a certain fury to the way she stomped at the ground. 'She'll be fine, you know what she's like.'

Irenka, their paternal great-aunt, had been on the brink of expiring the entire time the twins had been alive, but was much too stubborn to actually die. She liked instead to flirt with the afterlife, occasionally going almost all the way into the light before suddenly and dramatically recovering from her deathbed, doling out insults like Halloween sweets as her family, once again, relaxed their vigil.

'We can stay,' said a steady voice to Eva's right, and that made her smile, too. Hanna's husband Owen was a good egg. It helped that he had not yet been subjected to one of Ciocia Irenka's near-death jaunts, and as such had significantly more sympathy for her than the average member of the family.

Hanna shot her husband a look but softened almost immediately, still firmly in the grip of the honeymoon phase at 364 days of marriage. 'Fine,' she huffed, no edge to it this time. 'We can stay.' She tightened her foil blanket around herself, a smirk creeping onto her face. 'But can we at least talk about how Eva just nearly got arrested for burning down a stately home.'

'Hanna!' Eva shrieked in reply, sounding much more like her mother than she'd like. 'It is *not* a stately home. And I'm not getting arrested, the policeman said so.' Her anxiety about the whole situation hadn't lessened any, and she started to feel the familiar grip of it around her throat. 'Plus it wasn't even my fault. It was the curse.'

Sylvia laughed a little, tightening her own foil blanket even thought it was early evening on a perfectly mild August day, nowhere close to being cold. 'Oh my God, Eevs, I forgot about the curse!'

They all looked at her then, all at once; Eva's mother and her mother's German husband, Hanna and Owen, and sweet old Ciocia Nelka, all with varying degrees of concern on their faces as Eva herself spiralled into a pit of confusion.

'You forgot?' she asked, the words clumsy and slow. The very idea was incomprehensible. The curse sank its icy fingers into every day of Eva's life. In fact, she couldn't think of a single day – not one – where something hadn't gone wrong.

She looked up and five expectant faces looked back, each hovering a different distance between intrigued and concerned.

Like always, it was Hanna who broke the silence. 'You know,' she said, tucking a strand of her perfectly curled dark hair behind one ear, 'I feel like I've had much less bad luck this year.' Her eyes moved to her husband, who shrugged gently back at her. 'I can't remember the last time something even went wrong.' The smirk returned, and she motioned to the smouldering wall of the hotel behind them. 'Except for this whole business, *obviously*.'

'You broke the curse,' Sylvia said, her voice quiet and confident as she pushed her purple-rimmed glasses up her face with the heel of her hand. 'It was the same for me when I married Stefan. Everything just started'—she shrugged, as if searching for the right words—'going to plan.'

Eva couldn't process what was happening. 'But bad things still happen, *all* the time.' She motioned to the smoking mess behind her. 'I mean—'

'It's you,' Hanna interrupted. 'Bad things happen when *you're* with us. When you're not here, everything's gravy.'

Sweet old Ciocia Nelka, who hadn't said a word up until then, straightened up to her full height of not-quite five feet. 'Gravy is good, yes?'

'Yes, ciocia,' Owen said with a smile, resting a hand on her foil-covered shoulder. 'Gravy is good.'

Ordinarily, Eva would have been cheered by her elderly great-aunt's unexpected knowledge of slightly out-of-date slang, but at that particular moment she was feeling much too discombobulated to even react.

'Are you saying'—she almost couldn't get the words out—'that it's just…'

Sylvia's mouth hitched into a smile. 'Gone?'

'Well, for us it's gone.' Hanna stretched her arms out aimlessly, the foil blanket crinkling and creasing as she did. 'It's the Mallory curse. You're the only Mallory left. Well, you and Ciocia Irenka, but I doubt *she's* cursed.' One of her immaculately groomed eyebrows lifted. 'She's the one who curses.'

Eva felt her blood run cold, a shiver which started at the base of her neck and then crawled outwards, down her arms and around her ribcage. A secret she'd been suppressing suddenly sank sharp claws into the pit of her stomach.

Because there had been a time when she hadn't been a Mallory either. She'd changed her name once, by deed poll, when she was barely out of her teens. She'd chosen Smith, figuring that there were so many Smiths in the world that they couldn't all be either lucky or unlucky. A Smith curse would surely already have spelled disaster for the whole population.

So she walked out of the registry office one day as Eva Smith, and on that very day, her father dropped dead.

There was nothing they could have done, Sylvia had told the girls. No way they could have known. It was just one of those things.

Just random chance.

But Eva didn't believe in random chance. Only in the curse. And the curse, she was quite sure, was what had actually killed her father. That, and the fact that she had tried to outsmart it. Which meant, of course, all added up, that there was only one possible conclusion that a young Eva could possibly have come to.

She had killed her dad.

She changed her name back the day after his funeral, never telling a single other soul about the change while she submitted to a life of bad luck and small annoyances. It had been her penance, an extra weight draped across her shoulders as a reminder that she couldn't side-step the curse, nor could she outrun it.

It was here to stay.

At least, that was what she'd thought for the remainder of her thirty-one years.

But her mother had escaped the curse, and now so had her sister. Which must mean, she reasoned, her brain frantically grasping at ideas while her family looked at her with expressions of increasing concern, that it wasn't the change of name that the curse had objected to, but the fact that she had cheated fate.

It all made perfect sense in Eva's mind. She believed

wholeheartedly in such things, in fate and in chance. In the stars lining up, and conversely, in bad omens and destiny, whichever way the needle spun. But Eva was also a teacher, and she knew enough primary school level maths to know that in a sample size of three, two good outcomes was not something to ignore. And in their sample size of three, one of those things had not been like the others.

Which all added together to give one hypothesis: that the curse must see changing your name by deed poll as cheating, because taking someone's name in marriage was, thus far, the only known way to break the curse.

She sucked in a breath, holding it a moment before exhaling slowly and looking back up at her family, all now looking at her expectantly, blue lights flashing reflections in their silver capes. And in that moment, in the ridiculousness of that situation, she knew exactly what she had to do.

She didn't need to live in the shadow of the curse at all.

What she needed was a *husband*.

And fast.

Chapter Two

'A husband?' Ciocia Irenka shrieked from the wingback chair in her living room later that evening. 'Kochanie, we did not think it would ever happen. Did we, Nelka?' She looked over at her sister, perched like a tiny, delicate bird on the ageing sofa opposite, before looking back at Eva with a single eyebrow raised. 'Nelka has sold her hat.'

Ciocia Nelka waved her away, always hating to make a fuss. 'I can buy another one.'

'You always go straight to the hats.' Eva chuckled. 'I have to find him first.'

Ciocia Irenka did not acknowledge her words at all, just stuck steadfastly to her train of thought. 'At your age we thought you were the other kind, you know? Hitting at the other players? How you say?'

'Batting for the other team,' Stefan said, calmly, his accent clipping the tone of his perfect English.

Eva rolled her eyes.

Irenka ignored him completely. But that was nothing new.

She consistently refused to acknowledge Stefan's presence on account of him being German.

'There was a *war*, kochanie,' she'd said to Sylvia the first time the ciocias had met him, Irenka's brows drawn into a heavy line above her eyes. 'I don't know if you heard of it?'

'He wasn't even alive in the war,' Sylvia had replied, with the patience of a saint. Dealing with Irenka demanded such a thing.

Stefan had smiled, his manners impeccable. 'I wasn't born until 1958,' he'd offered, with a docile shrug, but Irenka had pretended she hadn't heard him at all, a habit she had stuck to faithfully ever since.

'There was maybe no war for you,' the old woman had said, addressing Sylvia. 'And there was maybe no war for *him*.' Her nose had crinkled in disgust at the acknowledgement, though she hadn't even looked Stefan's way. 'For us, there was a war.'

'It's OK,' Stefan had said then, to his future wife. 'I understand.'

And that had set the tone for their entire relationship. Irenka, though she had never directly acknowledged a single word Stefan had ever said to her, had not complained about his presence once since that first time, and Stefan, endlessly respectful and persistent, had never stopped talking to the older woman as if nothing at all was wrong.

'Batting for the other team, Irenka,' Ciocia Nelka parroted eventually, the self-appointed go-between for the two of them.

'Yes, *Nelka*,' Ciocia Irenka replied, stressing her sister's name as she always did whenever she was actually replying to Stefan. 'That is just what I am saying.'

Eva sighed. 'I'm single, ciocia, I'm not gay.'

'And even if she was,' Hanna piped up from across the room, legs draped over the arm of one sofa. 'It's not against the law.'

Ciocia Irenka's false teeth flew clean out of her mouth in shock. 'It's not?!'

'Irenka!' Nelka scolded gently, her brow tugging into as much of a frown as her temperament would allow. In truth both of the sisters were at least forty years behind modern thinking and values, but Ciocia Nelka, to her credit, at least knew well enough to be quiet.

Hanna sank her head back against the sofa cushions, doing a very poor job of hiding her rage. She'd dated a number of girls in the past who her old great-aunts had consistently refused to acknowledge as her girlfriends, referring to them instead as some variation of 'your lovely friend'.

Irenka tutted loudly as she searched her lap for her dentures, eventually popping them back in with an unholy slurp which only seemed to rile Hanna even more.

'Urgh, you know very well that it's not. We've been through this.'

Sylvia coughed once from across the room, raising one eyebrow as she caught her daughter's eye.

Hanna begrudging relented. 'Anyway, we were talking about Eva. Who *isn't* gay. But is horrifyingly single.'

In an instant, Ciocia Nelka's eyes lit up. 'Oh, we can help!'

'Oh no.' Hanna snorted a laugh. 'I'm not sure *your* help is what she needs.'

But maybe, Eva thought to herself, sitting on her great-aunt's ancient woven footstool with the acrid taste of smoke still at the back of her throat, it was.

Maybe that was *exactly* what she needed.

She'd had a few overwhelmingly disastrous romantic encounters in her youth, and some less frequent but no less disastrous flings more recently, but she'd always shied away from the idea of settling down. The truth was that she just couldn't face the idea of condemning any of her hypothetical loved ones to a life with the Mallory curse. But, if the curse could theoretically be lifted, then maybe that was less of an issue than she imagined.

Which meant that maybe she had a shot at happiness after all.

And, let's face it, at the speed she was hoping to find *and* wed said husband, she was going to need all the assistance she could get.

'I'd love your help, Ciocia Nelka,' she said, breaking into a huge and hopeful smile. 'I'd love everyone's help, actually. Consider this "Mission: Get Eva Married"!'

Four faces lit up in response.

Ciocia Irenka's face rarely moved from light disdain and today was no different.

And Eva's twin sister was looking at her as if she had fully lost her mind.

'Eevs,' Hanna said, almost carefully, as if the wrong word might cause a complete meltdown. 'I've got a couple of people I can set you up with. Are you sure that'—she lowered her voice, casting a glance around the assembled family members —'putting yourself *out to tender* is what you want? What if it's a catastrophe?'

Eva couldn't help but laugh. 'Han, my entire life has been one catastrophe after another. What's another disaster or two to add to the pile?'

'She's not wrong,' their mother piped up from across the

room, delight in her eyes the like of which Eva had rarely seen before. Sylvia had been gagging to matchmake her youngest daughter for the majority of Eva's adult life.

And after that all hell broke loose.

'I've got a friend you might like,' Owen offered, with a shrug.

Stefan nodded along. 'My nephew is single, and *very* handsome.'

'Is that incest?' Hanna muttered, before being lightly elbowed in the ribs by her mother.

'No, it's not incest, for goodness' sake,' Sylvia whisper-shouted, before abruptly changing her tone and chirping, 'Eevs, I have so many ideas about where we can find you a date!'

Ciocia Nelka smiled so widely that her eyes vanished from sight entirely, but she didn't say anything. No doubt she was mentally compiling a list of young, eligible Polish bachelors who frequented the Sunday morning mass she liked and might be open to taking a wife.

Only Ciocia Irenka was silent, casting her cool grey eyes over her assembled family members as age-worn fingers thumbed the buttons of her cardigan.

'That is not how love works,' she said, after a pause, her eyes narrowing at nobody in particular. 'You cannot *arrange* a marriage.'

Hanna huffed a laugh. 'You literally can. Half the world does exactly that.'

The old woman's undirected glare snapped immediately to Hanna. 'I'm not saying what *half the world* does. I'm saying only what I know.' Her accent caught at her words, adding extra consonants where they did not belong. 'That love comes when it wants to, like English buses. You cannot make it here sooner or to stop when it turns up.'

Nobody said anything for a moment, shocked, perhaps, as Eva was. Ciocia Irenka had never married, and Eva was not sure she had ever previously heard her great-aunt speak about love. She hadn't been entirely convinced the old woman was capable of such a thing.

It was Stefan who eventually broke the silence. 'That's actually very insightful.'

Ciocia Irenka, of course, ignored him completely, but her sister was there, as always, to relay his words.

'That's actually very insightful, Irenka.'

'Thank you, *Nelka*,' Irenka said, meeting her sister's gaze deliberately. 'You know, I *have* learned a thing or two in my life.'

And though Eva longed to be able to take Ciocia Irenka's advice, advice so rarely given, she already knew that she would be doing the exact opposite. Because, however much Eva supposed that after ninety-six years on the planet her great-aunt might be right, she didn't have the luxury of sitting around and waiting for a husband to turn up.

She needed to go out and flag one down right away.

It was pitch black when Eva got home, and she could tell by Lucky's strangled meows behind the door that it was later than she thought. Lucky got fed three times a day, at very specific times, and was *very* put out if those feeding times happened to stray a minute or two from the schedule he demanded.

Any more than an hour late, and Eva would need to sleep

with one eye open. When she'd adopted Lucky, named for the horseshoe-shaped patch of white on his otherwise entirely black coat, she'd had fanciful ideas of him being a talisman of sorts, but he'd turned out to be anything but. He was every bit as accident-prone as she was, and his hangriness knew no bounds.

She fed him quickly, so as not to incite any further rage on his part, kicked off her shoes, and plopped down on her olive-green sofa with an audible sigh.

It had been a hell of a day.

Like all the rest of them.

Between dropping her eyeliner brush down the toilet that morning and punching herself straight in the face while adjusting the strap on her bag, things had gone just exactly as she'd come to expect that things ever went. Though torching the venue for Hanna's anniversary meal and almost asphyxiating her elderly great-aunt was a little out of the ordinary, it probably said a lot about Eva's life that she wasn't even a little surprised by the whole affair.

But there was something else, something which had come as more of a shock. Some unfamiliar thread of hope, however small. An infinitesimal lifting of the weight across her shoulders. For the first time since her dad died, Eva felt like she had a real chance to escape the shadow of the curse. She wasn't even dreading the shower of total weirdos which her varying family members would inevitably set her up with, though she was a little worried about Ciocia Nelka's contributions.

Her phone buzzed with a message then, and she swiped to read it just as Lucky announced the completion of his meal via a series of increasingly loud yowls.

HANNA: OK, we've got your first husband candidate lined up. Are you free on Saturday?
EVA: Always.
HANNA: Then you're going on a date! Old friend of Owen's, I'll send you deets later.
EVA: That was quick!
HANNA: You wanted quick, no?
EVA: I guess.
HANNA: Don't overthink it. You'll get on like a house on fire.
EVA: …
HANNA: Too soon?
EVA: GOOD NIGHT HANNA.
HANNA: Night Eevs xx

Eva set her phone on the side table, unable to hold back the small smile pulling at her lips as she twisted her dark hair up into a loose bun. Her sister might be a first-class troll, but she never failed to come up with the goods. There were a million ways that Eva could imagine the date going horribly wrong, of course, but she wasn't going to let that stop her.

If she was being honest with herself she might have admitted to being a little concerned that her desperation was such that she would agree to marry the very first person who asked, regardless of whether she actually wanted to spend her life with him or not. But she decided that was a bridge she would cross if she came to it. For now she had to expend every ounce of her energy on finding potential husband candidates in the first place.

She would accept her family's matchmaking efforts where

they came, but she was very aware that they probably weren't to be counted on. She needed a plan of her own.

And so, with Lucky contentedly twisted into a softly purring pretzel in her lap, she set about on her search for the very best advice the internet had to offer.

How do people meet their spouse, she typed into the search engine, and clicked the first legitimate-looking link she came to, sliding on her reading glasses as she peered at the text on the screen.

Online, the first heading read, and her lip curled involuntarily away from her teeth as she scrolled through the information.

It was the modern way, she knew that, but there were a million potential red flags with internet dating which she just couldn't get past. With her luck she was bound to match with someone who kept their abducted trophy women in a soundproof bunker below their house or something similar. It just seemed safer to avoid the whole thing.

On a night out. Also hazardous, for the same kind of reasons.

Through family and friends. She smiled to herself, putting a mental tick in that box. Hanna had already come good on that front, and she had no doubt that the others would have no shortage of options for her, too. Of course, she couldn't rule out the very real possibility that the men in question might be completely horrifying, but she was willing to give them the benefit of the doubt. So far as she could see, she was not in a position to be fussy.

In the gym. Eva laughed out loud at that one. The last time she'd set foot inside a gym, she'd fallen off a stationary bike in a spinning class and broken both her wrists. That had been a dark time.

And then there was the last section.

At work.

Eva's instinct was to laugh at that suggestion too, but she didn't. It just seemed so unlikely. She'd taught at the same small primary school in the same area of suburban Leeds for the past ten years, and other than a brief crush she'd had on the peripatetic cello teacher, it had barely brought friendship into her life, let alone romance.

Her colleagues were overwhelmingly female but for Mr Myrtle, the year five teacher who was a stone's throw from retirement, and Monsieur Dubois, the overly flamboyant language lead. And when the cello teacher had failed to return after a low-key scandal in the regional choir event some years ago, she had mentally abandoned the idea of ever seeing the place as anything more than a place of employment. So finding love there seemed a bit of a non-starter.

Perhaps Mrs Abbott, the robust teaching assistant in Eva's class, could set up a date with one of her sons? Eva was sure they were around her age. She made a mental note to make subtle enquiries when they were in doing the back-to-school prep the following week.

She huffed a little to herself, disrupting Lucky, who wriggled and stretched in her lap. The internet had been no help. She was going to have to just see where her hunt took her.

Just hope for the best.

All while knowing that, inevitably, the universe would provide the worst.

Chapter Three

The evening of her first date arrived, not without incident of course, but Eva was well used to that. She'd planned to arrive an hour early, knowing that small misfortunes would inevitably delay her, as they always did. By the time she walked into the bar, albeit missing her umbrella and much of the thumbnail on her right hand, she was just about on time.

Hanna had chosen a bar a short walk from Eva's flat in Meanwood for that first meeting, and Eva fully expected her sister and brother-in-law to turn up at some point, probably in some kind of ridiculous disguise. It was quite a laid-back place, all bare wood and houseplants, with macramé hangings here and there among simple ink drawings of the bar itself in past times.

At the bar, three of the six wrought iron stools were occupied, though none of them, apparently, by Eva's date.

None of the people idly sipping craft beers and cocktails in the worn leather Chesterfield sofas appeared to be Eva's date either.

In fact, he was nowhere to be seen.

She checked her watch again, face falling into a frown. Three minutes past seven.

She wouldn't write him off right away, she decided, heading to the bar to offset her anxiety about being in the place alone, not to mention her pre-emptive hurt at the idea that she might have been stood up. Still, if anyone understood unexpected delays, it was Eva. She was the queen of them.

The bartender slid her drink towards her with a sombre nod, as if he might have read her mind, and she took it gratefully, scanning the room for an inconspicuous corner to sit in, before realising there were none. She hopped up on the furthest left of the bar stools instead, studying her phone in a weak attempt to feel less awkward as she hoped and prayed that Owen's friend would make an appearance.

Greg, that's what Hanna had said his name was. It seemed like a perfectly normal name, and the picture Owen had forwarded to them was nice enough too: just a reasonably good-looking man standing beside a landmark that she didn't recognise with a big, beaming smile on his face.

It would be fair to say that Eva was approaching the date, on the surface, with a healthy amount of cynicism, certainly the right amount for the unluckiest woman in the world, but bubbling beneath that was something altogether more positive: a deep-seated hope that this was it, that she might meet the love of her life tonight, and with that, her fortunes may just turn around.

She'd even gone so far as to dress up for the occasion, borrowing an emerald-green dress and heeled boots from Hanna, and allowing her sister to do her makeup – classic winged liner and ruby-red lips. She'd even freed her dark hair from its signature messy bun, and it hung in glossy waves down past her shoulder blades. She ran her fingers through the ends. She'd forgotten what it felt like to dress up, as opposed to her usual state of being half-covered in poster paint and playdough.

She scanned the bar one more time before turning her attention back to her phone, taking a long, slow sip of her drink as she tapped out a message to her sister.

EVA: He's a no-show at the moment.

EVA: Just my luck.

'Excuse me,' came a voice from beside her, so deep and smooth that for a moment she could do nothing but breathe, a knot of relief forming in her belly. 'Is anyone sitting here?'

Greg, her mind whispered, but when she turned to look, the man standing beside her bore no resemblance at all to the solid, outdoorsy man in the photo she'd seen. This man had deep russet hair where she had been expecting sandy brown, and his hazel eyes, a million miles from Greg's perfectly pleasant blue ones, reached deep into her chest as his mouth hitched into a smile, a grip on her throat so tight she felt as if she could barely breathe.

It was as if the earth had shifted a little, as if she were off-kilter now somehow, in a way that she couldn't quite explain. There was a buzz behind her breastbone which she wasn't sure she could explain away as mere nerves. It hadn't been there when she'd walked into the bar.

'Not at the moment,' she said, hoping she was smiling, but much too out of sorts to have full control over what her face was doing. 'I'm waiting for someone, but they haven't shown up yet.'

The dashing stranger's smirk widened into a full smile, and

that did strange things to Eva's insides too. 'A date?' he asked, and she didn't miss the slight raise of his eyebrow as he spoke.

An involuntary blush crept along her cheekbones. 'First date, actually.'

He nodded slowly, and his fingers went to his face, finding the light brush of stubble on his jaw. 'I see.'

There was something about his expression which riled her, or maybe it turned her on. She wasn't quite sure which. 'He's not that late.' She checked her watch. 'Only ten minutes. People get held up for all sorts of reasons.'

She knew it only too well.

He didn't say anything at that, just nodded again, and he didn't take his eyes off her either. It was driving her to distraction.

'You can sit if you want,' she said, desperately trying to come across as if she didn't care either way while also trying her hardest to tear her eyes away from the draw of his gaze. Her skin was on fire, goosebumps pricking at her arms and the back of her neck as her mind went straight to the gutter.

There was an intensity to his stare, those warm hazel eyes boring into her, undressing her. She coughed down a rush of emotion. It had been a long time since any man had looked at her like that.

He slid onto the stool beside her, and his scent hit her like a fist, fresh and warm and masculine. She needed to pull herself together.

'I'm waiting too,' he said, a lilt to his accent that she hadn't noticed before. Northern, for certain, and familiar in a way she couldn't quite place. 'I'm supposed to be meeting my friends here, but they're late.' There was a difference in his smile, then, the confidence replaced by something deeper. 'I should have known. Very unreliable.'

Eva couldn't help but laugh. 'My sister is the same way. We actually call it Hanna time. You have to tell her to be somewhere half an hour before you actually want her to arrive.' She sipped her drink and set it back carefully on the bar, wiping at the condensation on the glass with one thumb. 'We're twins, actually. But we couldn't be more different.'

He'd been watching her while she talked, his mouth falling a little way open, as if he were intoxicated by her, too. 'You have a twin?' he asked, a grate to his voice which made it at least twice as sexy.

Her heart leapt at the sound of it, and she smiled to herself as she took another sip. 'Cool it, Romeo. She's married.'

He shrugged, unapologetic. 'Just expressing my approval that there are two of you out in the world.'

It was definite. He was flirting with her. The most attractive man in the whole bar was flirting with her. She dug deep for whatever game she might possess while she quietly thanked the universe that she was looking her very best on this particular day.

'We're not identical.'

He raised an eyebrow. 'Shame.'

Another blush crept up her face. 'Maybe she's the hot one?'

That had been said before. Hanna was certainly the glamorous twin.

'Maybe.' He didn't break eye contact through a long sip of his beer, the purse of his lips around the bottle drawing her attention far more that it really ought to. And when he set his bottle back on the bar there was something different in his expression, something that made a warm shiver ripple its way down Eva's spine.

'What's that look for?' she asked, her voice little more than a whisper.

He huffed a little breath of a laugh. 'I was just thinking that there's no way in hell I'd stand you up.'

Her body roared to life, desire flaming in her belly. 'What about you? Your friends still not here?'

'No,' he said, mouth hitching into a smirk as he scanned the room. 'But they will be.' He snapped his gaze back to Eva. 'We're celebrating.'

'Celebrating?'

He nodded, slowly, the perfect curve of his smile turning her insides to molten metal.

She cleared her throat. 'Celebrating what?'

'I was offered a new job today.' His eyes lit up, and it made him look younger somehow. Younger and crushingly, *devastatingly* handsome.

Her chest tightened. 'Oh really?'

'Yep.' There was something like pride in his tone. 'I start next week.'

She couldn't help but smile in response. 'Congratulations.'

'Thank you.'

'What do you…' She tailed off. She had been curious to know what his new job was, what it was that had made his whole face brighten, but just then, at that exact moment, she spotted an almost-familiar figure over his shoulder. 'Oh crap.'

His brow furrowed. 'What?'

'I think my date is here.'

He checked his watch, raising an eyebrow dramatically. 'Only twenty-seven minutes late.'

She smirked. 'Your friends should be here soon, then.'

A laugh burst from him, his eyes dropping to her lips for a moment or two before they met hers again, dark and intense. 'Want to escape with me and pretend you were never here?'

Eva had rarely felt more conflicted in her life than deciding whether to blow off her carefully laid plans – not to mention *definitely* piss her sister off – just for the chance to spend more time with this alluring stranger.

She didn't even know his name.

But then she caught sight of Greg again, now casting panicked eyes around the bar, and her conscience kicked in, however hard her body was begging it not to. 'Urgh, I kind of do want to do that, but I can't.'

The stranger looked at her with fire in his eyes, and began to lean towards her. For a moment, she thought he was going to kiss her, but he didn't. Just brought his lips to her ear and whispered '*He's a lucky guy*', before sweeping off into the buzz of the bar, leaving Eva breathless.

But as it turned out, he wasn't.

Greg Wilson was, in fact, a very *unlucky* guy, even by Eva's standards.

He was still apologising for his delayed appearance an hour into their date, though Eva had thought it best to forgive him almost immediately after hearing the story of how a deer had run straight under the wheels of the train he was on, bringing it to a standstill just outside of the station for forty straight minutes, and all of this happening after his car, which he had originally planned to drive, had completely failed to start. It was definitely something that might have happened to her.

'This is just my life,' he'd said, a lopsided smile tugging at the corner of his mouth. 'I have the worst luck.'

That was the first red flag. Eva had enough catastrophes of her own. The last thing she needed was a share in someone else's.

The second red flag was when he said, some time later, that he thought marriage as a concept was flawed, and that he didn't need a piece of paper to prove that he loved someone. Eva respected it as a viewpoint, but it wasn't going to help her mission any. She idly wondered what the handsome stranger from the bar's views on marriage were, right before she accidentally caught his eye over the top of Greg's head. Now surrounded by his friends and clearly a few drinks in, he smiled and raised his glass at her.

She snatched her gaze away before Greg noticed, though couldn't help the small smile which pulled at the corner of her mouth as she did.

'What did you think about the—' Greg was saying, though as she looked back over at him, he accidentally inhaled a mouthful of his drink rather than swallowing it, and immediately launched into the most dramatic coughing fit that Eva had ever seen, which, considering that she had already worked with four-year-olds for a full decade, was really saying something.

She did her best to interpret his frantic signals, and after the ninth or tenth thump of his back his breathing seemed to settle a little. A few moments later, he sat back in his seat, smiling weakly over at her though streams of tears.

'Thank you,' he said, his voice still thick and awkward. 'God, I'm so embarrassed. Who chokes on *liquid*!?'

Eva did, all the time. And seeing as the man in front of

her appeared very much to be the male embodiment of her, she imagined that it was not an isolated incident for him, either.

'Don't worry about it,' she said, as gently as she could. 'These things happen.'

He smiled a response, though she noted that it didn't quite reach his eyes this time. 'I'm such an *idiot*,' he said, his brows tugging together. 'You must think so.'

Eva shook her head. 'Not at all.'

And that was the truth. But it was also, quite unfortunately, the third red flag. These things *did* happen. They happened to her all the time. And she simply couldn't face the idea of being with someone who couldn't take such misfortunes at least slightly in their stride.

Still, Greg seemed like a nice enough guy, and she did enjoy his company, so when he suggested another drink, she was happy to agree to it. And after that, when he asked if he could see her again, the tone of his voice told her that he had already knew that her answer would be no.

'I'm so sorry,' she said. 'Because you seem lovely, and I've really enjoyed tonight.'

His expression fell further, if that were possible.

'But I'm a really unlucky person,' she continued, with a shrug. 'And I've noticed that you are, too. I just don't think that it would be very wise for either of us to pool that bad luck.' She chuckled a little to herself. 'I'd be worried that the universe might implode or something.'

He looked a little cheered by that. 'You're unlucky too?'

'*So* unlucky,' she said, laughing again. 'Just on my way here this evening I tripped, twice, got my thumbnail caught in the button you press at a pelican crossing'—she held up her thumb, nail ripped off at the quick—'and I dropped my umbrella down a drain.'

'Down a *drain*?' His eyes widened, clearly unused to dealing with someone of similar fortunes.

She nodded. 'One of those metal grate ones in the road. Just slipped right down. Plop!' She laughed a little to herself. 'You wouldn't even have thought it would fit.'

He laughed too. 'That is unlucky.'

'That's me all over.'

'Same,' he said, acceptance in his voice, and then he reached a hand out just as she moved to hug him, and accidentally punched her in the stomach. 'Oh God, I'm sorry.'

'It's fine,' she replied, just a little winded, taking his outstretched hand and shaking it. 'It was lovely to meet you, Greg.'

He beamed. 'It was lovely to meet you, too. I hope that we both find ourselves more *fortunate* people to date in the future.'

She laughed at that, and as she said goodbye to Greg and watched him push back out of the door of the bar, her eyes darted to where she had last seen her handsome stranger.

He was nowhere to be seen.

'I take it he's one to cross off the list?' a familiar voice asked from the sofa next to hers, and Eva turned to see her sister, dressed fully in black, wearing gigantic sunglasses and the most ridiculous wig she'd even seen. She couldn't hold in her snort of laughter.

'Have you been there the whole time?'

Hanna removed her sunglasses theatrically. 'Long enough. Poor Greg.'

'Poor Greg,' Eva agreed, with a nod. 'He was nice.'

Hanna shook her head. 'Nice isn't going to cut it, Eevs. You need *mind-blowing*.'

'Mind-blowing?'

Hanna nodded, definitively. '*Eviscerating*.'

'Maybe not eviscerating,' Eva said, smiling at her sister. 'The way things go for me it'd be literal.'

Hanna huffed a breath out, putting her ridiculous sunglasses back on. 'I'm just saying that you should be with someone who makes you feel like you're on fire.' Her glossed lips cracked a smile. 'Ideally not *actual* fire though. You *have* got previous.'

Eva fixed her sister with a look, and it made Hanna laugh out loud.

'Come on, babycakes. I'll walk you home.'

And then the sisters linked arms and swept out of the bar, Hanna chatting about all the other avenues they had left to explore, while Eva made a mental note to cross anyone whose surname was Wilson off her list of potential husbands, just in case.

Not that her list was particularly long at the moment. In fact, it consisted of only one name.

Or at least it would, had she found out what his name actually *was*.

Oh, and the small matter that she was probably never going to see him again.

Just her luck.

Chapter Four

Eva's list of names did not stay short for long.

By the following Friday, between the efforts of Hanna, Stefan and Ciocia Nelka, it was running at eight names, and Eva couldn't resist trying to round up to ten as she sat sticking labels onto seemingly endless stacks of exercise books and reading folders. Mrs Abbott, her no-nonsense TA, had offered her help with setting up for the new term, even thought it was quite clear that the older woman would rather be almost anywhere in the entire world.

With that in mind, it probably wasn't the ideal time for Eva to ask if there was any chance she could be set up with one of the Abbott sons, but ideal times were rare in Eva's life, and she simply could not afford the luxury of waiting for one now.

She pulled a new set of books towards her as she went in for the kill. 'How are your boys doing these days?'

Mrs Abbott stopped abruptly, eyeing Eva with thinly veiled suspicion from beneath her blunt-cut fringe. And then, as if she could read Eva's mind, she simply said, 'They're both married,' before she returned to her stickering as if she'd never stopped.

So much for that.

'Oh, congratulations,' Eva chirped, her bright tone as forced as the smile on her face.

Mrs Abbott nodded once, before falling immediately back into her routine. She'd been a teaching assistant in the reception class for as long as anyone could remember, and it was fair to say that she saved every last scrap of joy in her personality for the little ones. It was rare that she so much as smiled at Eva, but Eva had become used to it over the years they'd worked together. What Mrs Abbott lacked in warmth, she made up for in efficiency, and Eva had the most organised classroom in the entire school.

Not to mention that Mrs Abbott deployed her stern front to maximum effect with the rest of the staff, too, which afforded Eva a certain level of protection from the coven further up the school, as well as guaranteeing that she never ran short of laminating pouches.

They didn't speak for a while then, falling into not so much an uncomfortable silence as a functional one, which Eva didn't mind one bit. She'd learned over the years not to take it personally, not to mention that the peace gave her time to ponder her mission a little more, and to dwell a while on the faceless list of names with which she had been presented.

Two offerings from Hanna, two from the combined efforts of her mother and Stefan, and a lightly concerning four from Ciocia Nelka, who had taken her assignment *very* seriously and handed over an actual list, handwritten in her spidery cursive on paper which smelled like the inside of an old cupboard. Eva had breathed it in with a smile, catching perhaps the slightest hint of the lilac-scented perfume which Nelka had religiously bought from the same seller on the outdoor market since the late seventies.

She didn't recognise any of the names, but they seemed harmless enough, and she aimlessly tried her name out with each of the surnames to see if anything struck a chord. There was a Wozniak and a Wright, a Nowak and an O'Leary. Two Wisniewskis, a Lewis and a Schwarz.

None of them jumped out at her, but none seemed offensive, either, and Eva sighed to herself as she pulled a differently coloured stack of books towards her and reached for the stickers just as the unmistakeable scratch of the deputy head clearing his throat came from her doorway.

She plastered a smile on her face before she looked up. Dealing with Nigel Carter demanded such niceties.

'Eva,' he said, by way of greeting, the edge of condescension in his tone managing to make her hate the sound of her own name. 'I trust we're all on track for Monday?'

Nigel, she had once worked out, couldn't possibly be older than his mid-thirties, but he acted as if he were twice that, not helped in the slightest by his slightly awkward dress sense or the steely determination with which he tried to conceal his thinning hair.

Her eyes flicked to the awkward thatch of his fringe by habit. 'Of course,' she said, before her to-do list popped into her head. 'Hey, have you seen Kelsey around today? I have a couple of additions to the handover notes I gave her in July.' The impossibly glamorous year-one teacher was flaky at best, but it wasn't like her to not show up at all, not when there was so much left to be done. She must be working somewhere else in school.

Nigel visibly stiffened in the doorway. 'Oh no, haven't you heard?' He toed the floor with his scuffed brown loafers, not looking at her. 'There was an incident. Anyway, it was decided that Miss Martin would not return for this school year.' He looked up at that, straight at Eva. 'We've secured temporary cover for her position until we can properly recruit.' And with that, he turned on his heel and strode off down the corridor, no doubt on his way to ruin someone else's day.

'Wow,' Eva said, to no one in particular, and she turned as she heard the small sound which escaped Mrs Abbott in reply – something between a huff and a tut.

'Well,' the older woman said, not looking at Eva. 'I hope she finds a position which is more...' She paused a moment, weighing her words. '*Suitable*. For her *skills*.'

Eva nearly swallowed her tongue. Mrs Abbott was staunchly anti-gossip, and Eva had never heard such a scathing comment on her lips in all the time they'd worked together. She narrowed her eyes. 'What do you know?'

But Mrs Abbot only shook her head as she stood, heaving the pile of books she'd been stickering into her arms before meeting Eva's eyes with a stern look. 'Maybe you should ask her,' she said, stiffly. 'I don't think it's my place to say.'

Eva laughed, just about to make a silly joke to ease the tension when her left hand twitched inexplicably, drawing the edge of one exercise book along the side of her thumb and leaving a familiar sting in its wake. She yelped, her thumb going automatically to her mouth as Mrs Abbott, who had just deposited the books into a drawer, whipped back to look at her, one eyebrow raised.

'Paper cut,' Eva muttered around the digit in her mouth, and the older woman nodded once before wordlessly retrieving an antiseptic wipe from the first aid box in the high cupboard. She tore open the packet and threw it into the bin without so much as a glance in its direction.

'There are more germs in your mouth than in any other part of your body,' Mrs Abbott said firmly, handing the wipe over, and Eva took it as obediently as if she'd been one of the children, pressing it onto her finger and grimacing at the familiar burn of the alcohol on her fresh wound.

'Jesus,' she said, through the grit of her teeth, 'I still can't believe we use these on the kids, they're like instruments of tor...' She tailed off, noticing that Mrs Abbott had stilled beside her. 'What?'

But the older woman said nothing, just stood, staring at the door for a moment with that look on her face like something was about to happen. Eva relied heavily on that look in her classroom. Mrs Abbott's early warning system was another gift that more than made up for the rest of their relationship.

'Mrs Sharma's on her way,' Mrs Abbott said, easing herself back down onto the child-size plastic chair she'd been sitting on as the dulcet tones of Neeta Sharma's best voice echoed down the corridor. Eva wondered who she was trying to impress.

'How did you even hear that?' Eva asked in a low voice, eyebrows tugging together. 'You must have the hearing of a—' But then she stopped dead as Neeta herself passed the doorway, resplendent even in casual wear in a rich maroon cardigan and bright red lipstick. But that wasn't what had made Eva's train of thought grind to an abrupt halt. Neeta looked glamorous every day of the year. She probably looked glamorous in her sleep.

No, the reason that Eva's heart had slammed to a sudden stop in her chest had absolutely nothing to do with her nattily dressed headteacher and everything to do with the strangely familiar man she'd been talking to.

Surely it *couldn't* be?

She was projecting, that was it. Seeing what she wanted to see. It wouldn't be the first time. Plus, there must be lots of other russet-haired strangers about. What were the chances that the one she'd spent almost a full week mentally tracing the sharp lines of would walk those sharp lines straight into her school? That would be lucky by anyone's standards, and Eva simply did not have that sort of luck on her side.

So why did her skin feel as if it had caught fire?

She heard Mrs Abbott cough pointedly, and it was only then that Eva even registered that the older woman had been talking.

'Sorry,' Eva said, lips twisting into a sheepish smile. 'I was distracted, nosying at what Neeta's doing. Would you mind repeating that?'

The truth, at least. Mrs Abbott just sighed. This wasn't Eva's first offence.

'I was saying,' the older woman said, her voice firm but not unkind, 'that we only have the welcome display to do, and then everything should be ready for next week.'

Eva frowned. Her to-do list was still a mile long. 'I'll do the display. You go enjoy the rest of your day. I need to label the water bottles anyway.'

Mrs Abbott raised an eyebrow. 'They're done.'

'Oh,' Eva smiled, her gratitude tinged with a little embarrassment. 'Thank you. Then I need to re-fill the sand pit.'

'Also done.'

Mrs Abbott was truly worth her weight in gold, however lacking in warmth or social skills she might be.

'Reading folders?'

'Labelled.'

'First aid kit?'

'Restocked.' The older woman glanced over at her. 'I put in extra wipes and plasters again.' The *for you* was implied. Eva's mishaps easily doubled the requirements of an already accident-prone year group.

'Construction area?'

'Disinfected.'

They'd had one child in particular in the previous cohort who'd had a habit of storing Stickle Bricks in his cheeks, like an oversized hamster.

Eva smiled, genuine relief flooding her chest. 'Have I ever told you you're an angel?'

'Yes.' Mrs Abbott rarely wasted her time or energy on unnecessary words, at least where adults were concerned. She nodded once and reached for her handbag, shouldering it with a half-shrug that Eva took as a goodbye.

'Enjoy your weekend,' she shouted to Mrs Abbott's vanishing back. 'See you Monday!'

And then sat back down on the tiny plastic chair and took a breath so deep that it made her head spin.

———————

Eva was still feeling dizzy an hour later as she thumbed through the different coloured sheets of A1 paper in the art cupboard, looking for just the right green for her welcome tree display. One of the greens was too pastel, the other too dark. She had just sighed in defeat when she noticed a corner sticking out, right at the bottom – just a hint of the perfect grass green for the leaves she had planned.

She tried to slide it out first, but it wouldn't budge, such was the weight of the packs of paper on top. But that was OK; she just had to ease the other two colours out of the way, and leaf display victory would be hers.

The wodge of pastel paper came easily, and she took great care when she balanced it on the stacked boxes of cellophane and then manhandled the darker green out. That was easier than she'd expected, too, and she freed the perfect sheet of green from its prison before sliding both packs of paper back onto the empty shelf with a smile. In fact, she was just thinking how straightforward the whole manoeuvre had been when the entirety of the pastel green paper bucked from its shelf like a freshly caught fish and flip-flopped down onto the floor of the cupboard. And then, as if that weren't bad enough, the brown paper wrapping split almost completely in two as it hit the lino tiles, spewing the whole lot into a heap of crumpled green waves at her feet.

Eva sighed. That was much more in keeping with what she'd come to expect from her life.

'Man *alive*,' she spat, with all the fury of the worst expletive she could imagine behind it. She had become conditioned, over the years, to only use child-friendly exclamations when she was within the school grounds. It was like a switch flipping: she could swear with the best of them in the outside world, but the second she stepped through those gates, she buried all of her contentious vocabulary deep down, somewhere where it would never manage to accidentally slip out.

She dropped to the floor, salvaging the heap of paper as best she could in the tiny space, and she was so focused on avoiding another lecture from Nigel bloody Carter on the global paper shortage that she didn't hear the door open.

But she felt it – the sudden shift of energy when it did.

And she definitely felt the rasp of the voice which followed, in every last cell of her body.

'Are you OK?' it asked, a familiarity about the tone settling into her bones. 'I heard a shout and—'

But then the voice paused, just exactly at the moment when Eva looked up, still on her hands and knees on the dusty art cupboard floor, to confirm something she had known in her heart from the beginning.

The dashing, russet-haired stranger didn't click straightaway, but she saw it happen in real time: that slight hitch between his eyebrows before his perfect lips pulled into a smirk.

'Well,' he began, his voice lighting Eva's skin on fire all over again. '*This* I was not expecting.' And then he dropped to his knees beside her. 'Here, let me help you.'

Together they collected and re-stacked the sheets, straightening them out as best they could and sliding them back onto the shelf, Eva taking extra care so as to avoid any further fish-flopping incidents.

When she had satisfied herself that they were definitely secure, and turned to brush the dust off the knees of her jeans, he was watching her. His gaze was intense, like it had been at the bar, and no less steady.

'So,' he said, in that deep grate of a voice.

'So,' she parroted in reply, almost embarrassingly breathless. His gaze on her made her chest tighten. It felt as if every last molecule of oxygen had been sucked out of the room.

'This is weird.' His perfect lips tipped up at one side into that half-smirk. She briefly wondered what it would feel like to bite down on them. 'You work here?'

She couldn't do much but nod. 'Reception teacher.'

His smirk grew into a broad smile. 'I'm the new teacher in year one.'

Just in the classroom straight across from hers, that's all. No reason to lose her damn mind or anything.

'I see.' She fought to keep control of her senses. He was overwhelming her. 'I guess this was what you were celebrating?'

His nod was slow, measured. 'What are the chances?'

She just smiled in response, as if her mouth didn't trust itself not to blurt out any of the words which were swimming around in her head. He took a step forward, and she breathed him in, that same scent of spearmint and sandalwood nipping at her throat.

'I'm Luke, by the way.'

Luke, her brain whispered to her, like it was significant.

'Eva,' she replied, and he repeated it once, and then a second time, testing the feel of it in his mouth. Warmth pooled deep in her belly.

He was a little taller than she remembered from the bar, and twice as handsome, his face a perfect balance of lines and curves. Those eyes – the eyes which had drawn her in from the start – were still trained on her, the span of his chest rising and falling with his breath.

'So this is the art cupboard,' she said, quickly, before her mouth had the chance to say something else, something like *kiss me* or *I should have left the bar with you* or *I want to drag my lips over every inch of your perfect skin*.

He chuckled at that, but there was a strain to the sound, like he was thinking all of those things too. 'It's cosy.'

Eva had never thought of the art cupboard as cosy before, but now she doubted that she'd ever think of it in any other way. 'Just watch out for the handle,' she said, fending off flashbacks of the five to ten times she'd accidentally trapped herself in here. 'The mechanism is broken, so make sure the lock is disengaged or you won't be able to open it from the inside.'

A laugh, little more than a breath. 'Noted.'

There was a moment's silence then, the crackle of tension in the air making the small hairs stand up on Eva's upper arms. She felt as if she were about to get struck by lightning, and maybe, in a way, she was.

'How was your date?' he asked, his voice dropping to a husk.

She blew a breath out. 'It was lovely. He was a good guy.' She saw a muscle knot at his jawline. 'But he wasn't right for me.'

His mouth fell open a little way, his breath catching on the inhale, and she thought for a moment that he was going to reply, but he didn't. And he didn't move for a long time either, but for the slightest twitch in his lips.

And then, before she knew what was happening, those lips were on hers, one of his hands sliding to the curve of her waist as he backed her up against the old brown gloss of the art cupboard door. His other hand knotted into her hair, sending a cascade of shivers down her spine at the brush of his fingers against the nape of her neck.

She'd thought her skin was on fire before, but this was *white hot*: the taste of him, the weight of his body as it pressed against her, his breath on her face. It was deliberate and unrestrained in equal measure, his mouth knowing exactly how to move against hers; when to push, when to pause; when to bite down gently on the flesh of her lips, just as she had imagined doing to him.

It all came together to turn her stomach to molten metal.

But she didn't even have the time to reach for him in return before he was pulling back, pulling away, cool air rushing to fill the space where he'd been. His cheeks flushed a little, something like doubt in his eyes.

'I'm sorry,' he said, after a beat, a coarse edge to his voice which made her pulse jump. 'That wasn't very professional.'

She stood, stock still, fists balled, as they had been the entire time. It wasn't that she hadn't wanted to respond, just that she'd been unable to, every muscle paralysed by the heat which was flooding her body. The same feeling she'd had in the bar was back: that feeling like she wasn't sure whether she wanted to sleep with him or slap him.

But there was another feeling roaring up inside her, too, something far more primal, and she wasn't sure she had the will or the want to ignore it. It had been a long time since a man had had his hands on her.

'I, um…' she muttered, every form of communication having deserted her.

Every form except one.

She was acting on some kind of base instinct when she grabbed for his shirt, feeling the vague warmth of his skin through the fabric as she reached to kiss him back, something like electricity firing through her as their lips met again. And this time, wild horses couldn't have stopped her.

The hands which had been balled in his shirt started to move, one reaching for the curve of his jaw while the other grabbed a shoulder, marvelling at the firm layer of muscle beneath her fingers. Her stomach tightened.

She felt those perfect lips smile against her before he kissed her back, deeper and more urgent, coaxing out the most carnal of sighs from deep in her throat. He hummed in appreciation, pulling her close. Dangerously close. So close that she could feel every inch of him, hard and hot and pressed against her in a way which was completely inappropriate for a place of education.

Not that she could bring herself to care. The children wouldn't be back until the following week, and Eva had abandoned every last scrap of willpower right about the time that Luke's hand had slid around her waist.

In that moment, half-drunk on lust, she didn't stop to think any of it through: not that she was almost certainly flouting multiple points of Neeta's code of conduct; not that come Monday she would be expected to behave like a professional as he taught less than ten metres away from her; certainly not that she was supposed to be looking for a husband, not surrendering herself to illicit encounters in storage spaces.

'I've got so much work to do,' he muttered, between kisses. 'I already hate myself for saying this, but I really need to get back to sorting out my classroom or there's no chance in hell it'll be ready for Monday.'

The sound she made in reply was as much a moan as it was a sigh, and she could feel his body respond to it through his clothes, pressing harder against her for a moment before letting out a small noise of his own. His head fell to her shoulder, the warmth of his breath in her ear sending ripples of pleasure down her spine.

He looked as disappointed as she felt when he pulled away, trying his best to disguise it with a look she could only describe as a smoulder. 'This isn't over,' he muttered, his voice so rough and deep that she felt halfway to orgasm just from the sound of it. 'We'll carry on this conversation later.'

'Yes,' she said, her voice thick. 'I definitely have more to say.'

His eyes darkened.

'My house.' His smirk was back. 'Tonight.'

She nodded her reply. At that moment she probably would have agreed to anything. And then she smiled to herself as he swung the cupboard door open and left, sucking half the air in the room out with him. She couldn't catch her breath for a while, and when she finally managed, she turned to find the single sheet of perfectly coloured green paper crumpled and torn at her feet.

Just my luck, she wanted to think, but she couldn't. Not with the way her whole body was buzzing. Instead she grabbed a sheet of the green she'd originally thought was too dark and practically skipped back to her classroom.

Chapter Five

By the time Eva got out of her car that evening, the sun was low in the sky, casting a golden glow over the three small terraced houses at the very end of the street. She checked the address – hastily scribbled on a Post-it – for the sixth or seventh time, a knot of anxiety tightening her throat.

Luke's was the middle house.

She took a deep breath before she started up to the door, a rich olive green against the worn red brick of the walls. A wooden trough sat underneath the window, planted full to bursting with fragrant herbs, a scent which made her heart skip that same, familiar beat: an old song of grief which caught her at the strangest of times. Her dad had been a chef, once upon a time.

Before she'd killed him, of course.

She snuck another lungful of rosemary and thyme and mint before she knocked on the door, and when it swung wide open in response, that made her heart skip too.

Luke was standing in the doorway wearing a smile so

broad that it changed his whole face, eyes crinkling to soft lines in the glow of the evening sun. He'd changed into a T-shirt and different jeans, and his hair – still wet from a shower, she assumed – had taken on a different quality too, falling forward on to his face and curling about his temples.

He was glorious there, and it made her forget every rational thought, her brain able to do little else but whisper his name over and over.

'Hi,' he said simply, moving back a little way to allow her in.

'Hi,' she said in return, and as she stepped into the hall she was suddenly surrounded by that same sweet scent of spearmint and sandalwood, the scent of *him*. She inhaled deeply, shamelessly.

Luke's hallway was tiny, but wouldn't have looked out of place in an interior design magazine, with a bold tiled floor and whitewashed walls, simple framed prints and shelves full of trailing plants. Eva had never met a plant she couldn't kill, but these were lush and vibrant, some in full bloom. She was so taken by the sight of them that she didn't notice that the strap of her handbag had caught around the lip of the waist-height vase which stood next to the front door.

Not until she took another step and the vase dropped like a bomb, shattering on impact and sending a thousand small shards skidding every which way across the tiles.

Eva almost stopped breathing.

She'd been in Luke's house less than ten seconds, that was it. That was all it had taken for the curse to show her up. She felt her cheeks flush with shame.

'Oh God, I'm so sorry,' she said, dropping to a crouch and

beginning to collect the bigger pieces in her palm. 'I'll replace it.'

She heard Luke's small chuckle above her before he reached down for her free hand and gently tugged her back to her feet. 'Don't worry about it, it's not even mine.' He carefully plucked the pieces of pot from her palm. 'It was left in the house when I bought it and I just never got round to throwing it out.'

Eva frowned. He was just being polite, surely. 'But the mess… There are bits everywhere.'

It was true. Every last inch of the floor was covered in a dusting of ceramic fragments, their edges glistening gold in the evening light.

But Luke just looked down at the floor and then back up at her with a shrug. 'I own a broom,' he said, that broad smile not leaving his face, as if it really wasn't a problem. 'Wait there. Don't move.'

He padded carefully through the wreckage and then disappeared into the room off to the right of the hall, appearing again a moment later with a broom in his hand and a triumphant grin on his face.

'I'm sorry,' she said, as he whisked around the hallway expertly, gathering the mess into a neat pile in one corner in no time. 'I'm kind of a disaster.'

He leaned the broom against the wall and turned to look at her, before his eyes dropped to her lips. 'That has not been my experience.'

A small knot of desire tugged at her belly, along with something else, maybe disbelief. 'It really doesn't bother you?'

He shook his head, wiping his palms on his denim-clad thighs. 'You know what does bother me?' He reached for her hand again, threading warm fingers into the spaces between hers. 'The fact that you've been inside my house for five full minutes and I haven't got to kiss you yet.'

That same hum started up again, just behind her breastbone. 'Oh yeah?'

'Yeah.'

He pulled her in with their joined hands, his free fingers going to her jaw as he bent to kiss her, his lips warm and familiar against hers. She'd memorised small things about him without even noticing it: the soft scratch of his stubble on her skin, the slide of his tongue against hers as he deepened the kiss, the small noise he made as she reciprocated, partway between a sigh and a growl.

God, this man. The way he was kissing her. She almost couldn't bear it. It was less urgent than their cupboard kiss, slow and deliberate, but with an edge of intent which made her whole body hum.

Eva didn't even recognise herself, in that moment. She was not, typically, a person who kissed strangers with abandon. She was far too cautious for that – much too busy thinking about the various ways in which her romantic endeavours could go wrong. And yet here she was, with fistfuls of this beautiful man's T-shirt, forgetting every last thing which usually made her hold back. Ignoring the list of eight names written on a piece of paper which she'd tucked into the back pocket of her purse. In that moment there was only the two of them, writing their names on each other, surrounded by the fine dust of a shattered vase.

Eva, emboldened by the rush of hormones raging through her veins, reached for the hem of his T-shirt and began to lift it up before he moved to stop her, his mouth curving to a smile against hers.

'I think'—he stole another kiss before he pulled away more definitely—'that we should eat first.'

A huff escaped her, a small sound of vexation. 'Who needs to eat?'

'Well,' he started, as his gaze dropped to assess her body, his eyes darkening, 'I can only speak for myself. But if I'm going to do what I'd like to do with you later, I'm going to need fuel.'

Eva almost melted to a puddle right there on the tiled floor. 'Fine,' she conceded, though she did allow one of her hands to slip underneath the shirt she'd been holding and trail over the warm ridges of his stomach for a moment before she released her grip with the other.

His eyes fluttered almost closed in response, but he held firm, taking her hand and leading her through into his kitchen, as small and perfectly formed as the hallway. Her fingers went to the smooth wood of his worktops, the texture sparking the vague whisper of a memory in her subconscious.

'Well,' he said, dropping her hand and swinging the fridge door open, 'I can't promise you a gourmet meal, but there's enough in here to knock something up. Any dietary restrictions?'

It was Eva, of course there was.

'I'm allergic to crustaceans and kiwi,' she said, with an apologetic shrug, but Luke just smiled that same easy smile at her.

'OK. So no lobster thermidor, then?' He chuckled to himself. 'Shame, that's my signature dish.'

Eva raised an eyebrow. 'Is it actually?

'No, that's an outrageous lie,' he said, a glint in his eye. 'I'm just an average home cook.'

But that turned out to be an outrageous lie, too. Eva knew it as soon as he started chopping vegetables. He had a confidence about him, his grip on the knife familiar in a way which made her heart swell and ache at the same time. And if she hadn't known then, she would definitely have known the second he slid the plate of pasta in front of her. It was a work of art.

She looked up at him as he sat on the stool beside her and twirled a forkful of linguine. 'Average cook, eh?' She took a bite, and couldn't help the noise she made in response.

But Luke just smiled. 'Under promise and over deliver,' he said, his smile hitching into a smirk. 'That's my whole vibe.'

It really wasn't, Eva thought, but she didn't voice it. The promises he'd been making, in the way that he looked at her, the way he kissed her, well. If he over delivered on those, it might tip her over the edge.

'So,' she started, needing a distraction from her thoughts on Luke's *delivery* before she spontaneously combusted. 'Tell me about you.'

He paused, another forkful partway to his mouth. 'What about me?'

'Everything.' And she really did mean *everything*.

'Everything?' His chuckle was low and warm, 'How long have you got?'

'Fine,' she fixed him with a look. 'Just the basics.'

That grin was back. The one which made her forget herself. 'OK,' he started, after a beat. 'I'm Luke. A very youthful thirty-two. Six foot one in shoes. Science nerd. Slightly above average home cook. Sagittarius.' He quirked an eyebrow. 'Anything else?'

Sex god.

She cleared her throat. 'Primary school teacher?'

'Yeah, now.' There was a note of something in his voice then, the slightest of shadows, and it made her brows tug together in curiosity.

'Now?'

'I retrained recently,' he said, and though he met her eyes it still felt like he wasn't looking at her. 'Still technically an NQT.'

'Technically?'

'Actually.' He smiled. 'But hopefully not for much longer.'

Eva had been teaching children long enough to know when something was being left unsaid, but she didn't push it. Just considered him for a moment or two before she forced her mind to move on.

'What did you do before?' she asked, and the question made the hunch of his shoulders drop a notch. She could almost feel his relief.

'I was a food stylist,' he replied, rubbing the scruff on his jaw.

She laughed. She couldn't help it. It was just that she'd expected him to say something like *model* or *firefighter* or *elite sportsman*. She realised, of course, that was very judgemental, but a more primitive part of her brain always seemed to take the wheel around Luke, and the last thing that part of her brain had imagined he'd say was food stylist. She didn't even know what a food stylist was.

'It's someone who makes food look good for photoshoots,' he said, as if he could read her mind. Or perhaps it was because he'd had to explain it to people a lot. Stupid people like her who laughed when he said it. She felt a nip of guilt, and when she smiled, there was an apology laced through it.

'So you know when you have a recipe book and the food looks incredible, but then you cook the recipe for yourself and even though you've followed all the steps perfectly, it never looks quite as good?'

She nodded. Her cooking was about as disastrous as the rest of her life, but she didn't tell him that.

'That's because,' he continued conspiratorially, 'the dish which was photographed was constructed by someone like me. The meat's definitely cold, probably half raw and brushed with fence paint to make it look richer. It's like being an artist, but for lying about food.'

'I didn't know that was a job,' she said, her mind blown.

But Luke just smiled wider, reaching over to take her hand in his. 'Now you do.'

'But you left?' Her brow creased.

He nodded. 'I turned thirty and … I dunno … I just wanted to do something which felt more'—he shrugged lightly—'important?'

He'd phrased it as a question, but Eva wasn't sure if it required an answer. Instead she squeezed his hand gently, her thumb rubbing slow circles on the knuckle of his index finger.

'It is,' she said, the skin contact making her feel as though she couldn't quite catch her breath. 'Important, I mean. And in year one especially. Don't even get me started on how valuable it is to have positive male role models lower down school.'

His hand tightened around hers, and for a moment she was swept away, ripples of heat flooding to the far reaches of her body.

'How long have you been teaching?' he asked, a tug in his voice which Eva could feel in her whole body.

'Ten years this year.' She smiled. It had gone in the blink of an eye, 'God, it sounds like such a long time.'

His nod was slight, but enough to shake a strand of dark red hair free. She wanted to muss the whole lot up. 'How many of those years have you worked at Burton Lane Primary?'

'All ten.'

'Seriously?' His brows flew up. 'Always in reception?'

She nodded, grinning broadly at him. 'The chaos is my happy place.' It made her own personal chaos stand out less. 'Plus my teacher voice doesn't work as well on the older ones.'

He laughed, and when he spoke, his voice was more gruff. 'I can't wait to hear your teacher voice. Maybe you could use it on me?'

Eva smiled, her cheeks heating in a blush. It wasn't the first time a man had asked, but on Luke's lips the question was playfully hot, nothing like the seedy requests she'd always found herself squirming out of.

'OK,' she said, trying her best to quieten the roar of arousal in her ears. 'Sit down.' She enunciated each word, biting off the syllables in that practised way which, more often than not, made her little ones fall into line.

It had the same effect on Luke initially, as he walked the three or four steps back to the heather-grey sofa, not taking his eyes off her for a second. He reached for her hand as the backs of his knees hit the cushions, and she tutted dramatically, though she didn't resist.

'Keep your hands to yourself, buster,' she said, in that same even tone, and he obliged, thrusting his hands into his back pockets with the filthiest grin she'd seen on him yet, before leaning down for a kiss.

She pulled back, an infinitesimal retreat, just enough so that their faces stopped short of actually touching as she deepened her voice for one single command.

'Sit.'

He immediately did, looking up at her from the sofa as if he wanted to devour her. 'Sit yourself.'

Ordinarily, Eva would have responded to that by sitting beside him, always one for the cautious route, but this was not an ordinary day, and Luke was definitely not an ordinary man. So instead she lowered one knee to the sofa, and then the other, so that she was straddling him, taking care not to break eye contact as a pulse thumped between her legs.

Luke's exhale escaped as a satisfied sigh. He'd taken his hands out of his pockets as he sat down, and they were now draped across the back of the sofa, his T-shirt sleeves pulling at the curve of his biceps. Her eyes swept shamelessly over them before they snapped back to meet his. The way he was looking at her was nothing short of a fire hazard, burning hot, even by Eva's standards.

'Still want me to keep my hands to myself?' he muttered, his voice low and rough. And in that moment there was absolutely nothing in the world that Eva wanted less.

The *no* that she muttered felt too quiet for the actual level of enthusiasm she had for Luke's hands to explore every inch of her, but it was enough. Enough for him to nod once in understanding. Enough for his hands to move to her ribcage, thumbs grazing her sides, sending ripples of electricity through her.

Truthfully, she was a little ashamed of the hunger which ripped into her at that point, but not so much that she did a single thing about it. It had been a year or more since she'd kissed anyone at all, much longer since it was anyone she had any kind of connection with. Even when she'd started thinking about the husband hunt, it had been a practical exercise in changing her fortunes. She hadn't actually thought at all about the simple fact that she was lonely, nor, clearly, that she was horny as all hell.

But between the heat of Luke's mouth on hers and the grip of his fingers dimpling the flesh of her body, it was all she could think about now. Her love life, much like the rest of her life, had been an unmitigated disaster from start to finish, so much so that she'd largely avoided even trying to meet someone.

And she'd done such a good job of packing away her needs, denied herself pleasure so efficiently, for so long, that it had become a habit. But all it had taken was one glance from Luke in the bar that night to wake her libido from its slumber, and now it had roared to life, wailing and thrashing against the bars of the cage she'd so carefully constructed to contain it.

She'd abandoned all hope of ever seeing him again, and then he walked straight into her life, less than a week later. Maybe if she had thought about it in any kind of detail, she might have wondered if that was the first sign of the curse starting to lift?

But she wasn't thinking at all, not about the curse, and honestly really not about anything other than the delicious drag of Luke's fingers across her heated skin.

She *wanted* him.

She wanted him so badly that it made her whole chest ache.

She reached for the hem of his shirt and tugged it up with greedy hands as he broke their kiss to help her, leaning away from the sofa so that she could get it over his head. And then she took a moment to marvel at the expanse of chest which she'd revealed, broad and toned, with a smattering of hair, the same deep red as the hair on his head. She burrowed her fingers into it, relaxing back against him with a sigh, which deepened once his lips found her neck.

He made her crazy, there was no other way to describe it. Something about the way that he looked at her, the way he kissed her. *God*, the way he touched her, the burn of his fingers on her skin was unlike anything she'd ever experienced. It made her want to throw her usual overabundance of caution to the wind.

But then, all of a sudden, there was something underneath that feeling, some quiet whisper of a voice which she ignored at first, until it grew so loud that she couldn't help but listen.

'I don't want you to think this is what I do,' she said, her breath coming as a pant.

'This?' he muttered, the words almost lost to the curve of her neck.

She couldn't stop the whimper of pleasure at the feeling of his warm breath on her skin. 'You know.' Her fingertips trailed down his sides, and she felt him tense underneath her. 'Kiss strangers in cupboards and then go home with them.'

She felt the curve of his smile against her ear. 'I'm pretty sure *I* was the one who kissed *you* in the cupboard.'

'Yes,' she said, unable to suppress a smile of her own. 'You were.'

His lips found the small hollow behind her ear. 'I'm just glad you kissed me back.'

She couldn't help but laugh at that, though the sound turned to a groan at the tug of his teeth on her earlobe. 'Have you seen yourself? Pretty sure a marble statue would kiss you back.'

He laughed too, the heat of his breath sending shivers down her spine. 'You'd be surprised,' he said eventually, and there was a darker tone to it, one she'd have thought more about if he weren't about to make her lose her damn mind.

'We can slow down if you want,' he muttered, from somewhere underneath her jaw.

'I don't want...' She wasn't actually sure what it was that she *did* want. She only knew what she feared. 'It's just...' His kisses had slowed to a gentle graze as he listened to her, but it was still enough for her to lose her train of thought every few seconds. 'I don't have the best of luck,' she managed, eventually, an understatement if ever there had been one. 'And as much as I want to – *God*, please believe that I *want* to—' She sighed, as much from disappointment she felt at the idea of stopping as from the small shivers of desire Luke's lips were sending through her.

She took a deep breath before she spoke again. 'I just don't want this to turn into another one of my disasters.'

He pulled back then, his hazel eyes suddenly soft, eyebrows hitching together as he studied her. 'Eva,' he murmured eventually, catching her face in his hands and kissing her once, carefully. 'It's OK. I want to, too. But I can wait.'

'But—' she started, but she was silenced by the press of his lips on hers, again. A single kiss, soft and slow.

'We have time,' he muttered, so close to her that she could feel his mouth brush against hers as he spoke.

She wasn't sure what to say to that, so she let her lips do the talking, her kiss full of grace and of gratitude. His tenderness in that moment, his understanding, despite his obvious arousal pressing into her, *well*…

Maybe he wasn't the bad influence she'd built him up to be in her head.

Maybe he was husband material after all.

Chapter Six

As a rule, Eva generally liked to spend the day before the start of the school year alone, perhaps with a book and a box of chocolates, revelling in her last hours of peace before the inevitable chaos of that first week with her new class.

This year, however, she was very definitely *not* alone. Not by any stretch of the imagination.

'Dab it, Eevs,' Hanna was saying, almost pressed up against her in what was surely the smallest toilet cubicle in all of Scarborough. The heat of the late summer day was making both of them sweat uncomfortably. 'If you rub it, it'll smear.'

Eva rolled her eyes, adjusting her grip on the single baby wipe they'd managed to lay their hands on. 'What are you, a stain-removal expert?'

'I used to be a Mallory,' Hanna said pointedly, wrestling the murky wipe out of Eva's hand. 'I've been shat on by my fair share of seagulls.'

'This wasn't a seagull.' Eva muttered, submitting to her sister's assault on the fabric of her brand-new shirt. 'A seagull couldn't have passed this...' She gestured vaguely to her front, stained a muddy green from chest-height downwards. 'It must have been a pterodactyl.' She glanced at herself in the murk of the old mirror. 'I think it's a lost cause, Han.'

But Hanna, as stubborn as they came, only shook her head, refolding the wipe before attacking the stain again, even more vigorously than the first time. Eva felt as if she were having a sports massage.

'I'll just buy something from one of the shops on the seafront,' Eva said, trying in vain to lean away from the more aggressive jabs.

'Urgh, what?' Hanna was talking as much to the stain as she was to Eva. 'A *kiss me quick* T-shirt? Though, I guess it wouldn't hurt your husband hunt. Fancy adding a rando from Scarbs to your list?'

Eva flushed, the sudden memory of Luke's lips on hers pulling her breath from her lungs. He was now very firmly on her list.

Her eyes fluttered closed involuntarily at the mere thought of him, a warm shiver slipping down her spine. She didn't clock, at first, that Hanna had stopped jabbing at the stain, and when she opened her eyes, she found her sister's cool, grey-blue eyes narrowed at her.

'What's that look for?' Hanna asked, her tone heavy with suspicion.

'What look?' Eva laughed, a little too quickly. 'I'm just having a hot flush because it's a million degrees in here.' And then she nearly jumped out of her skin at the sudden pounding on the door.

'Girls!' Sylvia shrieked, her voice uncharacteristically shrill. 'We need to leave for the church *now*.'

Sylvia was not ordinarily one to fret, but the weight of the day was getting to her, as it was to all of them. The twins freed themselves from the small toilet stall and stumbled out onto the seafront, temporarily blinded by the glare of the late morning sun.

'We couldn't get it off,' Eva started, looking in the direction in which she expected her mother to be while she waited for her eyes to adjust. She heard Sylvia's soft tut off to her right and adjusted her gaze accordingly. And, as Eva's vision returned to normal, there her mother was, looking at her with an expression somewhere close to pity as she clutched a small bundle of fluorescent pink cloth, almost as bright as the sun.

She offered it to Eva with a pre-emptive shrug of apology. 'The ciocias found this for you.' Her green eyes, ringed by darker shadows than usual, crinkled with her wince. 'There wasn't a lot of choice.'

Eva took the pink bundle from her mother's hands, shaking it free with more than a little dread building in her chest, which was entirely validated when she saw the depth of the horror which awaited her.

BEACHES BE CRAZY, the neon lettering said, its placement a hair off-centre of the main image, a poorly drawn cartoon shark wearing a bikini and sunglasses. Eva's stomach dropped like a stone.

'Well,' Hanna said, from over her shoulder, 'I'm not sure I can get behind either the sentiment *or* the presentation of that monstrosity.'

Eva turned back to her mother in a panic. 'I can't wear this in a church, I'll spontaneously combust.'

Hanna smirked.

'*Don't even*,' Eva muttered through gritted teeth, her pulse beginning to speed.

But Sylvia only sighed. 'Just do praying hands over it, you'll be fine.'

Hanna snorted a laugh at that, putting one hand on her twin's shoulder. 'I'm queer as hell, Eevs.' Her voice was steady, encouraging. 'We'll burn together.'

Eva took a deep breath and nipped back into the toilet stall. She swapped her top as quickly as she could before binning her ruined shirt and scrubbing her hands until they were raw.

As she re-emerged into the blinding sun, Sylvia nodded her relief, deliberately averting her gaze from her daughter's new outfit. 'OK, you two and Owen can go with Stefan. Irenka refuses to get in his car.' Her smile was weak. 'We'll meet you at the church.'

It was blissfully cool in the church when they arrived, and Eva crossed her arms firmly over her chest as she shuffled down to the wooden pew right at the front. She'd been able to see them from the door, the back of her mother's neat bob, streaked through with silver now, beside the ciocias' matching shampoo and set styles: Nelka's pure white next to Irenka's steel grey, like good and evil versions of each other. They all piled onto a single pew, the seven of them, despite the fact that there wasn't a single other soul in the church.

It had been a while since Eva had been in St Peter's. Not since the funeral, she thought, ten years ago almost to the day. There was a familiarity about it still: the feel of the wooden pew under her hands; the patterns of coloured light streaming in through the stained-glass windows; the smell of worn leather and dust.

It caught at Eva's throat, as she remembered.

They'd lived in Scarborough for a while, when the twins were younger. Their dad had landed a head chef job at one of the most highly rated restaurants on the seafront, and so they'd moved up from Leeds and rented a sweet two-bedroom house set just back from the North Bay.

The five years they'd spent there had been the best of their lives, they'd all agreed. They'd moved back to Leeds shortly after Ciocia Irenka's first near-death experience, not that Irenka had ever seemed to appreciate it. Despite that, Tomasz and Sylvia had always planned to return to the seaside when they retired. But plans, in the Mallory family, were rarely anything but a vain hope, and Sylvia simply couldn't bring herself to make the move back without her late husband. Instead they'd laid him to rest there, on the hill overlooking his favourite view in the world.

'The T-shirt fits!' Ciocia Nelka whispered excitedly, as Eva slid onto the pew next to her, Hanna wedging herself into Eva's other side.

Eva smiled. Nelka's spoken English was very good, certainly much better than Irenka's, but her reading and writing ability was weaker, and her understanding of stupid puns almost non-existent. She would have had no idea what she was subjecting her great-niece to. 'It does, thank you, ciocia. It's a little big, but I made it work.'

It was size extra-extra-large.

But Nelka just beamed in response, oblivious to the curl of embarrassment in Eva's shoulders. 'We wanted to give you space, kotku.'

What Eva wouldn't give for a little space right now.

A door opened then, and they all sat a little straighter as the priest took his place in the pulpit. Tomasz had been delighted to discover, all those years ago, that there was a Polish mass offered at their local church, and Sylvia had been delighted too when she managed to arrange for the Polish priest to do a small memorial service to mark the tenth anniversary of her first husband's death.

Ten years.

Eva took a breath, deep and even, warding off the subtle shake of her shoulders. It felt like weeks, sometimes. Sometimes more like centuries. She was able to live with her guilt most of the time, but sitting there, in the world's worst T-shirt, listening to a man of God celebrate her father's life, she couldn't help but feel as if she were suffocating, crushed under the weight of her responsibility for his death.

It came in waves, still, after all this time. Sometimes slight, just small laps of ice-cold water nipping at her ankles. Sometimes bigger; building to huge tidal waves of sorrow which pulled her down, deep beneath the surface.

Tomasz Mallory, she heard the priest say, between strings of Polish that she couldn't entirely translate. She couldn't help the sob which crept up her throat.

Hanna's words from the other day whispered to her, as Hanna herself took Eva's hand, squeezing gently.

You're the only Mallory left.

And as she returned the squeeze, a knot of gratitude in her throat, it had never felt more important that her plan should work.

It was mid-afternoon by the time they made it back to the beach, having stopped for lunch at Tomasz's old restaurant first. The tight grip of Eva's grief had settled back to a low hum, helped in part by the ice creams which Stefan had treated them to.

The twins sat together, backs against the sea wall, eating their ice creams and watching Owen help the ciocias haggle for deckchairs while Sylvia and Stefan paddled in the surf, a little way away.

'What did you get?' Hanna asked, nodding at Eva's cone.

Eva smiled. 'Mint and honeycomb. You?'

She knew the answer even before Hanna said it.

'Black cherry.'

Something about their predictability felt soothing. 'Classic.'

'Don't mess with the classics.' Hanna smiled back, looking out to sea. 'You OK?'

Eva adjusted her sunglasses. 'Yeah.'

It was almost true.

They watched together as Owen, having apparently secured two deckchairs, was helping lower Ciocia Irenka into one, her comically large hat slapping him in the face as the old woman ranted at him. Irenka was not built for sand, and even being near a beach made her twenty percent more furious.

Eva couldn't help but laugh. 'Looks like Owen's got his hands full.'

'He's a saint,' Hanna huffed, but there was pride in her voice. 'I'd have thrown her in the sea by now.' She nibbled around the edge of her cone, thumbing a deep red smear off her nose before peering back at her husband, who was now visibly sweating, his pale skin flushed red. 'Do you think he's

OK? He's balding and ginger, Eevs, I'm worried he'll frazzle. Have you still got that factor fifty?'

Eva was just about to reply when, from nowhere, she saw sudden movement just off to her left, a manic flurry of grey and dirty white swooping at her and snatching her ice cream clean out of her hand.

She shrieked, shocked, but – as always – not surprised.

'God damn,' she muttered, looking down at her feet, where the gigantic seagull was devouring what remained of the cone she had been enjoying. She could still see faint splatters of bird shit on her shirt and shoes. 'Reckon that's the same arsehole who bombed me earlier?'

Hanna snorted a laugh. 'With your luck, I'm going to say yes.' She popped the last of her own cone into her mouth, as if to add insult to injury. 'Speaking of which, how are you getting on with your hunt? Looks like that husband can't come quickly enough.'

Luke, Eva's mind whispered, making her smile so broadly her cheeks hurt.

'Whoa.' Hanna lifted her sunglasses to study her twin, eyes widening beneath their flicks of perfect eyeliner. 'That's a smile I haven't seen for a while. Did you go on another date?' Her eyebrows flew up. 'Oh my God, do not tell me it's one of Ciocia Nelka's. Did she put those brother-twins on there?'

Eva laughed. 'Give me a chance to talk, and I'll tell you.'

Her sister said nothing, only nodded slightly as she settled back against the sea wall.

'It's a new addition to the list, actually,' Eva said, trying to keep the excitement in her voice under control. 'Remember the guy from the bar?'

Hanna's brows pinched. 'What, Greg?' She pulled a face. 'I

thought we crossed him off? He came with his *own* curse, for God's sake.'

'No, not Greg.' Eva chuckled. 'Wait, you might not have seen him. Were you there right at the start?'

Hanna laughed at that. 'Have you ever known me be on time for anything?'

'Yeah,' Eva conceded. 'That was a stupid question.'

'You were talking to Greg when I arrived.'

Hanna time. Of course. She'd have missed the entire exchange with Luke.

'Well…' Eva grinned, her heart swelling as she began the story about her encounter with him at the bar, how he'd made her chest tighten from the very start, but how she'd assumed she'd never see him again. And then how he'd turned up at school mere days later and kissed her senseless in the art cupboard, invited her back to his, taken her out the following day.

Hanna's eyes had widened to the point where Eva genuinely feared they might pop out of their sockets. 'When will you see him again?'

'Tomorrow.' Eva laughed, warmth blooming in her chest at the idea. 'Every day. He's the new year one teacher. Literally the class across the hall from mine.'

Hanna studied her a moment or two, her face falling suddenly serious. 'Oof, Eevs, is that a bit close for comfort? You shouldn't shit where you eat.'

'Han!' Eva screwed her nose up.

'I'm just saying. Might be a recipe for disaster.'

Luke's face flitted into Eva's mind again. The way that he'd looked at her. The gentleness of his words.

We have time.

'I'll take my chances,' she said eventually, and it made her sister's energy change completely.

Hanna tucked a stray strand of dark hair behind her ear. 'You really like him.'

Eva shrugged. 'It just felt … different. With him. Like I'm where I'm supposed to be.' She looked away from Hanna, out to sea. 'Eh, it sounds stupid when I say it out loud.'

'It's fate,' Hanna said, beside her, a certainty in her voice which seemed ridiculous given that Hanna had never taken to such frivolities.

'You don't believe in fate.'

'No,' Hanna said kindly. 'But you do.'

'I do.' Eva turned back to look at Hanna then, her sister's smile so warm and broad she almost didn't look like herself. 'Argh, but I don't want to jinx it.'

But Hanna was already shaking her head, reaching one hand out to gently grip Eva's forearm. 'This is it, Eevs. I can feel it in my bones.'

And despite everything, with the sweet sound of Luke's voice ringing in her ears and memories of their short time together etched into her soul like co-ordinates, there was a part of Eva which really hoped – no, *believed* – that her sister was right.

Chapter Seven

It wasn't even lunchtime on the first Monday of the school year and there were only two children in the entirety of Eva's new class who hadn't cried yet. In fairness, this was not even nearly the first time she'd been in this position, so it hadn't exactly come as a shock.

What *had* come as a shock was Neeta's sudden and inexplicable decision not to exclude the youngest children from the school's traditional welcome assembly, less than three hours after they'd entered the school building for the first time in their short lives.

It was carnage.

Eva and Mrs Abbot were each comforting three children, mercifully now just sobbing quietly rather than the full-on screaming which had accompanied their entry into the hall. Over the head of the smallest child, who was clinging to her front like a baby koala, Eva was shooting daggers at two boys picking each other's noses, while one hand snaked around the back of the girl leaning against her right side to hold another small boy's shirt down. He'd been trying to squirrel out of his clothes since the moment he'd walked through her door, and Eva didn't fancy letting him finally succeed in his quest in front of a room of two hundred people.

She sighed, and was just tightening her grip on his yellow polo shirt – brand new and stiffly buttoned to the very top – when Neeta walked back onto the stage, her peacock-blue pencil dress popping against the old burgundy velvet of the curtains. Eva had long suspected that Neeta had a replica of the stage curtains somewhere in her home which she tried any potential new assembly outfits against, such was their perfection.

'Who's she?' one of Eva's new pupils shrieked at top volume, before being quickly shushed by Mrs Abbott, now almost completely hidden behind a mound of small children.

Neeta was speaking, and Eva was nodding, but she wasn't really listening. At least, she wasn't listening until the moment she saw Luke striding up the steps of the stage, smarter than she'd seen him before, his perfect buttocks enhanced by slim-fitting grey trousers, shirt sleeves rolled up around his toned forearms.

Good God.

It wasn't so much that she'd forgotten what an insanely attractive man he was, as that the events of that morning had managed to erase all other thoughts from her brain. But it all came rushing back at once, a knot in her stomach which was joined by heat pooling low in her belly as she remembered the feel of him against her, hard and ready and yet willing to wait.

For her.

Good God.

'—and I know you'll all join me,' Neeta was saying, 'in extending Mr Mallory a very warm welcome.'

And just like that, her heart skidded to a halt.

WHAT?

Luke's surname should really have been near the top of her list of questions, given her circumstances, but she'd been so distracted by the electricity which flowed between them that it was a detail she had not yet thought to clarify. She'd never met another Mallory in her life, outside of her own family, so the possibility hadn't even crossed her mind.

She must have misheard. It couldn't be true.

Could it?

As Eva headed, heart-first, into a tailspin, Luke met her eyes for a moment, breaking into a huge grin before he turned to address the rest of the school.

'Thank you, Mrs Sharma,' he said, his voice as warm as his smile. 'I'm very glad to be here.' And then he shot another look in Eva's direction as he headed back down the steps to re-join his class. She just about managed to smile back, a cold finger slipping down her spine as she did, a feeling she recognised well clutching at her throat.

Dread, maybe, or maybe guilt. She'd had enough of both in her life that she should have been able to tell them apart, but she couldn't. Not usually. They were so often tied up in each other.

Despite it all, she managed to keep it together for the rest of the assembly, and then through her class's chaotic exit from the hall. Eva deliberately avoided eye contact with anyone as she shepherded her now only partly sobbing shoal back to the safety of their classroom. She was just wrangling the last of them through the door when she felt someone step up behind her.

She knew it was Luke before she turned around.

'Mr Mallory,' she said, a desperate last-ditch grab towards the possibility that she *had* misheard after all, or that Neeta had somehow got confused. A reach for the fading chance that she wouldn't have to turn this magnificent man down on what amounted, on the surface, to such a trivial thing.

Not that the curse was trivial to Eva, of course. After all, it had killed her father.

Luke's smile then was like nothing she had even seen before – *devastating*, she would remember thinking afterwards – and it cracked her heart even wider open. 'Neeta told me you're a Mallory too. What are the chances?'

And with that, the last small fragments of hope slipped from her fingers, crushed to dust around her feet like the pieces of the vase she'd scattered across Luke's hallway floor.

What, indeed, were the chances?

She fought back tears. She'd been so entranced by the beautiful stranger from the bar, so completely pulled into his orbit, that she had almost forgotten about the curse.

But the curse had not forgotten about her.

Was it her penance, perhaps, for daring to cheat the curse last time? Or just her luck playing out as it always did? Either way, Eva was pretty sure that there was only one way her love story with Luke was going to end, and that was *badly*. Either she was going to have to end it herself, though it was going to shatter her to do it, or the curse would end it for her.

Would she accidentally set him on fire?

Unintentionally push him off a cliff?

Would he fall down and die one day, his heart

inexplicably stuttering to a stop, just like her father's had? She just couldn't take that chance, not with her history. So she took a deep breath and looked back into those warm hazel eyes, her fingers around the wrist of the small child at her side.

'Can we talk later?' she asked, grateful beyond words that the churn of emotion in her chest had not translated to her voice.

The smile which broke out across Luke's face in response was a work of art, endearing and somehow filthy at the same time. She already hated herself for what she was going to do.

'Mine, after work,' he said, a statement, not a question. 'I'll drive us both, if you want?'

She shook her head, carefully manoeuvring the wriggling child through the classroom door. 'It's OK,' she said, with the least fake smile she could muster under the circumstances. 'I'll meet you there.'

What she had to say wouldn't take long.

———

It was a little after six when Eva found herself back on Luke's doorstep.

The scent of the herbs in his window box hit her as she approached, just as it had the first time. Only this time it read like a warning; like Tomasz Mallory himself whispering words of caution from beyond the grave. Eva felt the hairs prick on the back of her arms, a shiver running through her even though it was a perfectly mild night.

She paused a moment before she knocked. Perhaps she wanted to prolong this, to just savour a moment more of her life actually being good before it inevitably plunged straight back to terrible.

Finally, still feeling a million miles from ready, she lifted her hand to knock, but the door swung wide open before her knuckles even made contact with the wood. When she looked up, Luke was right there in the doorway, still in the clothes she'd seen him wearing at school, but a little undone now.

It hit her all at once; the scent of him, the memory of his hands on her skin, the way his smile made his face light up, and, most of all, the way that all of it made Eva herself light up, at least for the split second until she remembered why she was there. He reached for her, but she stiffened before his lips could reach hers.

His eyebrows knotted into a frown as he pulled away. 'What's wrong?'

There was no good way to do this. Eva had struggled enough when she'd had to end catastrophic relationships she couldn't wait to be out of, so ending something she was completely into would have felt impossible at the best of times. And after the day that she'd had at school, this was very much not the best of times.

She tried to speak and promptly burst into tears.

He gathered her into his arms, his scent surrounding her, the warmth of his breath on her neck sending shivers across her skin as he muttered into her ear, 'What can I do?'

Her breath out was ragged, catching at her throat as it went. It all felt a hundred times harder with him there. 'I can't —' His arms tightened around her, thumbs stroking slow circles on the backs of her shoulders. It would be so easy to just re-think everything, to melt into his touch. 'You—'

But then her life played back in her head like a montage.

Every loss. Every disaster. The day she came home as Eva Smith to find Sylvia sobbing at the kitchen table. 'I mean—'

She needed the curse gone, fast. And marrying another Mallory wouldn't help in the slightest. Even if he did set her soul ablaze.

After all, she could set things ablaze all by herself.

'Let me help,' Luke said, his voice low and calm beside her ear, and she so wanted him to be able to. But—

'I can't,' she gritted out, finally, and whether it was the weight of her words or him sensing the tension gripping at her, his body language changed in an instant.

He took a step away, his eyes searching hers for a moment before he said a single word – her name – and in that moment it was clear.

He knew.

'I'm sorry,' she scratched out, her voice barely more than a whisper. 'But I don't think we can … do this.'

Another word, the effort of saying it forcing a deeper crease into his brow. 'Why?'

Why? Her body was screaming the same thing at her. Every cell in it wanted to take back the words, to melt into his arms and take her chances. But the chances were too high. She'd learned that the hard way.

'It's hard to explain,' she managed eventually.

His brow fell further, slashed so deeply across his face that she couldn't see the usual light in his eyes, and when he spoke, his voice was dark and rough. 'Try,' he said, one hand coming up a moment before falling back to his side, as if he'd been going to reach for her and then thought better of it.

His jaw flexed. 'I … really like you.' He couldn't meet her eyes, and she was glad of that, because the thread of vulnerability running through his voice might have broken her entirely, particularly when he said, quietly, 'It's been a while, for me.'

Tears began to nip at her eyes, all the breath in her lungs escaping in one long sigh. 'I really like you, too. Please believe that. It's not anything you've done or haven't done.' Anxiety rushed up into her throat, but there was no way out of this other than to tell the truth. 'It's because I'm cursed.'

His eyes snapped up to hers, one eyebrow raised. There was a chill to his expression now, but she had to explain. She owed him that much.

'My great-grandad changed his name to Mallory after the war, and two weeks later he was dead. Since then, all his descendants have been saddled with the worst luck in the world.' She looked down, away from the burn of his glare. 'It's the curse. The Mallory curse.'

'I've never had a problem.' He huffed a laugh, sharp and humourless. 'Well, until now.'

The sound of it went right through her. 'Our name literally comes from the word for unlucky.'

'I don't believe in luck,' he said. Every last ounce of warmth was gone from his voice.

It was her turn to frown. 'That's easy for you to say. The curse ruins everything.' Her hands balled into fists, nails digging into her palms. 'I need it gone.'

'I know someone who'll do you an exorcism for fifty quid,' he bit out, a harsh edge to his voice that she hadn't heard from him before. She didn't like it.

'I don't need an exorcism,' she nipped back. 'What I need is a *husband*.'

He reared away at that, the distance changing his face

again, so much so that he almost looked like a stranger. 'A husband?'

She nodded. 'So I'm not a Mallory anymore.'

'Just change your name,' he said, with the dry husk of a laugh. 'It costs less than a meal at a restaurant.'

'I tried that; it killed my dad.' There was a shake in her voice now, a shrill edge to the tone of it. She could hear it but there wasn't a damn thing she could do about it. 'Like a punishment.'

He just looked at her, the slightest of creases above his nose, as if he couldn't quite believe what he was hearing.

'But my mum and sister took their husbands' names, and the curse didn't punish them at all, and now their luck has changed.' She couldn't quite catch her breath. 'So that's what I'm going to do, too.'

'What, marry away the Mallory?' Incredulity raised the pitch of his voice.

She nodded again, one hand pushing against the churn of her stomach though it didn't help in the slightest.

He didn't reply for a moment or two, just looked at her with his arms folded across his chest, his eyes narrowed and trained on her. 'You know,' he said, eventually, 'if you weren't feeling it, you could just have said so. You didn't have to make up a crazy story.'

A single tear tracked down her face. If only it *were* just a crazy story. If only there were a way to make him see that this was actually a kindness. That she was saving him, if only from herself.

'I'm sorry,' she muttered, her voice catching on the lump in her throat. And she saw it – the very second he realised that she was serious. She watched the moment the final flicker of hope in his eyes turned to ash. She looked on as his walls flew up, the light she'd seen in him waning and dimming until there was nothing but darkness, and then a single sentence on his lips, five words which hollowed out her heart completely.

'I think you'd better go.'

Chapter Eight

I t was a week and two days before it happened.

Eva had been avoiding it, of course, but she couldn't put her family off for that long. Ciocia Nelka had brought it up first, which shouldn't have been surprising considering that Eva hadn't told anyone but Hanna about the Luke debacle. In fact, she hadn't told anyone but Hanna about Luke, full stop.

The last thing she'd wanted had been their pity.

Or, honestly, their help.

'So when are we starting on your husband list, kotku?' Nelka had asked, her cheeks folding like a Shar Pei as she smiled warmly at her great niece.

And that had been the slap in the face that Eva needed. She'd been so consumed by the Luke situation – by mourning him at home and avoiding him at school – that she'd almost forgotten about the husband hunt. But she couldn't afford to forget about it. After what she'd just lost, it was even more important that her plan should succeed. So instead she'd pulled herself together and plastered a smile onto her face.

And that was how she'd ended up here, another week and three days after that, sitting opposite Stefan's nephew as he swirled a straw in his Jack and coke.

She'd thought he might be a good bet, that perhaps some of Stefan's traits might run in the family. That he might be patient yet motivated, fascinating but humble, and unfailingly polite. But the man sitting opposite her could not have been less like his uncle if he'd tried.

He'd been on time, at least, strutting into the bar on legs clad in too-tight denim, which pulled and strained over the curves of his muscles. His T-shirt, at least one size too small, had a V-neck deep enough to reveal the entire centre section of his chest, hairless and tanned.

'Jonas,' he'd said, his mouth tipping into a smile as he'd offered out his hand. She'd smiled in return as she took it, not really registering the lack of fireworks as his skin touched hers.

'Eva,' she'd replied, and his smile had widened, his perfect teeth just a hair too big for his mouth.

'Pretty name.'

'Thanks.'

It hadn't been a bad start, in truth. There hadn't been anything in the way of sparks flying, but with Eva that wasn't necessarily a bad thing. She wasn't to be trusted with sparks anyway.

He'd smiled politely as she dropped her bag on their way to sit on the sofa, and helped her scoop up the contents, which had rolled out in all directions. He'd winced in sympathy as she'd then turned around to sit on the sofa and walked straight into it, whacking her thigh on the very edge of the wooden frame. He was even looking at her with a small smile now, in the aftermath of her sucking a much-needed mouthful of vodka and coke up her straw, only to have a good slosh of it splatter out of a hole she hadn't noticed on the side of the straw, catching her right in the eye.

'Not having a very lucky day, are you?' he said, his eyebrows angling into what she was sure was intended to be understanding, but it read a lot like pity.

She couldn't help but laugh, regardless. 'Not having a very lucky life.'

And he laughed a little too, as if she were joking. She very much was not.

'So Eva,' he said, dragging out the syllables of her name in a strange way. 'Tell me about yourself. What do you do?'

That was an easy one. Eva could have talked about her job all day. 'I'm a primary school teacher. In reception.'

He nodded, a quirk in his brows as if he were concentrating. 'They're the tiny ones, right?'

'Yep. I taught older children when I was first training, but then I got my last placement in reception and fell in love with the chaos.' She took a sip of her drink, from the rim of the glass this time. 'There's nothing quite like trying to tame a room full of four- and five-year-olds.'

There was a glimmer of something in his eyes, almost a wince. 'Sounds intense.'

'It's quite a workout.'

His ears perked up at the last word. 'You work out?'

She held in a laugh. Since the stationary bike incident, even the thought of going back to a gym brought her out in hives. 'Other than chasing kids around? No.'

'Oh.' He said nothing more, but his expression went on to say *maybe you should*. A flicker of self-consciousness sent Eva's hands skimming down her legs. She'd borrowed a pair of wet-look trousers from Hanna for the date and she regretted that now. She should have known to leave such things to her more fashionable sister. Eva definitely looked better dry.

'You're into working out?' she offered, seeing as the mere mention of exercise was the first thing that seemed to have captured his full interest on this date.

He beamed in response. 'I'm a personal trainer.'

OK, that made the physique make sense. He was looking at her expectantly, as if he expected a certain response to that, but she wasn't sure what it should be.

'Cool,' she settled on. 'You must be very busy.'

From the look on his face, that was not what he'd been hoping for.

'I'm in the gym six days a week,' he said, not breaking eye contact as he flexed the muscles in his shoulders and upper arms.

A smile tugged at her mouth. She got the impression that move typically had a very different effect on his dates. She also got the impression that she was not his typical audience.

'So what's your usual type?'

His body language shifted a little at her question, thumbs pressing awkwardly against his fingers.

She couldn't help but smile. 'You don't have to say "like you" just because I'm sitting here. I'm not that insecure.'

The sound he made was somewhere between a laugh and a sigh of relief. 'I know it's a stereotype, but I mostly go for girls who are tall, blonde, tanned, curvy.' His hands mimed comically large breasts. 'Plus lashes and lips, you know?'

She laughed. 'The absolute opposite of me in every way, then?'

In response, he laughed too, but it was awkward, as if he

wasn't sure if she were genuinely amused, or just waiting to drop a bomb on him. 'I mean, you're pretty too.'

Still chuckling, she waved him away. She was at peace with the way she looked. Working with children had driven her dignity away a long time ago. 'I'm kidding. Honestly, you're not my usual type either.'

He sat up at that. 'Oh really?'

'Really'

'So what is your type?'

Tall, russet-haired strangers who kiss the life out of you in storage spaces and can wear the actual hell out of a pair of tailored trousers?

She breathed past the rush of emotion in her chest. 'More … I don't know … low key.' She shrugged. 'Clark Kent rather than Superman.'

Jonas frowned. 'He's the same guy.'

'Different vibe, though.'

A nod. 'So it's a vibe thing?'

'I don't know.' She took another sip, the tightness in her chest now easing a little. 'It's undefinable, don't you think?'

'Maybe.' He was looking at her like he was studying her, a new fire in his eyes. 'Maybe it's a challenge.'

It wasn't intended to be, but what the hell. She'd let him try to seduce her. If nothing else, she needed something to try and chase away the thoughts of Luke, because there were times she felt as if she were drowning in them, and that was not conducive to finding a husband.

Not at all.

It didn't matter that she felt as if she couldn't breathe without Luke. She had made her decision, burned her bridges, and that was that. Now she needed to make an effort to move on.

This curse, quite clearly, was not going to go away by itself.

———————

By the time Eva was five drinks deep, she was a lot more on board with the idea. She still flinched every time she saw Jonas's clear blue eyes in the place of Luke's warm hazel ones, and she still couldn't quite get over how tight his trousers were, but she couldn't deny that there was the tiniest spark of *something*. It was a start, if nothing else.

'Truth or dare,' Jonas said then, eyes half-closing. He'd been drinking doubles to her singles and his game had taken a notable downward curve since the last Jack and coke. Not that she was in any position to criticise, of course.

'Dare,' she said, with a rush of boldness. She was, ordinarily, a die-hard *truth* girl, but they were where they were.

He bit his lip, eyes narrowing further. 'Kiss me.'

Other that the very obvious reason why not … why not?

From her current position on the sofa, Eva couldn't quite reach him, so she hauled her weight around, using her left leg for leverage as she pulled herself up. She focused on Jonas's mouth, pleasant and plump, and closed her eyes as she went in for the kill.

Their lips met without incident. Jonas's skin was soft and warm, and his breath smelt sweet, like sugar and bourbon. It wasn't a bad kiss at all, on the scale of things, but as Eva's scale had recently been recalibrated by a kiss of astronomical proportions, this one didn't even rank.

She smiled out of politeness as she pulled away, and was

just about to thank Jonas for the date and suggest they head home when, out of nowhere, the heel on her left shoe snapped, propelling her back towards him with a surprising amount of force. With his eyes still closed, he didn't even see her coming, but she heard his squeal, albeit dulled by the pain which had ripped through her jaw on impact.

'I'm so sorry,' she mumbled, grabbing wildly at her mouth.

Jonas had grabbed for his too, a reflex, but soon took his hands away, gingerly pressing against his mouth as he did.

'Jesus,' he muttered, fingertips still running along his perfect teeth, 'I thought for a minute you might have chipped my veneers.'

'My heel snapped.' Eva flushed with mortification. 'God, I'm so embarrassed. I hope I didn't hurt you.'

He smiled, but it didn't quite reach his eyes. 'I'm OK, don't worry.' The small laugh he forced out didn't help. 'I don't normally have women literally throwing themselves at me.'

Eva cringed. 'Anyway,' she said, a finality to her voice which she hoped he would catch on to.

'Anyway,' he said in return, with a slight nod, and he stood up from the sofas, offering out his hand again, just as he had at the start of the date. 'It's been…' He weighed his words. 'An experience.'

Eva might have taken more offence to his tone if she hadn't been so desperate to get the hell out of there, but as it was, she simply nodded in reply and reached to shake his hand with extra care. 'It was nice to meet you, Jonas.'

She'd rarely been more grateful for the cool night air on her cheeks as she was the moment she pushed through the heavy glass door of the bar. She pulled in a lungful, ignoring the notes of food scraps and fuel which hung in the city air.

The door swung open behind her, and for a moment she was seized by a rush of panic. But the figure that appeared beside her wasn't Jonas, though it was particularly familiar.

'Hanna?'

Her twin laughed, and the action made the bobbed platinum wig she was wearing swish around her cheeks. A moment later Owen appeared too, eyes dark under the peak of a baseball cap she had never seen him wear in all the time she'd known him.

Eva huffed. 'You two look like a latter-day Bonnie and Clyde.'

'That was the inspo,' Hanna said with a chuckle, turning to adjust the peak of Owen's cap, as he beamed down at her.

Eva's stomach knotted at the sight of them. She was happy that Hanna had found the love of her life, obviously, but that didn't stop the light prod of jealousy which poked at her as she watched them together. 'You're ridiculous,' she muttered, looking back out into the night. 'How many wigs do you own?'

'Less than twenty.' Hanna chirped, before she cut to the chase. 'So Jonas, eh? I guess he's another one to cross off.'

'Another one bites the dust,' Owen piped up then, bursting with unconcealed pride at his own joke.

'Owen!' Eva shrieked, in mock horror, but his joy was so pure that she couldn't even bring herself to be mad. 'She's rubbing off on you.' She nodded at Hanna, and her sister's scarlet lips pulled into a smirk.

'I'll rub—' Hanna started.

'No!' Eva interjected, raising one hand, palm out, as she did with the children in her class. Both Hanna and Owen stopped immediately, Owen's grin considerably more sheepish than his wife's.

'Sorry,' he mumbled, his cheeks flushing a little. 'I couldn't resist. Let me make it up to you by driving you home.'

And that *did* make Eva smile.

Not for long, though. Only for the few moments until her twin looked at her and gasped in very real horror.

'Eevs, your tooth!'

Eva's brows knotted, the tip of her tongue going to her front teeth and finding a small, sharp edge which had never previously been either sharp, or an edge. Panic roared back up in her belly.

'Did I chip it?' She ran her tongue back along the edge. 'It's not that bad, is it?'

Hanna was already half-buried in her bag, and she rifled through it for a few seconds before holding up a pocket mirror. Eva craned her neck to see in the light of the bar's neon sign, before her eyes pulled into focus and she reared back in horror.

'Oh Jesus, it's terrible.'

It was true. The entire corner of her front tooth was gone.

Hanna winced as she nodded. 'How the hell did you hit it that hard?'

'My heel snapped as we were, you know.' There was no point trying to hide anything. The two of them would have watched the whole thing. 'I had all my weight on it and then my foot just gave way, and I smashed my teeth *right* into his.'

Hanna frowned. 'What were his teeth made out of? Kevlar?'

It had felt a little like they could be. Teeth like that were not found in nature.

'Come on, Eevs,' Owen said, squeezing her shoulder

lightly. 'Let's get you home.' His smile pulled a little to the side, sympathy softening the edges. 'Get a good night's sleep, and then in the morning you can call the dentist.'

She nodded, the combination of alcohol and the fading traces of adrenaline making her eyelids grow heavy. 'OK,' she muttered, clinging to the arm which Owen offered as the mismatch of her shoes threw her stride off balance.

'You know,' Hanna said, falling into step beside her, 'you might have bitten off a little more than you can chew with this husband hunt.'

Eva groaned. If she knew her sister, she would have been waiting to get that one in ever since she'd witnessed the incident. Hanna was wrong though; Eva was sure of it. The night's events had only made it clearer to her that she was on the right path and should plough on with the husband hunt at any cost. Jonas might not have been the one, but she had seven names left on her list. Surely one of them would be a better fit.

They *had* to be.

She wasn't sure how much more of the curse she could take.

Chapter Nine

Eva rarely ventured into the staff room at lunchtime. It was almost a given that she'd end up hurting or embarrassing herself in some way. Either that, or get cornered by one of the trio of key stage two witches, which was enough to make her want to burn herself at the stake.

But, after one of her little ones had had a particularly prolific vomiting episode that morning, the cleaner had chased her out of her classroom for the whole lunch hour to allow enough time to thoroughly decontaminate the maths corner.

She'd tried to camp out in the library at first, settling down in the big orange sofa which ran almost all the way along one wall. But then Miss Presley, the English lead, had walked in and nearly had a coronary at the sight of Eva unwrapping her egg mayonnaise sandwich on the soft faux-leather of the sofa's arm. And so, Eva had no choice but to brave the rough plastic staff-room chairs instead.

As it turned out, there were only two people in there anyway: Mrs Abbott, who liked to eat in silence with only a gardening magazine for company, and Zahra, the sweet year two TA, who looked up from her book with a smile when Eva walked in before quickly burying herself back in it, twirling a single braid around her finger as she read.

Eva breathed a sigh of relief. These were the ideal conditions to decompress after the hellish morning she'd had. And it had been *bad*. The vomit-nado had just been the icing on the cake.

Absolutely none of it was helped, of course, by the man in the class across the hall.

She could hear his voice, she'd realised, even with both doors shut. Just the slightest of sounds: a baseline vibration in her chest, like the low hum of electricity. And that, coupled with her hyperawareness of his proximity to her at all times, well… She was exhausted.

She settled down into the scratch of one of the chairs with a sigh, re-opening her sandwich and tucking in hungrily. She was so relieved that she didn't even care when a lone fragment of egg broke free and slid down her front, plopping into her lap with a splat. She picked off the stray piece and dropped it onto her smoothed-out tinfoil. She'd had worse things than mayonnaise smeared down her.

In fact, by the time she'd finished her sandwich and polished off two Jaffa Cakes from the communal biscuit tin, she was feeling much better. That is, until the staff room door opened and a whiff of perfume entered the room ahead of the person wearing it. Eva groaned inwardly. There was only one person in school who was surrounded by a fragrance forcefield of that magnitude. She didn't even have time to roll her eyes before Jasmine Howell – year four TA and leader of the Burton Lane coven – plopped down next to her.

'Eva,' Jasmine said, dragging out the first syllable in a strange and yet familiar way. She either wanted something, or she was here to make Eva's godforsaken day even worse.

Nonetheless, Eva looked up with a smile. 'Hi Jasmine.'

She was just about to say more when Jasmine shuffled closer, eyes wide underneath her fake eyelashes. 'I heard you went on a date with one of my friends on Saturday.'

Eva's first instinct was to feign ignorance, but that lasted for somewhere in the region of three seconds into Jasmine's knowing stare. She'd have made a terrible spy.

'So you weren't on a date on Saturday night?'

Eva shuffled uncomfortably in the hard plastic chair. 'I mean yes, I was on a date, but I don't know if you know him.'

And that was when she heard the unmistakeable sound of the staff room door clicking shut. She'd been so caught off guard by Jasmine's interrogation that she hadn't even noticed it opening, but the very second she heard that familiar click she knew exactly who had just walked in. She could feel it in the prickle of her skin. And every cell in her body willed her not to look up and see for certain, but her traitorous eyes were moving by themselves by that point, up to meet Luke's, which were narrowed almost to nothing and fixed on her.

And then, just as quickly, he snapped his gaze away from her and set about making a cup of tea in silence.

'Jonas?' Jasmine continued, either completely oblivious to Luke glowering behind her or deliberately speaking loudly enough for him to hear. 'Clock tattoo on his forearm? Really fit?'

Mrs Abbott was absolutely not oblivious to the situation, and, having looked up from her gardening magazine when Jasmine entered the room, now raised a single eyebrow at Eva.

Jasmine's eyes widened. She wasn't going to let this lie. Eva wished for a sinkhole to suddenly open up beneath her.

'Yes,' Eva muttered, as quietly as she thought she could get away with without arousing suspicion. But from the clench of Luke's shoulder blades as she did, it did not appear to be quiet enough. He stirred his tea with renewed vigour, the spoon clattering against the side of the mug with every revolution.

Jasmine's lips pulled into as much of a smirk as the fillers would allow. 'Is it true that you chipped your tooth on his when you went to kiss him?'

Eva squirmed, her tongue automatically going to her tooth, which had been expertly reconstructed by the emergency dentist.

'Yes,' she said, even more quietly than the first time, but again, she could clearly read Luke's reaction to her admission through the grip of his fingers around the handle of the fridge. He froze in place for a split second before hauling the milk out and slamming it down next to his mug.

'I knew it!' Jasmine's manicured hands clasped together in glee which felt a little too forced, although Eva didn't doubt for a second that Jasmine was enjoying this. 'Him and his mates were calling you Jaws.'

At that, Luke threw his spoon into the sink in fury and strode out, Jasmine's eyes following him as far down the corridor as the angle would allow. She looked like she wanted to eat him for dinner.

'Sweet Jesus, he's fit,' she said to no one in particular, though loudly enough that everyone in the room could hear. 'I've never seen him mad before, but *oh my God*, am I right?'

Eva's fists clenched. It wasn't that she hadn't been expecting the bite of jealousy at Jasmine's words so much as she hadn't expected it to be quite so fierce. If she hadn't already been sitting down, she might have fallen over.

Jasmine clocked it straightaway. 'I'm not treading on your toes here, am I?' One deep red fingernail went to the corner of her mouth, wiping off a smear of lipstick which had migrated a little too far from her lip line. She didn't break eye contact with Eva the entire time. 'There was a rumour flying about that the two of you had something going on.'

Eva laughed a little too quickly at that, gripped by a sudden flashback of Luke draped back on his heather grey sofa, dark-eyed and breathing heavily. 'Just a rumour, I'm afraid,' she said, her decade of teaching experience helping ensure that there was absolutely no shake to her voice when she did. 'I'm a single Pringle. Hence the dating.'

Jasmine combed her fingers through her blonde waves. 'Good to know,' she said, her eyes still cast over towards the door. 'I might call dibs on Mr M, then.'

Eva's jaw clenched. 'By all means,' she said, her voice as cool as she was able to make it, but it wasn't enough to stop the small snort of derision from Mrs Abbott, who had turned her attention back to her magazine soon after Luke had entered the room but hadn't turned a single page since. Mrs Abbott took a dim view of staff members fraternising with each other.

'Anyway,' Jasmine said breezily, skipping back to her feet as if her sole reason for coming into the staff room *had* actually been to ruin Eva's day, 'I've got to run. It's more than just puppets and playdough at *our* end of school, you know.'

Eva managed to stop herself from rolling her eyes, but when she looked over at Mrs Abbott she was delighted to find that the older woman showed no such restraint.

'*Bye*, Jasmine,' Mrs Abbott said to the vanishing swish of

blonde curls, a little too loudly and without looking up from her magazine.

Eva had to hold in the giggle which had bubbled up her throat. She loved when Mrs Abbott's inner Rottweiler bared its teeth. 'She wouldn't last a morning with the littles. Can you imagine her playing hunt the poo?'

The older woman huffed, the nearest to a laugh that she ever got. 'That,' she said, snapping her magazine closed, 'I cannot.' She stood, her glance at the clock making Eva check it too.

Five to one.

'Right, Mrs A,' Eva said, balling up the foil from her sandwich and dropping it into the bin. 'You ready for round two?'

The afternoon, mercifully, was much less eventful than the morning. Other than the residual tug in Eva's chest every time she thought about the incident in the staff room, by mid-afternoon she was feeling somewhere close to OK.

Even when she saw Mrs Appleby, the secretary, quickly nip into her classroom and stick a Post-it to her laptop screen. Even after she read the scrawled note on it, asking her to pop into Neeta's office when she had a moment. It couldn't be anything bad, she reasoned, if Neeta was (a) sending a Post-it, and (b) asking Eva to pop in.

You didn't *pop* anywhere to be told bad news. Eva should know, she'd had more than her fair share of it.

And so, by the time she was loitering outside Neeta's office later that afternoon, she was feeling almost upbeat, humming a particularly catchy YouTube song about the oceans, as one finger lazily tracked the fattest of the fish in the school tank. She was just returning the faces he was pulling at her through the glass when she saw something else in the glass: a shape in the reflection which made her blood run simultaneously hot and cold, her senses as confused as she was.

Luke.

He met her eyes in the reflection before snapping them away quickly, turning to peruse the artwork along the corridor as if that had been his intention all along. Eva took a deep breath, and then another one, her eyes still fixed on the fish tank as she said his name, just loudly enough for him to hear.

He didn't react. Didn't even flinch.

She gathered up every scrap of courage that she had, along with what remained of her dignity, and then she turned to look at him.

'Look,' she said, her voice as straightforward as she could bear to make it, 'I just want to apologise for all that in the staff room earlier, I know it wasn't—'

'You have nothing to apologise for, Miss Mallory,' he said, cutting her off. He hadn't turned to face her. He'd barely reacted to her presence, in fact, other than to turn away from it.

It hurt more than she thought it would.

'I'm not…' She trailed off, weighing her words before she burned any bridges with them. Not that she hadn't absolutely decimated this particular bridge, of course, but she still felt compelled to explain herself. She didn't even know why. 'I'm not interested in him.'

He reached out to straighten a name label which had been knocked askew. 'That's really none of my business.' His voice was flat, with a drag to it so slight that she wouldn't have noticed if she wasn't studying him so intensely.

Was it hurt? Had she hurt him?

Embarrassed him, perhaps. That seemed more likely, now she thought about it. She imagined that men like him did not get dumped very often. The idea of it nipped at the pit of her stomach. The thought of other women he'd had. Other strangers he'd kissed in cupboards.

She couldn't be the only one.

Perhaps she was just the first to say no. However desperately she wished she hadn't had to.

'Luke…' she started again, not even knowing where she was going with it, and at the sound of his name, he finally turned to look at her, his eyes as cool as she'd ever seen them.

He hesitated for a moment, just the slightest hitch to his breathing, and then he spoke, with a finality which made her heart crumble to dust in her chest.

'I hope you find what you're looking for.'

She wanted to cry in that moment. And maybe she would have done had it not been for Neeta's door suddenly swinging open, and Neeta herself appearing, flanked by an older-looking man wearing a slim-fitting suit and a lopsided grin.

Neeta looked up at the two of them with a smile. 'Ah, you're both here, excellent. I was going to talk to each of you separately but this actually makes things a little easier.'

Eva and Luke exchanged a glance but Luke snatched it away quickly, his shoulders turning away from her. Eva felt it like a dart in the chest.

'Step into my office,' Neeta continued as her perfectly manicured hands swept over her dress, easing out the wrinkles which had started to form at her hips.

Luke gestured for Eva to go first without quite making eye contact with her, and they shuffled awkwardly into Neeta's office. Neeta nodded at the small conference table and all four of them sat, Eva deliberately choosing the seat next to Luke so she wouldn't have to look at him.

She took back everything she'd previously thought about not *popping in* to hear bad news. This was all feeling very ominous indeed.

'Thank you both for coming,' Neeta began, pushing an open packet of custard creams into the middle of the table. 'I'd like to introduce you to Mr Drummond.'

The older man beamed at each of them in turn, running a hand through his flop of greying curls. 'You can call me Ross.'

'Ross is from the advisory board who are helping us improve our OFSTED rating. His area of special interest is in the performing arts.'

Oh Lord. Eva didn't have the best of track records in that department. The last time the school had attempted a concert Eva had been put in charge of catering and accidentally fed the parents in the audience out-of-date hot dogs.

Nonetheless, Eva smiled at him and out of the corner of her eye she saw Luke smile too. Then she reached for a biscuit without a single ounce of shame. If she was going down, she was going to go down chock full of custard creams.

But the man was still smiling broadly, and so, for that matter, was Neeta.

'Ross, this is Eva Mallory.' Neeta nodded in Eva's direction. 'And our newest member of staff, Luke Mallory.'

'No relation,' Luke said quickly, and Eva spun to face him as if he'd slapped her. But Neeta and Ross just laughed. It had probably come across as a light-hearted quip, she realised, even though it had felt a lot like a dig. She gathered her dignity behind the smile she forced onto her face.

'Eva and Luke,' Neeta continued, a note of pride in her voice, 'are the most musical of all our teachers.'

Eva nearly swallowed her tongue. She was no stranger to belting out a tune for the little ones, often accompanied by her trusty ukulele, but she wouldn't describe herself as *musical*, and she couldn't help the snort which escaped her. 'I wouldn't go that far.'

Neeta leaned back a little way in her chair. 'Come on, Eva.' There was encouragement in her smile, but her voice was firm, the way it always was when she was trying to make her staff members do something they didn't really want to do. 'You have a beautiful singing voice and a real ear for rhythm.'

Eva blushed furiously. She hadn't been aware that anyone other than Mrs Abbott could even hear her singing. 'I mean, I can hold a tune, but I'm not exactly Elaine Paige.'

Ross laughed at that, not unkindly. 'Don't worry,' he said, with a wink so natural that she imagined he had spent time on the stage himself, 'this isn't exactly the West End.'

Fair.

'And Luke,' Neeta said, moving her attention to him, 'is the lead singer in a very successful local band.'

'I sing backing vocals,' Luke corrected, shades of indignation beneath the veneer of politeness in his voice, 'and play bass. And we're a moderately successful hobby band. We mostly do pubs and weddings.'

Eva's eyebrows shot up. He hadn't mentioned anything about this in the full day they'd spent together. She snuck a sideways look at him before immediately regretting it. He was just as handsome as ever, with his hair falling forward onto his face, the faint flush of colour on his cheeks mirroring the burn of her own.

Ross smiled his encouragement. 'Well, I watched one of your videos on YouTube and I enjoyed it very much. You're very talented.' There was the slightest flush in Ross's cheeks too, and it made Eva smile to herself. Perhaps she was not the only one who had noticed Luke's *talents*?

She made a mental note to search for the video at her earliest convenience.

'Anyway,' Neeta said, tucking a stray strand of glossy black hair behind her ear, 'the advisory board have identified a gap in our provision. They believe that beefing up our music and performing arts offering would really help boost our rating.'

Ross nodded. 'There's a new music programme being pushed by the local authority in this area which can, if you are successful, lead to accreditation as a centre for musical excellence.'

'We know that this is not an area we have flourished in previously,' Neeta said, her eyes settling on Eva, 'but it is something we need to improve if we want to become outstanding.'

Eva felt every word deep in her gut. She knew exactly what was happening. Neeta had shielded her after the hot dog incident, managed the response from parents and local news and Environmental Health.

It had been an easy mistake to make, Neeta had said, though it hadn't really. Eva had read the 09/12 best before date as the 9th of December, perfect for their October concert. It actually, of course, was September 2012, and twenty-two of the thirty-eight parents in the audience had come down with food poisoning, two so severely that they'd had to spend a night in hospital. It had been *bad*.

Eva could have been fired on the spot, but she wasn't. She didn't know why Neeta had chosen to take pity on her, but Eva had felt indebted to her ever since. It had been six years since then, and in that time Neeta had never brought it up, never once asked Eva to repay the debt.

She was asking now.

And there was absolutely no way Eva could say no. There was no way she *would* say no.

'So what would we have to do?' Eva asked, meeting Neeta's eye with a nod, and the other woman nodded in return, both understanding the exchange.

'Well, you can start small.' Neeta smiled broadly. 'Singing assemblies, reinstating the choir. Maybe a school band? Many of our older children play instruments.'

'All excellent suggestions,' Ross chirped, brushing a hand through his grey curls. 'And to achieve the full accreditation, you'll have to work up to something a little more spectacular.'

All of a sudden, Eva heard the rumble of Luke's voice beside her. 'Spectacular?' he asked, a note of something darker in the tone. Doubt, perhaps, or something deeper. Whatever it was, it made both Neeta and Ross snap their gazes to him.

'Think of it as an opportunity,' Neeta said, smiling, but without an ounce of give. 'Helping the school achieve this accreditation would go a long way towards proving you're Burton Lane material.'

That piqued Eva's interest. She recognised the tone of Neeta's voice: equal parts pleasant and firm, just as it had been a few minutes earlier. Neeta wasn't asking, she was telling.

'Yes, of course,' Luke replied, and there was something

strange about his tone too, a strange obedience to his words like he had his own debt. Even though he'd only been at the school for three weeks.

And as they listened to Neeta and Ross continue to outline the plan, Eva grabbed for another custard cream, fighting hard to suppress the creep of anxiety up her spine when she imagined how this whole endeavour might unfold. Because whatever had been behind the deliberate tone of Neeta's words, both she and Luke seemed to be in the same boat.

Together.

Unable to even look at each other.

What could possibly go wrong?

Chapter Ten

Eva was on the run when she got the message.

At least, she would have been, had she not been stuck fast. As it was, she was the exact opposite of on the run.

She'd had a bad feeling from the start. In fact, from before the start. From the very second that Ciocia Nelka gave her the lowdown on Bartek, her date for that evening, she'd had a knot of something tugging at the pit of her stomach like an omen. And ordinarily Eva would have listened to such a feeling. Ordinarily she would have given this walking red flag an extremely wide berth, but she didn't.

The trouble was that the date had come at the end of two particularly gruelling weeks at school, where she and Luke had begrudgingly tried to get their fledgling music programme off the ground with a resounding lack of success. They'd been uptight and out-of-sync, too busy avoiding each other between sessions to form any kind of cohesive plan. Not to mention that, ruffled by his mere presence, Eva had been even more of a disaster than usual.

So when Nelka mentioned that her friend's son, one of the potential husbands on Eva's list, had asked if he could invite Eva to a gig at a local bar that evening, she'd thrown caution to the wind. Despite a number of concerns raised by Nelka's description of Bartek and in particular by the demands he'd made of her prior to the date, she'd agreed to meet him.

Her need for an end to the godforsaken curse had never been greater.

But it didn't take her much longer than an hour to realise that Bartek Wozniak was utterly, and Eva did not use the word lightly, terrifying. Like hose-you-down-in-a-pit, wear-your-skin-as-a-dress terrifying.

And that was why, exactly one hour and seventeen minutes after meeting him, Eva was hanging halfway out of a toilet window, pinned fast by her hipbones and *deeply* regretting the miniskirt that Bartek had insisted she wear.

Hanna, who had sat through the entire thing six feet to Eva's left, was at her head end, wearing a long black wig and coaching her through the trauma. Meanwhile the bar manager, who had just happened to be passing the toilet door at such a time as to hear Eva's initial scream, was inside the toilet, trying to push her out from behind.

But Eva already knew the reality of her situation. She'd known it from the moment when she'd lost her grip and slipped, her hips screaming with pain where they'd wedged in the narrow window opening.

She was stuck.

Actually, properly *stuck*.

She winced as the bar manager tried to heave her through one last time, and again after that as Hanna tried to shove her back through the other way, but neither was achieving much at all.

'You know,' Hanna said, stopping to wipe a thin sheen of sweat from her forehead, 'you could have just done the secret signal and I would have whisked you away. You didn't have to actually climb out of a window.'

Eva shook her head, feeling the vibration of the action all the way to her hipbones. 'The situation was too grave for the secret signal. I didn't want him to see what you looked like.'

Her sister snorted a laugh.

'I'm serious,' Eva huffed. 'I was acting on instinct, Han. It was proper fight or flight.' She shuddered, remembering the cold shiver which had slipped down her spine when Bartek had grabbed her wrist over the table. 'That man is going to murder someone one day.'

'Maybe you can report him to the authorities when they turn up,' the bar manager said as she appeared out in the small courtyard, hands propped on her hips.

Eva's stomach nipped in shame. 'The police are coming?'

'Fire brigade actually,' the manager said cheerfully, shoulders hitching into a one-sided shrug.

Hanna huffed a laugh. 'Oh, your old pals.'

Eva glared at her, as far as she was able to, anyway, considering the angle she'd become stuck at. Her head was lower than her knees, folded at the hips, and she was beginning to feel the prickle of pins and needles in her extremities. She wanted to cry, but her eyes felt too swollen for the tears to form.

'Urgh,' she muttered instead, a scratch to her voice, 'this is all Luke's fault.'

Hanna's brows pinched. 'Luke?'

'You know.' Eva gestured vaguely. '*Luke* Luke.'

'Oh, kissed-you-in-a-cupboard Luke.'

Eva nodded, regretting the movement immediately. 'Since the whole…' She paused, scrabbling for a diplomatic way of putting it. '… *incident*, he's been making my life a misery.'

Hanna swiped a stray strand of black hair from the corner of her mouth where it had blown into. 'I thought he was just ignoring you.'

'He *is* just ignoring me.' Eva couldn't help the exasperation which crept into her voice. 'That's what's making it a misery.'

But her twin only laughed. 'What, are you expecting him to come to his senses and tell you he can't live without you?' She raised one eyebrow, an accusation. 'Didn't *you* dump *him*?'

'Yes, I did.' Eva rolled her eyes, feeling the pressure building in her face. 'And no, that's not what I'm expecting.'

'What *are* you expecting?' the bar manager asked, beside them all of a sudden, and both sisters turned to her in shock. 'Sorry,' she said, blushing, 'I didn't mean to be nosy. I'm just kind of invested.' An awkward laugh burst out of her. 'I'm Caitlyn, by the way. I feel like I should introduce myself after getting so, um, intimate with you.'

Eva laughed too, despite herself, and it made her hips strain and throb. 'Nice to meet you, Caitlyn. And I'm sorry about all this.' She motioned vaguely to herself. 'I'm kind of a disaster.'

Caitlyn chuckled. 'Don't worry about it. This is the most interesting shift of my whole week.'

'You're welcome,' Eva said, her exhale equal parts sigh and laugh. 'At least my pathetic life is good for something.'

Just then, Hanna paused, cocking one ear. 'Wait, did you hear that?'

All Eva could hear was the whooshing of blood through her ears.

'No.'

'Your phone just beeped.' Hanna raised one eyebrow like a cartoon sleuth. 'That's it. We've summoned him.'

Eva huffed a breath. 'You're an idiot.'

But Hanna, nothing if not determined, was already rifling through her sister's bag. She grabbed Eva's phone and held it aloft, a huge, smug grin stretching from ear to ear.

'Oh my God.' She waved the phone at her sister. 'We *have* summoned him.'

Eva's vision was beginning to darken and blur from the inversion. She couldn't see a thing. 'Shut up, that isn't him.'

Hanna was almost beside herself. 'It is!'

'Unless you know more than one Luke,' Caitlyn offered, from just over Hanna's right shoulder.

'What the hell?' Eva's heart skidded down into her throat, even more so than it already was from the squeeze of the window frame around her body. 'Give it to me.'

She swiped for it, but Hanna evaded her easily, tapping in a passcode before tutting and trying another. 'Unlock it, I want to see what the message says.'

'No!' Eva's voice came as an indignant squeak. 'Not like this.'

The other two women laughed, and Eva made a mental note to disown her twin as soon as was reasonably practicable.

'A-ha!' Hanna's smile grew. 'You *are* hoping he's telling you he can't live without you.'

Eva's chest squeezed, and she forced the feeling down. The reality was that it didn't matter how much she hoped that was the case. She had made her decision for a reason and she wasn't about to go back on it now, not while the curse was still wreaking such effective havoc on her life.

'It'll be about school,' she said, as calmly as she was able. 'We're working on a project together.'

Caitlyn sucked a breath in through her teeth. 'Woah, you're working on a project with your ex?' She shook her head, lips pinched tight. 'Must be pretty intense.'

Actually, it *was* intense, but again, that wasn't the point.

And so Eva opted for deflection.

'He's not even my ex.' She tried to shift her weight, only to be punished by a new rip of pain. 'We went on one date, for God's sake.'

Hanna tapped in another passcode, before swearing at the phone under her breath. She looked up at her sister. 'So how is any of this his fault?'

'Because he hates me now, probably with good reason.' A hot knife of guilt sliced through Eva's chest. 'And having to work near him makes me feel the full force of the curse.'

Caitlyn's ears pricked up. 'Curse?'

'Long story,' the twins replied in unison, and Eva sighed, a contrast with Hanna's smirk.

'So now.' Eva continued, the thump of her heartbeat growing behind her eyes, 'I'm having to go on all these dates with complete *weirdos* in the vain hope that one of them turns out to be a little less weird than the rest so I can marry them and stop making an utter fool of myself generally, but *especially* in front of Luke.'

Eva couldn't see the sudden rush of sympathy on her sister's face then, nor the slight widening of Caitlyn's eyes as she looked on. In fact, she couldn't see much of anything at that point. Just reflected flashes of blue light bouncing off the glass panels lining the courtyard as her vision slowly faded to black.

When she came round, she was looking up at four faces, only two of which she recognised.

'Hi Eva,' a man she hadn't seen before was saying. 'Welcome back.'

Wait.

She was looking *up*.

'I'm out,' she said, as much a question as it was a statement, and the man grinned in reply.

'You're out,' he said with a sure nod, and it was only then that she noticed the gleam of a reflective strip on his jacket, identical to the other man who was also standing over her. She didn't recognise either of the firefighters from the day at the hotel and she was immeasurably thankful for that.

Her hands went to her hips, finding a little soreness, but nothing which seemed catastrophic. 'Thank you,' she said, with her first genuine smile of the night, and the second firefighter nodded a *you're welcome*.

'We'd like if you popped to the hospital, just to get checked out,' he said, with a little half-smile which made Eva feel more at ease than at any point in the last couple of hours. 'You were pretty wedged in there. You won't need an ambulance, but we can drop you at A&E if you need? It's on our way back to the station.'

Eva looked at Hanna, who replied with an enthusiastic nod. 'Yes, please,' Eva said, taking the man's offered hand and smiling a little wider than was reasonable as she pulled herself to her feet.

The curse rarely came with benefits.

It was a short ride to the hospital, and Eva enjoyed every last second of it, despite the nag of pain in her hips and the residual pounding in her head. She still had a smile on her face when she turned to her sister.

Hanna had a faraway expression on her face, eyes looking straight out onto the road ahead. 'I still can't believe it,' she said, when she saw Eva looking at her.

Eva snorted a laugh. 'Can't you? This is my whole life.'

Her sister frowned in confusion a moment before she laughed too. 'I mean yeah, I can totally believe that you got stuck in a toilet window.' She'd taken her wig off and was twirling the strands around her fingers. 'What I can't believe is how the hell lovely Ciocia Nelka is such a terrible judge of character.'

That was a fair comment. Eva had wondered the same thing herself.

A small breath escaped through Hanna's nose as she shook her head. 'Where the hell did she meet him?'

'Church, apparently.'

Hanna's brows shot up. 'I don't believe that man could enter a house of God without being immediately struck by lightning.'

'Maybe he wasn't that bad,' Eva said with a shrug. 'I could be being overly dramatic about the whole thing.'

She felt the change in her sister's demeanour immediately.

'Eevs, no,' Hanna said, brandishing the wig as if it were a weapon. 'Don't do that thing you do.'

Eva scoffed. 'I don't do a thing.'

'You do. But don't do it now.' Hanna looked forward out of

the windscreen. 'We agreed no settling. No making excuses. You have plenty of other husband candidates.' At that, she suddenly spun back to her sister, her eyes wide. 'Oooh, speaking of which, did you ever check that message?'

Eva couldn't help but laugh. 'You mean you didn't manage to hack into my phone while I was passed out?'

Hanna's brows pinched together, 'No, I did not.'

'You tried though.'

'Obviously.' She shrugged. 'You've changed your code again, haven't you?'

But Eva didn't answer, just laughed and reached for her phone, a strange mix of dread and excitement churning in her stomach as she swiped to open the message. It was shorter than she expected. Just three words.

Three words which made her heart leap into her throat.

LUKE: *Can we talk?*

She felt her lungs empty of their own accord, her pulse kicking to a race in her ears. Maybe he *was* trying to win her back?

She'd be lying if she said the idea didn't make her chest swell. She'd never in her whole life connected with someone the way she had with him. She still jumped a little every time she heard his voice, the rasp of it reaching deep down into her body even when the words he was saying were perfectly ordinary.

The other day he'd popped his head round her door and said, 'You haven't seen the trundle wheel, have you?' and she hadn't been quite herself for the rest of the morning. They hadn't even made eye contact. The rumble of his voice in her chest was enough to make her want to fashion a trundle wheel just for him, purely to hear him say 'thank you' in that same tone.

She shivered just thinking about it.

But then, before she'd even had time to close her eyes and imagine it, her heart jumped again, this time down to her feet. Because there was a reason she'd walked away from him, and she couldn't allow herself to forget it. She couldn't willingly sign herself up for a lifetime of getting wedged in window frames and burning down buildings.

Not now that she knew there was a way out.

She sighed, seeing the familiar pattern of the hospital lights come into view. She'd spent enough time in the place that she knew it by heart now, and that in itself made her more determined to stick to her guns. She was only ever one misfortune away from total devastation, and she was never quite able to let herself forget it. She'd never forgive herself for not taking the chance to leave that worry behind.

Even if it meant leaving Luke behind too.

Even if it meant breaking her own heart all over again.

Chapter Eleven

By the time Eva walked into Luke's classroom the following morning she was barely limping. She had a hell of a bruise on each hipbone, and a matching one in a straight line across the top of her buttocks, but her X-rays had been clear and the doctor had been happy that there was nothing worse lurking beneath the surface.

A lucky escape, the doctor's exact words had been, and it had made Eva cringe.

An unlucky escape, perhaps.

She saw Luke react as she rounded the door, almost as if he'd known it was her, but he didn't look up. Not at first.

'Thanks for coming,' he said, his tone so flat that it felt as if he'd punched her in the chest. Her hand moved to her heart, but she directed it to her shoulder instead, adjusting the blouse she'd chosen that morning. It was the nicest one she owned, though she wouldn't have liked Luke to know that.

Her lips, painted a rosier shade than usual, pulled together, gathering up courage before she spoke.

'How can I help?' she asked, and immediately regretted it. It was so formal. *Too* formal. Not the way you should speak to someone who'd had their tongue in your mouth, she thought, before regretting bringing up that memory too.

And when he finally looked up at her, she regretted agreeing to come at all.

His face looked as if it had been carved out of a block of stone – cold and ungiving – to such an extent that she barely recognised him. This man wasn't the Luke she'd met in the bar all those weeks ago. He wasn't even the Mr Mallory she'd been acclimatising to, with his veneer of congeniality and a pleasant, if a little hollow, smile.

For the first time in a while, it was just the two of them. Again. But not in any of the ways they had been before. And as she looked at him, just a little before eight on that Friday morning, it was as if she were being introduced to a whole new side of him.

Eva knew, in that moment, that whatever Luke had to say it wasn't going to be good.

She took a deep breath, pushing off the desk that she'd been leaning on and walking a few steps more before perching gingerly on the corner of a table. Her hips ached and groaned as she moved, and her hands went to them almost without thinking, fingertips soothing the soreness as best they could.

She didn't notice him watching her until he spoke.

'Are you OK?'

It was a genuine question, but there was no warmth to it, and that in itself made Eva feel worse. She wondered if he even cared to know the answer.

'Yeah, I'm fine,' she said, fingers curling around the edge of the table. 'Just got stuck in a window and had to be rescued by the fire brigade. You know, a regular Thursday night.' She laughed a little, the sound weak and humourless. She wasn't sure what she'd been hoping for, perhaps some kind of lighter moment to prompt a truce, but Luke just looked at her from beneath the jut of his frown.

'OK,' he said, finally, and it felt worse than if he had said nothing at all.

It was always strangely quiet in school without the children, and that morning was no different. It made the awkward silences that much worse, the buzz of electricity filling the spaces where she had been hoping to hear the blissful rumble of his voice.

A muscle in his jaw flexed once or twice, and he looked away from her before he started to speak.

'It's not working,' he started, something straining at his voice as he did. 'This music thing.'

Eva's brows pulled into a frown, her heart spiralling to her feet. She'd been at the practices, of course, and as such could not fully disagree, but doing anything with young children was always disastrous at first. She'd been in the game long enough to know it always came together in the end.

Pretty much, anyway.

She cleared her throat. 'I mean it's still pretty rough, but we'll get there.' Her voice dropped a little. 'I can't let Neeta down.'

He looked straight at her, an expression she couldn't read playing on his features beneath the poker face he was forcing.

'No,' he said, his right hand going to the opposite shirt cuff, fingers working the button free. 'That's not an option for me, either. I'm just saying that there might be a workaround.'

Eva's frown deepened. 'A workaround?'

He unbuttoned the other cuff and began to roll one up, the action practised, meticulous. 'I'm saying I need to do it, but I can't do it with you.'

Eva, who had been staring shamelessly at the contours of Luke's newly revealed forearms, snapped her gaze up to his face then, indignation building in her chest at his words.

'What?'

'It's a mess,' he said, his voice straightforward. 'Us doing this together.'

She huffed a laugh, breathy and humourless. 'I do have that effect on proceedings.'

He was looking at her again, though she almost wished he wasn't. There was something behind his eyes, something which made her throat clench, and between that and the hard set of his mouth, it made her want to sink into the earth.

He was looking at her as if he wanted to say something, barely constrained words making the muscles in his jaw knot and flex, but behind his unrelenting stare it came across a lot like derision, and that made a completely new feeling flare in her chest.

When she'd first met Luke in the bar, she'd been gripped by a paradox, a simultaneous sense of attraction and annoyance. And that feeling had tipped in favour of attraction, after the incident in the art cupboard, and especially after the evening she'd spent at his house, and the full day they'd spent together afterwards. But now the gauge was swinging back, anger bubbling in the pit of her stomach as she looked at him. Her chest tightened as she took in his tense jaw, the slight clench of his fists, the narrowing of his eyes as they bore into hers.

'So, what are you proposing?' she asked, unable to keep the bite out of her voice.

'That we split it.' His jaw tipped up a little. Bravado, perhaps. 'Fifty-fifty.'

'Split it?'

He nodded slowly, as if it was obvious, as if she were the one slow to catch on, rather than him talking in riddles 'Straight down the middle. I'll take band, you take choir.' His stare was even, unrelenting. 'We can copy each other into emails and leave notes on practices. That way we'll each keep up with what the other is doing in case Neeta asks about it, but we won't both have to be at both.'

And that was the point at which the last remaining shreds of hope, misguided though it may have been, dropped like autumn leaves and fluttered to her feet. Perhaps she *had* been hoping that he was going to plead with her, to ask her to give *them* a chance. She'd certainly dressed like someone who expected to have undying love declared to them at any moment, though she hadn't been particularly proud of it.

But that wasn't it at all. She wasn't his *One*. She probably didn't even register on the scale.

She was a little more than a blip.

An inconvenience.

Someone he couldn't even bear to share a room with. And the way his words were making her feel right at that moment, well, she didn't much want to share a room with him either. But she had made a commitment, and her loyalty to Neeta was the only thing which kept her there, in that moment.

'What if Neeta notices that we're never in the same place at the same time?' Her fingers found the jut of her hip, rubbing away a sudden jolt of pain. 'She did ask us to work together on this.'

He shrugged, almost arrogant, and it made her teeth clench tightly. 'We'll cross that bridge when we come to it.'

But crossing bridges wasn't one of Eva's strengths; she was far more likely to burn them. It was accidental, most often, though that rarely seemed to matter.

It definitely was not going to matter now.

'It's probably for the best,' she replied, with as much bite in her tone as she could possibly muster. She saw when it connected, the way he bristled, teeth gritted, and before she could stop herself, she spoke again, the words slipping from her lips like an act of war.

'We don't work well together anyway.'

And then, before she had to suffer the sting of his narrowed eyes on her for a moment longer, she spun on her heel, and her feet – which clearly had much better instincts than she did – were walking her out of the room.

Back to the relative safety of her own classroom.

And, most importantly, far, *far* away from Luke Mallory.

Chapter Twelve

'Can you see it?' Eva asked, sprawled out on the cool tile of Sylvia's kitchen floor, one eye squinting under the fridge. Her twin, in a mirror image of her position, tutted loudly, her head pressing against Eva's as she squirmed.

'I think I...' Hanna muttered, swiping into the murk with a wire hanger she'd manipulated into a hook. 'Ah shit, no. That's just a random bolt.' She squirmed some more, readjusting her grip on the makeshift hook. 'Can you get the torch on your phone or something? It's darker than a bat's arsehole under here.'

Eva fumbled for her phone, tapping on the torch and angling the beam as far underneath the fridge as she could. She'd do anything she could to aid in the retrieval of her dad's ring. It was, after all, entirely her fault that it was under there.

She hadn't meant to drop it, it was just that there was something about it, an energy which got under her skin. It had been Jozef's wedding ring, originally, then Pawel, her grandfather's, and then finally Tomasz's. Two of the three men had died young, and while Pawel did not, the curse – and the cancer – had ensured that he lived the latter years of his life in terrible pain, withering to nothing before the family's eyes. Based on that, Eva couldn't help wanting to keep the ring at arm's length.

These days it lived in Sylvia's jewellery box and only came out every few years for a clean. This time Sylvia had entrusted the job to her daughters and they were messing it up spectacularly.

At least, Eva was. Hanna had passed the ring over while she rooted under the sink for Sylvia's polishing cloth and Eva had taken it in hesitant fingertips, not wanting to absorb too many of the bad vibes. But then she'd fumbled as she was grabbing it, almost catching it once, and then a second time before it landed on top of the fridge and somehow managed to roll all the way to the back before falling to the floor with a small metallic *thunk*.

'I think I've got it!' Hanna shrieked then, almost head butting her sister in her elation, but the joy did not last. 'Never mind, that's the leg of the bloody fridge.' She swore a little under her breath as she reached back in.

'Language, Hanna,' came a voice then, from behind them, and Eva almost jumped out of her skin.

'We haven't lost it,' she blurted, spinning round to meet her mother's eyes with the creep of dread in her chest. But Sylvia didn't look angry. She was just watching the two of them with her lips hitched into a half-smile, a vacuum cleaner sitting by her feet.

'Just misplaced it?' Sylvia asked, her smile widening as she pushed her glasses up her nose. 'Don't worry, this isn't my first rodeo.'

And then Eva watched as her mother shooed them both out of the way, produced a pop sock from her pocket like a low-budget magician and slid it onto the vacuum attachment in one smooth move. She crouched down, flicking the vacuum on and reaching it as far underneath the fridge as she was able, covering the whole area with wide, sweeping movements. After a moment or two, she pulled it back out carefully and switched the vacuum off, whereupon the formerly missing ring fell the short distance to the floor, landing amid a small heap of lint.

Hanna sucked a breath in through her teeth. 'You unlikely *genius*.'

But Sylvia just laughed, picking up the ring and putting it carefully in Hanna's open palm before dusting herself off. 'Finish cleaning it and then bring it through to the living room. The ciocias are watching *Catchphrase* together and you know how they get.' She shrugged, almost an apology. 'I can't handle it by myself for much longer.'

Eva laughed, watching her mother leave the room before turning to Hanna. 'I have no idea why they even watch it; I'm not sure I've ever known them to get one right.' She picked up the polishing cloth, abandoned on the worktop, and handed it to her sister. 'Why don't you just clean it so I don't get my curse on it again.'

'Any excuse,' Hanna replied, with a smirk, but she got to polishing straightaway, her fingers moving in quick, frantic strokes as if she didn't want to spend too much time touching it, either.

Hanna, unlike her sister, had never been particularly superstitious, but the ring was bothering her, Eva could tell. Her shoulders were hitched high, her glossed lips pressed into a flat line as she worked. When she finished polishing it, she breathed an audible sigh of relief before wrapping it carefully in the cloth itself.

'You don't like to touch it either,' Eva said gently, and her sister spun to face her, embarrassment colouring her cheeks.

'I don't think it's *cursed* or anything.'

'But?'

'But,' Hanna began, with a small sigh, 'seeing it like this, you know, not on his finger.' Her mouth twisted a little, the movement familiar. 'It feels like losing him all over again.' She looked away quickly, like she'd said something wrong. 'Sounds stupid, I know.'

Eva's breath caught in her throat. She knew exactly what Hanna meant – she'd felt it herself. Not just about the ring, but about everything, all of his things, and their absolute audacity to still exist in a world where he didn't.

'Doesn't sound stupid at all,' she managed, her throat thick. And then neither of them said anything for a while, just let the familiar waves of grief wash over them as they stood, together. It always felt easier when Hanna was there, particularly so when Eva felt her sister reach for her hand and squeeze gently.

'Come on,' Hanna said, a soft glint of tears in her eyes. 'Let's go see which well-loved saying the ciocias are butchering today.'

True to form, Irenka was shaking one age-worn fist at the TV when the twins walked into the living room. The ciocias were perched together on the sofa like two birds, though Irenka's bird looked as if it was spoiling for a fight.

'Stupid thing,' she said, as much to herself as to anyone else in the room. 'I never hear this in my whole life.'

Hanna snorted a laugh. 'It's a very common expression, ciocia.'

But the old woman did not even turn to look at her, muttering to herself in Polish as she settled back into the worn fabric of Sylvia's sofa.

'Surely there's a Polish version of this that we could stream from somewhere,' Hanna continued, oblivious to the quiet seethe of her great-aunt behind her. 'You might have more luck with it in your first language.'

At that, Irenka snapped her gaze back to Hanna, her frown deepening. 'I am trying to learn new things,' she said, sternly, her cool grey eyes searing into her great-niece. 'You think I am too old to learn?'

Hanna, to her credit, at least had the sense to look repentant. 'No, ciocia.'

And Irenka turned her attention back to the screen with an audible harrumph, reaching a hand as if to put her grey curls back into place even though they were caked in enough hairspray to withstand a nuclear blast.

Hanna, now suitably admonished, headed for her mother, settling on the arm of the loveseat Sylvia was nestling in and holding the ring out to her. Sylvia took it with a smile, unfolding the cloth and running her fingertips against the shine of the metal. And then, before Eva could even react, her mother had reached for her hand and was gently pressing the ring into the skin of Eva's palm.

'For your husband,' she said, 'when you find him.' Her voice was just loud enough for Eva to hear over the obscene volume Ciocia Irenka insisted on setting the TV at. 'Don't lose it this time.'

Hanna nearly fell off the arm of the chair. 'You have to be

kidding.' Her voice was plenty loud enough to hear over the TV, and Eva heard Irenka tut. 'You're going to give your husband, who you're marrying to escape a curse, a *cursed ring*?'

Eva couldn't help but smile, despite the thump of apprehension in her chest. 'I thought you said it wasn't cursed.'

Sylvia's brows tugged together. 'It's *not* cursed, don't be silly.'

'Isn't it?' Hanna's expression was a mirror of her mother's. 'What happened to the men who wore it?'

'Hanna.' Sylvia's voice as she muttered the name was many things, but most of all it was a warning. 'It wasn't the ring that caused it.'

But her elder daughter was never one to heed a warning. 'Not a great omen though, is it? Why didn't you give it to Stefan if you're that confident?'

Eva expected that her mother might tell Hanna off again, but she didn't, and when she spoke again, there was a softening to her voice that Eva hadn't been expecting at all.

'Because it wasn't my place to.' If anything, Sylvia was smiling. 'It wasn't my ring; it was your dad's. He would have wanted to pass it on to one of you.'

'For Bartek, maybe?' Ciocia Nelka piped up then, from across the room. The old woman had, in the past, claimed that she was losing her hearing, but that didn't seem likely. She had the auditory acuity of a bat in its prime. 'You liked him?'

Tension knotted in Eva's shoulders. Should she be honest about the full horror of the encounter? She wasn't sure she could bring herself to do it. Ciocia Nelka had been so pure in her intentions, and she looked like a small, elderly angel now, looking at Eva with such hope as her snow-white curls were illuminated like a halo by the wall lamp behind.

'I don't think I'll see him again,' Eva said eventually, trying hard to keep her tone positive. 'We ... we wanted different things.'

Hanna snorted. 'Yeah, *you* wanted to survive the night.'

Her snark was totally lost on the ciocias, but Sylvia almost did herself a mischief the way she snapped up tall in her chair.

'What?' She looked between her daughters from beneath her greying fringe, her expression a question. 'Eevs?'

Eva plastered on a smile. She never did like to worry her mother. 'He was just a bit strange.'

'He was more than just a bit strange,' Hanna said, adjusting herself on the arm of the chair. 'Eevs literally jumped out of a window to escape him.'

'Shooting the mouth,' Ciocia Irenka barked at the TV, paying no heed to any of them.

But Sylvia was focused only Eva. 'I hope you're being safe out there, Eva.'

'I am,' Eva replied, with a smile. 'I always have Hanna there. And I ran away as soon as I realised he was properly sinister.' She shrugged. 'I'll just choose a more appropriate window to climb out of next time.'

On the other sofa, Ciocia Irenka tutted so violently that she nearly lost her teeth again. 'Bite the bullet? What is?'

Eva caught Hanna's eye and barely held in her giggle. Hanna managed no such thing.

'Ah, you didn't like him.' Ciocia Nelka's eyes creased with her smile. 'Don't worry, you have lots of other names on your list. One of them will be right.'

Hanna laughed again. 'Yeah, I bet you can't wait to get back out there after your near miss with Bartek, the axe murderer.' She looked over at Nelka, whose smile had fallen to a frown. 'Did you really meet him in church?'

'Yes,' the older woman said, her tone light. 'He is always there for confession on Saturday mornings.'

Hanna eyebrows shot up so fast that Eva was concerned they would pop right off. 'Wait, he goes to confession *every* week?'

'Twenty-two balls!' Irenka boomed.

Hanna glanced her way for a moment before lifting one eyebrow even further. 'Maybe he commits a higher-than-average number of sins.'

'Maybe,' Nelka began, smiling fondly at her sister, who was now ranting in Polish in the direction of the TV, 'he is just very devout.'

Eva smiled gently at her great-aunt. Nelka was such a pure soul. She always saw the good in everyone.

Even axe murderers.

Behind her on the sofa, Irenka made a noise which fell somewhere between a laugh and a growl. 'Catch twenty-two.' She huffed a breath out. 'That is what I said, yes?'

'Yes, ciocia,' Hanna said, her voice dripping with sarcasm which Irenka did not pick up on, merely nodding curtly and turning her attention back to the programme. Hanna looked back at Eva. 'OK, I'll let you pick one of ours next.' Her voice dropped a little. 'You can trust me; Greg was nice, wasn't he?'

Eva thought back to that first date with Greg. It all seemed so long ago now, and for a moment she was transported back there, back when she didn't know Luke's name or how his mouth felt against hers.

She cleared her throat. 'Yeah, he was actually. At least he would have been, had he not been a male me.'

'Yeah, not ideal,' Hanna said, with a laugh. 'Anyway, onwards and upwards. I can offer you Gerard, the art director, or Justin, the accountant. Who do you like the sound of?'

Neither, honestly, but Eva wasn't in a position to be picky.

'Let's try Gerard,' she said, with a smile she hoped looked genuine. 'I don't even know what an art director does, but it sounds interesting.'

Hanna's smile lit up her whole face. 'I'll set it up!'

'And I'll take care of this until you find The One,' Sylvia said then, from between the twins, holding the now perfectly polished ring in delicate fingers.

Eva still wasn't convinced, but she smiled at her mother regardless. She couldn't bear to say anything, not with the hope which had begun to creep into Sylvia's expression.

'Perfect,' Hanna chirped. 'Now let's get back to *Catchphrase*.' She settled back on the arm of the chair, one knee propped up under her chin. 'Who do you think's going to win? My money's on Ciocia Irenka.'

Irenka broke away from the TV for a moment to glare at Hanna, her face falling into the frown lines it was so used to.

Hanna merely waved in return.

Chapter Thirteen

Eva's first solo choir practice was an unmitigated disaster. She was used to disasters, of course, but this one felt different, a bite of panic, cold and uneasy, rising in her chest as she smiled sweetly at the raven-haired year one child who had just burst into tears.

She wasn't the first child to cry in the session. Not even close. In all honesty, Eva was close to crying herself.

She had years of experience standing in front of classes. She'd taught every last child in the room at some point, for God's sake. It shouldn't have been difficult to get them to simultaneously belt out a few bars of 'Morning Has Broken', and yet it felt as if she were undertaking a mammoth task, her shaky grasp on the last remnants of her dignity overshadowed only by the sudden impossibility of keeping order.

The younger children were fidgeting, chewing on their cuffs and ponytail ends as they spun full 180s to laugh at their friends in the row behind. The older children looked as if they were moments from sleep. And little Bobby Hutchinson was, oh Lord…

'Bobby!' Eva called, the sound echoing off the shiny old paint on the walls. 'Stop licking the piano stool.'

Bobby's eyes snapped up to meet hers, though he didn't move an inch other than to close his mouth, those huge green eyes fixed on hers and widened in an expression of surprise. Eva hadn't even fully moved her eyes away from him before he lunged for the stool again, teeth bared like a tiny vampire.

Eva made the three strides towards him in a flash, grabbing one hand and guiding him back across the parquet floor, away from the temptation of the lush chartreuse velvet.

'Chairs are not food,' she muttered, as much to herself as to him, and she took a deep breath as she grabbed her sky-blue ukulele from the top of the piano.

'OK,' she started. 'Let's try that again, from the—'

'Miss,' came a voice from the middle row, stretching the vowel out far longer than was necessary.

Eva didn't even need to ask what the issue was. At this point in her career she could guess it from the intonation of the *Miiiissssssss*.

'You can go to the toilet in a minute, Grace,' she said, a good deal more patience in her voice than she felt.

Seven more hands flew up. A muscle clenched in her jaw.

'We just need to make it through one verse of the song,' she gritted out. 'Just *one*, and then it's playtime anyway.'

Eight hands reluctantly went down.

'Right.' She strummed a single chord, the ordinarily joyous jangle of the uke totally lost to the sombre mood of the room.

'Where's Mr Mallory?' Year-four Sienna blurted, her lip sucking into a pout. 'It's boring without him.'

A low rumble of chatter started at that, spreading through the rows of children like wildfire. Eva frowned, raising her palm and trying desperately to ignore the unreasonable lurch in her chest at the mention of his name. 'No thanks,' she said firmly, her fingers gripping the ukulele so tightly that for a moment she was afraid it would splinter. She looked back at Sienna, who was trying to hide her pride at the disruption she'd caused. 'No shouting out, please, Sienna. Put your hand up if you want to ask a question.'

Eva played another chord, slow and deliberate. 'Mr Mallory won't be joining us for choir practice anymore.' She was surprised the words even made it out, such was the tension in her jaw. 'It's going to be just me.'

Sienna's face fell. One of the children who had cried earlier in the session spontaneously burst into tears again. A couple of the year six girls exchanged loaded glances.

Eva sighed. They hadn't even managed one line.

Out of the corner of her eye she just about clocked Bobby, inches from making full-mouth contact with the cushion of the stool. How the hell had he got back there so quickly?

She set off walking again. If he managed to take a chunk out of it, Neeta would hold it against her forever. The piano was her pride and joy, despite the fact that Neeta herself couldn't play a note.

The thought stopped her in her tracks. That was it.

She needed to find someone who could play the piano.

It would help the children stay in time and on-key, in theory, anyway. At worst, it would drown out a bit of the singing. Not to mention that Bobby would be a lot less likely to try and eat the piano stool if there was someone sitting in it.

Perfect.

There must have been someone, maybe a TA or a parent volunteer or someone who could play – they probably didn't even need to be that good. She made a mental note to ask Mrs Abbott later. If anyone knew, it would be her.

'Right everyone,' she said brightly, fully revived by her new plan. 'One more time, from the top.'

'Mr Myrtle,' Mrs Abbott had said when Eva asked, poking dried-up playdough out of the underside of a Lego brick with a look of steely determination on her face.

Eva's brows had pulled together. 'Orson?'

She couldn't picture the ageing year-five teacher at a piano. He'd been at Burton Lane twice as long as she had, if not three times, and in that time the school had kind of grown around him, like a tree around railings. The busy comings and goings of school life had just seemed to swallow him up. At least, that was the impression she'd always had.

Mrs Abbott had snapped narrowed eyes at Eva. 'He's a classically trained pianist.'

'He is?'

But the older woman had just harrumphed, turning her attention back to the brick, nimble hands working the biro lid deep into the embedded dough. 'Ask him yourself.'

And that was how Eva had come to be here, hovering outside the year-five classroom, watching Orson Myrtle neaten a stack of exercise books, through the glass of the door. She didn't know the older man nearly as well as she should have done considering the time both of them had worked together, and she felt bad about that now, particularly as she was about to ask him for such a huge favour.

She took a deep breath, pushing away her regrets as she reached for the handle.

'Eva,' he said, before she was even all the way through the door. He hadn't even looked up.

'Mr Myrtle,' she replied, by way of greeting, and at that he looked up, his face falling along well-worn creases into a smile so broad that it made her smile, too.

'Orson, please,' he said, his words chased by the smallest of chuckles. 'We've known each other far too long for such formalities.' He pushed his gold-rimmed glasses up his nose, though he was still looking at Eva over the top of them. 'How can I help you?'

Eva hesitated a moment, her fingers knotting together. 'I'm looking for someone to play the piano for the choir.' She shrugged, trying to offset some of her awkwardness. 'I've heard that you play.'

He studied her a moment, his deep brown eyes soft and curious. Eva had seen him hundreds of times, but she'd never really *seen* him. He looked different from the impression of him she'd had in her head. She'd always thought of him as being a little lost, but that wasn't it at all. There was something unexpectedly bright etched along the lines of his face.

'*Played*,' he said, eventually, stretching the word out. 'I haven't even sat at a piano in a decade.'

Eva nodded, already edging out of the room. She was just about to apologise and thank him for his time when he spoke again.

'But if the choir you're talking about is the same one I heard through the hall doors earlier today then I don't suppose that will matter.'

She stopped dead, her brows pulling together. 'Are you saying—'

'I toured with the Royal Philharmonic Orchestra once.' His eyes twinkled, mischief folding the creases even more deeply. 'We played in front of the Queen a couple of times. I think I might be able to stretch to a few bars of "Morning Has Broken".'

Eva chest swelled, relief flooding through her. 'You should tell Neeta this; she somehow believes that I'm the most musical member of staff.'

She didn't mention Luke. Couldn't bring herself to even say his name. But Orson only smiled, adjusting his glasses on his nose.

'Neeta is well aware of my past life.' He chuckled again, and the sound was warm, like a beam of sunlight. 'She just knows better than to ask.'

Eva raised an eyebrow. It was a question, though she couldn't quite bring herself to raise it.

'When you're seven years past retirement age,' he said, leaning back a little way on his chair, 'no one asks you for anything. Too scared you'll leave.' There was a glint in his eyes, barely visible beyond the creases of his face. 'It's marvellous.'

Eva smiled, but there was a tug in her chest at the idea. Apparently, there was a lot she hadn't known about Orson Myrtle. She'd always thought of him as a quiet character, grey and dull. But that wasn't true at all.

They'd worked together longer than their pupils had been

alive. Why had she never taken the time to get to know him better?

'Why don't you?' she asked, a caution in her voice. She was not ordinarily one to ask something so intrusive. 'Retire, I mean. If that isn't a rude question.'

His eyes changed then, peering at her over the rims of those gold-framed glasses, and for a moment she feared that he wasn't going to answer, that she had completely overstepped.

But then he nodded once, his shoulders hitching up into a shrug. 'I'm happy here.' His eyes darted around the classroom, catching on colourful artwork displays and the full-height bookcases. 'The children make me feel like I'm still young.'

Eva's lips tightened. She'd been on the wrong side of a year five child more than once. 'They don't make fun of you?'

'Oh constantly.' His face folded again, back into that huge, deep-creased grin. 'I wouldn't have it any other way.'

She laughed at that; she couldn't help it. Orson's laid-back joy was infectious. In truth she felt a little annoyed with herself that she hadn't discovered it earlier.

'So,' he said. 'Tell me a little more about your choir situation. How are things going?'

How *were* things going? For a moment she fought the urge to sugar-coat it—the automatic need to try and hide her latest catastrophe. But she'd never thought of Orson as particularly judgemental, and, more importantly than that, she needed his help.

So instead she shrugged, lightly, as if it wasn't a big deal.

'Imagine a bit like *Sister Act*,' she said, 'except they're kids, not nuns, and we haven't gone through the montage where we discover they're actually good. Mainly because they're not.'

Orson nodded, his face breaking into an even wider smile, if that were possible. 'Not *yet*.'

Eva beamed in response. He had *buckets* of optimism, misguided though it may be. He was exactly what the choir needed, and she left him then with a song list, practice timetable and a veritable spring in her step.

Which lasted somewhere in the region of two minutes, just around the amount of time it took for her to run into Neeta on her way back to her classroom.

'Eva,' Neeta said, by way of greeting. Eva nodded in reply.

'Neeta.'

The older woman smiled, straightening the collar of her silk blouse as she looked back down the corridor towards the year one door. It was a door with which Eva was very well acquainted. She spent a great deal of time fixing her attention on the peeling brown gloss rather than on the man beyond it.

The mere act of thinking about him made her skin flush with heat, which in turn caused her to flush again, this time with annoyance. She'd replayed their last encounter in her head more times than she cared to admit, and each time the wound dug a little deeper

'I passed the library earlier,' Neeta said, her perfectly painted lips pulling into a smile. 'Sounds like band practice is going well.'

For a moment, Eva froze. Neeta couldn't have found out that they'd ignored her instructions.

Could she?

Panic rose like bile in Eva's throat, her pulse thundering in her ears. She tried to study Neeta's facial expression, but she gave little away. Knowing Eva's luck, Luke had probably thrown her under the bus and Neeta was trying to catch her in a lie.

Urgh, *Luke*.

There she was, thinking about him again. Even with the potential threat of Neeta's gaze on her, she made a sound, muffled and indistinct – a sound which fell somewhere between *urgh, I hate him* and *I'm not sure I can live without him*.

In that moment both and neither felt true.

'I knew I was right to team the two of you up,' Neeta continued, her voice pleasant, and for a moment Eva almost forgot to breathe, such was her relief. That was, until Neeta spoke again, her face erupting into a wide smile as she did.

'Team Mallory is going places.'

'Thanks,' Eva muttered, through the stab of guilt hitting under her ribcage. Because despite Neeta's obvious excitement about their project, *Team Mallory* had made her stomach tighten into a hard knot.

She didn't want them to be going places. Not together, anyway, unless that place was the surface of the sun. Knowing the curse, it probably wasn't outside the realm of possibility.

Before Eva had a chance to dwell on it too much, Neeta turned back to her, beautifully lined eyes widened. 'Ooh, Eva, before I forget, I've been meaning to ask you a favour.'

Eva braced herself. She'd had quite enough of Neeta's favours for this term. But there it was again, the debt of gratitude she owed to her boss. They both knew it.

'Of course.'

Neeta beamed. 'Years three and four are going on their trip to the leisure centre water park tomorrow, and Juniper's one-to-one has just been diagnosed with impetigo. Horribly infectious. She's not allowed in the water.'

Eva smiled, but it was strained. She already knew what was coming next.

'You had such a great rapport with Juniper when she was in your class,' Neeta continued, that magical persuasive tone slipping into her voice, 'and I know you understand her needs. I really hoped you might—'

'I'll go,' Eva said, quickly. She had a real soft spot for Juniper, a sweet autistic girl who was profoundly anxious and mostly nonspeaking. It had been challenging to connect with her initially, but the two had bonded deeply over the year Juniper had spent in Eva's class, and it was fair to say that Eva adored her.

Not to mention that it wouldn't hurt to stay in Neeta's good books in case she ever did catch wind of their deception, *and* a full day out of school with key stage two would give her a day off from the stifling presence of one Mr Mallory.

'Excellent!' Neeta chirped, her hands clapping together in relief. 'You are a *lifesaver*, Eva. I'll ask Marion to cover your class if you want to leave her any specific tasks.'

Eva barely had time to mutter *no problem* before Neeta was off again, gliding down the corridor on her lush cobalt wedges. 'Coach leaves at 8am,' she called over her shoulder. 'Bring an old T-shirt!'

It was quiet down Eva's end of the corridor when she got there, and she chanced a look at the door of the year one classroom, though she was cross with herself for it. But Luke was nowhere to be seen, and she breathed away some of the tension which always seemed to grip at her ribcage when she was in his vicinity.

She checked her watch: 4:30 He was probably gone by now, but—

'*Arghh*!' A rip of heat through her foot, followed by the unmistakeable throb of her big toe. 'Holy smokes,' she gritted out, clutching the wall a moment to collect herself. She was no stranger to a stubbed toe, but it never failed to suck the wind out of her. She hadn't even seen the doorframe she'd kicked, such had been her relief at Luke's absence.

But then, as she hobbled to the door of her own classroom, there he was, perched on one of the tables, his eyes boring into her through the gridded glass.

At once, that grip on her ribcage was back, tighter than ever, her pulse roaring to life like an old car as she fought to retain control over herself.

'Luke,' she said, by way of greeting, her feathers ruffled by the weight of it on her lips. But he just nodded, his expression neutral.

'I was looking for you.'

It was so matter-of-fact that it almost made her catch her breath. She wondered for a moment if she had imagined his warmth back at the start. If her brain had filled in all the gaps which wishful thinking had left.

'You found me,' she said eventually. 'I was just talking to Orson.'

There was a flicker of something in his expression, some infinitesimal change to the way he was looking at her that she couldn't quite quantify.

'Orson?' he asked, with a drag to his voice that hadn't been there before.

Her eyes narrowed a little, involuntarily. 'Myrtle?'

Surely he hadn't been—

'Ah yes.' And his expression reverted at once, back to that

neutral which had seemed so foreign at first but which now seemed to be his default state.

Jealous?

The audacity.

There was more of a snip to her tone than she had intended when she said, 'How can I help you?'

One hand went to his hair, a muscle ticking at his temple. 'We had an incident today, with Daniel Summers.' He took a breath, as if bracing himself. 'He put Cornflakes the hamster down his pants. I need to log it, of course, but it seemed out of character for him and I wanted to check if you'd seen any signs of it when he was in your class.'

Oh Daniel. She almost laughed out loud, though that seemed very inappropriate. She'd had endless problems with him hiding things in his underwear. They'd never been alive before, but she wasn't at all surprised.

'Yeah, he's got previous,' she said, mercifully managing to keep all of the mirth out of her voice. 'Sorry, I probably should have mentioned that.'

She felt the change in his stance like a shockwave – the way he straightened, vertebrae stacking on top of each other as he tipped his chin up, his eyes not leaving hers for a split second.

'Yes,' he said, the scratch of his voice stopping every atom in the room in its tracks. 'There are a lot of things which you should have mentioned.'

Perhaps it was the audacity of his fleeting jealousy which riled her in that moment. Or his tone, maybe. Maybe just the residual thump of pain in her big toe. Whatever it was, it bypassed every single one of her usual filters, and her rage, unbidden, spilled straight out of her mouth.

'What is your problem?' she demanded, hands finding her

hips. 'I know it's a bit awkward, after … you know.' She couldn't even bring herself to say it. 'But it happened and now it's over and I'm trying my best to just get along with you, but you're making it *so hard*.'

His eyes flared, widening a moment before they narrowed, the burn of his glare making her skin prickle. She should have stopped herself talking at that point, but she didn't.

'You need to get over it.' She huffed out a breath and the smallest of laughs, but without the slightest trace of humour. 'It was twenty-four hours, that's all. It didn't even mean anything.'

As soon as the words left her mouth, she regretted them. She wasn't a habitual liar, but this one was a whopper. If anything, those twenty-four hours had meant too much. She'd tried repeatedly to scrub them from her mind, but she'd failed. They were permanent now – a raised scar on the very foundations of her consciousness. She didn't even know why she'd said it.

Actually, that wasn't true at all. She knew exactly why she'd said it. She'd wanted to try to minimise things, to get him to forget, so that the two of them could finally get on with their lives. She'd wanted to quieten the roar of fire in her chest whenever he was around so that she could focus on her plan, to finally get rid of her damn curse.

But, as was usual for Eva, things hadn't quite gone to plan. Instead of the truce she'd misguidedly assumed might come about, she actually seemed to have stoked the fires of war. That did seem obvious, now that she stopped to think about it.

But it was too late.

She saw the moment her words registered, how they made Luke's perfect lips flatten, his hands drawing into fists by his sides. Something like hurt flashed in his eyes before he coughed it away, his eyes darting down to the floor.

'Well,' he said, his expression a perfect balance of pain and fury, 'If that's how it felt to you, we should probably never talk about it again.'

'Wait,' she said, as he stood and strode to the door. 'I didn't mean—'

But he didn't stop, didn't even turn to look at her as he bit out three words and left the room.

'Goodbye, Miss Mallory.'

Chapter Fourteen

Gerard the art director, as it turned out, *was* a nice guy. Eva had been right to trust her sister on that. He was punctual and polite and funny and quite handsome and she didn't consider jumping out of a window even once.

Unfortunately, it didn't take much longer than an hour for Eva to deduce Gerard's one critical flaw: he was absolutely in love with her sister.

She asked him outright, in the end, after he'd said Hanna's name somewhere in the region of fifty times in the first half hour of their date.

'Don't tell her,' he replied, in a panic. 'I know she's married now; I don't want to mess anything up.'

Eva scanned the room for Hanna and Owen, who had ventured as far as the pool table this time, obviously feeling relatively confident with how the date was going. Either that or Owen had also noticed that Gerard was in love with his wife and was trying to keep her as far away as possible. That was a definite possibility.

'Voice down,' Eva said, quietly and calmly, as if she were trying to placate one of the children in her class. 'She's over there.'

Gerard nearly hit the roof. '*What?*'

'She always comes along on my dates,' Eva said, through a chuckle. 'It's a safety thing, you know? In case I need an out.'

'I can't see her.' Gerard was looking vaguely in the direction that Eva had pointed, his eyes straining into the crowd, and that made Eva laugh too.

'She's in disguise.'

He looked as if he wasn't sure whether to be terrified or impressed. 'Why?'

'Who knows?' She looked back at her sister, her huge curly wig glowing almost fluorescent orange against the burn of the bar's lights. 'It makes her stand out more, if anything.'

She felt Gerard's sigh to her bones. A sigh a lot like that had escaped her on more than one occasion recently.

Luke.

There he was again, invading her thoughts when he had absolutely no right to. Sometimes it seemed like her brain just liked to whisper his name now and again. Just that single syllable over and over, like a heartbeat: *Luke, Luke, Luke.*

She tried to shake it away, turning her attention back to the man sitting opposite her, who was now smiling a very apologetic smile in her direction.

'I'm so sorry to have wasted your time,' he said, that lilt of a Dublin accent warming his words like fingers around a steaming mug. 'I don't think I should have agreed to come.'

Eva smiled gently at him. 'Why did you, if you don't mind me asking?'

He laughed at that, softly, and his eyes found Hanna again

through the buzz of the bar. 'I'd do anything for her.' He huffed a small breath out, and when he turned back to look at Eva, he looked almost embarrassed. 'I suppose you'll tell me there are plenty more fish in the sea.'

There wasn't a sadness to his words, so much as a quiet resignation, and something about it caught at Eva's chest.

She shook her head. 'I mean there *are*.' Her shoulders hitched into a shrug. 'But I'm guessing you know that.'

'Don't I just,' he said, fingertips tracing a lattice across the tabletop, dipping high and low along the grain of the wood as he thought. 'Hey, can I ask you a question?'

Eva nodded.

'Do you believe there's only one person for us?'

She thought for a moment. She had *used* to think that. Young Eva had believed in all of it: in destiny and soulmates; in The One; in love at first sight. She'd assumed that she'd know when it happened, that it would hit her like a thunderbolt, an undeniable connection between them that was impossible to shy away from. But the only time she'd ever felt anything close to that was when she was with Luke, and she'd managed to walk away from him.

In body, anyway. The spirit was a little more stubborn. But none of that mattered because if Luke was her soulmate. then that would mean either giving up on her one true love or taking the very real risk of losing him forever anyway.

'I do and I don't,' she said, eventually. 'I mean, I believe in The One, but I don't think there's only *one* One, if that makes sense?'

At least, she hoped not.

Gerard smiled at her, then, broad and genuine. 'Has anyone ever told you you're nothing at all like your sister?'

'Constantly,' she said, grinning in return, and she lifted her glass in the air. 'Cheers to that.'

'Cheers,' he singsonged, raising his glass to clink hers. 'And cheers to finding The One. The *Other* One.'

How Eva longed to do just that.

'Told you he was nice,' Hanna said smugly, picking pieces of chicken kebab out of her pitta and stuffing them into her mouth like a woman starved, even as she strode full-speed through the streets of Leeds.

Eva nibbled at her falafel. She wasn't so bold as to try to walk and eat at the same time. With her luck, she'd definitely choke. 'He *was* nice.' She thumbed a smear of garlic sauce off her lower lip. 'But he's in love with someone else.'

Hanna nearly inhaled a piece of tomato. 'He's what?'

'I don't think it's requited.' Eva shrugged, careful to keep Gerard's confidence. 'He was probably too embarrassed to tell you.'

'Maybe,' Hanna replied, with an edge of something more in her voice, and Eva was glad when she didn't ask anything else. 'We're not doing very well with this husband hunt, are we, Eevs?'

Eva couldn't help but laugh. 'Welcome to my life.'

Hanna snorted and shoved more food in her mouth. When she spoke again it was around a mouthful of kebab. ' God, this is good. I'm not used to eating these so early in the night. I'm normally so drunk I can barely taste them.'

Owen said nothing, just took steady bites of his doner as he strived to keep up with the velocity of his wife.

They turned off the neon glow of Albion Street, cutting across towards Briggate, the rise and fall of doorways stretching out as far as Eva could see. There was a figure leaning against a doorway in the middle distance, his contours picked out by the streetlights. A small thump of recognition hit her in the pit of the stomach, something familiar about the man's silhouette, about the way he leaned against the stone.

But that didn't make any sense at all.

So she shook the idea off, taking a tentative bite of pitta and trotting along obediently a half-step behind her sister.

'Who's next?' Hanna was asking. 'We've only got one more potential husband on the list from us and then you're thrown largely to the chaos of Ciocia Nelka's horrendous taste in men.'

Eva chuckled. 'Stefan's was OK.'

Hanna stopped dead at Eva's words, and Eva slammed straight into her, the force of her sudden halt sending her entire partially eaten falafel wrap tumbling across the cobbles.

She took a step away, doing a quick check up and down her person for sauce splatters but finding only a tiny smear on the toe of one shoe. 'Dammit!'

Hanna's face pinched into a grimace of repentance. 'Sorry, Eevs.' She extended one hand, gripping a paper bag full of scraps of chicken and salad and pitta. 'You want some of my kebab?'

Eva shook her head. 'Don't worry, I wasn't hungry anyway.'

And that was the truth. Too busy thinking about—

'*Wait*!' Eva shrieked, grabbing handfuls of her sister and brother-in-law's jackets and dragging them behind a stone pillar.

This time it was Hanna who dropped her kebab.

'Eva, what the hell?' she shrieked, toeing the scraps which had tumbled out of the paper, which she was still gripping as though her life depended on it.

'Shhhh!'

Eva peeked around the pillar, her eyes settling back on the figure, his breath now sending plumes of mist out into the nip of the late autumn night. His head was thrown back, one leg bent back at the knee and propped on the wall behind him.

Her heart leapt in her chest, knocking butterflies into her stomach as her breath caught, the pattern of his name ghosting through her brain.

Luke, Luke, Luke.

As if it had ever gone away.

'That's *him*,' she hissed, her voice low, nodding at the shadowy figure fifty metres up the road. 'You know, *Luke*.'

Hanna's breath out was almost a laugh. '*That's* cupboard boy?'

'Yeah.'

The three of them peered around the pillar like a trio of cartoon bandits.

'Huh.' Hanna screwed her paper into a tight ball, but her eyes stayed locked on Luke. 'He's fit.'

Eva couldn't help the snort of a laugh which escaped her. Never had a truer word been spoken. 'Yeah.'

'And you can't go out with him because…?' Hanna turned to her sister, a single eyebrow raised in judgement. 'Remind me.'

Eva sighed. 'Because of the curse, Han. You know how it is.' A stab of longing hit her clean in the chest. 'I'd end up maiming him or setting him on fire for sure.' There was a shake to her exhale. 'Best case.'

'But the husband thing?' Owen asked gently, from her other side. 'I thought that was the way to stop it?'

'He's a Mallory too,' the twins replied, in unison, and then burst into fits of giggles.

Owen, four beers in and feeling it, simply nodded. 'Ah.'

'But what's he doing out there?' Hanna strained to see past the blowing of orange curls in her face.

'Looks like he needs a break from that bar,' Eva said, with a soft tut. 'And he's out in town on a school night.'

Owen turned to look at her, his blue eyes steady. '*You're* out in town on a school night.'

'All right, voice of reason.' She brushed him away with a smile. 'When I want logic, I'll ask for him. Until then, can it.'

Hanna was still transfixed, and her eyes widened as Luke pushed off the wall and disappeared back through the door, into the bar.

'Wait, he's going back in!' she said, leaping out from their hiding place and extending her hand to Eva. 'And we should, too.'

Eva probably should have said no. In fact, she definitely would have said no had it not been for the three to four drinks she'd downed with Gerard, his plans to find his Other One getting sketchier and more outlandish with every sip. Those same drinks were giving her a quite uncharacteristic burst of adventurousness now, and she grabbed her sister's hand tightly.

'Let's go investigate!'

Owen made a sound like he'd had quite enough nonsense for one day, but like the dutiful husband that he was, he fell into step behind the women and together they walked down the road and into the bar.

It wasn't much lighter in the bar than it had been in the street, and the air was clammy and close despite the bite of the night air outside. There was a vibration through the whole place, a dull *thump thump thump* which nagged at the pit of Eva's belly as she slipstreamed Hanna through a throng of averagely drunk millennials.

And then they turned a corner and she saw the stage, three men around her age huddled around a drum kit as one of them tapped the bass drum lightly with his foot again, thump thump thump. And then, all at once, they scattered, a perfectly rehearsed dance across the stage to their positions, one man slipping a forest green electric guitar over his head as the other adjusted the microphone stand and tapped it once before he began to speak.

'OK folks,' he said, the buzz of the pub-quality sound system distorting his words slightly, 'I'm Benny, we are The Ordinaries and we're here to rock your Wednesday night.'

A rumble started in the crowd, before it swelled and grew into a low roar. Eva had never heard the band name before, but everyone around her was cheering, and then so was Hanna, Owen stepping up behind her and wrapping his arms protectively around her shoulders.

And then she saw something in her periphery: a flash of movement, which turned into the shadow of a person, and then finally a figure. A very familiar figure, easing his bass guitar over his head as he began to play the first distinctive notes of 'Seven Nation Army'.

The crowd went wild.

And so, for that matter, did Eva's stupid, traitorous heart.

Chapter Fifteen

Eva was rooted to the spot for the entirety of the song, and at least the first verse of the second, which she didn't recognise.

Luke, a vision in low-slung black jeans and a V-neck slashed to the sternum, played bass like he was making love to it; his fingers skipping deftly over the fretboard as muscles in his arms flexed, his head alternately thrown back and hung low. Occasionally his lips – lips she had spent rather a lot of time staring at – would start to move, half-singing along with his eyes closed as his hair began to dampen at the temples.

She was *transfixed*.

'They're pretty good,' Owen leaned to yell, over the music, and Eva nodded in return, though her eyes didn't leave the stage for even a second.

It was true. They *were* pretty good. Not amazing, not even very good, but certainly far from terrible. Now and again the singer would catch a note a little off-key, or the guitarist would change chord a second too late. Luke turned at one point and a squeal of feedback ripped through the speaker, but it didn't matter. Not to Eva, and not to the rest of the audience, by the sound of it. They were bouncing in time to the beat, whistling and singing along to parts they knew as Eva stood, unmoving, on the spot.

The entire band had a kind of hypnotic energy, but Luke was mesmerising. He wasn't the buttoned-up Mr Mallory she'd come to know over the past weeks – the man who had emerged from the ashes of the stranger she'd met at the bar that day. This man was stranger at the bar *with bells on*.

She must have looked like a top-tier stalker, watching him the way she was, but she couldn't tear her eyes away. There was an energy about him as he played which outstripped even the memory of him, lust-drunk and heavy-lidded, draped back on his heather-grey sofa as she moulded herself around him.

Hanna shouted something over to her then, but she didn't hear it. She didn't even pretend that she had. Her entire body was a heartbeat, her limbs tensed, fingers coiled into fists at her sides.

And then he looked right at her, like he'd known she was there, those intense hazel eyes widening where she thought they might narrow, a muscle ticking in his jaw as he held the eye contact.

They were playing a song she didn't recognise – an original, perhaps, and as she watched he began to sing again, his lips barely moving with the words as his eyes burned into her.

Hey girl
Let's not fight
You're still the song I sing

When nothing feels right

Eva's skin burned, a breath catching in her throat as she watched his fingers dancing up and down the strings of his bass. Was that how he felt? It was what she'd wanted, if she were honest, but it felt wrong now, like she'd cheated him out of something.

And with that it all came together, building to the chorus as a hum built in her body too, something about the four drinks she'd had or the unabashed eye contact or the swell of the melody sending a rush of emotion through her. Her vision blurred as tears stung her eyes, and she looked away in shame. She didn't even know why she was crying.

It was a moment or two before she chanced a look back at him, and when she did he was still watching her, his brows quirked in a question. The smallest of sobs caught in her throat, and as he saw it, he looked away, his Adam's apple bobbing in a hard swallow, teeth gritted.

It felt as if something had just happened between them, some unspoken exchange, and certainly there was something about Luke's energy which seemed to have shifted into a different gear now. She felt exhausted just watching him.

Exhausted and wildly turned on, that was. Even through her residual tears.

And then, as if to dampen the flames of desire roaring through her body, something hit her from the side, connecting hard with one cheek before the shock of the cold made her yelp out loud.

A plastic cup clattered to the floor beside her, the tang of beer biting at her nostrils as she feebly wiped froth from her clothes. But it was no good. She was soaked.

'What the hell happened?' Hanna said, leaning in close to her ear before rearing back in disgust. 'Urgh, you smell like a brewery.'

Eva blew a breath out. Of *course* she would be the one person in the crowd to be hit by a flying pint. She tried again to brush herself off with her hands, though, just like the last time, it had absolutely no effect on her saturation levels.

'At least it was beer and not pee,' Owen chirped, with a kind smile, and though she couldn't argue with his point, she'd have really rather preferred to be not covered in any random fluids at all. The lump in her throat was back. It was as if the universe itself had thrown the glass, a timely reminder that lusting after Luke was the very last thing she should be doing if she wanted rid of the curse.

And right then, standing in the dimly lit bar with beer seeping into her knickers, she really, *really*, wanted rid of it.

That thought only made her want to cry more, and she excused herself and darted off to the toilets, both to deal with the beer situation, and to get herself together. The lock on the cubicle was stiff, and she worried for a moment or two that it would snap off in her hands. It wouldn't be the first time that Eva had accidentally locked herself in a toilet. But mercifully she managed to wiggle it shut without incident, and she plopped down on the closed lid of the toilet with a sigh.

She gingerly dabbed at the soggiest parts of herself with a rolled-up wad of toilet paper, and when she'd dealt with the worst of it, she put herself under the hand dryer for a few minutes too, the warm air making her feel a little better, though it made the smell three times worse.

Then she washed her hands and cleaned her face as best she could around her date-level eyeliner and fading lipstick. It didn't really matter, she told herself. Because once she went back out into the bar and found Hanna and Owen, she was leaving.

Before anything else happened.

Before her brain could have any more impure thoughts about Luke Mallory.

So the very last thing she expected to find when she swung open the heavy toilet door was Luke himself, flushed and breathing hard, leaning against the rough brick of the corridor outside. She hadn't even noticed that the music had stopped.

Those hazel eyes flew up to hers, his stare almost too much for her to stand. It rooted her to the spot. And when he reached for the handle over her hand and walked the two of them back into the toilet there wasn't a lot she could do about that either.

'Luke,' she said dumbly, as if it were her lifeline, but then she heard the click of the lock behind him.

It was a small cubicle, maybe five feet in both directions and all of a sudden it was like they were in the art cupboard all over again, their eyes locking over a heap of fallen paper. But there was a different energy between them this time: something dark and desperate, a last cry out before they slipped underwater.

Luke had circled her before she knew it, and then in one swift move he grabbed her thighs and hauled her up onto the ledge of the sink, pressing his body between her spread legs, his lips grazing her ear as he spoke.

'I can't stop thinking about you,' he muttered, the rumble of his voice sending ripples of electricity down her spine.

She breathed him in. He smelt even better than she remembered – like salt and soap and sandalwood, and with the sweet tang of whiskey on his breath, although he didn't appear drunk.

'I should forget all about you, I know.' His lips brushed against her neck, lighting small fires on her skin. 'It's what you want.'

It wasn't, but it was definitely what she needed. Her arms slipped around his body and she closed her eyes against the feeling of him, warm and solid in her arms. She wanted to stay there forever.

'I just…' She heard him swallow, a ripple of tension moving through his body before he let out a sigh. 'I've tried so hard. But I can't stop.'

'I don't want you to,' she heard herself say, before her rational brain made her follow up with, 'But I can't—'

His groan cut her off. 'Please? Just…'

But there was no *just*. Just the grip of Luke's nimble fingers on her thighs, the press of his body against hers, his heart beating a riot through his chest as she fought the urge to melt into him. His breath came heavy and fast against her ear, the hair at his temples soaked through with sweat where it brushed against the side of her face. Heat pooled between her legs.

It would have been so easy to give in to it. All she'd have had to do was slightly turn her head and they'd be kissing. Kissing and who knows what else. Because the way that he was making her feel right at that moment, she didn't trust herself not to abandon herself to him right there on the cold porcelain of the sink.

But she hadn't walked away from him for no reason. And she'd had her warning from the curse once already that night, she didn't want to provoke it to try something else – something worse than a beer shower.

She pulled a deep breath in, and when she let it go there was a shake to it, a hesitancy which made him pull back, his eyes searching hers as if they held the answer to his prayers. But all her eyes held at that particular moment were a fresh batch of tears, and perhaps a few odd traces of some stranger's beer.

'You need to move on,' she gritted out, before taking another breath and speaking again, with more conviction this time. '*We* need to move on.'

His brows pulled into a frown, and he huffed the smallest of laughs, breathy and humourless. 'I'm trying,' he said roughly, his thumb tracing the very edge of her cheekbone. 'But you're everywhere.'

She summoned every last scrap of willpower not to give in to his touch. 'I'll try not to be.'

His face fell to her shoulder as he gathered her up in his arms, just for a moment, his breath on her skin tracing a line of fire down deep into her belly.

'Don't,' he muttered into her neck, and then, as quickly as he'd appeared, he was gone, leaving Eva breathless and cold on the edge of the sink, mourning the space he had left even though it was her who had asked for it.

It took her a moment or two to get herself together and when she finally emerged from the corridor, she found Hanna and Owen, a united front, with the most spectacular look of judgement on each of their faces.

'Nothing happened,' Eva said, in response to her sister's raised eyebrow.

Hanna barked a laugh. 'Course it didn't.' Her eyes darted

left, up to the stage, where Luke had re-joined his band, now packing up their equipment. 'That's why Cupboard Boy came stomping out ahead of you with a face like you'd just murdered his puppy.'

Eva winced. 'Can we not call him Cupboard Boy?'

'Cupboard Man?' Owen suggested. Hanna was a bad influence on him.

'That's no better,' Eva said frowning as dramatically as she could at the two of them. 'Anyway, I think it's time we left.' She pulled her jacket around her beer-soaked body. 'I'm going swimming with a bunch of eight-year-olds in about nine hours' time.'

And then she sneaked one last glance in Luke's direction and headed off, out into the chill of the autumn night before anything else could happen.

Chapter Sixteen

It was one minute to eight when Eva ran up the steps of the coach the following morning, and though she was sure Nigel Carter would have a few choice words to say about it later, all the deputy head actually said was, 'Good morning, Miss Mallory.'

She almost laughed. She'd been expecting a *nice of you to finally join us*, at least. Then again, she was in the rare position of doing him a favour, so she supposed it was in his interests to keep her on side.

'Miss Mal,' a small voice said, from the front seat, and in that moment it eclipsed everything else. Juniper hadn't said Eva's name until she'd spent almost eight months in her class, and when she finally did it had brought tears to Eva's eyes. Even now she could feel a lump forming in her throat.

'Juni,' she singsonged, plopping down on the empty seat next to the youngster, and though Juniper didn't look at her, her head tilted in response. Eva held out a palm, and after a moment or two, Juniper touched it with her own.

'High five,' she said, quietly, pressing her small palm against Eva's. 'High five, Miss Mal.'

Eva made a mental note to tell Mrs Abbott about it when she got back to school. She had been the one to teach Juni to high five in the first place, something that had shocked the both of them. It remained to this day one of the only times Eva had known Mrs Abbott to soften.

'Swimming,' Juniper said, resting her little body against Eva's as the coach lurched into action, and then she said nothing more for the entirety of the forty-five-minute ride to the leisure centre.

———

'Swimming,' Juni said again, an hour or so later, as Eva led her out of the changing rooms, and they headed down towards the small toddler pool at the back of the swimming area, tucked away from the hubbub of the main pools and, if Eva remembered correctly, a few degrees warmer.

She headed for the steps and then motioned for Juni to sit. The little girl lit up as warm water licked at her ankles, muttering a phrase Eva couldn't quite pick out, over and over as she rocked gently, one hand flapping towards her face. She had always loved water.

Eva grabbed for the armbands which the leisure centre had lent them and handed one to Juniper to inspect.

'Can we put these on you?' Eva asked gently, stretching her legs down further into the pool.

Juni grabbed at the armband, touched it against her cheek once or twice and then looked back at Eva with undisguised suspicion.

'To keep you safe,' Eva said, with a nod, pointing to the armband. 'If you put these on, you can get all the way in. They'll help you float.'

'Float,' Juni repeated, touching the plastic to her cheek again before extending it back out to Eva. 'Miss Mal. Help.'

Eva beamed. 'I *will* help.' And then she gently eased the armbands on to Juni's little arms before lowering them both down into the water. It was a lovely temperature in the toddler pool, calm and relaxing, and Eva appreciated it every bit as much as Juniper seemed to. It had been almost midnight by the time Hanna and Owen had dropped her at her flat, and she couldn't sleep for an hour or two after that, her brain replaying the encounter with Luke over and over. The way he'd looked performing on stage. The brush of his lips against her ear. The pressure of his fingers on her thighs. She couldn't stop thinking about it.

She was glad of the space this trip had afforded her. She wasn't sure how she would have reacted to seeing him over the corridor this morning, not knowing whether she would have seen any traces of the undone Luke, or whether he'd be back to buttoned-up Mr Mallory.

With a sigh, she turned her attention back to the little girl in her arms, manoeuvring her tiny body so that she was stretched out on her back, limbs flung wide. Eva slipped one hand underneath Juni's head and one under her shoulders. And then she began to move, pulling Juni's body in long, smooth movements in the water, small waves lapping over the little girl's chest and against her face as she grinned broadly, her arms turning aimless circles in the water.

'Water,' Juni muttered to herself. 'Splash.'

And Eva couldn't help but smile in response. Juni hadn't

had any words at all that first day she'd walked into Eva's classroom, and when she'd left the following summer she had more than twenty. Though that was three years ago now, Eva still felt that same giddy rush of joy with every new word she heard.

They stayed there in the toddler pool for almost an hour, floating and splashing and blowing bubbles and enjoying *being*, in a way Eva rarely got to when she had a full class. She could hear the shriek of children beyond the boundary of the toddler pool, but it was dulled, her focus completely on the little girl in front of her, who was now floating independently, just within grabbing distance.

Until, all of a sudden, Juniper started fussing.

'Out,' she said, almost a cry, and Eva's heart rocketed to her throat.

'What happened, Juni?' she asked, with a bite of panic in her throat. Neeta had trusted her to look after Juniper; she couldn't mess it up. She'd had a way with the youngster when she was in her class, but that had been a few years ago now. What if she was doing it all completely wrong now?

She swept Juni – now wailing and curled into a foetal position – out of the pool and onto the side in one smooth move, whereupon the little girl immediately quieted, merrily trotting the few steps away from the pool to the low glass wall which separated the smaller pool from the main waterpark.

'Splash,' Juni said, one small palm pressing against the glass. 'There.'

Eva frowned. She'd planned to keep Juni away from the main pool area, thought it too busy, too loud, too overwhelming for her to deal with.

'You want to go on a slide?' she asked, already feeling a

hum of dread building beneath her ribcage. She definitely didn't want to be the person responsible for drowning Juni on one of the rides.

But Juni was clear. 'Yes,' she said, her voice clipped, defiant. 'There.' She pointed through the glass to one of the shorter slides.

'Wow, OK.' Eva scanned the area, mentally risk assessing the slide which Juni had picked out. It was maybe ten feet high, if that, and built up on both sides, definitely the safest of all the available waterpark options. She'd need help, though, to be totally cautious, either someone to help Juniper up the steps, or to catch her at the bottom.

She took a deep breath. 'Come on then, lovely.' She held out a hand, which Juni took without hesitation. 'Let's go splash.'

Eva spied Maxine, the year three teacher, standing ankle-deep in the wave pool, her dark coily hair piled high on her head, the T-shirt of a band Eva didn't recognise clinging to her shoulders and her hips. She turned as she saw Eva and Juni, smiling brightly at the little girl before looking back up at Eva.

'Thanks so much for stepping in at the last moment,' she said, her eyes sweeping back out around her pupils in the pool, a habit. 'You're a star.'

Eva shook her head. 'Don't even worry about it.' Her hand closed a little around Juni's, feeling the smallest of squeezes in return. 'Maybe you can help us out?'

Maxine's brows quirked up a little in a question.

'Juniper has asked to go on a slide,' Eva continued, 'so I thought the best idea was if we have one adult to help her up the steps, and then another at the bottom of the slide to catch her.'

Maxine beamed. 'Great idea.' She adjusted her damp T-shirt. 'Do you want to take steps duty, and I'll catch her at the bottom?'

'Absolutely.' Eva dropped to Juniper's level, feeling the scratch of the pool tiles against her knees. 'Come on, Juni. Let's go splash.'

Eva did not need to ask her twice. She was off, almost before Eva could get back to her feet, trotting excitedly around the back of the slide as if she'd been on it a hundred times. Eva held a guiding hand to her back as she climbed the tiled steps and then helped her into position at the top of the slide.

'You going down, Miss?' a voice asked to her right, and she turned to see Aaron and Noah from year four smirking at her. They were both in the choir, though Eva suspected that was only so they could get away with missing the first ten minutes of their weekly RE lesson.

'I'm helping Juniper,' she said, keeping her voice as neutral as possible. She could handle the little ones all day long, but nine-year-olds knew exactly how to push her buttons.

They both laughed, and for a moment Eva felt as if she was their age rather than the fully grown woman that she was. She turned her attention back to Juniper, trying to will away the flush in her cheeks.

'Ready, steady—' Eva started.

But almost before the words were out of her mouth, Juni yelled *go*, propelling herself down the slide at such speed that she sent a wave of water towards Maxine, splashing her all the way up to chest level.

Juniper laughed first, lolling back into the water as Maxine reflexively grabbed her and jumped the little girl to her feet, the two of them giggling together.

Eva's heart swelled a little at the sound of it, and it grew bigger with every circuit Juni did: down the slide, splash the onlookers, pad back round to the steps and begin again. By the time she'd done it twenty or so times, all three of them were laughing, Eva almost forgetting herself when Juni patted the other lane of the slide, to her right.

'Miss Mal, slide,' she said sternly, and Eva didn't even hesitate.

'Readysteadygo!' Juniper bellowed as she launched herself down towards Maxine, and Eva was so panicked about the speed at which Juni was travelling that she launched herself too, her proportionally heavier form picking up speed at an almost alarming rate before she ploughed down into the shallow water at the bottom with a grunt.

A rush of anxiety gripped her, arms flailing wildly. It would have been just her luck to drown in water which must have been at least ten percent urine, given the current clientele. But then her feet found the texture of tiles beneath her and she stood to find herself calf-deep in water, her hair obscuring much of her view, but with the sound of laughter surrounding her. Except for the year four boys. They weren't laughing. They were making the very specific sound which children make when someone embarrasses themselves in public.

That was somehow worse.

But not in any way as bad as what came next.

'All right boys,' a voice boomed from what sounded like the middle distance, 'settle down.' The strange acoustics of the pool distorted the sound to a point, but even so, Eva was in absolutely no doubt as to who the owner of that voice was. Her heart rocketed into her throat, and she peeled her hair from her face just in time to see Luke Mallory striding out of the waves like he was James Bond.

Her brain, and her body, went into complete meltdown.

She could do nothing but stare as he got closer, maroon swimming shorts sitting low on his hips as a wet V-neck T-shirt clung to every last curve of his torso, igniting flames within her that even a dunking in the verruca end of the wave pool couldn't extinguish.

Good God, he was a beautiful man.

But...

That wasn't the point.

Why the hell is he here?

'I'm filling in for Mr Crowther,' Luke said, which was right about the time that Eva realised that she'd said that last bit out loud. 'He has cryptosporidium poisoning and isn't allowed to go swimming for two weeks.' His eyes narrowed, those beautiful lips pressed together tightly. 'I might ask you the same question.'

It came flooding back, all at once. His hands on her body, his breath against her ear. Every emotion she'd felt the night before, growing and churning in her chest. But then she remembered his words, words which she could almost see now, reflected in the hard set of his stare.

You're everywhere.

'Similar story for me,' she said, past the tug in her throat. 'Miss Granger has impetigo and was banned from swimming in public pools until it clears up.'

His eyes narrowed even further, if that were possible, and she tried not to look at the angle of his cheekbones, nor the flop of his hair, gloriously undone and beginning to curl where it was drying at his temples.

'There are a suspicious number of infectious diseases at Burton Lane,' he said, cool and emotionless.

He did have a point, but that really wasn't Eva's doing, and she'd be damned if she was going to take any kind of blame for it, curse or otherwise. She narrowed her eyes right back at him.

'I'm just here for Juniper.'

'Miss Mal,' Juni said as she heard her name, but when Eva looked, the little girl wasn't looking at her, but gazing adoringly at Luke.

Traitor.

'She doesn't differentiate between titles at the moment,' Maxine said, with a shrug, her lips quirked in a knowing smile, as though she was enjoying every second of the display in front of her. 'Everyone is Miss to her.'

Eva could have died on the spot, particularly when she felt the full force of Luke's glare for a split-second, before he crouched down in the shallow water.

'Hey Juni,' he said to the little girl, his tone completely different, soft and upbeat, and he held out his palm to her in exactly the way that she liked. Eva's heart melted, despite herself.

Juniper met Luke's palm with hers, hesitantly, and when they made contact she paused a moment, her whole body tensing slightly. Eva wondered if she were witnessing Luke's first ever Juniper high five, and for a moment she thought he might have pushed a little too far, but then she saw Juni's shoulders relax, just a moment before she spoke.

'High five.'

And then she reached for Eva's hand again and tugged, her gaze focused on a point just left of Eva's eyes.

'Miss Mal,' she said, directing it to Eva this time. 'Splash.'

Luke straightened to his full height, his face open and warm and all of the things it hadn't been a moment ago. His voice, when he spoke, was completely different too, his lips curling almost into a smirk as he said, not for the first time, 'I think you'd better go.'

Chapter Seventeen

'You ready?'

Eva toed the floor, looking at the water flowing into the slide in front of her and disappearing into the darkness. She really wasn't ready. But she'd made a bet and she wasn't about to back out now, definitely not at that moment, with the year four boys standing right behind her.

So she looked back at the slide attendant and smiled, taking a step closer with her heartbeat thundering like a train in her ears. 'Absolutely.'

She'd been happily jumping waves with Maxine and Juni when the boys had passed her the second time, and she'd been having such good fun in that moment that she'd made the mistake of asking what slide they were going on next.

'That one,' Aaron had said, gesturing to the space bowl slide, just as another child dropped out of it, freefalling into the pool below with a joyful shriek. 'It's the best one here.'

'Looks pretty scary,' Eva had mused, with a smile. The slide she'd raced Juniper on had been bad enough.

'It's not that bad Miss,' Noah had said, then. 'I bet even *you* could go on it.'

The two boys had shared a look.

'Dare you to go on it,' they'd said in unison, before laughing out loud, and Eva had laughed too.

'Don't be daft.'

Aaron had raised one eyebrow. 'Double dare you.'

She'd laughed in response, despite the growing creep of dread swelling behind her breastbone. 'Double dare doesn't work on grown-ups.'

Aaron's huff of breath had stopped short of a laugh, his small chin tipping up in defiance. 'Mr Mallory did it.'

A rush of energy had coursed through her stomach at the mention of his name, like it always did. And, like always, she ignored it.

'He didn't.'

'He did!' Noah's huge grin had bared teeth much too large and awkward for his mouth. 'Should have seen the splash he made!'

She couldn't deny that she would quite like to have seen it. But she hadn't even had time to reply as much when Aaron had spoken again.

'Miss, are you and Mr Mallory married?'

The sound that Maxine made had fallen somewhere between a cough and a laugh.

Eva had felt the sting of a blush creeping along her cheeks and she'd tried to sound as neutral as possible when she'd said, 'We're not.'

Noah's brow had crinkled. 'Are you his mum?'

She'd reared back. 'What? No!'

'All right, boys,' Maxine had said then, obviously trying to suppress a laugh. 'Why don't you just go on the slide and leave Miss Mallory alone.'

And then the two boys had started to shuffle away, repentant heads bowed, and they would have shuffled all the way away if it hadn't been for the idea which had sprung into Eva's head right at that moment.

Even then, she would never have ended up standing at the top of the damn slide if she hadn't voiced it. But she did, and now she was here, regretting every second and yet much, much too stubborn to back out now.

'I'm ready,' she said to the attendant, her voice a little shaky now, and she took the two steps to the mouth of the slide, lowering herself into the gush of water and gripping the metal handles for dear life.

'OK, ready?' the attendant started, and then without any kind of reasonable time to allow her to actually *get* ready, 'Go!'

And with that Eva pushed off with all her might, before she got any crazy ideas about backing out. After all, there were stakes now. In honesty, she probably pushed a little *too* hard, but that hardly seemed to matter as she plunged down into the dimly lit slide like she was being sucked into a vortex.

It was dark and fast and scary in the slide, water splashing into her face and the joins in the plastic catching at the backs of her legs. And then all of a sudden she saw light, and then a second later shot out into the bowl, much faster than she'd been able to gauge in the darkness. She flew around the side in a full loop and then up high up on the opposite side.

Higher and higher she went, *too* high really, and then she hit the metal pipe spraying out water just a split-second after she'd realised she was going to.

'Holy moly!' she shrieked at the graze of metal on her spine as her ascent peaked, something like relief easing her chest as she began to fall. But then she stopped, almost immediately, caught like a fish on a line as the water rushed past her, her limbs flailing wildly as she struggled to free herself.

Flailing turned to twisting, and then finally to bracing her feet on the wall of the bowl and pushing hard, but all of it to no avail.

She reached a hand around her back, fumbling further and further up until she reached the metal pipe she'd grazed herself on. There was a gap in the pipe, she could feel it with her fingers, and then a bunch of fabric twisted tightly around the end of it; the back of her swimming costume, she assumed, from the way it was pulled tight around her and cutting into her skin under her arms.

She tried to untwist it, to pull it, even to rip it off the pipe, but with the combination of her bodyweight and the industrial strength, pull-you-in-in-all-the-right-places fabric of the costume she'd worn, it was a lost cause.

She was *stuck*.

It shouldn't have come as a surprise, really. Other than the unexpected presence of one Mr Mallory, the day had been going rather well. She was long overdue a visit from the curse. She briefly worried that she might die here, suspended over the gaping chasm of water like drying seaweed on a fishing net before realising the rather more realistic outcome – that they would have to stop the whole ride, drain it and then send in a slide assistant and a ladder. Her gut clenched, pre-emptive embarrassment flushing her cheeks as a wave of panic made her stomach tighten and her heart race and skip in her throat.

She was so preoccupied by her full-scale fight-or-flight response that she didn't notice the increased rush of water around her, nor the creak of movement in the slide above. In fact, she didn't notice anything happening at all until she saw the figure shoot past her, following the same overly ambitious loop that she had done before suddenly appearing next to her, shooting a hand up to grab the metal pipe in some kind of superhero move that she was panicking far too much to fully appreciate.

Her anxiety wasn't helped one bit when she saw who it was.

Luke raised a single eyebrow, a curious expression on his face. It wasn't humour, but it wasn't concern either, something about the angle of his mouth speeding her heart beyond the parameters which felt healthy.

'You're everywhere,' adrenaline made her blurt, her voice echoing around the bowl of the slide.

There was a flicker of something in his eyes. 'That's my line.'

'Sorry, yes.' She gulped a breath, chlorine burning her lungs. 'It's just that … urgh.' She shrugged as best she could with her entire body dangling by her shoulder straps. 'Why are you here?'

'I'm saving you,' he said matter-of-factly, and his tone sent prickles of annoyance up her spine.

'What if I don't need saving?'

He fixed her with a look. 'You do.'

She did.

'OK fine.' Her cheeks burned in indignation, but she wasn't really in a position to turn down assistance, however much it got her back up. 'How did you know?'

He did smile at that, pointing up a little way, over their heads, to a small black globe. 'You're on camera.'

Her stomach dropped. 'Oh Jesus.'

'Smile.'

The last shreds of her dignity fluttered away, sucked down by the constant flow of the water around them. 'This is the worst day of my life.'

His grin widened. 'The year fours are loving it.'

'Urgh.' She blew a breath out. 'They dared me to come on here.'

Luke's eyes twinkled. 'I think you've just made their day. This is all anyone's going to be talking about for weeks.'

It was, she knew it. The thought of if made her stomach churn. 'I'm genuinely mortified.'

He laughed properly then, a sound which she hadn't heard from him for such a long time, and it probably should have annoyed her, given her current predicament, but it didn't. Instead it made the grip of anxiety in her throat relax a notch, small ripples of warmth radiating out through her shivering body as his eyes scanned her.

'OK,' he said eventually, hauling himself higher. 'I can see where you're stuck.'

He leaned in towards her, his brows knotting into a frown as he peered behind her, to where she was suspended by a knot of military-grade Lycra.

'Still,' she blurted, feeling she needed to keep speaking to deal with his proximity to her. 'At least I satisfied my part in the deal.'

His frown deepened, and his free arm worked at the tangle of fabric behind her. 'Deal?'

'I told Aaron and Noah I'd come on here if they both did solos in the carol concert.'

'Nice,' he said with a nod, vague, as if he were only half

listening. 'OK, I think I can get it. Give me a minute.

'I'm not going anywhere,' she said, laughing we
own joke, but Luke didn't even crack a smile.

Instead, concentration pulled his lips into a pout. 'Ah, I
need a better angle. Can you lean this way a little bit more?'

She tried to lean, but her costume was so tight around her
that only her head and neck moved. He assessed her, brow
heavy in thought.

'OK,' he said finally. 'I'll come to you' And he shuffled his
body closer to her, so close that she could feel the warmth of
his breath on her face. Her belly clenched even further, her gut
twisting into knots tighter than the one she was suspended
from.

'Grab on,' he said, an edge to his voice that she was almost
positive she wasn't imagining. 'Put your weight on me.'

She reached out for him and her arms settled around his
shoulders, warm through the thin layer of his wet T-shirt. Her
breath caught, and she could have sworn his did too. That
feeling consumed her again – the feeling like she was aflame.

It was just like it had been the previous night – dark and
desperate, the messy pounding of their hearts joining as one
rhythm.

Eva cleared her throat, not even clear on what she was
about to say. 'Listen, about last night—'

But then, in one swift, almost supernatural move, Luke
tightened his free arm around her and hauled her upwards,
unhooking her from the pipe before he released his own grip
on it. And before he could hear what she had to say – before
she discovered it herself – the two of them plunged, still
attached, into a spiral in the bowl of the slide before eventually,
finally, falling into the pool below.

Chapter Eighteen

Eva was still shot through with residual adrenaline that evening, and as she sat at the old, veneered dining table, every sudden noise was making her jump out of her skin. A few minutes previously, Hanna had accidentally dropped the pastry board onto the worktop behind her and for a moment Eva could have sworn she felt her soul leave her body.

'Are you OK, Eevs?' Sylvia asked, her eyes flooded with concern as she considered her daughter carefully. 'You don't seem yourself this evening.'

'It's cause you're working us to the bone,' Hanna shouted from the other side of the kitchen, even though the kitchen was perhaps three metres across, if that. It made Eva jump again.

Sylvia tutted softly, her attention not straying from Eva even as she replied to her other daughter. 'Hardly to the bone,' she said, a smile playing at the corner of her mouth. 'And this is part of the deal, you know that.' She looked over at Ciocia Nelka for confirmation and the older woman nodded sagely in reply.

'If you want pierogi at Christmas,' Nelka said, her voice as gentle as it was firm, 'then you must help to make them.' Her eyes vanished into the folds of her smile. 'One day soon I will be too old to do it, and after that, if you do not do them, then they will not be done.'

Ciocia Irenka was at that point already, the gnarl of arthritis in her fingers much too severe for her to effectively pinch the little dumplings closed, and so she was afforded a pass to sit and watch TV in the other room while the others worked. In all honesty, that in itself afforded the others a pass: to not have their pinching techniques razed to dust by Irenka's overly harsh criticism.

'It's OK, ciocia,' Eva said, smiling past the knot of tension which had been lodged in her throat ever since the situation on the slide that morning. 'I'm not complaining, just had a tough day.'

She hadn't told her family about the incident, not at all ready for the almost guaranteed ribbing she'd get about it. *You'll laugh about this one day*, Maxine had said earlier as she met a dripping, mortified Eva at the steps of the plunge pool to hand Juni back over, and maybe one day she would.

But not this day.

This day she was just worn down by the whole thing, suffocated by embarrassment and completely and totally over being the unluckiest woman in the world.

That and exhausted by the effort of keeping up this charade that she wanted nothing to do with Luke Mallory. She was tired – bone tired – of trying not to imagine how things could have played out between them.

Had he not been a Mallory.

Had she not been cursed.

But he was, and *she* was, so she had no choice but to go on pretending.

She turned her attention back to the pierogi then, her practised scoop and fold and pinch, honed through years of doing just this: sitting with her favourite people in the world around an old-fashioned dining table, each playing their part in the dumpling assembly line.

Nelka, whose own joints were not too far behind her sister's, stuck to the less fiddly jobs – the rolling out of pastry, the cutting of small circles. Eva and Sylvia were in charge of assembly: first a scoop of the filling in the centre of the circle, then the all-important pinching close of the pastry, a job which had been heavily supervised by Ciocia Irenka in past years, but which the two women had now perfected.

Hanna, who they had learned early on did not have the patience for any part of the assembly line, took cooking duty, boiling the small parcels until they floated before leaving them to cool on laid-out tea towels.

It was calming, the ritual, though always underscored by a note of sadness. Tomasz had been the only male permitted to attend their annual pre-Christmas pierogi making night, on account of him being an award-winning chef. Even then, Ciocia Irenka had steadfastly refused to accept his input on any aspect of the process.

'It is tradition,' she'd snapped, that one year he'd suggested a different filling, and though he'd deferred to his aunt at the time, that hadn't stopped the twins from doing the same every year since. It had started a running joke, the proposed fillings growing more and more ridiculous every year, and after he died the joke had remained in his honour, though it had been twenty-two years now since he'd first made it, and Ciocia Irenka had yet to laugh.

Speaking of Ciocia Irenka, she was yelling something from the other room, a strange quality to her voice which made Eva's blood run cold for a second until she realised why the old woman's tone was so alien.

She actually sounded excited.

'Eva! *Ewunia!*' she shrieked again, louder this time. 'You are making the TV!'

Confusion tugged Eva's brows into a frown. 'Sorry, *what*?'

'Come quickly!' Irenka bellowed, with genuine delight in her tone, and the other women were so intrigued as to what could finally be amusing her that they almost fell over each other trying to get into the living room. Nobody wanted to miss whatever miracle it was which had finally lit a fire under Ciocia Irenka.

'What is i... Oh my *God*,' Hanna said, stopping abruptly in front of Eva as she clapped eyes on whatever was playing on the ageing TV.

Eva rubbed at her shoulder where it had collided with her sister's back. 'God, Han, you make a better door than a window, y—'

And then it registered what was actually on the screen: a clip playing over and over in a loop – grainy CCTV footage of a waterslide. A very familiar waterslide. A very familiar waterslide with two very familiar figures suspended from the pipe right at the very top.

Eva's heart dropped to her feet. The roughness of the footage shielded her identity a little, but to anyone who knew her well it was definitely, undeniably her.

'How did they get this?' she muttered, more to herself than

the others, as her eyes fixed on the segment title.

'Teacher's *Wet*,' Hanna barked, as if she could read her twin's mind, laughing so hard at the title that her breath came in raspy wheezes. 'That's the worst pun I've ever seen.' She swiped at the tears forming in her eyes. 'Ah, local news. I love it.'

'Eevs, when was this?' her mother was asking, from her left. 'Were you hurt?'

She shook her head in response. 'Other than leaving my dignity at the top of that slide, I was fine. And it happened this morning. How is it already on the news?'

'You have to move fast with news of this calibre,' Hanna said with another snort, before her gaze fell to her phone, which she had automatically reached for as they'd rushed to see what the hubbub was about. 'Eevs, you're trending on TikTok too!'

She lifted the phone and Eva and Sylvia craned their necks to see. Sure enough, there it was, the same grainy footage playing in a loop to an obnoxious soundtrack.

'This is the worst day of my life,' Eva muttered, unable to look away.

It wasn't, though. Not even close.

'They've put that "oh no" song on it,' Hanna managed, between honks of laughter. 'Oh my God, this is hilarious.'

She was still watching it a few moments later, as Ciocia Nelka ushered them back into the kitchen,

'OK,' Hanna said, as she regained her composure. 'A couple of questions. Firstly, who *is* that?'

Eva sighed. There was no point evading this; they had ways and means of finding out the truth eventually.

'It's Luke.'

Hanna's brows shot skyward. 'Cupboard Boy?'

'Yes.' Eva resumed her role in the pierogi production line, if only so that she wouldn't have to meet Hanna's eyes. 'And can you stop calling him that?'

She heard her sister's low chuckle, a sure sign that she would be doing nothing of the sort.

'He looks different with his clothes off. Anyway, second question,' Hanna said. She was loving this. 'Is he a literal superhero?'

Eva's eyes couldn't quite decide whether to opt for a roll or a glare, so they settled somewhere in between.

'I'm just saying,' Hanna continued, 'That manoeuvre. Holy sh—'

'Hanna!' Eva and Sylvia exclaimed, in unison. Eva did look up at her sister then, and she didn't miss the smug curl of Hanna's mouth. She'd always said that Eva would be the one to turn into their mother.

'Third and final question.'

Eva turned her attention back to the pierogi at that point, but she could see Hanna brandishing the slotted spoon in her periphery. She didn't respond, though she doubted that would matter much to Hanna.

'The two of you look *awfully* cosy there.'

Eva huffed a laugh, defensive, though she needn't be. 'Not a question.'

'And yet,' Hanna said, slowly, as though she were solving a puzzle, 'it seems to require an answer.'

'We weren't *cosy*.' Eva's answer came too quickly, and she saw her mother's ears prick up. 'He was helping me.'

Hanna coughed out a laugh. 'I bet he was.'

'Hanna!'

Hanna relented at that, turning back to her bubbling cauldron of dumplings while the others worked, mostly in silence, save for the occasionally waver of a whistle from Ciocia Nelka and the vague hum of the TV, still on in the other room.

'All I'm saying,' Hanna blurted few minutes later, just as Eva was finally starting to decompress from the whole ordeal, 'is if you still want to get rid of the curse, and you're *really* not boning Cupboard Boy…'

Eva couldn't help but cringe. She didn't even have the energy to *Hanna!* at Hanna.

'Then you really need to get a crack on with the husband hunt.'

Eva shook her head, trying to swallow down the flare of anxiety she felt in her chest when she thought about the hunt. It hadn't been there at the start. She never would have settled on the plan if it had been. Maybe it was down to her startling lack of success thus far, but somewhere along the line it had started to become a penance, a punishment which she felt she had to endure in order to finally set herself free.

But she didn't voice her concerns, not then, and not an hour later when the twins were alone in the kitchen, bagging batches of pierogi for the freezer.

'I'm sorry I laughed at your traumatic morning,' Hanna said, more gently than her usual manner, her expression so earnest that it made Eva laugh.

'You're not.'

Hanna's mouth twisted into a sheepish smile. 'You're right, I'm not, but I do genuinely hope you're not scarred by it.'

She offered a hand out and Eva took it, grateful as always for her sister.

'I'll live,' Eva said, smiling past the drag in her chest, and it made Hanna's smile fade immediately, her brows hitching into a frown.

'You sound tired, Eevs.'

Eva shook her head, barely convincing herself. 'I just need a break. You know, from…'—she motioned vaguely with her hands—'everything.'

'Which is why the hunt has to work,' Hanna said, and it was a question and an answer all at once.

Eva couldn't bring herself to reply, so she simply nodded. Her sister nodded too, in response, her lips pressed together in thought for a moment or two before she spoke again.

'I hate to say it, but I think it might be time to try one of Ciocia Nelka's brother-cousins.'

Eva chuckled, even past the growing lump in her throat. 'I hate to agree.'

'But you agree?'

Eva's *yeah* was little more than a breath out, a whisper of desperation out into the vast abyss of her fate. After all, what were the chances that Nelka would know more than one sociopath? Pretty slim, Eva wanted to believe.

'Oh Eevs, I so want this to work out for you.' Hanna's face softened way past the benchmark to which Eva had become accustomed. It was just enough to put a little wind back into Eva's sails.

'It has to,' she said, and whatever it was that Hanna heard in her voice, it made her brighten a little, and she reached out a hand to squeeze Eva's shoulder lightly.

'Come on,' Hanna said, with a conspiratorial wink, 'let's go tell Ciocia Irenka that we're planning to stuff next year's pierogi with a parfait of goat's cheese and rhubarb.'

Chapter Nineteen

'It's all anyone's talked about since,' Orson said lazily playing scales on the school's ramshackle piano as the children filed into their choir rehearsal. It was a good few weeks after the waterslide debacle, but the children still made a joke about it at least once every other day. It didn't feel as bad as Eva had feared, though. Somehow speaking to Orson about it had faded the burn of embarrassment somewhat, even though he still brought it up all the time.

He had that effect on things, his easy manner managing to take the sting out of even the worst of Eva's incidents. He was the perfect balance of resigned and optimistic, his soft chuckle as she recounted events pushing her infinitesimally closer to seeing the funny side herself.

With every day that passed she was a little more glad that she'd walked into Orson Myrtle's classroom that day. She'd asked for his help, but he'd given her something else, too.

Sanctuary.

She spent most lunchtimes in his classroom now, the two of

them laughing about catastrophic choir rehearsals or Eva's ridiculous mishaps. Eva would tell him all about her family, or about her husband hunt, and Orson talked about his beloved Jules with such affection that at times it made Eva feel hollowed out and full to the brim at the same time, her only aim in life to be loved as deeply and fully as Orson loved Jules.

Also, with the sum of their efforts, the choir was finally coming together. They still sounded a little like a group of cats whose tails had simultaneously been stood on, but they were all howling more or less in time these days. Bobby hadn't tried to eat the piano stool once since Orson's behind had taken up residence there, and the two year-four boys had absolutely held up their end of the deal, each singing a verse of 'Away in a Manger' to a standard which was actually surprisingly acceptable. It almost made Eva's national humiliation worth it.

Almost.

'So,' Orson said, hands still moving effortlessly across the keys as he swept an experienced eye over the assembling children, 'is it a date night tonight?'

Eva paused to glare at one of the year one children with a full finger up their friend's nose before turning back to him with a smile. 'It is. And I'm actually looking forward to it this time.'

A half-truth, perhaps. She had been looking forward to it until she'd made the mistake of peering into the year-one classroom earlier to see Luke cheering for one of his pupils like they'd won an Oscar, the look of pure delight on both of their faces hitting Eva right in the chest. Nevertheless, Marcel Wisniewski seemed like a decent guy on the face of it, and she needed nothing more than someone to distract her from the deep burn of those feelings.

'That's good,' Orson said, seamlessly switching from scales to a classical piece which Eva vaguely recognised.

She nodded, eyes following his fingers, marvelling at the ease with which they moved across the piano. 'It'll be refreshing to talk to someone who knows nothing at all about the whole slide situation.'

'I mean, unless he watches local TV news or has any social media accounts,' Orson deadpanned, the crinkle of his eyes beneath gold-framed glasses the only giveaway that he was joking. Eva wailed theatrically in response.

The gentle lilt of Orson's chuckle settled her a little, as it always did. 'I'm sure he won't bring it up. You'll enjoy it.'

'I hope so.' She grabbed for her ukulele. 'What are your plans for tonight?'

Orson's smile widened, though he didn't look up from the keys. 'I'm going out too, actually. It's Jules's birthday so we're going out to our favourite restaurant.'

That familiar pang caught her in the stomach. It wasn't jealousy so much as it was hope, and most likely it was somewhere in between – a longing for someone's face to crease along those same lines whenever they mentioned her.

'Sounds lovely,' she said, her smile genuine. 'Hope you're celebrating in style.'

He stopped playing abruptly at that, his eyes focusing on the piano for a beat until he looked up at her, his face alight. 'Oh we will be.'

And Eva beamed back at him before striding out away from the piano, ukulele tucked under one arm.

'OK gang, everyone in your places!'

Eva had just flopped down at her desk after ushering the last child out of the building when Neeta popped her head around the door.

She'd been expecting it, honestly, ever since she'd clocked Neeta slipping into the back of the hall just as they were starting the last song of their rehearsal. There was a weight to Neeta's expression, an edge to the way in which she leaned against the stack of blue plastic chairs which had made Eva and Orson exchange wide-eyed glances. They'd both recognised it.

Neeta had something to say.

She hadn't said anything at the time though, just watched the final song, motionless and unreadable, before pushing back out of the doors and vanishing up the corridor. A small wave of panic crept up Eva's throat as the clack of heels on lino grew quieter and quieter.

Had Neeta finally realised that Eva and Luke had gone off piste with the music project? Eva had made an effort to mention his name whenever she spoke to Neeta about choir, and to pretend to know what was going on every time Neeta discussed the band performance with her. She had thought she'd got away with it, but Luke's obvious absence at the rehearsal had been damning.

'Eva, a word,' Neeta said, voice neutral.

Shit.

She followed Neeta the two dozen steps to her office, rounding the corner to see Luke, already there, shifting uncomfortably in one of the chairs. He made eye contact as she sat, the closest she'd been to him since they'd emerged from the plunge pool together.

Busted, his expression seemed to say, a look of solidarity which surprised her a little. She'd half expected him to throw her under the bus. And when she met his gaze, a single nod her reply, she almost thought she could see one corner of his mouth lifting in a smirk.

It felt like a peace offering.

Neeta motioned for her to sit and she did, not deliberately choosing the seat across from Luke, but being left with it as an only reasonable option. Going all the way around the table in order to sit next to him would just have appeared awkward, and Eva was wary of giving Neeta any more ammunition.

'Eva, Luke,' Neeta began, her tone as formal as always. It was impossible to tell if she was cross. 'I wanted to talk to you about the music project.'

They both nodded, a small, noncommittal noise escaping each of them simultaneously, and Eva braced herself against the incoming fallout.

'I noticed that you've roped Orson Myrtle into the choir,' Neeta started, her eyes meeting Eva's under their perfect flicks of eyeliner.

Eva hands knotted together underneath the table. 'Yes.'

'And Luke has sought assistance from Fran Parkes for the band.'

Eva had known that, of course. She'd spotted the two of them giggling together after band practice one day and had to try very hard not to combust with jealousy. It didn't help that Fran was unspeakably pretty, all flawless olive skin and dark, shiny curls. Eva had had to make a real effort not to stalk the two of them as she fended off all manner of irrational thoughts about how they were going to fall in love and get married and have beautiful, musically talented offspring. Her throat began to tighten at the mere mention of Fran's name.

'Yes,' Luke replied, his voice steady, the rumble of it making Eva's chest ache, as it always did.

And then there was a moment, heavy, like the wait between a bolt of lightning and a rumble of thunder, tension snapping through the air as they braced themselves for a dressing down.

Except that wasn't what happened at all.

'What a great idea,' Neeta said then, 'to involve more of our staff members in the music project. I love it.'

Eva braced herself. Neeta was usually straightforward but she couldn't help but worry that this was a trap.

'I've heard Orson play, and he is just outstanding.' Neeta continued, 'And who knew Fran had a voice like that?'

Eva was speechless at first, sneaking a look at Luke and almost yelping out loud when she found he was already looking at her.

'Right?' he said, turning back to Neeta. 'I heard her singing in the staff room when she didn't know anyone was there and I was mesmerised.'

Mesmerised.

Eva's guts tied themselves into a tight knot. Once upon a time he'd said something similar about her. She took a deep breath and reminded herself all over again that *she* was the one who'd ended things. It wasn't the first time in her life that she'd felt a surge of pure hatred for the curse, and she doubted it would be the last.

'I knew I was right to trust the two of you with this,' Neeta was saying, and Eva turned her attention back to her boss. 'You make a fantastic team.'

Eva ignored the tiny huff of a breath which she heard from Luke, and smiled past the awkward grip of tension between them.

'Um, thanks?'

Eva wasn't entirely sure why she had phrased that as a question.

'Which is why,' Neeta said, smoothing a neatly manicured hand over one lapel of her coral blazer, 'I know you'll be able to handle the next part of the plan.'

She saw Luke glance back up at her out of the corner of her eye but she didn't dare return the look.

'A whole school production!' Neeta finished with a flourish. She was grinning from ear to ear, an expression of pure optimism on her face.

Eva's throat tightened as Neeta quickly ran though the details. They'd have to think of an idea this side of Christmas in order to get Ross and his colleagues to sign off on it. Then rehearsals would start in January with the performance itself being mid-March, just before for the deadline for their music accreditation application.

In truth, it was a perfectly reasonable timescale, but Eva's brain hadn't fixated on that part. It was stuck, right back at the beginning, when Neeta had uttered the words *whole school production*.

Whole. School. Production.

There would be no way they could split it. Not something on that kind of scale. It would take one hundred percent from each of them and most probably everything Orson and Fran had, too.

They had no choice.

They had to take it on together.

Shit.

By the time Eva arrived home an hour later, she was in a tailspin. Between the familiar bite of anxiety in her throat and the whirl of ideas in her head, she was so distracted that she didn't see Lucky in the doorway of her flat until she'd fallen over him, tumbling into a heap on the tile with an inelegant grunt.

She clambered gingerly to her feet, running a hand over her left hip and forearm, which had taken the brunt of the impact, and blowing out a breath of relief when she found no real damage.

'Didn't see you there, buddy,' she said to the now-retreating feline as she locked the door behind her. There was more haughtiness to the rise and fall of his haunches than usual, and his baseline was already pretty high. He meowed once, and then vanished off into the darkness of the flat.

Eva always felt a certain sadness coming home at this time of the year, though she wasn't always completely aware of it. It was always just there, in the background, a feeling so slight and so constant that she had grown entirely used to it.

It was the faint reflection of Christmas lights from the house over the road. A light trail of glitter shed from handmade Christmas cards, which headed up the steps in the hallway. It was snatches of carols sung in the street below, small reminders that it was almost Christmas, and she was largely alone, again.

She'd spend Christmas Eve at Sylvia's, of course, and Christmas Day too, but after the busy warmth of both celebrations she'd come back to that dark, silent flat, with only a belligerent old cat for company. She sighed, then, without really knowing why, pulling her laptop out of her bag and flicking on the kettle as she waited for her disappointing microwave meal for one.

By the time she settled at the table with a cup of tea and a cottage pie heated to approximately the temperature of the sun, she was filled with a buzz of nervous energy. Neeta had asked them to submit their initial ideas by the following Monday, so in reality they had a little time, but it didn't feel like that to Eva. It felt like a test, and she was determined not to fail it.

Especially not in front of Luke.

She started searching for primary school production ideas, and was almost to the bottom of page three when she saw *The Springing of Spring* and had a sudden memory of the first time they'd sat around Neeta's table with Ross. Hadn't he said that was one of his favourites?

It seemed too obvious to pick the same play that he'd explicitly mentioned, though. As if they'd not really thought about it at all. So instead Eva used her tried-and-tested method of googling *plays like The Springing of Spring,* and she was just about to hit the search button when she remembered something else that Ross had said – in particular the almost inappropriate way he'd gushed about Luke's band video.

Eva had been a little concerned by Ross's enthusiasm at the time, though her curiosity *had* lead her to search extensively for the video in question back then. But she never found it, and so completely forgot that it existed. But she had new intel now; she knew the name of his band. Plus, after watching them play that night in the pub, she absolutely *got* it. If the video was even half as captivating as the live performance, she would be bookmarking it in a heartbeat.

She shovelled a palate-scalding forkful of cottage pie into

her mouth as she deleted *plays like The Springing of Spring* out of the search bar and typed in *The Ordinaries band video* instead.

Three results.

She clicked on the first.

Her heart skipped up into her throat as the music started, the first twenty seconds focusing on the singer before all of a sudden there was Luke, dressed in that same low-cut V-neck, the strap of his bass pulling it a little way down, exposing the small hollow underneath his collarbone.

She gaped, shameless, her cottage pie forgotten as the fork loosened in her grasp, her breath speeding and a small flicker of heat edging its way down her spine. Of all the versions of him that she'd come across, Music Luke was her absolute favourite.

The video finished, and she huffed a small breath out into the sudden silence, mouth open, heart racing. And then she hit the play button and started watching it again from the beginning.

So maybe she couldn't marry another Mallory, but it couldn't hurt to save this video to her favourites to watch on repeat when she'd had a particularly bad day.

She was just getting to the best part – the build to the second chorus in which Luke seemed to lose himself to the music, his head thrown back and beads of sweat tracking down his temples – when her phone vibrated on the table next to her and she jumped so violently that she inadvertently flung her fork halfway across the room. Lucky appeared from nowhere and trotted off to investigate while Eva picked up her phone. She nearly threw that across the room too when she saw who the message was from, and then clicked off the video as fast as if he'd actually walked into the room.

LUKE: Truce?

Her heart jumped, and she almost lost her breath as she read that single word again and again. Had he known she'd been watching him? Impossible, surely, and yet the timing was absolutely perfect. It was as if she'd summoned him, just like Hanna had said that time she got stuck in the window. She stared at the message for a minute, then two, then fifteen, then forty, typing and deleting reply after reply as she tried to find the perfect response to his olive branch.

Of course.

No way in the world.

Didn't even realise we were at war.

I can't make my peace with you because then I'll fall in love with you.

But none of it felt right. She almost didn't reply, but that in itself felt like a statement, and that wasn't the message she wanted to send either. After all, it wasn't Luke's fault that she was cursed. She'd hurt him, however much she'd hurt herself in the process, and he deserved better than that.

And so, in the end, she managed a single word in reply, sending it quickly, before she could talk herself out of it.

EVA: Truce.

Chapter Twenty

Marcel Wisniewski was indeed a decent guy.

In fact, he was more than *decent*. He was polite and intelligent and objectively good-looking, not to mention that he had arrived for their date four minutes early and had taken Eva's inevitable string of minor disasters absolutely in his stride.

'Life happens,' he said with a chuckle, the slightest tug of an accent at his words. 'If we don't laugh at our mishaps, they will laugh at us.'

They talked for a while, the conversation coming easily, with Marcel throwing his head back into a wonderful, warm laugh at even the most feeble of Eva's jokes. On the face of it, he was the perfect man.

And yet, there was something which wasn't quite right. Nothing sinister, like with Bartek, whom she'd crawled out of window to escape from, but something quieter, in the way that he spoke to her, or maybe in the way he looked at her. It was a sadness, perhaps, or a longing. Something frail and bittersweet that caught at Eva's chest every now and again.

It was more like the sixth sense she had with the children in her class. It was the feeling that something had happened, or that something *was* happening, and that she was not a party to it.

Not yet.

They talked about their families, and were delighted to discover they were both twins, although Eva did not mention that hers was sitting at the other side of the bar, and Marcel reared back in horror when Eva let slip that Ciocia Nelka had also suggested Marcel's brother as a potential date for her.

'Oh no, petal,' Marcel said, his use of the term of endearment seeming overfamiliar and yet strangely distant at the same time. 'Mariusz is not a good prospect.'

She barked a laugh. 'Prospect! You sound like my ciocias.'

'Sometimes ciocias are right,' he said, the warmth of a laugh in his voice too. 'I love my brother, but I know that he would not treat you with the respect that you deserve.'

His dark eyes crinkled with his smile, and that action set off the rest of his features: perfect olive skin; dark hair styled to perfection; a million-dollar smile. God, he was handsome. And respectful too. All in all, the perfect man,

Why didn't *he* make her chest tighten the way that Luke did?

'In fairness,' she began, smiling past the tug of longing in her belly, 'my ciocias are rarely right about relationships. I mean I love them to death, but I've lost count of the number of times I've had to explain to them that catcalling isn't a compliment or that homosexuality is both legal and completely acceptable.'

His face changed at that. Was it shock, perhaps? She wouldn't have clocked him as a bigot, but there had been a noticeable shift in his body language when she'd uttered the word *homosexuality*, and the small *oh* which he muttered in response had seemed strained too.

'Oh yeah,' she said, putting as much conviction as she could behind the sentiment so as to call him out, if that were necessary. 'My sister's bisexual so we've had this conversation a lot. She's married to a man now, so they think she's cured, and I think we've both lost the will to explain why that's offensive.'

His gaze dropped to his feet, and for a moment or two Eva was concerned that she'd been right. But as he looked back up, his brown eyes not quite meeting hers, she suddenly realised that wasn't what had been happening at all.

And when he said, tentatively, 'Eva, I must confess something to you,' she knew exactly what it was that he was about to say. Perhaps it was the way that he was studying her, or the hitch in his breath as he spoke. Whatever it was, something compelled her to offer her hand, outstretched, which he took with the slightest hint of a smile. And yet, when he spoke, she was surprised to find not sadness, but something akin to guilt in his voice.

'I'm gay,' he said, his beautiful face earnest and perhaps a little sheepish, 'And I'm so sorry that I have led you on by agreeing to come on this date.' His free hand went to his chin, scrubbing at the perfectly clipped stubble. 'I love my life. I don't feel any shame, not even an ounce.' He took a breath, slow and deliberate. 'But my mama, she is like your ciocias. Not hateful, just…'—he paused, weighing his words—'of her time.'

Eva nodded slowly. 'That's exactly it.'

'Maybe one day I will tell her,' he said, a smile pulling at one corner of his mouth. 'But for now she has enough prayers to say for the soul of my womanising brother. I don't need to burden her with the salvation of mine, too.' His smile grew. 'She'll wear her rosary beads down to dust.'

Eva couldn't help but laugh.

'So until then,' he continued, a glint in his eye, 'as and when she tries her hand as matchmaker, I will have to put up with evenings spent in conversation with beautiful, fascinating women.' He squeezed her hand lightly. 'I have enjoyed your company immensely. I can't for the life of me fathom why you are still single.'

Eva chuckled, about to launch into her spiel about how she was the unluckiest woman in the world when she noticed something over Marcel's shoulder – a familiar figure moving towards a table in the restaurant section of the bar, white hair combed neatly back from his face and his usual gold-rimmed glasses conspicuously absent.

'Oh hey,' she said, absentmindedly grabbing onto the bunched fabric at Marcel's elbows. 'My friend is here!'

Warmth bloomed in Eva's chest as she said the word. She wasn't entirely sure when she had stopped thinking of Orson solely as a colleague, but she was so grateful that she had.

Marcel followed her gaze over to the table where Orson was pulling out a chair. 'You should go say hi. I don't mind you abandoning me.'

Eva shook her head. 'He's out with his wife this evening. It's her birthday.' She studied Orson, so familiar to her now and yet so out of context in this new setting, 'I wouldn't feel right intruding.'

Orson looked up, then, and for a moment Eva thought that he would look her way. She ducked behind the bulk of Marcel's body. 'Quick, hide me!'

Marcel chuckled, moving himself a little way in his chair so as to hide her more efficiently. 'I thought you were friends?'

'We are,' she said, still clutching his shirt sleeves, 'but I don't want him to think I'm spying on him when he's just out trying to enjoy a lovely meal with his wife.' She chanced a peek back round Marcel's body to the table where Orson, still alone, was now wrestling something from the canvas bag he'd been holding. 'Wait, where *is* his wife?'

She could feel the vibration of Marcel's laugh through his arms. 'I thought you weren't spying?'

'Oh no,' she said, tightening her grip on Marcel as she peered back around him. 'I'm definitely spying. I just don't want him to *know* that I'm spying.'

'I see.'

'I thought they'd be… Wait, what is he doing?'

Orson finally won his fight with the bag, and pulled out a small, leather-bound frame, setting it on the table across from him before sitting back in his chair with a smile. Eva's brow creased in confusion, and she tugged at Marcel's sleeves to get him to turn too, not fully convinced she wasn't seeing things. The frame was a little worse for wear, the leather cracked and split around the edges, but that wasn't the thing that had caught Eva's attention.

It was the photograph inside.

They were a little way away from Orson's table, maybe five metres or more, but even at that distance Eva could see that that it was a picture of a man. She couldn't make out the details – just the contrast of his huge, toothy smile against dark brown skin, the sprinkling of grey in his beard and hair the only reason she could see them at all.

Her frown deepened. 'Wait, what? He said he was going out with his wife, Jules?' She spoke slowly, the cogs in her brain lurching into action. 'That today was her birthday.'

But when she looked up at Marcel, he was looking at her with a soft expression, head tilted slightly to one side. 'Did he ever explicitly say that Jules was his *wife*?'

Oh.

Oh.

She thought back, skimming though mental index cards of all the conversations they'd had, and she couldn't pinpoint a single time he'd used the word. 'I just assumed!'

She was an idiot.

But Marcel just shook his head, that same almost-smile on his face. 'It's easy to do.'

'Oh God, what if I said it to him?' Her cheeks burned. 'I never even asked.'

'But he never offered.'

'That's true.' Her lips pursed in thought. 'I wonder why?'

Marcel shrugged. 'Self-preservation? Habit?'

Her heart sank. They were becoming friends, that's what she'd thought. But friends shared things like this with each other.

Didn't they?

She'd given him a running commentary on her husband hunt. They'd laughed for hours about the night the fire brigade had to free her from the window, and he'd given her great advice for her date tonight, not that any of it had turned out to be of any use. She'd been an open book.

Almost.

With everything except…

Ah.

She hadn't breathed a single word about Luke. Not about meeting him in the bar, or kissing him in the cupboard, or the days and nights since then that she'd spend burning for him, wishing that he'd just had a different surname. And she'd told herself that the reason she hadn't said anything about it to Orson was because she didn't want to seem unprofessional, that there would be no way that any rumours about her would get back to the upper school coven, but that wasn't quite true.

It was because it hurt too much.

It was hard enough having him there all the time, the constant hum of temptation across the hall, so close in some respects, but in others, a million miles away. Like he was there, but he wasn't there.

The realisation gripped her like a vice, forcing all the air out of her lungs at once as her eyes found the leather-bound frame again.

He was there, but he wasn't there.

'He told me that he was going out with Jules,' she said, quietly, all the pieces of the puzzle finally slotting into place as she spoke, and Marcel nodded lightly in response.

'He's dead, isn't he?'

Marcel winced. 'That would be the conclusion I'd draw from this, yes.'

Tears welled in her eyes, grief rushing to fill the space in her chest that her exhale had left. It was such a familiar emotion for her now that she almost couldn't believe that she hadn't noticed it in her friend. But then she remembered all the times Orson had mentioned Jules, the pure joy which had taken over his features when he'd described their evenings out, their weekends away. She couldn't remember a single time when that expression had wavered. Not even for a second.

'He didn't tell me that either.' She blew a breath out. 'Do I tell him I know?'

Marcel raised a single perfect eyebrow. 'Do you want him to know you spied on him?'

'No, OK.' She nodded. 'Good point.' She snuck one final look at Orson now focusing his attention entirely on the laminated menu card in front of him, before shifting herself around, deliberately putting her back to him. 'So what do I do? When I next see him, I mean.'

'Nothing?'

'*Nothing?*' She frowned, fingers tapping a frenzied rhythm on the worn wood of their table. 'How do I do nothing?'

'Just imagine you never saw him tonight. However you would usually act around him, act like that.' He reached for her forearm and squeezed gently, a strangely reassuring gesture. 'Nothing's changed.'

'Nothing's changed,' she parroted, and though she knew Marcel was right, there was another feeling behind it, something uncomfortable sitting low in her chest.

It made perfect sense now that Jules was a man; that revelation hadn't shaken her at all. It stung a little that Orson had never told her as much, nor had he told her that, when he was going out with Jules, he was going out alone with only the memory of him for company, but he didn't owe her that either. No, there was something else, something darker and less defined. A small tug in her throat. A drag to her inhale, as if she might start crying any moment.

It felt like a warning, though she couldn't begin to say why. Like a sign from the universe, as so many things which happened to her seemed to her to be. But she didn't say anything about that to Marcel.

All she said was, 'Let's get another drink,' as she mentally crossed both Mariusz and Marcel Wisniewski off her list of potential husbands.

Her list which was now down to three. Three more chances to change her life.

One of them *had* to work out.

Chapter Twenty-One

Marcel's words echoed around Eva's brain for the entirety of the following day.

He doesn't know you spied on him, he'd said. Just act normal.

Yet, in her attempts to act normal, Eva was acting as far outside the realm of normal as was humanly possible. She hadn't spent lunchtime with Orson, as she normally did, and though that had actually been circumstantial – a poorly-timed nosebleed followed by an email from Neeta which had apparently been deemed so urgent that the subject line was three exclamation marks and nothing else – Eva couldn't help but feel as though she had done something wrong.

So when she saw Orson walking down the corridor just as school was finishing for the day, she panicked. She wasn't proud of herself, but in that moment her instincts took the wheel, and before she knew it, she'd dived into the art cupboard, flicked off the lights, and was now hiding, breath held, behind a crate of crepe paper.

'I'm sorry,' she whispered into the darkness as she heard his footsteps pass. 'I'm sorry you lost the love of your life.'

And then she heard the unmistakeable sound of Luke Mallory clearing his throat behind her and her soul almost left her body. When she flicked the lights back on, there he was, four feet away from her, one arm propped on a neat stack of new exercise books, a question in his eyes.

'What?' he asked, his voice veering nearer to shock than to irritation, though Eva suspected it could take a turn at any moment. 'Who's the love of … *what*?'

Eva's base reaction swelled to a full-scale panic response in the blink of an eye, and before she knew it, she was bent almost double, her fingers whitening as they tightened their grip around a spare guillotine propped against the stacks of paper. Her heart sped, beating a riot in her chest as her breath caught, hoarse and tight. It wasn't just Luke being there, or her absolutely inability to act like a normal person. It wasn't even the way she'd felt her heart shatter when she'd seen that Jules was a photograph on a table and not a living, breathing person, nor her own residual grief, a fresh wave crashing over her now, just as it had then.

It was all of those things, all at once. And it was more. Everything coming together at once, like a weight pressing down on her until she had no choice but to submit to it. It was awkwardness and lust and loneliness and inadequacy, all swirling into the perfect storm in her chest.

She hadn't had a panic attack for years, not since the early days of mourning for her dad, but she was having one now, her vision darkening around the edges as she wheezed out a plea into the heavy air of the cupboard.

That was when she felt Luke's hands close around her

upper arms, steady and comforting, guiding her to the old wooden step stool in the corner and carefully lowering her to sit on it, speaking to her the whole time. His voice was even, counting her breaths steadily, every fourth number replaced by whispered words of support.

Breathe, Eva.

Don't worry.

I'm here.

You're OK.

She closed her eyes, leaning into his words, and after a minute or two the tight grip around her chest began to ease, the wheeze of her breath coming easier and easier, slowing with his counting as her panic settled.

When she opened her eyes, he was right there, crouching in front of her, concern just barely pressing his lips together. It was an expression she'd seen on him before, when he was dealing with the children, but he wore it differently with her, and something about it made her breath catch.

'You OK?' he asked, after a beat, and she nodded, slowly, as if not quite sure.

When she reached for him that was an instinct too, and he responded in kind, her head falling to his shoulder as his arms wrapped around her back, thumbs stroking small circles. She breathed in the almost-familiar scent of him, notes of PVA glue and coffee mingling with the fading traces of his aftershave, settling somewhere in her chest, just to the left of her sternum.

'Thank you,' she whispered into the curve of his neck, stubble scratching at her lips as she did, and she felt the small breath he blew out in response as it scattered over the heated skin of her cheek.

'Anytime,' he muttered, and the scratch in his voice made

her throat tighten again, for a different reason this time. She lifted her head, putting distance between them before she did something stupid.

'How did you know what to do?'

He smiled weakly. 'You'd know this if you ever read your staff bulletin, but I just finished training as a mental health first aider.'

'Oh.' Her laugh was sharp, catching in her throat. 'Lucky for me.'

He lifted one eyebrow. 'Not like you to be lucky.'

She smiled, wider this time, and he reciprocated, reaching to pull a rogue strand of hair from where it had become caught on her eyelashes. She tried her best to ignore the lurch of her heart, but it was difficult with him so close, particularly with the way his hazel eyes were locked on hers.

'Can I help?' he asked, his voice low.

She shook her head. 'I don't think so.'

He studied her a while then, his fingers skimming the perimeter of her face. His fingertips brushed along her jawline, her forehead, her temples. And when his eyes dropped to her lips, she thought for a moment that he was going to kiss her, but he didn't. After a beat he pulled away from her completely, sitting back on his heels.

'I guess this must be the go-to cupboard for emotional breakdowns,' he said, the gruff of his voice thick in his throat and it made her thoughts stop in their tracks, a sudden realisation gripping her.

'You were in here with the door closed,' she muttered, slowly, as it came to her, and he looked away as he nodded.

'Yup.'

Her face fell into a frown. 'You were hiding too.'

'I was…'—he huffed a small breath, fingers tugging at his hair, which she just realised looked more tousled than normal—'having a moment.'

Her chest tightened. She'd been so caught up in her own panic that she hadn't even noticed that he was struggling with something too. 'Can I help?'

The shake of his head was so slight she almost missed it. 'It's something I have to do.' His voice dropped, almost to a whisper. 'That's the problem.'

Confusion tugged at Eva's expression, and her heart sped a little with anxiety as she watched him wrestle with whatever it was that he was about to say. One hand went to his face, rubbing at the stubble she had just realised was a little longer than usual.

'It's my final NQT assessment next week,' he said eventually, and when he did, the vulnerability running through his words almost broke her heart in two.

'Ah, OK.' She nodded in solidarity, remembering the stress only too well. 'But you'll smash it.'

The breath he huffed out wasn't quite a laugh or a sigh. Perhaps somewhere between the two.

'Won't you?'

He didn't look at her at first, and when he did, his face was pinched, not at all like his usual confident expression. It made him look younger, like a lost boy. Eva's protective instincts roared to life.

'I had a meeting with Nigel today, and—'

'Urgh, Nigel,' she couldn't help but blurt. 'What does he know? Want me to beat him up for you?'

At that, his face broke into a smile, small but genuine. 'He was actually saying nice things. He's a great mentor.'

Eva nearly fell off the stool she was sitting on. 'He *is*?'

A nod. 'He's a strange man, I grant you, but a brilliant teacher. His support has turned my lesson planning around.' Luke paused a moment, his hand going back to his hair before he spoke again. 'That was what I was going to fail on last time.'

She drew a breath in, her heart aching for him. She would never have guessed that he struggled with any of it. He always seemed to be at the top of his game in the classroom.

'This is my last chance,' he continued, not quite meeting her eyes. 'I left my last school before the assessment, thought I was going to have to give up on the whole teaching thing. But then my old mentor sent me a message saying that his friend was in desperate need of someone to cover a year one class, and was willing to let me retake the term.'

'Neeta.'

He huffed a small laugh. 'Saved my ass.'

'Which is why you had to say yes to the music project,' she said, as she made the connection, and he smiled as confirmation.

'I owe her, big.'

She bumped his knee with hers. 'Same.'

His brows knotted. 'What did you do?'

'Accidentally poisoned twenty-two parents with wildly out-of-date hot dog sausages.'

A laugh burst out of him, warm and unchecked. It was almost worth reliving the darkest moment of her educational career to hear it.

'What?' he managed, shock raising the pitch of his voice, and she shrugged as casually as she was able.

'It was an honest mistake. Neeta shielded me from as much of the fallout as she could.'

His eyes held hers a moment as he nodded. 'She's a good egg.'

Eva smiled. 'She is.'

There was a moment then, the air between them charged, just like it had been the last time they were both in the art cupboard. Luke's jaw twitched, and his eyes dropped to the ground before they came back up to meet hers.

'Luke?' Eva muttered, past the knot of warmth in her throat.

'Yeah?'

'You're going to pass, I know it.'

His teeth nibbled at his lower lip for a moment before he replied.

'Thanks. And remind me never to let you cook for me.'

'Deal,' she replied with a smile, so wide that it made her cheeks ache a little, and his grin in return was everything.

'Now,' he said, scrambling to his feet and holding out a hand for her, 'how about we both get out of this cupboard?'

'Sounds good.'

But there was a thump in her chest as she did, disappointment grating at her as she took his outstretched hand and hauled herself to her feet. She mentally scolded herself for it, but it didn't seem to make the slightest bit of difference. She doubted she'd ever stop wanting to be near him.

His fingers slipped out of hers and she mourned the loss of his touch, her eyes following him as he went to the door. Only, as he reached the handle he stopped, suddenly looking back at her with wide eyes.

'It won't open.'

She frowned past the rush of panic in her throat, going to

the door and trying the handle for herself, but feeling only resistance, the handle stopping abruptly just above the halfway point. But this was not Eva's first rodeo.

'It's stuck,' she said, turning to meet his eyes. 'Remember, I told you about the mechanism.'

He nodded, lightly. 'I *do* remember. I check it every time because of that.' He raised an eyebrow. 'Including this time.'

A familiar sinking feeling hit Eva's stomach. 'Oh no, sorry, I must have knocked it in my rush to get in and re-engaged it somehow.'

But Luke just blew out a breath, one corner of his mouth pulling into the lightest of smirks. 'That does sound pretty on-brand for you.'

Her exhale was almost a laugh, even as something turned over in her chest. She hadn't heard that tone in his voice for a while. He was joking with her. Were they OK?

She couldn't help but grin. 'Told you I was cursed.'

His smile broadened too, taking over his whole face in a way which she hadn't seen since the day they'd spent together all those weeks ago. The buzzing behind her breastbone, which had never entirely disappeared, now swelled, pushing against the walls of her chest with a ferocity that took her breath away.

Luke was leaning against the doorway like a catalogue model: the prop of one leg across the other making the weave of his tailored trousers pull at his hip and knee; dark red hair displaced by a day of tugging at it; forest-green jumper sleeves pushed up to his forearms; hazel eyes laser-beam focused on her. He looked like a work of art, wildly out of place in a primary school art cupboard, and yet somehow exactly where he should be.

She cleared her throat, coughing down the wave of longing

which had rushed up it. 'I don't think I ever thanked you for the waterslide incident,' she said, hurrying to change the subject before it veered over to the dangerous side, but Luke's chuckle in response was dangerous enough—a deep rumble low in his chest.

'Anytime,' he said again, his voice dark and rough, and it made Eva reach back for the door behind her, her fingers splaying against the dark brown gloss as she fought to calm herself, to ground herself, to stop herself from reaching for him right there and then.

She felt a blush spread up her cheeks. 'Hopefully not *anytime*.'

But he just smiled, steady and knowing, a crackle of electricity between them which she fought to temper.

'Maybe we should talk about the production,' she blurted, flailing for anything which would help dispel the tension. 'We have to present our ideas to Neeta next week.'

'OK,' he said, voice steady, not breaking eye contact even for a second. 'Or – and this might be a crazy idea – we could try to get out of this cupboard.'

Eva wished, not for the first time, for a hole to open in the earth beneath her. She hadn't even considered that as a course of action. She wasn't even sure her brain was capable of firing on all cylinders when she was in Luke's immediate vicinity.

'Yes,' she said, hating the fury of heat rushing to her cheeks. 'Let's do that.'

He nodded, but he made no move to try the door or get help, and he didn't take his eyes off her, either. 'We can get together tomorrow to talk about it. Maybe you could bring Orson along? And I'd love to get Fran involved too. She's been amazing with the band.'

Eva felt the slither of jealousy around her throat again. 'Yeah, of course.'

'And she has yet to lock me in a cupboard with her,' he continued, 'which probably should score her a bonus point.'

Eva's heart sank to her feet. Of course. Who wouldn't prefer to spend time with someone that didn't attract disaster wherever they went? Fran was beautiful, nice, available, and not a walking liability. She was, Eva thought, the sensible choice.

The *better* choice.

It didn't matter to Eva's reasoning that she'd been the one to walk away in the first place, nor that she had actively spent the last few months searching for a husband, a husband who was anyone except the man standing in front of her. It didn't even matter that she actually had no idea whether or not Luke and Fran were even interested in each other. It took mere seconds for her imagination to conjure up visions of the two of them together: laughing, playing music, *kissing*.

Eva wasn't ordinarily a jealous person, but a roll of nausea pulled at her gullet at the idea, and she cast her eyes down to hide the sudden well of tears.

'God, sorry,' she said, swallowing down the knot in her throat. 'I'm being a chaotic mess as usual.'

She heard his small huff of a laugh – soft, not unkind – and when he spoke there was a softening to his voice, too.

'Not that I *hate* being trapped in small spaces with you.'

Her eyes flew up to meet his, heart beating ten to the dozen. There was something about his expression then, something vital, like the answer to a question she wasn't sure she'd even asked. And whether it was the way he was looking at her, or the residual adrenaline from her earlier panic attack, or the way she was suddenly completely surrounded by that familiar scent of him, something changed. In the blink of an eye, some primitive part of her brain took a sledgehammer to all rational thought, drowning out all her carefully constructed objections beneath a giant wave of emotion.

After that it all came undone.

She felt her skin prickle with heat, her needs and her fears colliding into one feeling, heavy and relentless. And when she reached out for him, settling one hand against the soft knit of his jumper, she felt his body coil in response, as if he was ready. As if he'd been ready the whole time.

'We can't…' she began, with far less conviction than the last time she'd uttered those words, and she saw his eyes darken. 'It's not fair on you if we—'

He straightened, his chest pushing into her hand as he leaned closer. 'Why don't you let me decide what's fair on me.'

And with that, the last remnants of Eva's resolve shattered into small fragments and fell away.

It was too much. *He* was too much.

They were back in the stuffy old art cupboard, just like before, and just like before she was powerless to resist his pull.

She couldn't even have described it as a kiss. It was like a shockwave, the snap of lightning cutting through the air. They crashed together as one entity against the door, his body pinning her fast against the brown gloss as his mouth sought hers out.

There was no finesse to it this time. It was hungry and raw, the occasional clash of teeth punctuating the urgent press of their tongues as they each surrendered themselves to the pull of desire. She felt his hands close around her thighs, edging up underneath the hem of her dress, finding the swell of her hips and pulling her closer than she'd thought possible.

She broke away, dragging her mouth down his throat and humming with pleasure at the groan that earned her. His grip around her hips tightened, and when he pressed himself into her again his hardness made her groan too. It only seemed to spur him on, and as his kisses deepened his hips started to move, just a little. The slightest of rocks, just exactly where she needed him.

She muttered his name but it was bitten off by another kiss, and her hands, moving of their own accord now, found the hem of his jumper and slipped beneath, reaching around the warmth of his sides and up the heated skin of his back, holding on for dear life.

Eva had never been more turned on.

Luke's mouth grazed her collarbone, and as he muttered broken words and half promises into the crook of her neck, the gravel in his voice sent ripples of need deep down into her belly. And then he stopped and pulled back a little, just for a second, his eyes searching hers.

'Eva,' he gritted out, his breath warm against her swollen lips, and it sounded like a question, although she didn't know what he was asking. Not that she would have had any answers for him anyway.

Instead she responded with a kiss, soft and slow. An apology, perhaps, or maybe permission. Whatever it was, it seemed to make lightning strike again, and he grasped the whole of her face in one hand as he kissed her, his body pushing her back into the door.

Somewhere along the line one of them must have knocked the light switch because it was dark now, but that only heightened the sensations. She could feel his growl as a rumble through his chest, feel the beat of his heart through the skin of his back. His mouth was on hers, hot and demanding, the press of his body relentless. And when his hand slipped from her face and trailed a firm line down the centre of her body, she thought for a moment she might just burst into flames where she stood.

She was alight with need, lit up like a flare and entirely unconcerned, for that moment, about any of the consequences.

That was, until the door opened without warning, and the two of them tumbled out into the brightness of the corridor. Eva took the brunt of the impact, losing her footing as she fell, and ending up crashing down, limbs akimbo, onto the rough industrial carpet.

'God, are you OK?'

Eva was still squinting against the light, but she recognised Fran's voice, and as her eyes adjusted she saw the younger woman there, brows pulled into a frown, her expression partway between concern and confusion. Luke was off to the side, straightening himself up as well as he was able.

Eva scrambled to her feet and dusted her dress off. She adjusted her weight from foot to foot, but nothing seemed to be hurt.

Just her pride.

'I'm sorry,' Fran was saying. 'I didn't mean to shock you. I heard you knocking and just assumed the lock had stuck again.'

There was something in her expression as she studied Eva, something about the way that she gravitated towards Luke that Eva recognised completely.

Fran was jealous. Not the bitter kind of jealousy, but

something softer. Something deeper. She wasn't staking her claim so much as watching it be taken from her, and something about it made Eva's heart tighten. She'd already told Luke they couldn't be together and yet here she was, ruining his potential chances of happiness with someone who was, by the look of it, available. And interested. And, crucially, not cursed.

'Yes,' Eva said, biting back the remorse at the back of her throat. 'Knocking is definitely what we were doing. Good job you heard us.'

Fran nodded, her smile looking every bit as fake as Eva's felt. 'Why was the light off?'

'Was it?' Eva squeaked out, and then she sneaked a look at Luke and almost jumped out of her skin when she found him staring straight back at her, eyes on fire and his lips, still pink from kissing, curled into the slightest of smirks.

Her whole body ignited in a blush which felt as if it stretched from her toes to her scalp. Had Fran seen that? God, she hoped not.

'Oh Eva, Orson was looking for you,' Fran said, her voice returning to its usual pleasant tone. 'Something about sheet music for the nativity?'

Shit.

She was supposed to get the music to him in the morning but she'd been so distracted she'd totally forgotten. But any residual awkwardness she might have felt about her illicit snooping was blown out of the water now, and she took off in the direction of Orson's classroom, muttering a thank you over her shoulder.

After all, she had a new mistake to hide from now.

Chapter Twenty-Two

Eva was walking out to her car that evening when he caught her.

She'd known it was him before he spoke. It was all so familiar to her now: the pattern of his footsteps; the slightest scent of his aftershave; the very specific, strangely hot way that he cleared his throat. She wasn't surprised at all when he said her name. It was dark in the car park at that time, with fine rain settling like tiny gems on Eva's eyelashes, so when she finally turned to look at Luke, he looked as if he were glowing.

He grabbed her wrist over her coat and pulled her into the small alcove by the kitchen door, letting her go once they were sheltered as if he wasn't really sure what he'd been going to say. He took a step back, leaned back against the brick at the other side of the alcove. She'd rarely seen him look anything less than completely in control of any situation, and it made her heart leap, a feeling she couldn't place nagging at her.

'Eva,' he said again after a while, and after that he said

nothing. Just studied her with those eyes, his dark red hair appearing warmer in the golden glow of the streetlight.

She took a deep breath, bracing herself against the feeling she always got when she was this close to him – like she wanted to hold on to him tightly and never let him go. Because she'd realised something as she'd stood in Orson's classroom, not five minutes ago. She finally recognised that curious feeling that she'd had watching her friend eat his meal alone.

It had been a warning. A reminder that that could be her. She'd protected her heart so well for so long, and now it was open, exposed and vulnerable, at the mercy of whatever the curse could throw at it.

If she got too close to Luke then perhaps one day it would be *her* sitting at a table with only a photograph of her one true love for company. A lump formed in her throat at the very idea. The way she saw it, there was only one way to stop that from happening.

'I know,' she said, not quite meeting his eyes. 'Whatever this is, me and you, I feel it. But it doesn't change the fact that this was a mistake.'

He drew a sharp breath in, his mouth falling open a little way as his brows pinched together, those dark hazel eyes lined by hurt. 'Eva,' he said again, and it sounded different again this time – melancholic, defeated. She almost couldn't bear it.

'OK, fine,' she said quickly. 'It wasn't a mistake. I enjoyed every single second.'

He took a step forward at that, but she put out a hand to stop him.

'But we shouldn't do it again.'

He stopped just short of her hand, so close she could feel the warmth of his chest through his clothes. 'I've been trying so hard to keep my distance.' A muscle flexed in his jaw. 'But then when I'm near you ... when I *kiss* you, I...' He trailed off, one hand going to rub at the stubble on his jaw. 'It's not easy,' he said, eventually. 'To ignore.'

She huffed a small breath out. She ached to touch him, longed to just fold into his arms. It would feel so good, she knew it would.

But at what cost?

'I know.' She gritted her teeth against the feeling. 'But—'

The plea in his eyes just about broke her down the middle. 'There doesn't need to be a but.'

Eva would have moved mountains for there not to be.

'I so wish that there wasn't.'

He studied her a moment or two before his face fell into a frown. She saw one of his hands flex and then relax, as if he were about to reach for her. Instead he just breathed out a sigh, his eyes not moving off her for a moment.

'If this is about that stupid curse.'

'It's not stupid to me.' Her voice was high and tight, the threat of tears heavy behind her eyes. 'My dad is dead because I thought I could outsmart the curse and I know you don't believe that it's real, but believe this.' A lone tear tracked down one cheek and he reached a thumb out to brush it away. 'I have lived under the weight of that guilt for ten years, and I can't do it anymore. The husband hunt, it's not even about finding love. Not anymore. It's about setting myself free.'

His thumb hadn't moved from her cheek, and at the small sob which escaped her, it started to move, tracing the smallest, softest of circles on her face. She leaned into his touch. She couldn't help it.

'If you and me...' Her voice caught on the words. 'If we

were together, I would be constantly bracing for impact, just waiting for something to happen to you too, and I can't. It's too much.'

He took a step closer, his breath sending plumes of mist out into the cold night air as his hand moved across her face, his fingertips burrowing into the hair at the nape of her neck.

All she could do was shake her head. 'I can't be the reason you…'

She couldn't bring herself to finish her sentence, and she didn't need to. Something about the change in Luke's stance told her that he was finally seeing her point, or maybe he was just accepting it.

He took a moment, drew the deepest of breaths in and then out, like he was grounding himself, steadying himself. And then, before she knew what was happening, he leaned in to kiss her, so tenderly that it made her cry all over again. It was written through the slight shake of his lips, through the catch to his breath and the gentle grip of his hand in her hair.

Everything about the way he kissed her this time was different. It was gentle, *deliberate*. More like the whisper of words that the scream of desire.

He wasn't staking a claim. Not this time.

He was letting her go.

'Don't move,' Hanna barked, yanking at the Christmas ornament in Eva's hair with all the finesse of an irate nit nurse.

Eva harrumphed. 'I'm not moving; you're pulling me.'

'I'm definitely not.' Hanna pulled again, harder this time, scooting Eva and the stool she was sitting on a foot or more over the tile of Sylvia's kitchen. 'I'm helping.'

'Oof, Eevs,' Owen said, through his teeth. 'It's stuck in there pretty good. We might need to cut it out.'

Sylvia's voice added to the furore. 'We're not cutting it out. Look how tight it is to her head. She'll look like a monk.'

Eva winced, her fists clenching tightly. '*Very* uninterested in that outcome.'

'You should let Stefan have a go,' Sylvia said, in a voice which came across more as someone trying to act calm than someone who actually *was* calm. 'He's good at this kind of thing.'

'The man does have the patience of a saint,' Hanna

conceded, dropping both the ornament and the chunk of Eva's hair which was coiled messily around it. It landed on top of Eva's head with a thunk. 'I've taken it as far as I can.'

'I think you made it worse, if anything,' Owen piped up, leaning over to look, and Hanna swatted at him playfully.

Sylvia tutted at them both. 'I'll go get him. You should have seen him untangling Nelka's Christmas lights the other day. Unbelievable.'

She scurried off into the living room, and Hanna plopped down on the stool next to Eva, a drink in her hand that Eva had not known about. No wonder she hadn't helped at all on the hair front.

Eva's laugh could just as easily have been a sigh. 'Merry Christmas to me.'

'Don't worry, Eevs,' Owen said, from a few feet away. 'Stefan will fix it for sure.'

Hanna just chuckled, knocking Eva's shoulder lightly with her own. 'And if he doesn't then I think you'd make a really attractive monk.'

Eva managed a half smile. She actually wanted to cry, but she knew what Ciocia Nelka would say: that if she cried on Christmas Eve then she would be crying all year. She very much did not want that to happen, and so she held it in, bracing herself against the feeling as she had learned to do so well over the course of her catastrophic life.

It didn't take long for Stefan to appear, and when he did he was holding a tail comb and a bottle of conditioner.

'I'm ready,' he said with a kindly smile. 'Let's set you free.'

There was nothing Eva wanted more.

Stefan worked with a good deal less vigour than her sister. She could feel occasional dabs of conditioner, followed by small tugs, gentle and methodical, as he hummed quietly to himself, occasionally pausing to make cheery comments like *great, that part's off*, and *nearly there.* He'd just managed to extricate it from Eva's hair and smooth over the strands carefully when Orson appeared, flanked by Sylvia and a very excited-looking Nelka. Eva hadn't even heard the doorbell go.

He looked curious and out-of-context standing there in Sylvia's living room, as if he were an invader from another world, two separate parts of her life colliding in a way that Eva would never have imagined.

She hadn't been intending to invite him. It had just sort of happened. They'd been sitting together in the staff room, sneaking a little more than their fair share of mince pies and Quality Street while they basked in the relief of the last day of term. The choir concert had … well, it had happened, and the nativity would go down in history as one of the school's most entertaining, if not for the reasons they'd been hoping. Everything had been winding down for the holidays, in the very best of ways.

'Got any plans for Christmas?' Eva had asked, popping a toffee penny into her mouth, and Orson had just smiled as he brushed pastry crumbs from his fingers.

'It's just me and Jules this year,' he'd said, making Eva's chest tighten. 'We normally spend it with my sister and her family but they're all going to Tenerife.' His smile had been so bright and warm that Eva had doubted she'd even have noticed the small note of grief in his voice had she not been looking for it. 'It's her son-in-law's fortieth, you see.'

'You should join us on Christmas Eve,' she'd offered, all in a rush. She couldn't bear the image of him eating alone with only the photo for company. 'If you want to, of course. We have enough food to feed the five thousand and there's nothing my family love more than a guest.'

He'd paused a moment, white brows knotting in thought. For a moment Eva had thought he would say no, that he wouldn't want to expose his secret in such a way, but after a few moments, he'd looked back at her, his face falling back into that familiar smile.

'Can I bring Jules?' he'd asked, some vague, unasked question sitting alongside his words and Eva had nodded effusively.

'Of course.'

Eva's family, as predicted, had been delighted about welcoming an extra body. At least, the younger generations had been. Ciocia Irenka had eyed them all with deep suspicion, and Ciocia Nelka? Well, Nelka had apparently forgotten that anything at all had been mentioned, and was now studying Orson with barely-contained glee.

'Misiu, is this…' She adjusted her glasses on her nose. 'Are you *courting*?'

Eva and Orson burst out laughing in unison.

'Oh my, no!' Orson said, that soft chuckle still in his voice. 'I'm old enough to be Eva's grandfather.'

'*Father*.' Eva smiled at him. Then she actually did the maths. 'OK, maybe grandfather.'

Orson shot her a mock offended look and they both laughed again.

'We're colleagues,' Eva said.

Orson nodded. 'And friends.'

Eva's heart swelled. 'Of course.'

His smile was so wide it hid his eyes almost completely. 'I was honoured to be invited to spend this evening with all of you.' His smile faltered, just for a second. 'I've brought my partner; I hope that's not a problem.'

'No, of course.' Sylvia chirped, pure delight in her voice. She always loved hosting new people. 'The more the merrier!'

Orson didn't move for a moment or two, and Eva noticed her mother and Nelka scanning the room, just in case there was a whole other person there they might have missed. Eva hadn't mentioned the photo when she'd asked her mother if she could invite Orson. She hadn't thought it was her story to tell. Not to mention that there was still a part of her which thought that perhaps she'd been mistaken, that maybe a very real, very alive Jules might step into the room any moment now.

But he didn't, and as Orson began to rummage in that old canvas bag on his shoulder, Eva couldn't help but brace herself. Ciocia Irenka in particular was a loose cannon, but all of them had been known, in the past, to ruin a moment. She hadn't thought this through at all.

Orson pulled out a bottle of wine first, offering it to Sylvia with a small smile. 'A thank you for welcoming me to your beautiful home.'

Sylvia beamed.

Then his hands want back into the bag, and he pulled out the frame, holding it out a little way in front of himself, head bowed.

At that distance, Eva could see Jules's face more clearly, and it broke her heart just a little more than the last time. He appeared younger than she'd thought, or perhaps he just wore it well, with just a little grey in his close-cropped curls, his warm brown eyes shining with joy.

For a moment or two nobody moved, or spoke, the tension

growing in the room like a held breath. After a beat, Orson looked up, straight at Eva, his brows pulled into a question, and as she smiled in reply she saw relief flood his expression.

And then she saw Nelka nod once, one of her gnarled old hands gesturing vaguely at Jules's photo.

'He's very handsome.'

Orson flushed with pride. 'He is.'

Then Ciocia Irenka, who had been watching the whole exchange with narrowed eyes, cleared her throat, and all the breath left Eva's body at once. Irenka was not the most open-minded of people, nor the most tactful. In fact, experience had taught the twins that if there was an offensive comment to be made in any situation, Ciocia Irenka would be the one to make it. So when she began to amble towards Orson, both of the sisters drew a sharp breath in.

But then she stopped, just a few feet away from him, studying the picture from underneath heavy brows for a while before she looked back up at Orson.

And then, against all odds, she gestured to the table, set out beautifully in Sylvia's finest linen. 'Please,' she said, gesturing to the photo of Jules, and then to the dinner table. 'Here.'

'What's happening?' Hanna whispered to Eva's left, as Orson set Jules down in the centre of the table, taking care to adjust him just so. Irenka had now shuffled off somewhere, as fast as her slippered feet could take her. Eva almost couldn't look.

But then she reappeared, clutching something to her chest. And when she propped the photo of Tomasz Mallory beside Jules, Eva's eyes filled with tears. She had looked at that picture a thousand times – so often that it was as if she never saw it at all now. But right then, with the two men taking pride of place on the table, a shrine to love lost, she was seeing it more clearly than ever.

'Now the whole family is here,' Irenka said, her bark of a voice no less gruff than usual, and completely oblivious to the disbelieving gasps from her family, 'we will eat.'

And they did eat. The table was alive with warmth as they sat together, talking and laughing as they filled their bellies with freshly baked bread and gherkins, the huge fish platter that Owen had made and steaming bowls full of Nelka's barszcz. As usual, Stefan had made traditional German potato fritters, and as usual Irenka had refused to eat them. And then, just as they reached the point that they were quite sure they couldn't eat another thing, out came the pierogi they'd made together, fried with butter and onions.

Afterwards they sat back in their chairs, loosening waistbands with small noises of contentment as the conversation turned, as it so often did, back to Eva's love life.

'She's told you about the husband hunt, hasn't she?' Sylvia asked, nudging Orson lightly with her shoulder. He'd eaten every last morsel served to him and so it seemed Sylvia now considered him family.

Orson nodded, seriously. 'Of course.'

'Not that we're getting anywhere with it, are we, Eevs?' Sylvia shot a cheerful smile over the table. She'd had one too many shots of Nelka's home-brewed cytrynowka to have any kind of subtlety about anything.

It's been...'—Eva sighed—'enlightening.'

Hanna snorted a laugh. 'It's been disastrous.'

Eva shrugged. 'Story of my life.'

'How many left on the list?' Owen, also partial to the

cytrynowka, asked, without looking up from the satsuma he was peeling. He'd been at it for five minutes.

'Three.'

Owen's eyes widened. 'Only three?'

'And isn't one of them Ciocia Nelka's?' Hanna got louder with every unit of alcohol she consumed. The neighbours could probably hear her now. 'Did you meet *him* at confession too, ciocia?'

Nelka shrugged, eyes wide and innocent. 'Yes, actually.'

Hanna nodded, nose scrunched. 'Yeah, I'd scratch that one upfront. So two.'

'All it takes is one,' Ciocia Nelka chirped, as if she alone hadn't contributed three wildly unsuitable men to Eva's cause.

Owen had finally managed to get the last of the peel off his satsuma and was now brandishing it as if it were a weapon. 'Maybe we need some fresh blood?'

Eva cringed. 'Don't say it like that.'

Ciocia Irenka, who had drunk just as much cytrynowka as the rest of them but who appeared entirely unaffected by it, frowned deeply at no one in particular. 'I'm telling you,' she boomed, 'you cannot arrange these things.'

Orson adjusted his glasses on his nose, his eyes widening behind them. 'I actually know someone who's just perfect for you. Maybe you have room on your list for just one more?'

Irenka huffed. The rest of the family froze in anticipation, their attention darting from Orson to Eva to Irenka like they were spectating a three-way game of tennis.

There was a part of Eva which wanted to say no, that enough was enough. She'd suffered through enough of these dates now to know that Ciocia Irenka was at least half right. But she couldn't give up on the husband hunt completely, not when there was still so much at stake. And, given what she knew about Orson, she was willing to bet that he probably had pretty decent taste in men. Certainly better than Ciocia Nelka, anyway.

'OK,' she said finally. 'I don't suppose he can be any worse that the rest of them.'

Orson's face broke into a huge grin, his eyes vanishing beneath the folds of skin like a delighted mole.

Irenka huffed, but Eva could have sworn she saw the slightest flicker of interest in her great-aunt's eyes. 'Set up a date, Orville.'

'It's actually Orson, Ciocia Irenka,' Stefan said, gently.

Irenka ignored him, of course.

'It's *Orson*, Irenka,' Nelka parroted, and Irenka looked over at her sister with a nod.

'Oh yes, thank you, *Nelka*.' She turned back to Orson, her face as close to repentant as it ever got. 'Sorry, I muddled a little.'

But Orson just waved her away. 'I actually prefer Orville,' he said, with a pleasant chuckle. 'I might start going by that.'

And at that, everyone laughed, even Ciocia Irenka, which Eva would not have believed had she not seen it with her own eyes. And, despite the residual ache in her scalp, not to mention the ever-looming presence of the curse, there was a moment where everything felt just exactly as it should be.

It was so easy for Eva to get lost in all of the things that went wrong in her life that she didn't often stop to appreciate all the things that were right. Her ridiculous family. Her lovely new friend. And the half-ton of dumplings and potato cakes which were slowly ram-raiding their way through her digestive system. It was enough, she thought, to see her through the rest of the night and the following morning, alone.

In fact, she was still smiling a few hours later as she curled up on her sofa, with Lucky nestled underneath her chin and purring furiously as she perused her YouTube favourites. And then, without the slightest ounce of guilt, she scrolled to the favourited video of Luke's band, and shamelessly clicked play.

It was Christmas, after all.

Chapter Twenty-Four

I t was a few days later when Eva stumbled into the bar. It was the bar with bare wood and houseplants, the same one that she'd gone to on the date with Greg, and by the time she arrived she was missing the umbrella she'd bought to replace the one lost on that date, and also some of the skin on her right thumb.

The day marked exactly a week into her Christmas break, and though she had gone very much to seed by that point, she'd made a special effort to scrub up for her hotly anticipated date with Orson's *perfect for her* guy. It wasn't desperation, she told herself, but genuine excitement, and she had repeated the mantra in her head so frequently that she was almost beginning to believe it.

Orson had given her next to no information about the date, just that this perfect man would meet her at the bar at exactly six thirty. But when she arrived, the bar was empty.

She checked her watch: 6:23pm. Earlier than she'd thought.

That thumb trapping incident must have delayed her by less than it had felt. Her anxiety dropped a notch, and she clambered up on the furthest left of the six wrought iron stools. The fact that it was the same stool she'd been sitting on the night she'd first met Luke wasn't lost on her, and so she almost fell clean off it when she saw Luke himself, sliding onto the stool next to her.

He looked incredible: russet hair styled back with just the right amount of nonchalance; midnight-blue shirt fitted enough that it lingered on the muscles of his arms and shoulders; hazel eyes fixed on her like a laser-beam. For a moment or two she lost the power of speech completely and just looked at him, the churn in her stomach a perfect balance between longing and lust.

It was him who broke the silence, looking away from her with a grin before he spoke.

'God, take a photo, it'll last longer.'

Her cheeks flushed. She hadn't been staring. *Had she?*

'Sorry,' she muttered, trying to recapture the feeling she'd had as she was getting ready – like she could take on the world. Right now she just felt like she was taking on water. 'I just wasn't expecting to see you here.'

He nodded, a small smile tugging at his lips. 'Likewise.' He still wasn't looking at her, and it was beginning to feel deliberate. 'I'm, er, I'm meeting someone.'

A cannonball of jealousy hit her straight in the chest.

'So am I,' she said, hating the fact that her voice wavered a little as she spoke. 'Don't worry, I won't cramp your style.'

He spun back round to look at her then, eyes soft, and his hand moved a little like he was going to reach for her, but he didn't.

'Oh no,' he said, his brows tugging together. 'I didn't mean…' But he didn't finish his sentence, and she wasn't sure that she wanted him to. Instead, they sat in silence for a minute or two, Eva tracing lines in the condensation on the outside of her glass as Luke spun his beer bottle in his fingers. She didn't dare look at him at first, worried that she might get pulled back into his orbit, but after a while she couldn't resist, bracing herself against the pull of his gravity as she sneaked a glimpse at him. Her gaze caught again on the styling of his hair, on his perfectly ironed shirt. He looked as if he'd made a real effort.

For someone else.

'So you're moving on, huh?' Her voice was almost a whisper. She was surprised that he heard her at all, but he must have done, because he turned to her with a sad smile.

'You told me to.'

Absolutely true, for the record. But that didn't dull the slam of Eva's heart against her ribcage any.

She took a deep breath, emotions fighting a battle inside her chest, but at the end of it all, she knew that he was right. She'd told him to move on. That was it. She couldn't stand in the way of that now, however sick it made her feel. It wasn't fair. Not that *any* of this was fair.

'So what time are you meeting her?' she asked, smiling past the rise of acid in her throat.

'Half six.' He looked at his watch. 'Supposed to be, anyway.'

She nodded. 'Same. What time is it now?'

'Six forty-two.'

Her brows pinched into a frown. Twelve minutes was easily explainable, she knew that better than anyone, but she couldn't help the jolt of panic which surged through her at the idea of being stood up. Of being stood up in front of *Luke*, of all people.

'Weird,' she said, more to herself than to him. 'Orson said he was very punctual.'

He froze beside her. 'Wait,' he started, slowly, as if he were figuring out a puzzle. '*Orson* set up this date for you? Orson Myrtle?'

Her frown deepened 'Yeah, why?'

But then his body language changed entirely, mirth sweeping through his whole body like a wave until he was laughing so hard that he could barely breathe. 'Oh my God,' he muttered, and he paused to wipe his eyes before immediately bursting into laughter again.

Eva, if she were being honest, felt a little put out. He knew she and Orson were friends and she couldn't for the life of her see what was so funny about that.

'What?' she asked, more bite in her tone than she'd intended. There had always been something about Luke which riled her.

He took a few deep breaths, each one settling his breathing a little more, before he finally managed to say, 'Orson set up *my* date too.'

'At the same time and place?' Her stomach dropped. In fairness, she hadn't told Orson about any of the situation with Luke, but she still would have thought he'd know better than to send colleagues out on a date at the same place, especially at the same time.

Unless…

'Wait…'

He nodded. 'Yup.'

'He set us up with *each other*?'

Luke chuckled, one hand going to the scruff of his stubble. 'Well, he told us both to meet our dates here, at six-thirty.' He checked his watch again. 'And now it's six-forty-eight and we're still the only ones here.'

She laughed too, but the sound was swallowed up by the swell of disbelief. What were the chances that the *perfect for her* guy would be the one man who was off limits? At least she'd been right to trust Orson's taste in men, though he had, of course, forgotten the entire purpose of the husband hunt.

She looked back up at Luke, feeling the burn of her skin under his gaze, like always. 'So what do we do now?'

'Well,' he said, one shoulder tipped into a shrug. 'We could finish our drinks and then go home and pretend none of this happened.'

She nodded. 'We could.' There was a tug in the pit of her stomach, and she couldn't tell if it was relief ... or disappointment.

'Or,' he continued, ducking his head a little so as to catch her eyes, 'we could go on the date anyway, so I don't waste my evening or, if I'm honest, this haircut.'

Her traitorous heart did a flip in her chest. 'Luke,' she pleaded, though she wasn't entirely sure what she was asking.

His lips quirked into a smile, dangerously close to smirk territory. 'Cost me twenty-two quid.'

Worth every penny, she thought, but she didn't voice it. Instead she eyed him carefully, and as he caught her eye, he nodded once.

'Just as friends.' His voice was steady, genuine. 'No funny business'

Her brows pulled together. 'No funny business?'

That smirk again. God, it was dangerous. 'Only if you ask.'

'I won't.' She couldn't.

'Then no funny business,' he said, and despite the underlying edge of heat in the way he was looking at her, his voice was genuine. She could trust him, she knew it.

Could she trust herself? Less likely. But they were here, both in the same boat, and so there was no reason they couldn't enjoy a nice evening together. They were adults, after all.

'OK,' she said, eventually, and she held out her hand for him to shake.

He beamed in response. 'OK,' he said in reply, and he took her hand, shaking it firmly and lingering just a split second too long, sending a wave of warmth through her whole body.

What could go wrong?

They fell back into the rhythm of each other's company so easily. It was probably a little too easy, if Eva had been looking out for warning signs, but she wasn't. She was having too much fun.

So when Luke stopped her as she went to order another drink, she was a little taken aback.

'We're not staying,' he said, going to pay for both of their tabs before she could even find her handbag.

She looked at him in shock, confusion stealing her words. She'd thought they were getting on well. And no funny business, as promised.

He burst out laughing as he turned back to her, and the sound of it set something alight in her chest. 'I mean we're not staying here,' he said, head cocking to one side. 'I planned to take my date for food. I made reservations with a friend.' His shrug was almost an apology. 'Best tapas in town.'

Eva almost squeaked with relief. 'You had me at *food*. '

And he laughed again, the warmth of it making its way underneath her skin, settling somewhere deep inside her as she pulled her coat around herself and they made their way out into the bite of the winter night.

———

Alejandro's restaurant looked like nothing much, from the outside. Eva had never even noticed it before, nestled as it was between two big chain stores, the engraved brass plaque the only clue that there was anything lying beyond the door at all. Her confusion must have translated through her expression, because Luke paused a moment in front of the stone steps, his brows pulling together as he studied her.

'Trust me,' he said, in a low voice, and then he pushed through the heavy black door into the riot of colour beyond.

It was a small place, with no more than twelve tables carefully laid out in a grid, their rich red tablecloths clipped fast onto them as candles in the same shade of red protruded from the necks of wine bottles, flames flickering every which way.

Eva made a mental note to try not to knock any of them over.

Beyond the tables were whitewashed walls decorated with vibrant pottery and trailing plants, huge picture frames painted bright yellow around textured paintings of Mediterranean scenes. And then there was the smell, which had hit Eva as soon as she crossed the threshold – a delicious combination of garlic and onions underpinning the scent of fresh tomatoes and wine. She hadn't even noticed how hungry she was until that exact moment, when a furious growl burst from her stomach.

'This looks amazing,' she said, as a waiter swept past in the background, his tray laden with small terracotta dishes. But, before Luke had a chance to reply, a man appeared in front of them with a broad grin on his face.

'Luke,' the man said, offering out his hand, and Luke took it, pulling him into a quick hug before stepping back beside Eva.

'And this,' the man continued, now with a twinkle in his dark brown eyes, 'must be your date.' He opened his mouth to say more, but Luke held a hand up before he could.

'Yes and no,' he said, shooting a reassuring look at Eva. 'I mean, there was a misunderstanding. Eva's actually my colleague, but she agreed to come out with me anyway. As friends.'

He dragged out the last word a little and her heart at once soared and shattered. That was what she'd wanted, for the two of them to be friends, but hearing it from his mouth didn't come with the relief she'd thought it would.

She forced a smile. 'He told me there'd be food.'

The man laughed at that. 'I like her, Luke.'

'I like her too,' Luke said, and the tone of it drew all the air out of Eva's lungs. 'But I promised her no funny business and I am a man of my word.'

She froze to the spot, looking up at him with her heart galloping like wild horses in her chest. The way he'd said it, so straightforwardly, but with no weight, no expectation. Well, it just about tore her in two.

'Eva,' Luke was saying now, though she barely heard him over the rush of blood in her ears, 'this is Alex. Alex, Eva.'

She smiled at the man, who was now leaning against the whitewashed brick of the wall wearing an expression only halfway to a smile. 'Nice to meet you,' she said, as evenly as she could, given the pandemonium in her circulatory system. 'Your restaurant is beautiful.'

'Actually it's my dad's restaurant,' Alex said, his eyes sweeping around the small space. 'He's Alejandro. I'm just plain old half-English Alex.' His face broke into a grin. 'But we're pretty proud of it. Wait till you taste the food.' And then he swiped a chalkboard menu from the stack behind him and ushered them to a small table, tucked into the far corner of the room.

'Any allergies?' Alex asked, his voice all business, but Luke spoke before Eva could say anything.

'Kiwi and crustaceans,' he said, easily, like he reeled it off every day, and Alex nodded, his eyes scanning the menu before he dug a piece of chalk out from his apron and drew a thick line through two of the items.

'You'll be OK with the rest,' he said, popping the chalk down next to the menu. 'Just check the dishes you want to order, and I'll collect the board when you're ready. Can I get you some drinks?'

They ordered drinks and as Alex left with a nod, Eva turned back to Luke.

'You remembered.' Her throat felt tight, and it tightened even further when Luke smiled at her in response.

'Of course,' he said. 'Didn't fancy a date in A&E, if I'm honest.'

She laughed. 'You've met me before, right? Could still happen.'

'It could.' He nodded, eyes on hers, lighting all the same fires they always had. 'Still wouldn't be the worst date I've ever had.'

She leaned forward, forearms on the table.

'Now *that* is a story I would be very interested in hearing.'

Chapter Twenty-Five

'This,' Eva said, sitting back in her chair, 'was a fantastic date. I feel a bit sorry for the woman who missed out on it.'

Luke popped the last olive into his mouth and chewed thoughtfully for a moment. 'There *was* no woman who missed out.'

'You know what I mean.'

He was studying her again, a curious expression on his face. 'I know what you *think* you mean, but you're wrong.' He pre-empted her retort with one raised hand. 'It's not like I was desperately looking for women. I wouldn't have even come on this date if it hadn't been for Orson talking about this amazing person that he knew – a *once-in-a-lifetime kind of girl* I believe his exact words were.'

A furious blush raced up to Eva's face, her awkwardness bursting out as a giggle. But Luke wasn't laughing. He was still looking at her, his chin resting on one cupped hand, hazel eyes reaching into the very depths of her soul.

'And for what it's worth,' he said slowly, each word careful and deliberate. 'I think he's probably right.'

She stopped giggling with a start, her heart clenching into a tight knot. She didn't know what to say, so she said, 'I'm sorry.' But he just shook his head, the slightest hint of a smile tugging at the corners of his mouth.

'You don't need to be,' he replied in that same tone, and Eva wasn't sure whether to be relieved or disappointed when Alex appeared out of nowhere to clear their dishes away.

'Was everything OK?' Alex asked, and they both nodded enthusiastically.

Everything *had* been OK. In fact it had been more than OK. The food, as Luke had predicted, was delicious, rich and flavourful, hands down the best tapas that Eva had ever eaten. And obviously the night itself had not been without incident, Eva was there after all, but Luke had taken every mishap absolutely in his stride. He'd caught the drink she'd knocked over, his lightning reflexes returning the glass to the table with little more than a small splash on the tablecloth. He'd laughed when a rogue piece of tortilla inexplicably fired off Eva's fork as she went to take a bite, hitting him square in the eye. He'd even wordlessly freed her skirt from the knot of her waistband when she came back from the toilet with liberal amounts of her opaque-tights clad arse on display,

All in all, he'd acted like the chaos which followed her was no big deal, and that had made it *feel* like less of a big deal. He was, she thought, exactly the kind of person she'd want to be with, if only there wasn't the small matter of his name. If only she didn't have this persistent, underlying fear in the pit of her stomach that he might drop dead at any second and it'd all be entirely her fault.

But perhaps that was the work of the curse too.

They paid for the meal and headed out onto the street, Luke leaving Alex with another handshake and a promise that he wouldn't leave things so long next time. It was a clear night, with a glimmer of frost starting to form on windows and the bite of the air turning their breath to mist.

'How do you two know each other, anyway?' Eva asked. The two men had seemed genuinely close, so it had surprised Eva that they hadn't seen each other for a while.

Luke took a deep breath and held it for a moment or two before blowing it out all at once as clouds into the night air. 'We're both failed chefs. Worked in the same kitchen. I was a fresh graduate; he was an apprentice.' He laughed a little. 'But as far as the head chef was concerned, we were both dogsbodies. Never worked so hard in my life.'

Eva's brows creased into a frown, a whisper of grief tugging at her chest. 'You wanted to be a chef?'

He nodded, his smile barely a movement. 'That was plan A.'

'My dad was a chef.' Her voice was thick.

He looked over at her, his eyes so full of compassion that it almost made her burst into tears on the spot. 'Was he good?'

It made her heart swell, both with pride for her father, and with gratitude at Luke actually asking a real question. It felt like she hadn't talked about him for a long time. 'He was really good. He was head chef at a restaurant in Scarborough. Won a few awards while he was there, just local things, but still.'

'*Still* nothing.' Luke nudged her shoulder with his own. 'Being an award-winning chef on any level is not easy.' She wasn't looking at him, but she saw him smile in her periphery. 'Believe me, I've tried. He must have been pretty special.'

Eva huffed out a small breath, pride and pain combining to one feeling. 'He was.'

'I wasn't,' Luke said. His voice was steady, matter-of-fact, and when she turned to look at him there wasn't a trace of bitterness on his face. Just acceptance. 'Don't look at me like that, I wasn't. And I wasn't the world's greatest food stylist either. But then when I got into teaching it felt like coming home, you know?' His mouth tipped into a smile. 'Not that *that* whole journey was straightforward either.'

Her brows pulled together. It suddenly dawned on her that the term had finished and she had no idea how his assessment had gone. She hadn't even asked.

'But you got there in the end?' she asked, tentatively, and his smile grew, so wide that it made her breath catch.

'I did,' he said simply. It was explanation enough. 'Neeta extended my contract to the end of the year, with a chance to go permanent after that. If I don't make a balls-up of anything else, of course.'

She squealed out of genuine delight for him, and without thinking she flung her arms around his waist. 'I knew it! I'm so happy for you,' she said, the words distorting with the press of her face against the scratch of his wool coat.

He didn't respond at first, and she worried that she had made a mistake, but just as she went to pull away from him, she felt him begin to move, his breath catching as his arms closed around her.

They stopped like that, for a while. Just the two of them in each other's arms in the dark of the evening. It felt right and wrong at the same time, equal measures illicit and pure, the drumbeat of a feeling Eva wasn't sure she recognised in her chest. She probably should have pulled away, but she couldn't.

Not at that moment. She told herself it was because it was a cold night and she couldn't bear to leave the warmth of Luke body, but that wasn't true at all. It was because she didn't want to leave him.

But, of course, she already had.

She'd *had* to.

'What?' he asked after a beat, his breath warm against the top of her head.

'Nothing.'

He blew out a breath. 'It's not nothing.'

It wasn't, but how could she explain?

'I just wish that things were different,' she said, eventually, and it didn't seem like enough. Not until she heard the weight of his sigh, anyway.

'Me too,' he muttered, his voice gravelly and thick, and when he tightened his arms around her she could feel the pounding of his heart even through his clothes.

There was a part of her which longed to lean into it, to grab fistfuls of his wool coat and kiss him until she couldn't remember her own name, let alone his. And when his hands began to move, tracing up her back and threading into her hair, there was a part of her which almost acted on it, her resolve weakening with every slow stroke of his fingers against her skin. But then she thought about the risk, about the idea of losing him, and with the thoughts of her dad still fresh in her mind, it felt like too much.

'Hey,' she said with a smile, backing away from him a little as her hands came to rest at his sides. 'No funny business, remember?'

He tilted his head a little to the side, looking at her with the sort of intensity she'd come to expect from him. 'This isn't funny business; this is just *business*.' He reached to tuck a stray strand of hair behind her ear, the trail of his fingers sending shivers over her skin. 'But, you know, hit me up if you ever change your mind about the funny. I *love* the funny.'

If only, she thought, but all she said was, 'I will.'

He nodded, once, before moving out of her grip completely, offering his elbow as he turned to walk back down the street. She looped her arm through with a smile. It felt safe, this amount of contact. She wasn't sure she was ready to pull away from him completely.

'This has been a lovely date,' she said, falling into step beside him. 'Your *perfect woman* would have loved it.'

She heard him blow out a small breath, a sigh, maybe, or maybe a laugh. 'It's not over yet.'

'It's not?' she asked, before one of her feet slipped sideways into a pothole and she lurched towards the road.

Luke laughed, his arm catching hers and righting her almost before she knew it, like he'd seen it coming. 'Eva, it's not even nine.'

She wanted to look at him then, but she didn't dare take her eyes off the pavement ahead, just in case she tripped properly next time. 'I'm just saying, this is a very elaborate first date,'

'Well, yeah.' She could hear the smile in his voice. 'I put extra effort into planning it because I was trying to get over *you.*'

Another thump in her chest, something darker this time. It felt a lot like guilt. 'Ah. Sorry.'

'Don't be.' The light tone in his voice hadn't lessened any. 'And anyway, each stage was dependent on the last. So drinks first, if that went well we'd progress to the meal, and if we were both still feeling it after that I had an ace card up my sleeve.'

'Go on.'

'It's salsa night at a little dance club I know.'

'You dance?' she half-squealed. She nearly fell over again just from the sudden hot flush which rose through her body. It was completely unfair how hot Luke was.

He chuckled. 'A little.'

'Are you good?'

'Quite good, not great.' He huffed a breath, an almost-laugh. 'Like with everything.'

Not everything, Eva thought, but she didn't say it. She had a sudden flashback to the art cupboard – the way he'd cradled her chin and kissed her senseless. That had been the work of an expert. She wasn't sure she'd be able to endure dancing with him. She definitely couldn't be trusted in his arms.

Sweating.

Gyrating.

Good God.

'So we're going dancing?' Her voice was so high and tight that it was a wonder he heard it at all, but he chuckled again in response, the sound so easy and warm that it turned Eva's hot flush up at least a couple of degrees.

'No, we're not going dancing,' he said, and before he could continue, her legs had stopped dead in protest.

'But…' she started, her tone almost petulant, and he turned to look at her, his eyes dark.

'If I go dancing with you,' he said, rough and deep, 'I'm going to want to have sex with you, and we already decided that was off the table.'

If she was hot before, the look in his eyes almost turned her to ash. It took every last scrap of willpower she possessed to not immediately launch herself into his arms.

'So we're going home?' she asked instead, trying and failing to keep the disappointment out of her voice.

He blew a breath out, as if he were having the exact same thoughts. 'I'm not quite ready for that, either,' he said, his mouth edging into a smile.

'So…'

'So, I've got an idea,' he said, all at once, like it had suddenly come to him. He held his elbow out for her again. 'Come on.'

Chapter Twenty-Six

'It's rocking,' Eva said, tightening her grip on the bars of the pod, suspended, as they were, a hundred feet in the air. She wasn't hugely comfortable with heights, but the look on Luke's face as he'd presented her with the idea had been too good to pass up. That said, she hadn't seen that look on his face for a while, as she'd clamped her eyes shut the second that the giant wheel had begun to move.

'It's meant to rock,' he said evenly. 'The thing that makes it rock is the same thing which keeps you vertical as the wheel goes round.'

She cracked one eye open. 'Is that true?'

'I have no idea,' he said, smiling around the words. 'I'm not an expert on Ferris wheel physics.'

She eyed him, but he just looked straight back at her, his face soft and reassuring. She'd seen him make the same face in school many a time, though she'd never been the object before.

She frowned, one eye still closed. 'Are we really high up?'

His smile grew. 'Have a look for yourself.'

'I can't!' An icy gust whipped around them, making the pod rock again, and the resulting wave of panic made Eva snatch her eye shut. And then she felt it shift again, a different motion than the rocking. Her anxiety intensified for a minute or two, and she almost leapt out of her skin when she felt something brush against her arm. But then she felt Luke's hand on her forearm, the weight of it settling her nerves, just a little. Just enough for her to brave opening that one eye again.

'Are you actually scared of this,' he muttered, a foot away from her face, 'or are you just thinking about all the different ways it could go wrong?'

She opened both eyes at that, something in her chest squeezing tight as she met his gaze, warm and unflappable. He was asking about the wheel, of course, but maybe he was asking about more.

'Is there a difference?' she asked, quietly.

His brow furrowed, but he didn't say anything. Not at first. Just looked at her with that same expression, like he was trying to figure out the answer himself.

'Maybe not,' he said eventually, and then he held his hands out and motioned for her to hold on to them. 'But humour me. Let's try something.'

She took a deep breath, steeling herself, before she released her death grip on the metal pole and quickly slipped her hands into Luke's. She could feel the warmth of them through the thin wool of her gloves and that felt comforting too, like the easy lilt of his voice and the even expression on his face.

'OK,' he said, slowly, as if anything more might spook her. 'Hold on tight. We're going to turn around.'

It happened so quickly that she didn't have the time to overthink it. And then, all of a sudden, she was looking out, nose pressed against the Perspex cage, the skyline cast in pinks and blues and greens from the wheel's illuminations. Her breath misted on the cold plastic, blurring the small clusters of festive lights scattered throughout the city, strings of streetlights stretching out in all directions, the neon signs of shops and takeaways. The city, her home, in a way she'd never seen it before. It was captivating.

At some point Luke had let go of her hands, and she slipped them through the gap under the bottom of the Perspex, her fingers closing around the metal bar beneath.

'This is amazing,' she said, wonder stretching out the syllables in her mouth.

'Yes,' Luke replied. 'It is.' But when she glanced in his direction, she found that he wasn't looking out at the view at all. He was looking at her.

Something passed between them, a moment in time frozen like Eva's breath on the cage. She felt something rearrange itself in her chest – a memory being made in real time – and it didn't make any sense then, but it felt important.

She was just about to open her mouth and say as much when a sudden waft of air made her scream out in shock seconds before she felt the impact on her right hand, sudden and fleeting, an attack which stopped almost as soon as it had started. Her heart raced in her ears, thumping and skipping as she snatched both hands in towards her chest.

'What the hell was that?' she yelped, peering out into the night with her eyes half shut, just in case her attacker reappeared.

It was then that Luke started to chuckle, just around the time that Eva noticed the bite of the cold on her fingers. She looked down, bracing herself for any eventuality, but—

'Has that bloody sky monster just stolen my glove?'

She felt the change in Luke's laughter before she heard it, silent convulsions shaking his body over and over before he drew in a breath with a low wheeze.

'Sky monster!' he repeated, his mirth such that the words were almost inaudible, shattered and breathy, and at the sound of it Eva couldn't help but laugh too, just a little at first until it swelled like a wave, gathering pace little by little until she was crashing into him, hooting and gasping as they each wiped tears from their eyes.

'I think,' Luke said, his words still broken by the rumble of humour running through them, 'that your sky monster is a bird. Look.' And he pointed the short distance to the town hall clock tower, the outline of a large bird clearly visible in the glow of the wheel's lights.

'Unbelievable,' Eva muttered, being careful not to stick her other hand out of the cage. 'What the hell kind of bird is that?'

He huffed a breath. 'Looks like a bird of prey. Kestrel, maybe.' His mouth pulled into a smirk. 'Maybe the lesser-spotted glove-eater?'

She swatted at him, a giggle rising in her throat, and he ducked away deftly, making the pod start to rock again. Eva barely noticed this time.

'You think you're unlucky?' Luke said, nodding at the clock tower. 'Just wait till that fella finds out his dormouse dinner is actually a glove.'

She couldn't even begin to hold her laughter in that time, and as it spilled out Luke began to laugh again too, the two of them flopping back together on the cold plastic bench seat, clutching at their aching bellies. And then slowly, without further incident, the pod made its way back to earth beneath the velvety darkness of the night sky. But Eva was caught somewhere between; she was having the best date of her entire life with someone she couldn't be with.

It was all the things it couldn't be, and it was more. *So much* more.

Which was, she thought, entirely what she had come to expect from her life. From the curse. From all of it.

'Dammit Orson,' Eva said the first Monday of the new year, following the sound of Beethoven's fifth piano sonata to the corner of the hall. He was sitting at the keys, playing the notes lazily. He wasn't even looking at his fingers, he was looking at her, with a grin on his face so enormous that his eyes had almost completely vanished.

He looked very pleased with himself indeed.

'*Luke?*' she ground out, palms to the sky, and he nodded, still playing evenly with that big smile on his face.

'I didn't know you two were friends,' she said, and he laughed out loud at the accusatory tone in her voice.

'We go to the same barbers.'

Her brow furrowed. 'Do you actually?'

'Yes!' One hand went to his chest in mock offence, the other hand still playing the melody. 'Don't say it like that. I'm not totally past it, you know. He was pretty new to the school; I saw him when I was having a haircut and we talked.' The same hand moved up, adjusting his glasses before seamlessly returning to the keys. 'He mentioned you more than once, I noticed.' One white eyebrow hitched high on his forehead. 'You know, I wouldn't have survived working with pre-teens this long without being able to sniff out a crush.'

His eyes flicked to the keys for a moment before returning to her, studying her. 'You don't like him? I think you're pretty perfect for each other. And you *are* looking for a husband. He'd make an excellent one, that's all I'm saying.' A low chuckle rumbled through him. 'You know, the single ladies of key stage two would kill each other for a chance to go out with him.'

Eva's heart dropped, a lead weight in her chest. 'We have the same last name.'

'Exactly,' Orson chirped. 'So you won't have to change it. Think of the admin.'

'The name I'm desperately trying to lose.'

'Oh.' He stopped playing abruptly, looking up at her with wide eyes. '*Oh.*'

'Yeah.'

His smile had completely fallen, white brows pinching into a frown. 'Wow, that's unlucky.'

She huffed a laugh. 'That's me all over.'

'So you *do* like him?'

She scanned the room before answering. 'Yes.'

'And he likes you?'

'Apparently.'

Orson's face softened again in a moment, cheeks folding back into well-worn lines. 'I knew I hadn't lost my touch.' He paused for a beat, splayed fingers resting back on the keys, though he didn't play anything. 'And Neeta's really done a number on you, making you do this production together, hasn't she?'

She laughed. 'Tell me about it.'

He smiled at her then, his face soft and understanding, and

it made her feel a little better. Orson had a way about him that always made her feel a little better. She wasn't surprised Neeta had been careful not to make him leave; she'd hazard a guess he was an expert at defusing tensions in the ordinarily volatile year fives.

'Speak of the devil,' Orson muttered through his teeth, smiling at a point somewhere over Eva's shoulder, and she turned to see Luke and Fran walking into the hall. Luke was smiling broadly; Fran, a little way behind him, was nursing a travel mug and yawning. Eva all of a sudden felt as though she could relate to her more easily.

'You ready to make some magic?' Luke asked, coming up behind the piano and leaning his forearms on the top, and Eva heard Orson chuckle beside her.

'Magic?' the older man said in that lovely, gentle tone – the one which allowed him to say whatever he wanted.

Luke grinned at him, warm and familiar. Eva couldn't believe she'd never known they were friends. 'You ready to make … *something*?'

They all laughed at that.

'*Something* sounds good,' Fran said, and she propped herself next to Luke, but at her height she was resting her chin on the back of the piano, nestled on her joined fingers.

And for the first time, on that cold January morning, the music project felt a little bit less like a punishment to Eva and a little bit more like an opportunity. It had already brought her Orson, and helped her smooth things over with Luke, not to mention that she was starting to feel like she was repaying her debt to Neeta. It was true that they had a hell of a lot of work to do, but perhaps, for once, that work might actually be fun?

As Luke had said, it was definitely going to be something.

Chapter Twenty-Seven

Eva smiled to herself as she shrugged off her jacket and put it on the seat beside her. It felt like spring – unseasonably warm for the first week in March – and she was basking in the heat of the sun streaming through the window of the train.

She hadn't been on a train for years, and in truth was quite enjoying the whole thing, though she had got stuck at the automatic ticket barrier when it had closed on her before she was all the way through. It hadn't made her any less chipper, though.

Fewer things did, these days.

It was fair to say that she was still a walking disaster area. That hadn't changed. Mrs Abbott had already had to restock the first aid kit five times and they were only halfway through the year. But when she stood back and looked at the bigger picture, her life was actually going quite well, for once.

The production, a faintly terrifying three weeks away now,

was finally starting to come together, as much as they suspected it ever could. Neeta had been right, she and Luke *did* make a good team, especially when aided by Orson's endless musical talents, and the lovely Fran, of course, who Eva had actually grown rather fond of. They'd all become close, in fact, forever bonded by the shared trauma of those first few rehearsals.

There had been times where Eva had honestly thought that they couldn't pull it off. The day George Beeney projectile-vomited into the pigtails of the girl in front of him, sending a secondary wave of puke right down the year two line, and ensuring that someone, somewhere would make a retching noise at that same part of the song for the next few weeks. The first time they'd tried to run through the whole thing and Eva had almost thrown her laptop out of the window in frustration. The time that she'd taken her eyes off her class for a second – just a *split second* – and little Benji, the budding naturist in her class, had quietly stripped out of every last item of clothing he was wearing.

But then there had been moment of brilliance, too. They'd all cheered together when the children had finally managed to start singing upon seeing Fran's massively exaggerated cue from the back of the hall. They'd stood in awe when Orson, sick of waiting for his year five class to be quiet, instead launched into a powerful rendition of 'Fur Elise', shushing the children in seconds. And Eva, less publicly, had never stopped watching Luke: the way he effortlessly commanded respect from the children when it mattered; the way his class absolutely doted on him, even the trickier characters she'd taught the previous year; the way he'd become a role model for all of them, children and adults, without even realising.

She'd known that he was nice, and funny, and hot as all hell. None of that had come as a surprise. But over the past couple of months she'd learned new things about Luke too. She'd seen how resilient he was, how driven. How, when things went wrong, which they almost constantly did, he wouldn't fuss, or fret. He'd just regroup, rethink, redirect. When something didn't work, he'd change it. When something broke, he'd fix it. He was the master of plan B, and plan C and far beyond.

He'd kept the promise that he'd made on their accidental date: no funny business. They'd grown, both of them, in lots of ways, channelling their chemistry into more platonic routes to the point that they were now fast friends. It wasn't the relationship Eva wanted, given the choice. She'd never stopped feeling the flicker of flames in her belly in his presence, but she had seen even more now that he was much too precious to sacrifice to the curse. So it was enough, their friendship.

It had to be.

Meanwhile, she'd cautiously dipped her toe back into the husband hunt. Only the previous week, Hanna had rescued her from a date with an old colleague of Sylvia's so dull that Eva had literally fallen asleep in her dinner.

And that was how she'd found herself here: on a train to York, speeding towards the last man on the list. Her sister and Owen would be there already, having chosen to extend their obligatory spying into a full weekend break, and Eva was enjoying making the journey by herself. This date was her last chance, she'd said, and maybe a few months ago she'd have believed it, but things were different now. *She* was different now.

Since her date with Luke, since seeing first-hand how good things could be, she was finding it awfully hard to come to terms with the idea of settling for any less. She was even, now she'd fully thrown herself into something bigger than herself, starting to become less and less bothered by the curse.

By most of the curse, anyway. She just couldn't shake the idea that it might kill Luke.

And so she had taken a leaf out of his book, and figured out a plan B. And then a plan C. She would go to meet Justin the accountant, by all accounts a grand specimen of a man, and if things didn't work out, she would make her peace with being unlucky and alone. Because if the start of this year was anything to go by, unlucky and alone actually didn't feel too bad. Not anymore.

And for all she knew, Justin the accountant might be the love of her life.

Next station stop … York, came a crackly voice over the tannoy, and Eva gathered her things together and hauled herself up out of her seat. It was surprisingly quiet on the train for a Saturday afternoon, but Eva didn't mind that. It was nice to have a bit of space after the utter claustrophobia that was school at the moment.

The train pulled up at the station and she pressed the button to open the doors. But the doors didn't budge. She sighed a little. It had all been going a bit too well. She pressed the button again and breathed a sigh of relief when the doors began to open. But then, before they had even opened six inches, they slammed shut again.

Eva swore under her breath and picked up her bag, planning to go to the next set of doors. She should have time.

And she *would* have had time, had the hem of her dress not been caught in the doors. She tried to prise it out, but it was no use. She was stuck.

Of course. Of *course* her last date of the list would be a disaster. Just like the other dates had been disasters. Just like her whole life had been a disaster.

She felt her earlier optimism crumble to dust, and as the train pulled away from the station, she made one last ditch attempt to free her skirt, pulling at it as hard as she was able. But all that did was sound an alarm.

She could have cried, and maybe she would have had a conductor not suddenly appeared in the carriage and eyed her with confusion.

'You tampered with these doors, petal?' she asked, in a much gruffer voice than Eva had expected would come out of such a small person.

Eva shook her head, stepping aside to display her predicament. 'I was trying to get off at York, but the door wouldn't open, and then it did open, but immediately shut again and now…' She gestured to the chunk of skirt still firmly wedged in the doors.

The conductor looked at the trapped section of skirt, then at Eva, and to her credit, she didn't laugh, though it was obvious that she wanted to. 'That's bad luck,' she said, 'but don't worry. I'll give you a ticket to the next station, and then another from there back to York. No charge.'

Eva's anxiety settled a little. 'OK, thank you. Any chance you can free me?'

''Fraid not, love.' The conductor shrugged, gently. 'Can't open these doors until the train stops. Safety mechanism.' She nodded at Eva's skirt. 'But I'll pop back when we get to the next station, and if they don't open this time I can open them manually.'

Eva nodded, watching as the conductor spotted something up the carriage. 'What's the next stop?' she called, to her retreating back.

'Newcastle,' the conductor yelled back, before she vanished from sight completely.

Eva nearly swallowed her tongue. *Newcastle?*

She fished her phone out of her bag and searched *train time York to Newcastle*, wincing at the result.

An hour and five minutes.

She swore aloud that time, navigating to Hanna's number and pressing *call*.

Her sister answered after two rings.

'You here?' Hanna asked, undisguised excitement in her voice. 'Your date just walked in and he is fitter than I remember.' She barely paused for breath. 'This is it, Eevs, I know it.'

Eva's heart sank. 'There's been a bit of a problem.'

'I'd expect nothing less from you.'

'OK,' Eva said, with a sigh. 'I'm going to be late. *Really* late.'

The breath Hanna sucked in was so loud that Eva could hear it over the line.

'What happened?'

It was almost three hours later when Eva pulled into York station for the second, and hopefully final time, and she wasn't at all surprised to see her sister and Owen waiting on the platform for her, Hanna clutching a ruby-red wig in her hand. Nor was she surprised to see them both looking a little worse for wear. They had been waiting hours for her, after all.

She was, however, a little surprised to see someone else standing with them.

As the train slowed, she could see him more clearly. He was tall, just a little taller than Owen, and well-dressed, his dirty blond hair grown out to his chin and swept back, away from his perfect face. He was laughing at something Hanna had said, and his laugh seemed to make him glow, his perfect white teeth gleaming in the light.

She stepped off the train, beyond relieved when the doors opened without incident this time, and walked to the spot, a little way down the platform, where they were standing. Hanna squealed when she saw Eva approaching, skipping forward to envelop her in a big, boozy hug.

Eva had to laugh, even after everything.

'Can't believe you're still here,' she muttered into her sister's hair, squeezing her tight.

Hanna laughed. 'We needed to make sure you actually got off this time and didn't get stuck again and end up in Plymouth.'

'Glad you made it, Eevs,' Owen said from beside her.

'Thanks, mate.'

'Anyway, this…' Hanna untangled herself from Eva's grip and stepped back, motioning towards the god of a man beside her. 'This … is Justin the accountant.'

'That's actually my weekday name,' Justin said, a note of humour in his gravelly voice. 'At the weekends I just go by Justin.'

Eva smiled. Even his voice was sexy. 'Nice to meet you, Justin.'

And it *was* nice to meet him. Justin, as it turned out, was a good guy. In addition to his superhero looks and leading man voice, he was interesting and polite and good-natured. Not to mention that he'd stayed an extra three hours after the time they'd arranged the date, without even having met her.

He was everything she'd want in a husband, and more. Which is why it was odd that, as they were nearing the end of their rearranged date, Eva had a realisation: she was admiring Justin, certainly, but she was doing it the same way she'd admire a painting. Her eyes would catch on the shapes of his face, noticing the way the colour in his irises faded from pure blue at the outside to sea green in the middle. She looked at the swell of his lips, how well they framed his perfect teeth, as if someone had purposely designed him.

She didn't, not for one second, imagine those teeth grazing her skin.

She didn't feel her body flushing with want when his hand touched hers, nor have to look away at the intensity of his stare. Would she kiss him at the end of the date? She probably would, and she would probably enjoy it, but she felt no desperate need to. And her skin didn't feel like it was on fire just from looking at him. In fact, her skin didn't feel like it was on fire at all. She imagined that she could accidentally find herself locked in a small cupboard with Justin and they would end up having rather a lovely conversation about art supplies.

She swallowed back a wave of anxiety. Justin was the ideal man. She couldn't fault him on a single thing. And yet there was no buzz behind her breastbone the way there had been when she'd first met Luke. The way there still was, every time she was near him.

Luke.

God, even thinking his name made her pulse leap.

Justin, as if he'd noticed the change in her energy, suddenly stopped talking, his brow creasing. 'What's the matter?' he asked, concern making his face even more handsome.

She paused for a beat. What was the right answer to that question?

She decided that honesty was her only option. He deserved that. He'd been nothing but an absolute gentleman the entire time.

'You are perfect,' she said, guilt knocking at her ribcage.

His frown deepened. 'Thank you?'

'You are,' she went on. 'You're honestly perfect. You're kind, and funny, and polite and *really* hot. Like actually kind of disgustingly hot. Like save some for the others kind of hot.'

He laughed at that, but she saw him brace himself when he said, 'There's a *but* coming, isn't there?'

She winced. 'But…'

'There's someone else?'

'No,' she said. 'But kind of yes. I mean, we're not together, and we can't be together, but, essentially, yes.' She cast her eyes down, rearranging the skirt of her dress to hide the V-shaped area of filth that the eighty-five-mile trip on the outside of a train had bestowed upon it.

'Thank you for being honest,' he said, after a moment or two, and she was surprised to find no anger in his voice. Just acceptance.

She looked up, and his face looked pleasant enough, too. 'You're not mad about it?'

'Why would I be mad?' He smiled softly, only the slightest hint of defeat tugging at the movement. 'I mean I'm a little disappointed, but I appreciate you being straight with me.'

Urgh, he was respectful and gracious as well. Why couldn't her stupid brain just *like* him?

'What's your surname, just out of interest?' she asked aimlessly. She wasn't even sure why it mattered at this point.

'Anderson.' One eye narrowed, studying her. 'Why? Is that a dealbreaker?'

She huffed out a little breath. 'Not on this occasion.'

His other eye narrowed, at that, and one hand went to his chin as he looked at her, puzzling, trying to work her out. 'You know,' he said, eventually. 'It's actually not the first time that going out with me has made a woman realise they're in love with someone else.'

Eva's heart, which had been thumping hard in her chest, almost skidded to a stop at his words.

'I'm not in *love* with him.'

Justin raised a single eyebrow. 'OK.'

'I'm not!' she exclaimed, her voice so high and tight that she barely believed herself. 'I'm just…' She paused, searching for the words. 'It's complicated.'

He blew out a small breath, a smile playing at his mouth. 'Love always is.'

'Stop saying it!'

He chuckled a little. 'What, *love*?'

'You did it again!' Her eyes widened but that only made him laugh more. It was such a lovely sound – deep and warm, a rumble through him – stretching his smile so wide that a small, secret dimple appeared on his chin. He was so hot when he laughed, so boyish and handsome that she felt pretty annoyed with herself. Justin would make a great husband, and here she was, all turned upside down by Luke's voodoo eye magic.

'He's a lucky guy,' Justin managed eventually, raking his hair back from his face, 'That's all I'm saying.'

But luck, as Eva knew only too well, had very little to do with it.

Chapter Twenty-Eight

'It's looking at me,' Eva said, half hiding behind Fran as they hauled boxes out of the PE shed, which despite its name was neither a shed nor particularly full of PE equipment. Instead, the large cupboard at the back of the hall had become a dumping ground for anything and everything, including the huge crates of costumes they were retrieving, and a full-sized mannequin, its painted-on features just naive and childlike enough to be completely terrifying.

'It's not looking at you,' Luke said from somewhere outside the door. 'It's not looking at anything. It's inanimate.' He appeared then, grabbing the crate from Eva's hands as if it were nothing and swinging it up onto the pile he'd created against the hall wall.

'Yeah,' Eva muttered, hands on hips, taking a moment to shamelessly watch him before she went to get the next crate. 'That's what a possessed mannequin would *want* you to think.'

Fran, who was at the coal face mining for anything which didn't look like another box of shepherd costumes, laughed, brushing dust off her skinny jeans. 'Maybe we should let him be in the production? Might distract from Harry showing everyone his pants every three minutes?'

Eva shuddered, sneaking another look at the mannequin before she got back to work, hauling box after box towards Luke as she tried to ignore the feel of those cracked-paint eyes on her.

'I've just got a bad feeling about it, that's all,' she said, and after that she deliberately turned her back to the mannequin until they were done hauling all the boxes. Bad feelings, in Eva's experience, were not to be ignored.

With the three of them working in tandem it took barely any time until they'd identified all the useful costumes, stacking the boxes high in the staff room where they'd be more easily accessible, before consolidating all the items they didn't need.

'I'll take these boxes back,' Luke said, nodding to the two women. 'You two can get off home. It's getting late.'

Eva and Fran looked at their watches in unison. 5:30pm.

Fran gasped. 'Oh no, it is getting late! I'm supposed to be meeting up with my mum in half an hour.' She swallowed the last gulp of tea from her mug and quickly rammed it into the dishwasher. 'Gotta run,' she called, already halfway out of the door. 'See you tomorrow!'

Eva shouted an aimless *bye* after her, and then turned to assess the stack of boxes by the door. 'This is one trip's worth, if I help you.' She reached for the boxes before he could argue. 'Come on.'

She was most of the way down the corridor before she heard him pick up the rest, and she smiled to herself, pleased at the idea of winning a point, somehow, though they weren't exactly playing a game. She was feeling so smug about it, in fact, that she completely forgot about the painted mannequin, and as she rushed into the cupboard and unceremoniously dropped the crates on the floor, she just caught, out of the corner of her eye, a face turning to look at her. A very creepy, supposedly inanimate face.

A scream tore out of her even without her knowledge, a survival instinct roaring to the surface as she flung herself away, as far away from the mannequin as possible. Only in her haste, she tripped on the boxes she'd just dropped, propelling her into the propped-open door with a thud.

Within moments, Luke was there, eyes wide, ready to fight Eva's attacker. He scanned the cupboard before dropping to his knees in front of her, brows pinched in confusion.

'What happened?' he asked, his voice strained. 'Are you hurt?

Was she? She'd certainly gone down like a sack of potatoes, but she couldn't locate any particular point of pain.

'I don't think so,' she said, giving herself a quick pat down. 'Just shocked myself.'

His mouth edged into a smile. 'Shocked me, too. I thought there was someone in here.'

'It was that bloody thing.' She pointed an accusatory finger at the mannequin. 'I swear on my *life* that it just turned its head to look at me.'

He turned, contemplating the mannequin for a moment or two, and then looked back at her, his brows more pinched than they had been before. 'It actually does look like it's looking in a different direction now.'

A shiver ran down Eva's spine.

Luke pushed to his feet and Eva held her breath as he

approached the godforsaken effigy. She didn't want to look but simultaneously could not tear her eyes away, anxiety creeping up her neck as he edged closer and closer. His foot hit the box she'd dropped, and as it did, the head turned again and Eva could not help the shriek which ripped out of her, particularly when she heard Luke yell out, not quite a scream, but enough to get her heart pounding, the shock distorting the sound of his voice before the acoustics of the cupboard changed it again. She clamped her eyes shut, her fists clenching tightly, involuntarily.

Then she heard him laugh.

'Eva,' he said, his voice gentle. 'Open your eyes.'

She opened one.

'Watch,' he said, kicking the box again. With the impact the head moved, just as it had the other times, swinging to and fro before it settled back into place, upon which Luke poked it with his finger, making it swing again.

'It's loose,' he said steadily, but with a thread of relief in his voice, like he hadn't believed the thing was possessed in the first place, but was still glad to have ruled it out. 'You must have knocked it when you dropped the box.'

Eva opened the other eye, her brows creasing in concentration. She stood and tiptoed towards Luke as if the painted demon were a bomb which could go off at any time. She prodded it herself when she reached it, noting the way it gave easily, swinging back into place.

'Thank God,' she muttered, replicating the movement a couple more times until she was satisfied that it was not moving of its own accord. Then she, too, began to laugh, and as she did, Luke joined her, the two of them hooting and wheezing as the rush of relief flooded through them.

Neither of them noticed that Eva's fall had shoved the door stop out into the hall. Not at first. Not until the door suddenly slammed shut and they jumped in unison, residual adrenaline pulling squawks of shock out of each of them.

But this was not Eva's first rodeo.

'Don't worry,' she said, nodding to the shut door. 'This one opens from the inside too. You just need the key. It's like a double Yale lock.' She rooted around, a clear picture in her head of the cupboard keys, and the safe place she'd wedged them. 'I put the keys in the … wait, where are the other two boxes?'

Luke frowned. 'I dropped them when I heard you screaming.'

'OK, where? She scanned the floor nearer the door. 'The keys are tucked in the blue one.'

But the boxes weren't immediately apparent, and when she looked up, back at Luke, he was pale, his eyes peering out of the small strip window in the door, She followed his gaze beyond the gridded glass to where the blue box sat, merrily, six feet beyond the door.

Shit.

'OK,' she said, ignoring the rush of panic in her chest. 'Give Fran a call. Maybe she hasn't left yet?'

'My phone's on my desk.' His frown deepened. 'Where's yours?'

Her heart plummeted to her feet. 'Coat pocket. In the cloakroom.'

'Oh.' She saw her own alarm reflected in his eyes. 'OK, let's try making a bit of noise.' His hand went to his face, scratching at his stubble the way she'd learned he did when he was stressed. 'Will anyone still be in?'

She checked her watch. 5:44. 'What time do the cleaners finish?'

'Half five?' He shrugged. 'Maybe later? Let's try it anyway.'

And they did, banging and knocking and stamping and yelling solidly for five minutes or more, but not a single soul materialised.

'This is a disaster,' Eva said, exhausted, as she flopped against the painted brick of the cupboard walls.

'You should be used to that,' he replied, with what sounded like an edge to it, but when she spun to look at him, she was surprised to find not annoyance, but humour in his expression. 'Get comfy, Miss Mallory,' he said, a smile pulling at his lips. 'We might be here for a while.'

'Look,' Luke dragged out, excitement clear in his voice. 'Were these always here?'

It was nearing ten now, and they were still discovering new things about the cupboard which had unexpectedly become their home for the night. The PTA stash had been their first port of call, and they'd dined like six-year-olds on crisps and chocolate bars, washed down with so many cup drinks that Eva had been forced to make their second discovery: a secret toilet just off the cleaning corner at the back of the cupboard. It must have been a relic from an earlier layout of the school, and it definitely looked as though it hadn't been used for a few decades or so, but Eva was delighted and wholly relieved to find that it still functioned perfectly well.

After that, Luke, buzzing slightly from the effects of the cup drinks, had thrown himself into exploring the huge stacks of crates and boxes along the side wall, which in turn had led him to his latest find: four pristine acoustic guitars, each painted a different bright colour. Luke had carefully freed the lime-green one, and was wincing as he plucked the strings, wildly out of tune.

He dropped down to sit next to Eva on the makeshift sofa they'd fashioned out of four gym mats and two huge stuffed sheep, and started roughly tuning each string in turn.

'You play the *real* guitar?' Eva asked, regretting the small squeak of surprise which she hadn't managed to keep from her voice.

Luke huffed a low rumble of a laugh as he continued tuning. 'I'm not going to tell my bass you said that,' he said, through a smile, 'but yes, I can play the *real* guitar.' He finished tuning the last string and played a chord dramatically, looking back up at her as he began to play something almost familiar.

'You're a man of many talents,' she said, trying not to watch the dance of his fingers on the fretboard. She'd watched *that* video enough times to know how her body responded to Music Luke.

He laughed again, but he didn't reply, and when he got to the chorus, she suddenly realised which song he was playing.

'Wait, is that "Stuck With You"?'

He lifted his eyes to hers and smiled as he sang, his singing voice rougher than his speaking voice and, she tried not to think, ten times sexier. He looked back down at his fingers then, and she was glad he wouldn't be able to see the blush racing up her cheeks.

By the time he'd finished the song she had just about got herself together. That was, until he turned to her, one hand resting across the strings, and asked, 'Any requests?'

She remembered the songs his band had played in the bar that night, how she hadn't recognised all of them. 'Do you write songs?'

He smiled, aimlessly playing a chord. 'Benny's the brain behind most of our originals, but I have written one.'

She could feel the hesitancy pulling at him, his shoulders hunching a little as he played the same notes, over and over.

'Can you play me it?' she asked carefully, frowning as his shoulders tightened more. 'You don't have to.'

He shook his head. 'It's not that I don't want to, it's just...' He tailed off, plucking a single string and letting the note hang in the air.

'I'm sorry,' she said quickly, 'I shouldn't have asked. Didn't mean to put you on the spot.'

'It's not that.' There was a grate to his voice. 'It's just...'

But he didn't finish his sentence that time either, and as the last vibrations of the note he'd played faded to nothing they were replaced with something else in the air, a taut string stretched tight between then.

'It's about you,' he said finally, so quietly that she almost didn't hear, and then before she could say anything in response his fingers started to move, coaxing something close to beautiful music out of the child-size lime-green guitar in his arms. And when he started to sing, that was almost beautiful too, his voice rich and soulful with a roughness to it which reached down into the very centre of her chest.

Once again, she was entranced.

He sang about chances taken and chances missed, about bolts of lightning and the scars they left, and then one phrase, over and over, a repeated refrain which pulled a little more air from her lungs every time she heard it.

I forgot to draw my line in the sand
I lost way too much land
To you

Her head was swimming, her heart beating a riot in her chest. His song was like a sledgehammer straight to her guts, his words a knock on her ribs, over and over, the string between them pulling tighter and tighter with every word from his mouth. By the time he played the final note there were tears in her eyes, and a lump in her throat which was growing by the second.

'I'm sorry,' she whispered, but he only shook his head again, not quite meeting her eyes.

'You don't have to be.'

She blew a small breath out, a smile catching at her lips. 'You keep saying that.'

'Because it's true,' he said, and turned to look at her for the first time in a while. She was struck, then by how handsome he was, but beyond that, how *real*. How raw. 'You don't owe me feelings just because I have feelings for you,' he muttered, as his hand reached for her face, one thumb tracing the curve of her jaw.

She closed her eyes against the feeling, leaning into the palm of his hand. 'You know I do though. Have feelings for you, I mean.'

It had tumbled out quickly, before she could stop it, and his hand stopped moving, frozen in place. When she opened her eyes his were fixed on her, dark and intense.

Her heart was in her throat, but she didn't stop. She'd lost all will to keep the words in. 'Just because I can't be with you doesn't mean I don't *want* to be, every single second of every single—'

He cut her off with an almost-kiss before he caught himself, his mouth halted four inches from hers as he muttered, 'I'm sorry, I know you don't want this.'

But she did. That was the truth of it.

She always had.

She hadn't pulled back from him any of the times because she wasn't into it. She'd pulled back because she'd been quite sure that by getting into a relationship with him, she might as well be putting a price on his head. But something about their closeness, or their captivity, or the song he'd sung her, or maybe just the sheer amount of real sugar and artificial colourings coursing through her veins was giving her pause.

It all came together in that moment, a feeling so intense that she half-forgot about the curse, forgot about all the things which had gone before. In that moment she couldn't help herself from pulling him closer, couldn't stop, couldn't resist. And as their lips met, all that existed was the two of them, together, the way it was always meant to be.

Impossible.

Inevitable.

Chapter Twenty-Nine

If their other kisses had been earth-shattering, this one could have destroyed a galaxy.

Eva wished she could have frozen it in time, every detail preserved forever. The taste of Luke's lips, still sweet from the last blue raspberry drink he'd downed, moving against hers with a rhythm so innate that it couldn't have been learned in a lifetime. The graze of his hand, still on her cheek, which moved to clasp her jaw lightly as the kiss deepened. The warmth of his tongue, moving against hers, so softly and yet with such intent it made her stomach clench. And then it clenched again with a pang of disappointment as he pulled away from her, still holding her face in his hand, his eyes half-closed but trained on her.

'But—' he started, and she shook her head.

'There's no but.'

He frowned, his breath coming hard. 'You said no funny business.'

'I know what I said,' she muttered, slowly easing the guitar out of his hands and standing to rest it against the wall a little way away.

When she looked back at him, her breath caught. He was still sitting there, on the pile of gym mats, hands balled into loose fists beside him as if he were readying himself. His mouth had fallen open, those hazel eyes as dark as she'd ever seen them, dragging down the length of her body before they met hers again.

If they'd needed a spark to light the touchpaper, that would have been it. But the truth was that their fire had been smouldering for a while, a slow burn which had gradually gained pace, inch by inch, until it was inextinguishable.

She walked the two paces it took until she was in front of him and he reached for her, his fingers closing around her hipbones as he pressed a kiss low down on her belly. And with that, the smoulder ignited, and she dropped to straddle him, knees digging into the blue pleather of the gym mats as she leaned in to kiss him again.

He pulled her into him with a groan which reverberated in every part of her body, goosebumps scattering over her skin at the warmth of his breath on her face. His hands were everywhere: closing around her sides; knotting into her hair; tucking around the curve of her hips and driving her out of her mind.

She fumbled the buttons on his olive-green shirt open and slipped it off his shoulders, her fingers trailing the warmth of his skin unashamedly, reacquainting themselves with the contours of his body. She felt him trying to lift her top over her head and shifted to help him, shivering at the delicious nip of the cold air on her newly exposed skin and shivering again when the cold air was replaced by the heat of his hands, moving over her body like he was learning it. His fingertips mapped the valley of her sternum, the length of her neck and the curve of her breasts through the thin fabric of her bra before he did away with that, too.

He pulled back for a moment to look at her, and she heard him mutter something under his breath before he spoke again, raspy and low, while his thumbs absentmindedly grazed her nipples.

'You are perfect,' he gritted out, the pause between each word longer than it ought to be by rights. He held her there for a moment or two, fingers wrapped around her ribcage as his thumbs continued their slow circles, winding Eva up tightly, like a spring.

She wasn't quite sure what to do with herself.

She'd had sex before, of course, but a side effect of avoiding relationships was that she had only ever had rushed, elbowy first-time sex, and awkward, *is-this-a-relationship* second-time sex before losing her nerve and cutting loose. So this, whatever was happening here, was unprecedented.

Luke was looking at her like he wanted to devour her, but there was an undertone of something more, something quiet and reverent in his gaze, and in the slow movements of his hands. She had no fire metaphors to describe this feeling at all. It was more than the lick of flames, more than the smoulder of ashes.

It was more like a star exploding, a fundamental shift in the fabric of her universe.

His brow quirked in a question, but she had no words for him, no answers that would have made any kind of sense, anyway. Instead she reached for his belt buckle with a slow nod which she hoped would convey the churn of emotions swelling in her chest, all the things she could not voice and yet, she hoped, none of the things she had no right to promise him.

She clambered off him and pulled him to his feet by his waistband, the bare lightbulb casting crisp shadows which made his features look sharper, the muscles of his body more defined. In three buttons his jeans were undone, and he helped her slide them down, kicking off his shoes and socks as elegantly as such a movement would allow. And then he stood tall again, naked but for his underwear and with his heart beating so hard she could see it through the skin of his chest. He reached for her, kissed her slow and deep as his fingers worked the button of her trousers, and then the zip, thumbs hooking into the waistband as he dispensed with them in one smooth move. And then he broke the kiss as she pulled off her shoes, drawing in a long breath as his eyes swept over her, drinking in every last curve.

'This is very inappropriate, Mr Mallory,' she said with a smile, barely enough breath in her to get the words out, and his laugh turned her on even more. His hands went to her hips, picking her up and perching her on the edge of the old vaulting horse at the very back of the cupboard.

The ageing wood creaked underneath them as he leaned into her, the worn-smooth suede of the top cool against the heated skin of her thighs. Ordinarily Eva would have been worried about the possibility that it would just collapse underneath her weight – such things were often part of her experience, after all – but she wasn't thinking about any of those things in that moment. All she could focus on was Luke: the warmth of his skin against hers; the slip of his tongue in her mouth; the press of him, hard as hell, right up again the heat of her body.

She cried out when his hands moved from her hips round to the inside of her thighs, tracing a teasing trail up to the lace of her underwear.

'You sure you want this?' he asked, his fingers paused in place, and she blew out a breath of frustration.

'I'm tired of pretending I don't.'

There was the truth of it.

And the way his face changed with her answer told her that he understood.

A white-hot bolt shot through her stomach as his fingers resumed their path, grazing over the lace, making her hips buck skyward. Those beautiful lips, swollen from kissing, pulled into the filthiest smile she'd seen on him yet, a vision, she knew, that would stay with her for a long time. Perhaps forever.

He dragged her underwear off and her eyes fell closed, seemingly of their own accord. After that, her head fell against his shoulder and she felt his fingers on her, the pattern of his touch both familiar and new, like everything about him. At times it felt like he was exploring her body for the first time, and at others like he knew exactly where to touch her, how she wanted him, how to bring on shudders of pleasure so intense that she could do nothing but cling to him, muttering his name into the warmth of his neck as explosions of stars burst behind her closed lids.

When she opened her eyes again he was looking right at her, an expression on his face that she could have written poetry about.

'Need you,' he muttered. That was it. As if he was so focused on her that he didn't want to waste a single ounce of energy on needless syllables.

'I...' She wasn't any more coherent, her voice lost to the things she'd muttered into his skin. 'Same,' she managed eventually. 'But...'

'Condom?'

'Yeah.'

'Don't have one.' His voice was rough, words ground out between breaths. 'Wasn't expecting...' He tailed off as she reached for him, trailing a finger from the centre of his chest down, through the valley where his abs met, and then lower, fingers hooking into the waistband of his boxers. His eyes fluttered closed.

'Me neither,' she said, heat surging through her as his hands gripped her hips again.

'So...' The disappointment in his voice was palpable, but it was soon replaced by a different quality as her hand slipped beyond his waistband, closing around his erection. '*Jesus*, Eva.' He sucked a breath in, head thrown back, just like in the band video she had watched once or twice or twenty-five times. She couldn't help but smile. She'd never look at it in the same way again.

'Haven't slept with anyone in over a year,' he muttered.

She smiled, pleased about that, though she had no right to be. 'Longer for me.'

His head snapped back up, eyes searing into her. 'But...'

'I'm protected,' she said quickly, though she couldn't in good conscience leave it at that. 'But unlucky.'

He nodded, brows pinched, eyes so dark they looked as if they were all pupil. It didn't look as if he were deciding what his next move should be, more like he had already decided, and was savouring every last second of it.

One hand came to her face, his fingers carefully tracing the edge of her jaw and the curve of her lips. And then, as they caught the tip of her chin, he brought his face to hers, forehead to forehead, their breath mingling in a syncopated rhythm.

'I'll take my chances,' he said, gruffly, his lips brushing against hers with his words.

She nodded, eyes fluttering closed. 'Me too.'

And then he kissed her like the world was ending.

Her name fell from his lips like a prayer as he pushed inside her, and just like that the fabric of her universe changed again, something in the very pit of her chest growing and swelling with every thrust, every muttered word, every drag of his mouth across her skin.

He was marking her, whether he knew it or not, carving his name into her blueprints and rewriting the foundations of everything she thought she knew. Except there was one thing she did know for certain: after they got out of this cupboard, everything was going to change.

Somewhere in her consciousness she registered that sleeping with him would make it ten times harder to walk away again, but it was a force she couldn't fight; a riptide pulling her away from the shore. Every kiss pulled her further under, every groan dragging the air from her lungs until she was drowning. And right then, she wasn't sure that she even wanted to be saved.

She watched him unravel piece by piece: first in the dampening of his hair around his temples, then in the pressure of his fingers dimpling her skin. And then, finally, in the way the rhythm of his movements changed gradually, quickening and then falling out of time. He was losing his grip, losing control and the exquisite joy of knowing that it was because of her made another wave of pleasure rattle through her like a freight train.

In the end it was that which tipped him over the edge, a low growl rising in his throat as he clung to her, his muscles twitching underneath the grip of her fingers. For those few seconds it was as if he was entirely hers, and she his. She didn't catch the words he muttered into the crook of her neck afterwards, but she felt the kiss which followed them – a lingering brush of his lips so tender that it almost made her cry.

Because as she sat there in his arms, her body still riding out the waning aftershocks of her orgasm, Eva had realised something. Or, perhaps more accurately, a truth which she had been trying to evade for a while finally lit itself up like a flare – loud and blatant and undeniable.

She was in love with Luke Mallory.

And she had absolutely no idea what she was going to do about it.

Chapter Thirty

By the time Eva lowered herself on to Sylvia's ageing sofa that Saturday morning, five separate people had asked her if she was OK.

The first person to ask had been Luke, as they lay together on the small stack of gym mats, huddling together in their clothes against the chill of the bare-brick cupboard. They'd had sex twice more after the first time, and neither occasion had done a single thing to convince Eva that the realisation she'd had was wrong. So when Luke pulled her back against the warmth of his body, surrounding her with that delicious scent of spearmint and sandalwood as his mouth grazed her ear with the question, she *had* been OK. At that point, she'd been more than OK.

And when the caretaker had asked, when he'd freed the two of them from the cupboard early on Friday morning with the slightest of smirks and a knowing nod of his head, she'd been OK then, too.

Mrs Abbott had asked twice. First as Eva skidded into her

classroom two minutes before the doors were due to open, breathing hard and with her hair still damp from the shower, and then again as the two of them tidied up at the end of the day. Mrs Abbott did not ask questions she didn't genuinely want the answer to, and she certainly was not one to repeat herself, so the second time she asked, Eva paused, pencil part-sharpened, and gave the older woman her full attention.

It had also happened that from the beginning of the school day to the end, her answer had begun to change. She'd been feeling pretty close to perfect the first time Mrs Abbott had asked, still buzzing from the previous night and the not-insubstantial amount of espresso she'd had to down in order to get herself ready for school in those ninety-six minutes between them being released from the cupboard and actually having to teach. But it had been a long day – and on approximately three hours of broken sleep, a particularly *gruelling* day – so by three-thirty both her body and her heart were flagging.

She'd hoped to see Luke at lunchtime to organise the production costumes they'd dug out, but she hadn't. One of the Jameson twins had taken a flying leap off the climbing frame and she'd had to accompany him and his banana-shaped forearm to the local A&E department before his dad arrived to take over. By the time she got back they were partway through afternoon registration, and the costumes were already sorted, racked up and clearly labelled, which she was quite sure must have been Fran's doing.

She'd heard him though, all day long, the low rumble of his voice through the walls which reverberated in her body. She'd even caught his eye once through the glass of their respective classroom doors, his lips lifting into a small smile before she'd heard a crash on the other side of her classroom and had to rush over to save Jerome the class gerbil from an untimely demise.

So the second time that Mrs Abbott asked the question, Eva had reason to pause. And when she looked across at her ordinarily stern TA, she saw something she hadn't been expecting in her eyes: genuine curiosity, and more than the older woman's usual amount of compassion, too. It was almost enough for Eva to pour out the whole story, then and there, but she didn't. She couldn't, not with the situation still so mixed up in her own head. And so she replied the same way she had the first time, though the energy and the implication had been a million miles away.

'Yes,' she said. 'I'm OK.'

And Mrs Abbott had replied in just the same way as before. 'Right.'

But there had been a difference to the tone of the older woman's voice that time, a change in the curt nod of her head. A conversation had passed between them, as much in the things they weren't saying as the things they were. It was the same way they spoke across a crowded classroom sometimes: in the widening of their eyes and the subtle movements of their heads.

Tell me what needs to be done, Mrs Abbott's question had really meant.

And Eva's reply: *I don't know yet.*

OK, the response. *I am here when you do.*

And then Mrs Abbott had busied herself disinfecting the water tray – out of sight but not quite out of reach. It had made something tighten in Eva's chest. The two women had never been what Eva would describe as close, but any time it counted, Mrs Abbott had been in her corner. Even if all she had done was scowl while cleaning said corner.

They'd finished cleaning together, then gone their separate ways, and when Eva had wished Mrs Abbott a lovely weekend she had never meant it more. Then she'd gone home, shovelled a hastily cooked pizza into her mouth and collapsed into bed.

The following morning, Sylvia asked her if she was OK on her front step. Eva hadn't even got through the door.

'I'm fine,' she'd said gently, pulling her mother into a hug. 'Just tired.' It was automatic, now, the need to put a brave face on. She worried Sylvia enough just with the day-to-day happenings of her life without piling on any extra concerns. The image of Sylvia sitting at the dining room table the day Tomasz died had been etched so deeply into Eva's consciousness that she would do anything in her power to avoid being the reason her mother made that face again.

Mercifully, Sylvia just nodded, smiling back at her as she adjusted a few stray strands of hair which had fallen out of Eva's messier-than-usual messy bun. 'I'll make you some tea,' she said, vanishing into the kitchen.

Behind her, Eva caught sight of her sister perching on the stairs, one eyebrow raised.

'OK,' Hanna said, her body unfurling like a cartoon villain. 'Maybe you'll tell *me* the truth.'

Eva's eyebrows pinched. 'What do you mean?'

'Well,' Hanna stood, lowering her voice a notch. 'You didn't reply to the text I sent you on Thursday evening until yesterday lunchtime.' She paused, taking another step towards Eva. 'And you look like you were dragged here *behind* your car rather than sitting at the wheel and driving it, so I'll ask again: are you OK?'

'*Yes,*' Eva insisted, sending her sister a silent plea to drop it. She knew that Hanna would be able to read her like a book but she did not have the energy to go through it with her. Not yet.

And maybe Hanna understood, because after studying her a moment or two she stood and nodded. She turned to follow Sylvia into the kitchen, but paused as she passed Eva, resting a hand on her shoulder and leaning in, her voice hushed.

'Just let me know if you want him kneecapped.'

Eva reared back in horror. 'What? *Who.*'

'Cupboard Boy,' Hanna whisper-shouted. 'Oh don't pull that face, we both know this is about him. I'm just saying I know a guy.' She widened her eyes. 'You know, if you want to teach him a lesson.'

Eva almost laughed at the ridiculousness, though she was a little short of breath at the mere mention of Luke. 'You do not.'

'I do. He'll do it for fifty quid, no questions asked.'

Eva's breath escaped as a snort. 'Sometimes you legitimately scare me.'

Hanna shrugged lightly, as if she hadn't just suggested maiming a man. 'Or, you know, we could just set Ciocia Irenka on him. For free.'

'Stand down.' Eva widened her eyes back at her sister. 'I don't want you kneecapping anyone. *Least* of all Cupb…' She caught herself. '*Luke.*'

'Least of all, eh?' Hanna said, the tone of her voice changing in an instant, and she walked off with a smirk.

Eva rolled her eyes and followed her sister into the kitchen. It was a bright day, and in the sunlight pouring through the windows of Sylvia's kitchen she didn't recognise the person sitting with Stefan at the table, a complicated array of playing cards in front of them. Not until he spoke, anyway.

'Hey, stranger,' came the warmth of that familiar voice. 'Fancy meeting you here.'

She almost laughed with the surprise of it. '*Orson*?'

'Orson mentioned at Christmas that he misses having a card partner,' Stefan said, with a small smile. 'I can never convince your mother to play with me.'

'He always wins,' Sylvia shouted over her shoulder, making Stefan smile warmly in her direction before turning his attention back to the cards.

'So now we play together a couple of times a week,' he finished, drawing a card from the deck and frowning at it.

Orson nodded at Stefan, his face crinkling into a smile. 'He still always wins. But I don't mind.' He looked up at Sylvia, who had put a steaming cup of tea in front of him, and mouthed a *thank you* before speaking again, to no one in particular. 'It's just nice to feel like a part of a family again. I have my sister of course, but she…' He paused a moment, a flicker of some emotion crossing his face. 'She has her own family now.' A breath blew away the expression as quickly as it had arrived, and his eyes met Eva's again, his lips twisting back into a smile. 'Plus, who could resist watching Challenge TV with your great-aunts?'

Sylvia carried two more mugs to the table, putting one in front of Stefan, and one in front of Eva. They each smiled their thanks.

'The ciocias adore having you around too,' she said to Orson, before heading back to grab two more mugs.

'I just hope they're not being weird about it,' Eva said, as she watched her mother take the mugs through to the living room where the ciocias would no doubt be decamped.

Orson's brows pulled together in confusion. 'About?'

'You know, *Jules*.' Eva blew the steam off her tea before taking a cautious sip. 'I mean, I love them to death, but they're deeply Catholic and they have a combined age of about five hundred years so they have been known to be a little bit homophobic.'

She heard Hanna snort from across the room.

But Orson just chuckled. 'Well, Nelka has tried three times to set me up with her church friend's widowed daughter, so I'm not sure how much of that bit actually registered.' His smile had grown so wide that the skin around his eyes had blanched. 'But I'm having a good time.' And then he turned back to Stefan, groaning good-naturedly at the run of cards which Stefan had laid out in front of himself.

Eva couldn't help but laugh, a wash of warmth seeping over the cold knot which had been slowly tightening in her stomach. Even at that moment, with her life in more chaos than was usual, there was one thing which was absolutely as it should be. She drew in the energy of this house at that exact moment, with all the people she loved the most underneath its roof.

Well, almost all.

The feeling hit her like a slap in the face and she tightened her fingers around her mug, appreciating the warmth it offered her, though it was far from cold in Sylvia's house. Luke's face flashed into her mind, flushed red and awkwardly lit by the bare lightbulb. She thought of the way he'd kissed her as they heard the caretaker whistling that morning – like it was the last chance he'd ever have – and the words he'd said half under his breath as they heard the twist of the lock.

If this is all we get, he'd said. I'll take it.

All at once it was as if her legs couldn't support her, and

she grabbed her tea, muttering some frail excuse as she shuffled off into the living room and all but collapsed on the sofa next to the scowling form of Ciocia Irenka.

Irenka was the first person who didn't ask Eva if she was OK, and Eva revelled in the freedom of not having to lie. Because by that point, she wasn't OK. She wasn't OK at all.

It had been twenty-eight hours since she'd last kissed Luke, untwined her fingers from his and stepped out into the sharp light of the hall.

Twenty-seven since she'd reluctantly showered every last trace of his scent off her skin.

Nineteen since she'd knocked on his classroom door, finding it empty, his coat conspicuously missing from its peg.

Fifteen since she'd clambered into her own bed, bone tired and with a sharp spear of loneliness piercing her chest with every breath.

Three since she'd woken in that same bed, breathing though the fading traces of a dream she'd had. A dream which had gripped her windpipe so tightly that she could barely breathe. A dream she could barely remember now, the pieces lost to the passing minutes of the morning.

As she'd laid in bed, her pulse gradually returning to normal, there had been only one thing she knew for certain.

She was not OK.

She was in love.

Absolutely, completely, *irrevocably* in love, with a man who she was almost certain she would end up killing somehow. With a man so wholesome, so *good*, that she would never be able to forgive herself for it. And now she'd had a taste of him she was genuinely at a loss as to how she was ever going to be able to function without him.

But Ciocia Irenka didn't ask, just looked sideways at Eva as she nodded her head at the TV, her lip curling upwards in disgust at the sharply dressed presenter filling the screen.

'*Idiota*,' she growled, gesturing vaguely at the unusually smooth TV man. 'He is cheating. Nobody can know this.'

Eva smiled to herself as she took another sip of her tea. 'He's the host, ciocia. They *give* him the answers. He's the one who's supposed to know.'

But the old woman just shook her head, her eyes darting towards Eva for a moment before she fixed them back on the screen, sucking in a breath through her teeth. And that was when Eva realised what was really happening.

Ciocia Irenka didn't ask, because she *knew*. She always had. She had very poor knowledge of English catchphrases or popular culture or even the structure of the average game show, but she knew a thing or two about people. About love.

She'd been trying to tell her all along.

I am telling you, you cannot arrange these things.

Love comes when it wants to, like English buses. You cannot make it here sooner or to stop when it turns up.

How right she had been.

Something tugged at Eva's throat then, a question forming from nowhere, which suddenly felt too important to ignore. 'Did you ever fall in love, ciocia?'

The old woman looked sharply at her, before turning away, her thin lips curling downwards even more than usual.

'Yes,' she said eventually, age-worn fingers closing around the edge of her cardigan cuffs. 'Krzysztof.' She flinched as she said the name, her brow falling into its usual heavy crease. 'We were in Polish Army together. He was a good man.'

She looked back at the TV and tutted loudly at the

presenter. For a while Eva thought she wasn't going to say more, but then she drew a sharp breath in and spoke again. 'War was not good time for love, but love did not listen. We did not listen either. We made promise to marry, to have a family when war was over.'

'But you didn't,' Eva whispered, already knowing the answer.

'No,' Irenka said. 'We didn't.' Her voice was even, a little lighter than usual, Eva thought, though that made no sense. 'When we came to England, he was put on different boat, sent to different camp. I never see him again.'

Eva drew a sharp breath in, her heart squeezing for the old woman. 'You never tried to find him?'

'It was different world then,' Irenka said, sternly. 'We didn't have computer everything like now. Not so easy to find.'

'You could have tried.' Eva's voice almost caught on the words. 'Maybe you'd have been lucky?'

'I could have. Maybe if we did again, I would have, but there was a war; we were not in our country. Nothing was the same.' Her eyes narrowed, still focused on the TV. 'But I was alive, Nelka was alive, Pawel was alive. I … how you say? … count my blessings?'

'But…' Eva started, without really knowing where she was going to go with it, and it made Irenka's cool grey eyes dart back to meet hers.

'You talk a lot about luck,' Irenka said firmly, 'but there are things in life more important than luck.'

Eva's brows pulled into a question, but she didn't dare interrupt her great-aunt.

'You are twin. Did you know I am twin too?'

Eva shook her head, a ball of something cold and heavy in her stomach.

'Dorota,' Irenka said, the syllables strangely drawn out, as if she hadn't said them in a long time. 'She died in war. When they came for us, the Russians, she had a sickness. And when we were put on the wagons, she died.' Her fingers knotted into each other, knuckles whitening. 'They threw her from the train, the guards. Not just Dorota, but lot of people. Lot of people thrown away, like rubbish.'

Acid rose in Eva's throat. She'd listened to war stories from the ciocias before, but it never got easier to hear. And she'd never known that they'd had a fourth sibling, let alone Irenka's twin. She imagined losing Hanna in such a traumatic way, and ice gripped at her spine.

'Was I lucky that she died and not me?' Irenka continued, still staring at the TV as if it were her lifeline. 'Maybe. But what was my luck? I go then to Siberia. I live, I work in the camps— it was terrible.'

She turned then, her eyes fixing on Eva's, and when she spoke it was slowly, her English as good as it ever was. 'Was she lucky that she never saw any of this? Maybe. I have a life now, and she didn't have chance. But every day of this life I think about things she never had to see.' Her bony hand reached for Eva's, the skin of her fingers warm and smooth. 'Both unlucky, maybe. Both lucky, maybe. It is the same with you. Not one way or the other way.'

Eva's brows knotted together, her great-aunt's words working their way into her mind, prodding at the things she thought she knew.

'So now,' Irenka said, gripping Eva's hands just a little too tightly, as if she were about to say something of grave importance, 'I don't think about luck; I think about living. Bad things happen, a lot of. But around them, good. You look too hard at the bad; you don't know the good.'

Eva drew in a breath, and then released it all in a rush, realisation hit like a punch in the stomach. She'd been playing it safe, trying to protect Luke from her chaos, but she wasn't protecting him at all. She was only hurting him more. And herself, too.

She could avoid her feelings for him all she wanted, but where would that leave her? Sitting on an old sofa fifty years from now looking back at her lost love? Flinching when she said his name?

She could see the weight of regret etched into every line of Ciocia Irenka's face as she held Eva's gaze. It was like a flash forward, a warning from the universe. She saw the reflection of herself in the future, only it wasn't a war keeping her from Luke, nor the turmoil of being displaced from her homeland, a stranger in a new place, her heart riddled with still-healing scars. It was her own fear. It was the idea that something would go wrong, as if things didn't go wrong every second of every day.

As if people didn't die without being cursed.

All at once she knew what she had to do. She downed the biggest gulp of tea she could manage before slamming her mug back on the side table. She kissed Ciocia Irenka on the cheek, much to the older woman's surprise, grabbed her bag and sprinted out to her car.

She raced to Luke's house like it was on fire, so much so that she was completely out of breath by the time she pulled up outside.

Her phone started to ring, and as she glanced at the screen

she saw that her mother was calling. Probably wondering where she'd vanished to in such a hurry, she thought. On another day she'd probably have picked it up, and they would have laughed about it together, but right at that moment the ringing of her phone simply served as a distraction from the task in hand, and so Eva declined the call.

Nothing mattered more than seeing Luke.

Or so she thought. Because not even ten seconds later her phone began to ring again, lighting the whole screen up with Sylvia's ridiculous selfie. And, with that, Eva's blood ran cold.

Sylvia was not the kind of person to call twice in quick succession. In fact, Eva could only think of one occasion in her whole life when she'd done it: it was as Eva was walking out of the registry office clutching her deed poll certificate in optimistic hands as her dad lay dead on the kitchen floor.

She hadn't answered either call that time.

She would not be making that mistake again.

One finger swiped to answer, dread creeping up the back of her throat.

'Mum?'

She heard her mother's sob first, raw and biting, and a wave of panic hit her. Had something happened to Irenka, perhaps? Nelka? God forbid it was Stefan, Eva couldn't even bear to think it.

'What's wrong?' she gritted out, in a voice which didn't even sound like hers.

And then Sylvia replied through her sobs. Two words which struck ice into Eva's veins.

'It's Hanna.'

Chapter Thirty-One

Eva didn't remember the drive to the hospital. She wouldn't remember it as long as she lived. It was like something primal had taken over, an invisible guide which swept her up, pulling her towards her sister like they were two halves of one soul, which perhaps they were.

She sprinted though the automatic doors at the main entrance, her mother's words ringing in her ears the whole time.

'She was absolutely fine,' Sylvia had said. 'And then the next minute she was on the ground.'

If Eva hadn't been panicking just from the desperate grate in Sylvia's voice, that sentence would have done it. She'd said exactly the same thing about Tomasz. Word for word.

Sylvia was sitting near the entrance as Eva burst though. She couldn't see her mother's face, but she could see the shake of her shoulders, silent tears shuddering through her whole body as Stefan sat wordlessly beside her.

Eva's heart fell to her feet.

She dropped down into the seat beside Sylvia and reached a hand out for her mother's shoulder. She didn't dare ask what had happened, completely unprepared to hear bad news. Her dad dying had been devastating. She'd barely survived it. She was almost positive she would not survive losing Hanna.

Particularly if she were the one who'd caused it.

The timing wasn't lost on Eva. She should have been expecting it. No sooner had she decided that luck was of her own making and that she'd take her chances, than the curse had swooped in. Teaching her a lesson, just like always.

'She's…' Sylvia started, but her words were swallowed by a sob, the sound of it making Eva's heart pound, heavy drumbeats which wracked her whole body and made her vision slowly fade to black.

No.

She squeezed her eyes shut, silently bracing against the rip of pain which she was quite sure was coming.

'She's alive,' Stefan said quickly, taking the slightest edge off Eva's panic. 'We don't know any more, but we know she's alive. Owen is with her.'

Eva nodded. It was all she was able to do. And then she took her mother's hand, the one Stefan wasn't holding, and the three of them held on for dear life.

———

It was about forty minutes later when Owen appeared, his complexion pale and his hands clenched into tight fists. But Eva didn't notice that at first. No, the first thing she noticed was the expression on his face. It looked almost like…

Relief?

He flopped down in the seat next to Eva, bones going slack all of a sudden as though they'd been pulled tight so long he couldn't stand it anymore. His head lolled back on the curve of the seat, his Adam's apple jutting out of his neck.

'She's OK,' he said, more an exhale than actual words, like his lungs had been filled by panic, pre-emptive grief pushing against the walls of his chest. 'They're running a few more tests, but she's sitting up and making stupid jokes, so I'm pretty sure she's…'

'She's OK,' Eva parroted, but that didn't feel real either. She wouldn't believe it until she'd seen her sister with her own eyes.

Beside her, she barely registered her mother bursting into huge, wheezing sobs.

'I'm going to go back in,' Owen said, as he hauled himself to his feet. 'I just wanted you all to, y'know.'

He didn't have to say it. They all knew.

Almost another hour passed before Eva finally pushed through the faded blue curtain of her sister's cubicle. Hanna's nurse had allowed a second visitor, and so Sylvia had gone in with Owen first, while Stefan stayed in the rough burgundy chairs with Eva. And then, once they'd both returned, a little colour back in Owen's face and the faintest of smiles on Sylvia's, it was Eva's turn to accompany Owen.

Hanna was sitting up on the trolley in her cubicle, and she took a gulp of water from a plastic cup before stretching both arms wide with a smile, exposing electrodes stuck to the skin on her chest and wrists.

'Surprise,' she hooted, a little louder than was probably advisable. 'I'm alive!'

'Hanna!' Eva scolded, in what sounded a lot like her mother's voice, and Hanna shrugged sheepishly.

'Sorry, that was in bad taste, but … I'm alive!'

The relief which Eva had been holding back on suddenly burst from her chest in a giggle, a small bubble of joy which rippled out of her, cascading into full laughter which bounced off all the shiny surfaces of the small cubicle. She bounded over to her sister and wrapped her in a cautious hug, which Hanna returned with double the enthusiasm.

'I was so worried,' she muttered into Hanna's hair, and she felt the arms around her tighten in response. 'I thought—'

'I know what you thought.' Hanna's voice was quiet, no trace of her usual snark. 'But it's OK. *I'm* OK.'

Eva squeezed again, a little more boldly this time, before untangling herself from Hanna's arms and stepping back. She noted that one of the electrodes from Hanna's chest had somehow come unstuck and tangled itself in her hair, but she'd deal with that later. For now, there were more important things.

'What have they said?'

Hanna blew a breath out. 'I fainted, essentially. But I was out for a little while, and then when I came around they were a bit worried about my heart, so they've done a couple of extra tests but—'

'Your heart?' Eva couldn't hold back her concern. It wouldn't have been the first time that the curse went for the heart of someone she loved.

'Listen,' Hanna said, as gently as she was capable of. 'I said they *were* worried about that, but then they did more tests and it turns out I didn't pass out because I have a problem with my heart, I passed out because—'

'You're pregnant?' Eva couldn't stop her eyes from widening.

But Hanna only recoiled in horror. 'What? No! I'm anaemic.'

'Oh.'

'Yeah.' Hanna's smile turned sheepish again. 'Apparently having a diet like a three-year-old at a birthday party isn't good for your health.'

Eva laughed, her mouth pulling into a wry grin as the churn of anxiety in her gut began to settle. 'Who knew?'

'Calm yourself.' Hanna rolled her eyes. 'They're going to give me supplements and I've got to eat iron-rich foods, whatever.'

Eva was about to open her mouth and tell her sister that she was glad she'd been felled by her chicken nugget addiction and not something more serious when the curtain swished open again, making Eva jump out of her skin.

'Sorry,' said the woman, a tone in her voice which implied she really was sorry, but she had far too little time to dwell on it. She was shorter than the twins, and slight, but she had more presence than the both of them put together. 'Hi Hanna, I'm Dr Cheng, one of the cardiology registrars. I'd like to have a quick word about your test results, so if you'd like to be alone, or just with your husband…' Her eyes flicked to Eva, the *let me know and I'll throw this one out* implied. Eva completely believed that she could, and *would*.

But Hanna shook her head, nodding at Eva. 'This is my sister.'

With that, Dr Cheng's demeanour changed, and she

considered Eva through her tortoiseshell glasses. 'Ah, OK. Then you should probably stay for this, too.'

There was a weight to her words, a gravity which made Eva's recently hushed panic rise back up in her chest.

'As you know,' Dr Cheng continued, pushing her glasses up her nose as she did, 'there were a few things your heart was doing when we first examined you that we weren't completely comfortable with.'

Hanna nodded silently, which only sped the thunder of Eva's own heart. She watched Owen take a step closer to his wife and reach for her hand.

'But the ECG test we did on your heart didn't show anything worrying, which was good news. It means that the irregularities I mentioned are likely benign.'

The slap of the orange card file on the end of the trolley made Eva jump again, but this time the doctor didn't apologise. She was much too busy leafing slender fingers through the papers in the file. 'However,' she continued, a strange weight to the word, 'I noticed when I was scanning your notes that you were never screened for the condition that your father had, so with your consent I'd like to arrange a couple more tests on an outpatient basis.' Her dark eyes lifted from the file, moving to meet Hanna's eyes, and then Eva's. 'For both of you, if possible.'

Eva's throat tightened. 'Both of us?'

'Yes.' Dr Cheng met Eva's eyes, her voice even and straightforward. 'The condition can be hereditary, and there is a risk of sudden cardiac arrest if it's not treated.'

And with those words, it was as if Eva had been plunged underwater. She vaguely registered the doctor asking if they had any other siblings and her sister replying, but the sound was fuzzy, muffled by the words that the doctor had said as her vision faded around the edges.

A condition.

Which put him at risk of sudden death.

'I'm sorry,' Eva blurted, the room fading back into focus. 'You said our dad had a condition?'

Dr Cheng's lips lifted into a small smile, her expression pleasant, but no-nonsense. If ever she had to hear bad news, Eva thought, she would want it to be from this doctor.

'Yes,' she said, adjusting the stethoscope on her neck, 'he had a type of cardiomyopathy, which is a problem with the muscle of the heart. It was discovered at his post-mortem. You should both have been invited for screening at the time, but it seems it was never followed up on. I strongly advise you to follow up on it now. Have there been any other sudden or unexplained deaths in your family?

Eva looked over at her sister to find Hanna already looking her way. 'Our great-grandad,' Hanna said, without moving her gaze away. 'We were told it was a heart attack, but no one was really sure. His wife didn't speak much English and it was a long time ago.'

The doctor nodded her understanding. 'I imagine it was difficult with a language barrier there. They wouldn't have had the translation resources we have now.'

'We always thought it was random chance,' Eva said, some semblance of the belief she'd held for so long still lingering within her grasp. 'Just one of those things. That's what we were told.'

'That's not the case,' Dr Cheng said, gathering the file back up into her arms. 'I really can't understate the importance of screening here. There is a strong hereditary link. This condition killed your father and it likely killed your great-grandfather too. But the good news is that the tests for it are simple and non-invasive and there are treatment options available. I can refer you both right away, with your consent.'

Eva nodded. 'Absolutely.'

'Yes, of course,' Hanna said. 'Thank you.'

'Great.' Dr Cheng smiled quickly, tucking the file under her arm. 'OK, so I'm happy to let you go home now, and we'll contact you soon about the screening. Once the nurse comes along with your prescription, you're free to go.'

And then she slipped through a gap in the curtain that Eva couldn't even see, moving like she had a million other things to do, which, to be fair, she definitely did.

Eva eased herself down in the cold plastic chair next to the one Owen was sitting in and blew a long breath out. Her mind was swimming, long-held beliefs unfurling like petals, one after the other.

It wasn't the curse that had killed her dad or her great-grandad. It was a medical condition. An anomaly in his heart which had been there all along, ticking in the background like a bomb waiting to go off.

Which meant…

'If this cardiowotsit killed dad, that means … that I didn't?'

The feeling rushed through Eva's chest, so powerful that she could barely breathe, the years of guilt and fears starting to loosen their shackles on her as, one by one, they fell away. It felt like the sun on her face, like coming up for air.

Like she was finally free.

It all came together to send a rough chuckle up her throat, and when she looked up both Hanna and Owen were looking at her, each wearing an equally bewildered expression.

'Of course *you* didn't kill him,' Hanna said, frowning so hard that a deep crease cut up her forehead. 'Why would you think that?'

'It was the curse,' Eva said, still smiling. 'That's what I thought. The day he died I changed my name. I was so sick of the Mallory curse that I thought if I had some other name, some more common name, then maybe it would stop. So I changed my name to Eva Smith and by the time I got home from the registry office, he was dead. I thought the curse was punishing me for trying to cheat it.'

'The curse isn't sentient, Eva,' Hanna said gently.

'It's not *real*.'

Both sisters jumped at the sound of Owen's voice. There was a note of insistence running through it which made him sound quite unlike himself, and when Eva looked at him, his face looked different, too.

'You think you broke the curse by marrying me?' he asked his wife, who was looking at him like he had three heads.

Eva had never seen her sister speechless before.

'I … I *did*.'

Owen shook his head, his features starting to soften back into the man they knew. 'You were never cursed, just chaotic.' He smiled, reaching out a thumb to trace Hanna's cheek. 'I went along with the whole curse line 'cause it was a thing in your family, like a running joke, I thought.' He raised one eyebrow. 'You think you're less chaotic since we got married?'

'Yes?' Hanna squeaked, her brows still drawn together in surprise.

'No,' Owen replied, with a chuckle. 'Definitely no. You're a walking catastrophe. I mean maybe you never burned down a stately home or anything—'

Eva huffed. 'It was a hotel, and it was moderately scorched at worst.'

'But you're late for everything,' he continued, his lips quirking into a smile at Eva's words, 'you lose things constantly; you have a million *wigs* for some bizarre reason, and you're always up to the eyeballs in some crazy scheme.'

Hanna opened her mouth to speak, but Owen silenced her with a raised finger. 'But that's just *you*.' His raised hand went to cup her chin. 'And I love it. I don't feel cursed at all; I feel like the luckiest man alive.'

He paused, turning to look at Eva. 'And I might be making assumptions here, but I would hazard a guess that Cupboard Boy might feel the same way.' His mouth tipped into a smile. 'You Mallory women are one of a kind.' He looked between them. 'Two of a kind. Whatever.'

'OK firstly,' Eva said, 'can we stop calling him Cupboard Boy? And secondly, oh my God, *Cupboard Boy*! If I didn't...' She felt like she couldn't breathe, the words sticking in her throat. 'That means...'

It dawned on her all at once, the implications of this new information fitting into place like a jigsaw. The only part of being with Luke which she hadn't been able to make her peace with was the idea that she would somehow inflict real harm on him by subjecting him to the whims of the curse. But the curse hadn't been out for blood in quite the way she'd thought. In fact, she was beginning to wonder if the curse, as she'd believed in it, existed at all.

Ciocia Irenka's words ghosted through her mind. *Bad things happen, a lot of. But around them, good. You look too hard at the bad, you don't know the good.*

Was that what she'd been doing?

She looked back on the last six months through the new lens. There *had* been a lot of bad things, it was true. There had been the fire, the Jaws incident, Ciocia Nelka's terrifying taste in men, getting locked in every cupboard in school, national embarrassment on a waterslide, and all the rest. But around them, just as Irenka had said, there was good. She'd found firm friendship with Orson, and with Fran, she'd finally got back into Neeta's good books after the hot dog debacle, and then there had been Luke.

God, there had been Luke.

He'd set her skin on fire from the very second she'd met him, but over the months she'd begun to see past the leaping flames to the slow and steady burn of something more. Even when trying her best to distance herself from him, she'd seen him. The way he'd gently high-fived Juniper, who now hollered *Miss Mal* at him any time she saw him around school. The way he'd rallied her, and Fran and Orson, pushing through to make the production, well, not *good* exactly, but hugely less catastrophic than it could have been. How his class had flourished under his guidance. Because, as Eva was beginning to learn, Luke was a man who might never be the best at anything himself, but was always able to get the best out of others.

Even her.

Even after everything.

Three hours ago, Eva had pulled up outside Luke's house, ready to tell him that she was prepared to give it a go, that she'd rather have him and lose him than never have him at all. But now that wasn't quite true. Now the last barrier had crumbled away, she wasn't just going to give it a go. She was already gone.

She just hoped like hell that he was too.

She jumped to her feet, pulling on her jacket and grabbing her bag. But Hanna stopped her, calling out her name before she'd even managed to locate the gap in the curtains.

Eva walked back to her sister, her brows pulling together. 'I've got to go.'

Hanna nodded, a slow smile spreading across her face as she reached out to tug the rogue electrode out of Eva's hair with exactly none of Stefan's hair-detangling finesse. And then she gestured to Owen, now holding the curtain open with a strange expression of pride on his face.

'Go get him, Eevs,' Owen said, at the same time as Hanna said, 'Don't get caught on CCTV this time,' and the resulting cackle of her sister's laughter rang in Eva's ears until she was out of the hospital doors and running full pelt to her car.

Chapter Thirty-Two

Eva was exactly three miles down the road when her car stuttered to a stop. She'd noticed the petrol light was on when she was driving to the hospital, in fairness, but she'd been much too focused on getting to Hanna to have paid heed to the insistent blink of orange behind the wheel.

She was regretting that now.

She'd managed to pull half onto the kerb before it had completely given out, and it was just enough to keep the lane clear, but versed as she was in worst-case scenarios, Eva grabbed her bag and got out of the car, walking a few metres clear of it before she dug her phone out and dialled Hanna. She answered after three rings. 'That was quick.'

Eva huffed. 'I ran out of petrol.'

'OK,' Hanna said, a note of amusement in her voice. 'And?'

'And,' Eva started, that familiar swirl of doubt catching at her throat, 'what if it's a sign from the universe?'

'Yeah, it *is* a sign from the universe. The sign says *fill up your car before the petrol light starts blinking*.' Hanna's laugh was low and scratchy , like she was trying to keep the noise down. 'How long have you been driving it with the light on?'

Eva screwed her nose up. Her sister knew her too well.

'Come on, Eevs,' Hanna said, her voice uncharacteristically gentle. 'We said *go get him*, not *try to go get him but then get discouraged by the first obstacle you encounter*. You're a Mallory, fixing problems is in your DNA.'

Eva laughed at that. 'No, *creating* problems is in my DNA.'

'Whatever,' her sister scoffed. 'If you'd never learned to fix a problem in your life, you'd still be stuck back at the first problem you ever had. So fix this one.' There was a noise in the background, and then an unfamiliar voice in the background. 'Anyway I've got to go, the nurse is here with my prescription.' She paused for a moment, and when she spoke again, her voice was quiet. 'Eevs?'

'Yeah?'

She heard Hanna blow out a small breath.

'You've got this.'

And then she hung up before Eva could make any more excuses.

The second number Eva dialled was Luke's. He took much longer to answer, almost the point at which Eva was going to give up on him, and when he answered she heard him breathing hard before he spoke.

'Eva.' It was a hard breath out, barely even sounding like her name. But though it felt significant, words were already primed to tumble out of her, and there was very little she could do to stop them.

'I didn't kill my dad.'

She heard him huff out a little breath. 'Weird opener, but yeah.' Another breath. Almost a laugh. 'I mean … good?'

'It *is* good,' she said, aware that she wasn't making a lot of sense, but enjoying the feeling of saying it out loud too much to care.

I didn't kill my dad.

'So what's up?' Luke said, his breath coming a little more easily now, and for the first time, Eva wondered what he'd been doing.

'I've run out of petrol,' she said, pushing her visions of him having energetic sex with someone else to the far reaches of her mind. 'I was on my way to your house, and I ran out of petrol. I'm stranded.'

He laughed, not unkindly. 'That does sound like you. Anyway, it's a good job you didn't make it. I'm not at my house.'

'What? That's not how it works.' She shook her head, her face pinching into a frown. 'In romcoms, when the character goes to profess their undying love, the other person's *always* in.'

There was a pause before he spoke again, and when he did, his voice sounded different, a weight to it that she couldn't read. 'This isn't a romcom, Eva.'

Her heart dropped, a small knot of dread forming in her throat. 'Right,' she said. She couldn't bring herself to say anything more and she was glad he couldn't see the blush which raced up her cheeks. She's been so full of hope, so distracted by the worry for Hanna and then the huge waves of emotion the day had brought that she'd almost forgotten that she was Eva Mallory: one-woman disaster.

She'd been so focused on the fact that her last barrier had fallen that she hadn't even considered that Luke might not want *her*. He *had* made a swift getaway after the night they'd got trapped in the cupboard. What if he'd changed his mind?

Maybe she had been kidding herself that this wouldn't go wrong too.

Maybe, after everything, it was just too late.

'But,' he said after a beat, his voice different again, 'in light of the words I just heard coming from your mouth, I am now diverting my course to wherever you are.'

And with that, her heart did a full about turn, her chest swelling with hope. Maybe it wasn't too late.

Maybe she would get her happy ending after all.

'Text me your location, Miss Mallory,' he said, and her heart beat faster at the sound of his teacher voice. 'I'm coming to get you.'

'OK.' She was smiling so wide that her cheeks were beginning to ache. 'Bring petrol!'

He didn't answer, just chuckled and hung up, and Eva stood right there on the side of the A58, clutching her phone to her chest with a huge, stupid smile on her face.

She was still smiling twenty minutes later when Luke's car pulled in behind hers, and her heart leapt into her mouth at the sight of him. He was wearing a hoodie and shorts despite the nip in the air, his lower legs streaked with mud which was also splattered across his trainers and up his back. He grabbed a petrol can out of the boot and walked over to her, all sweat and dirt and as beautiful as she'd ever seen him.

'Ah,' she said, past the thunder of her heart in her ears. 'My knight in ... muddy shorts.'

He laughed, that beautiful rumble of a laugh which made him throw his head back. Eva's heart swelled even more, if that were possible.

'I was out on my bike,' he said, his free hand brushing his russet mop out of his face. 'Threw it down a few hills, trying to get out of my own head.' His mouth lifted into a half smile and it made Eva's breath catch.

'Because of me?'

His smile widened infinitesimally. 'Yeah.'

She breathed past the tightness of her throat. 'I'm sorry.'

'I'm not.' His gaze was steady, trained on her, and there was a moment where she nearly blurted it all out, right there on the roadside. But then he took a step away and nodded to the petrol can in his hand, breaking the spell. Eva was glad of it. What she had to say was too precious for the grass verge of an A-road, surrounded by diesel fumes and rubberneckers.

'Come on,' he said, patting the roof of Eva's Corsa. 'Let's get this fella back up and running and then I'll meet you at my house.'

He emptied the can into her fuel tank while Eva searched on her map app for the nearest petrol station – an infuriatingly close 0.2 miles away. Luke left her with a smile which kept her going through filling her car up and driving the mile and a half to his. When she pulled up, he was outside, locking up the small metal shed beside his house.

'So,' he said, wiping his hands down his shorts, an action which couldn't possibly have made them cleaner.

But it did make her smile. 'So.'

Neither of them said anything for a while then, not while Luke unlocked the door and let Eva in first, and not while they both kicked off their shoes at the door, Eva noticing that the space previous filled by the vase she'd broken was now occupied by a small side table with yet more plants on. Her smile widened, and she straightened to see Luke leaning lightly against the kitchen doorframe, the quirk of a grin pulling at his perfect lips.

'So,' he said again, clearing his throat in that very specific, strangely hot way. 'I heard you wanted to declare your undying love to me.'

Time felt like it slowed, in that moment, as Eva tried to hold on to the feeling she had, the feeling of possibility. It felt just like the first evening they'd spent together, giddy and breathless, where all she'd wanted to do was grab hold of this man and never let him go.

Hopefully this time she wouldn't have to.

'Oh yeah?'

He nodded, slowly, eyes burning into her. 'That's what I heard.'

She bit back a smile. 'From who?'

'This woman I know.' One of his shoulders lifted in a shrug. 'A *once-in-a-lifetime kind of girl*, some might say.'

'Some?'

His eyed darkened. 'Me.'

She had to draw in a breath against the burst of warmth in her chest, torn between wanting to make the moment last forever and not wanting to spend another second out of his arms. She took a step towards him and saw his breath hitch in response as the slightest of smiles ghosted over his face.

'What changed?'

Eva shrugged. 'I had some sense slapped into me by a ninety-six-year-old.'

He laughed, the sound warm and vital, and it connected with a point somewhere deep in her chest. 'Literally?'

'No, not literally.' Eva grinned. 'She's ninety-six; she'd have broken something.' She took another step closer. 'I had a talk with my elderly great-aunt who basically told me war stories and then said luck is nonsense and everybody dies anyway.'

'Dark,' he replied, with a shrug, 'but I can't argue with her.'

Eva nodded. 'I paraphrased; it was more uplifting than that.' She thought about Ciocia Irenka, felt a sharp tug in her chest when she thought about the way her great-aunt had flinched at the mention of her sister, and then again when she'd talked about Krzysztof, remembered the deep cut of her brow as she'd recounted her time in Siberia. 'OK, it was quite dark, but she was bang on. She made me think about luck in a totally different way. Told me that if I focus too hard on that bad things in my life that I won't see the good.'

He nodded. 'OK, that *is* good advice.'

'What I'm saying,' she took one more step, now only a foot away from him, 'is that *you're* the good, and I pushed you away because I was scared.'

He visibly swallowed. 'But you're not scared now?'

'Oh no, I'm absolutely shitting myself.' A laugh rushed out of her, the tears which had been glazing her eyes just starting to blur the edges of his face. 'I'm a disaster. I attract the most ridiculous of misfortunes, and being with me will almost certainly subject you to them, too.'

His smile appeared soft through her tears, and he reached out to brush one off her cheek. 'You think I'd change my life to spend thirty hours a week with six-year-olds if I didn't love chaos?'

The contact warmed her. 'I suppose not. But anyway, I

came here to tell you that I would rather have you and lose you than never have you at all.' One hand moved to his chest, feeling the thump of his heart beneath the mud-splattered fabric. 'I came here this morning, actually. To tell you that. But then my sister got rushed into hospital.'

His brows pinched, suddenly serious, but she waved his concern away. 'She's fine, long story. *Anyway*, while we were there I found out I didn't kill my dad. It wasn't the curse and it wasn't me; it was a medical condition. It was nobody's fault. And I'm not even sure if the curse exists anymore, but if it does, I'm not worried about it anymore. Not when I'm with you. You make everything better.'

One of his hands reached for her, his fingers settling around her waist. 'This is quite long-winded, but I'm here for it.'

She moved closer to him, chest to chest, their hearts beating wildly together. Every inch of her skin burned with the contact, but it was more than that. More than the spark of attraction. It was like coming home after a long journey; the sweet relief of being right back where she belonged.

With him.

'I'll give you the short version,' she said, as she slid her arms around his neck, a lump forming in her throat. 'I love you.'

It rushed out of her with the words, everything she'd been afraid of, lost to the air around them, as if love itself was denser.

'And I'm probably not going to kill you,' she continued, through the rush of a giggle, 'although I wouldn't rule it out completely, and I'm sorry for everything. Including in advance, for killing you, if that happens.'

Luke said nothing at first, only reached to trace a thumb

gently along the curve of her bottom lip, those hazel eyes alive. His other hand went to her jaw, fingers lacing into the loose hairs behind her ear. A warm shiver danced down her spine.

'I said before that I'd take my chances,' he said eventually, his voice rough, but every word measured, exacting. 'And I meant it.'

He leaned down to kiss her but she closed the gap first, and as their lips met, the lick of flames hurried through her, settling at a point just behind her breastbone where the buzz had been. It was a gentle kiss, soft and unhurried, but by the time he broke away they were both breathless.

'Eva,' he muttered softly, their foreheads touching.

'What?'

'I love you, too.' She could feel the tiny huff of a breath he blew out, as if all his fears were rushing out of him as well. 'You are amazing and infuriating and catastrophic and funny and clumsy and beautiful, and I love you.' His arms tightened around her, and when he kissed her again it was deeper, the low rumble of a growl vibrating though his chest. 'I'd take you to bed right now if I didn't have to shower half of Otley Chevin off myself.'

She backed off a little way, just enough to look him in the eye while her thumbs hooked into his belt loops, pulling his body into hers. 'I could be persuaded to have a shower.'

She saw the moment the realisation landed, his eyes burning into her all of a sudden as his hands traced her sides. And then they were moving, as one, kicking off socks and shrugging out of layers, teeth clashing as they punctuated their dance with kisses from the strangest of angles.

He reached to turn on the shower, accidentally pushing her half-naked bottom onto the scorch of the towel radiator and the shriek which burst out of her was so loud that it made them both laugh, the sound of it lost to each other's mouths, swallowed up by kisses.

By the time they stepped under the flow of the water Eva was aching for the feel of him against her. It had been less than two days since she'd last seen him naked, and she hadn't forgotten a single detail: not the slope of his shoulders, nor the cut of his abs covered with that fine trail of hair which darkened and curled in the shower's spray. She admired him like a work of art, this beautiful man naked in front of her. And most of all, she noticed the way he looked back at her with all the heat, all the yearning she felt reflected in his eyes.

There was a small shelf in the corner of the shower and he eased her onto it, his fingers gripping her thighs as bottles of shampoo and shower gel clattered to the floor. When he kissed her again there was an urgency to it, the slide of his tongue in her mouth igniting sparks of raw need as she hooked her heels around his hips, fingers knotting into his hair, body aflame. And when he pushed inside her, they both moaned, a shared cry of pleasure which echoed off the wet tile of the shower walls.

It was everything, all at once. It was equal measures dirty and pure: bitten off curses muttered into the crook of her neck and gentle words whispered in her ear. It was the rough grip of his fingers on her skin, a finger stroked lovingly across her cheek. It was the look of absolute adoration in his eyes, promises woven into the rhythm of his mouth on hers. And it was her name on his lips as she shuddered against him, eyes clenched tight as they held on to each other for dear life.

And when they tumbled, still a little damp, into Luke's bed, she found her place there too, nestled into the warmth of his arms without a care in the world. In fact, as she eventually felt herself falling towards sleep, her body heavy and blissfully sore, Eva felt something that she wasn't sure she ever had before.

She felt like the luckiest woman alive.

Chapter Thirty-Three

'Does this feel a bit like before you played for the Queen?' Eva asked Orson, passing him a cup of tea, and he chuckled in response and accepted it with a smile.

'Oh, this is much worse.' He blew steam off the top before taking a thoughtful sip. 'She was charming, and very complimentary.'

Fran nearly fell off the table she was perching on. 'You *met* her?'

He chuckled again. In the three months the four of them had been working on the production, they'd all become close, and it made Eva's heart sing to see that Fran adored Orson just as much as she did.

'We all did,' he said, beaming with pride. 'She had a backstage tour of the auditorium.'

Fran was gazing at him like he was a celebrity, eyes wide. Fran, like Eva, had only ever worked in schools, so Orson and Luke's glamorous former lives were always a source of great interest for them. Particularly now, as they were all trying to

329

distract themselves from the fact that their first performance was less than two hours away.

'That's amazing,' Fran said, a bashful smile taking over her face. 'You've literally performed for royalty and my biggest claim to fame is making these costumes.' She gestured to the table behind them, where four of the most ridiculous outfits Eva had ever seen were laid out.

'Speaking of which,' Eva said, downing half her tea in one long gulp. 'Do we want to get them on now, before any of the kids are dropped off?'

Luke huffed a breath from behind her. 'I still can't believe I agreed to this.'

Eva turned to look at him as he eyed the table with suspicion, smiling to herself as she did. It had been three days since he'd rescued her from the roadside. Three days since she'd kissed him in his hallway.

Three days since her life had changed, in the very best of ways.

She had found herself, that morning, looking forward to the future, a feeling which was almost totally alien to her, but also completely wonderful. She was trying to focus on the good, just like Ciocia Irenka had told her, and she'd been surprised to learn just how much good there was, now she was actively seeking it out.

There was still a lot of bad, of course. Things hadn't changed that much. Only that morning Eva had managed to slice open her palm on a broken box lid. Mrs Abbott had patched her up as best she could with Steri-Strips and gauze, but there was a decent chance Eva would be visiting A&E again before the night was over. It hadn't seemed so bad, though, after she'd loped through into the year one classroom at lunch, holding out her injured paw to Luke, and he'd pulled her into a warm hug.

Forgetting her lunch on Monday hadn't felt as catastrophic either after Fran reached into her desk drawer and offered Eva a choice of three different emergency noodle pots.

And only that morning she'd gone into the art cupboard and seen a single sheet of pristine grass green display paper sitting on top of the still slightly crumpled pile of pale green. She still absolutely took it as a sign from the universe, but while in the past she would have seen it as a taunt, this time she imagined that the universe was whispering to her, showing her a small memory of how it all started. Of how Luke had kissed her against the old brown door and changed everything.

She couldn't wait to see how things would go from here, how different her life could be now that she'd crawled out from underneath the overwhelming weight of guilt. She was so excited to see where she'd be in a year, or five years, or twenty years if she kept looking for the good and reaching for the things that she wanted.

She couldn't wait to spend a lifetime with the man that she loved, to bask in the glow of being happy, finally, after all this time.

Plus she really, *really* couldn't wait to see him in his costume.

'How come I have to be the daffodil?' he asked, poking the giant papier-mâché hat with thinly veiled suspicion.

'Because you're the tallest,' Fran replied, with an easy smile that Eva was quite sure must be suppressing a giggle. 'You're the daffodil, Eva's the crocus and I'm the snowdrop. We're the cornerstones of the *The Great Springtime Musical*.'

He blew a breath out. 'What about Orson?'

Orson didn't have even half of Fran's composure and was laughing so hard that he had to wipe away tears.

'Orson played piano for the Queen,' Fran replied, in a matter-of-fact voice that Eva had often heard her use on the children, 'so he gets to wear a suit. Have you ever performed for royalty?'

Luke mumbled something to himself that none of them could quite hear and gathered the daffodil costume into his arms.

At that, Fran's held-in giggle finally surfaced. 'Didn't think so.'

When they regrouped in the year five classroom a few minutes later they were each in their costumes, bent over with laughter at how ridiculous they looked. Well, all of them except Orson. He was looking dapper in a pea-green suit that Eva had sourced from the local charity shop. Dapper-ish, anyway. He did look a little bit like a holiday camp rep.

'You'll get used to it,' Eva said to Luke, through the wheeze of her laughter. 'Looking like a doughnut is par for the course at our end of school. On World Book Day last year Neeta convinced me to come as the piece of cheese from *The Very Hungry Caterpillar*.'

'I remember that!' Orson took his glasses off to more thoroughly wipe the tears of laughter from his eyes. 'Mrs Abbott was the sausage. Sternest sausage I've ever seen.'

And then, as if saying her name had summoned her, Neeta herself appeared in the doorway, flanked by Ross Drummond.

Neither batted an eyelid at the three staff members dressed as giant flowers.

'Eva, Luke, could we borrow you for a minute, please?'

Eva glanced at Luke, who was looking back at her, eyes wide and ringed with concern.

'My office, please,' Neeta said, already turning to stride back down the corridor on her striking seafoam wedges.

Eva and Luke shuffled after her as best they could in their cocoons of papier-mâché and craft cotton. At one point Eva tripped over her own feet and Luke caught her without a word, pushing her back up until she found her balance. She smiled at him as her heart skipped merrily in her chest. She'd never been rescued by a daffodil before.

They reached Neeta's office and took their places at the table, Eva's throat tightening as she did. She'd given up trying to predict how these meetings with Neeta would go, though experience had taught her to err on the side of caution.

'I won't keep you long,' Neeta said, hands linked in front of her, her expression giving nothing away. 'I know you've got a big night ahead.'

Eva nodded, though she wasn't sure that an answer had been required.

Ross sat up a little straighter, his red tartan blazer falling open. 'We just wanted to be the first to congratulate you,' he said, and as he finished, his face broke into a huge smile which tugged at his eyes and the corners of his mouth.

Eva and Luke shared a look. They hadn't told a soul that they were together, least of all Neeta, and they'd been very careful not to get up to any funny business on school grounds. Apart from the whole sex in the PE shed situation, *obviously*.

Oh God, what if Neeta knew about the sex in the PE shed situation?

Neeta continued talking, perfectly oblivious to the roar of panic in Eva's throat. 'We're all very excited about watching the show, but at this point it won't have any effect on the decision by the arts council.'

Relief flooded Eva's chest for a moment before it was replaced by a new wave of anxiety. *The arts council.* That must mean the conversation was about the performing arts accreditation. But if the performance wouldn't have any effect on the outcome, did that mean they hadn't done it? It seemed unlikely to be the case, given the size of the smile on Ross's face, but—

'As of this morning,' Ross blurted, completely unable to curb his enthusiasm, 'Burton Lane is officially the newest StageMark accredited school.'

What?

They'd actually done it?

Eva's brain immediately started down its usual track of second guessing, until she felt the slightest press of Luke's knee against hers under the table, and it was as comforting as if he'd reached out and taken her hand.

'The assessor popped in on your dress rehearsal the other day and was blown away,' Neeta said, looking between the two of them with an expression of pure pride. 'She particularly commented on the collaborative effort of the adults and on the general feeling of joy in the room. Said you never stopped smiling, children and adults.'

Eva nudged Luke's knee back in response to that. The assessor must have come early in the rehearsal, cause Eva was very definitely not smiling by the end. She heard Luke disguise a giggle as a cough.

'And,' Neeta continued, smoothing a strand of glossy black hair back into place, 'I think that joy has stemmed from the two of you.' She looked between them for a moment or two before focusing her attention on Eva. 'Eva.'

There was a weight to it. Eva sat straighter than she ever had in her life, even under the weight of her giant crocus head.

'When I said that I thought you two were the most musical staff members, that wasn't quite the truth. I've known about Orson Myrtle's past career since I moved to Burton Lane, and when Ross came to me with the idea for this music project, he was the first person I thought of. But I didn't want to burden him.' Her matte-red lips curled in a smile, wistful and knowing at the same time. 'But you didn't burden him. You made him feel useful again. After he lost Jules he was…'—she paused, weighing her words—'adrift. You brought him back to shore.'

Warmth settled in Eva's chest, the nip of tears rushing to her eyes. Orson had been her salvation every bit as much as she'd been his. She'd had no idea, on that first day she'd shuffled awkwardly into his classroom, how important he'd become to her – to all of them. She'd been hunting for a husband, but it had been finding a friend the real catalyst for change in her life.

'And Luke,' Neeta said then, shaking Eva from her thoughts. 'We agreed that we'd review your contract at the end of the academic year, but I've seen what I need to see,'

Luke stiffened beside her and in the silence of the room Eva could hear him swallow. She nudged his knee with hers again.

Neeta sat back in her chair as she considered him. 'I don't mind if my staff members make mistakes,' she said, after a beat. 'I'm more interested in how they work to rectify them. I've seen that in you. Tenacity. Adaptability. Resilience.' Her fingers laced together, the heels of her hands resting on the table. 'The permanent position is yours if you want it.'

Eva could feel the long breath Luke pulled in in every bone of her body, felt him straighten beside her before he reached a hand across the table.

'I would love it,' he said simply, emotion tugging at his words, and Neeta beamed in response, reaching for his hand and shaking it firmly.

'You will be an asset to our school,' she said, with a sure nod of her head, gripping his hand a moment or two more as she said, carefully, 'You *are* an asset to our school.'

Luke's thank you was barely audible, and upon hearing the scratch in his voice when he said it, Eva let her leg rest against his – the nearest thing she could think to holding him. She wasn't proud of much in her life, but she was proud of this, of him, of everything they'd achieved. She thought of her life so often in terms of the curse, but this, all of it, had been a blessing.

'So,' Ross said, in that rumble of a Scottish accent, 'I think you have the small matter of a whole school production to see to?'

They all stood as Neeta did, Eva and Luke thanking her and Ross as they shuffled to the door, their oversized flower heads occasionally clattering together as they moved.

'I knew you'd work well together,' Neeta said quietly as she turned to close the door behind them, and as she did, they could just see the faintest of smirks pulling at her scarlet lips.

Eva whipped around in shock, finding Luke already

looking back at her, one eyebrow raised. 'Did we...' she started, but Luke had the words before she could find them.

'Get played?' His giant flower head tilted to the side. 'Yes.'

'Neeta set us up on purpose?'

He smiled, broad and bright. 'She's a very efficient woman.'

Eva laughed; she couldn't help it. 'I'm not even mad.'

'Same,' he replied, and even dressed as an enormous flower he made prickles of heat scatter across her skin.

'You're the hottest daffodil I've ever seen,' she whispered, quietly, so that Neeta and Ross couldn't hear her through the door.

Luke laughed out loud, shrugging as best he could under the weight of his outfit. 'I mean, I should hope so, but thanks.'

'Come on,' Eva said, her heart singing, 'let's go tell the others our news.'

And they set off walking together down through school, the occasional brush of their hands against each other lighting small sparks as they did.

Past the art cupboard, their secrets lingering among the stacks of paper and tubs of half-used glue.

Past the staff room where Eva had felt the full force of his wrath for the first time, a part of her still flinching every time she thought of the rip of embarrassment she'd felt at the sound of the spoon clattering into the steel sink.

Past the old brown gloss of the year-one classroom door, which Eva had memorised every last dent and ridge of at this point.

And down, further, to Orson Myrtle's classroom, where their colleagues – their *friends* – would be waiting, anxious, for them to get back.

After all, they had a show to put on.

Chapter Thirty-Four

Three years later

E va watched from the wings as Luke strode out onto the stage, admiring him out of habit as he addressed the audience. She'd heard his speech so often that she knew by the reactions of the audience which part he'd reached, even when she couldn't hear his words.

They were a well-oiled machine at this point. It was all muscle memory: the props, the cues, the occasional cajoling of a reticent pupil out onto the stage. Eva barely had to think about it.

After all, this was now the fourth year that they'd been working on Neeta's increasingly elaborate performance ideas. The end-of-year talent show that they'd pulled together in the wake of their uproarious success with the objectively terrible springtime musical had been such a hit with the parents that they'd had requests to do it every year since.

Though the talents that they'd had to work with had often been somewhat thin on the ground, the audience never seemed to care. Eva thought sometimes that they actually preferred when it was bad. It made the show much funnier, and all the more endearing, she supposed.

On stage, Luke finished his speech to a small round of applause, and then went out to the wings on the other side to collect the first act.

Juniper, now in her final year at Burton Lane, was opening the show. She was wearing headphones and had her eyes clamped shut, but she was standing on the stage nonetheless, the spotlight bouncing rays off the neon pink tambourine in her left hand.

As Luke left the stage, the music began, timed to the music playing simultaneously in Juni's headphones, and her whole face lit in delight as the beat dropped. At that, she became a blur of motion, shaking her tambourine just off time to the beat, dancing and whirling, her free hand flapping in unbridled joy as she moved on the stage.

The rhythm was like a heartbeat, and it made Eva's hand go to the hollow beneath her collarbone, fingers brushing the small bump under the skin. The twins had been screened for cardiomyopathy soon after Hanna's trip to hospital, and while it turned out that Hanna didn't have the condition, Eva was not at all surprised to find that she did.

'Just my luck,' she'd told Dr Cheng, who'd delivered the news, and the doctor had shaken her head firmly in response.

'On the contrary,' she'd said, with a smile. 'This test might just have saved your life. That makes you pretty lucky in my book.'

And Eva did feel pretty lucky these days. Most of the time, anyway.

She'd had an operation to fit an implantable defibrillator a few months after that, and someone had called her a very lucky woman then, too. She hadn't argued that time, and she'd had the thought many a time since, her fingers tracing the outline of the device beneath the skin of her chest.

She was doing the same thing now – finding the edges. It soothed her, knowing it was there, should the worst happen. The device hadn't fired yet. Perhaps it never would.

On stage, Juniper's song was coming to an end, and she scampered off stage into the arms of her support worker while the hall erupted in applause, parents, teachers and siblings rising from their seats in an ovation that Juni could neither see nor hear. Perhaps someone would tell her about it later, not that Eva supposed that it mattered. The joy of being lost in her favourite music, to dancing as she did without a care in the world would mean much more to the youngster than any amount of applause.

Two girls with trumpets came on next, squeaking their way through 'When the Saints Go Marching In' with entirely misplaced confidence, and Eva looked over at Luke in the wings opposite. He was herding together a small group of year-ones in sheep costumes as they prepared for their appearance in a comedy skit that a few of the year six boys were performing. Once they were all together, he crouched to their level, talking to them in a low voice with a very serious expression on his face.

Once his pep talk was done, he caught Eva's eye over the stage and grinned, making her chest flood with warmth. He'd blossomed since taking up his permanent position at Burton Lane, and she thought, not for the first time, how good he was, how important to both her and the school. How many little minds he'd helped shape. Heal. Inspire.

She couldn't be prouder.

She heard a pointed cough and turned to see her TA sitting just out of sight of the audience at the front of the stage, clipboard in hand. Mrs Abbott had taken the production reins from Orson when he'd retired two years ago and though she had still yet to soften even an inch, every single production they'd done since had gone off without a single hitch. Whether it was because Mrs Abbott was so organised or because all of the adults and many of the children were a little scared of her, Eva couldn't say.

Either way, as always, she was glad to have Mrs Abbott in her corner. She wasn't a replacement for Orson, but another thing entirely. Something special all of her own.

And Orson, now he'd finally retired, had taken to going travelling at a moment's notice, just as he and Jules had always said they would. As a leaving present for his first trip, Eva had presented him with a half size photo of Jules, in a smaller, lighter frame. *Travel Jules*, she'd called it, and Orson had been so touched by the gift that he'd hugged her tightly and held on for a long time.

He was currently on an extended tour of Scandinavia, and from the postcards he'd been sending, looked to be having an absolute riot of a time. Eva kept the postcards in a joyful display on her fridge, each one signed *love, Orson and Jules xx*.

In between destinations, he was around. Since the first Christmas he'd spent at Sylvia's he'd just become one of the family, and they'd welcomed him with open arms. Eva often found him playing cards with Stefan, talking about music with Owen, or at her house, drinking a beer with Luke. Once she'd walked into her mother's house to find him sitting on the sofa with Ciocia Nelka, shouting the wrong answers at an episode of *Catchphrase*.

Ciocia Irenka would have been proud.

But, after Irenka's wildly dramatic spate of near-death experiences, when she actually did die it was a quiet affair, three weeks shy of her ninety-ninth birthday. She slipped away peacefully in her sleep one night with no fuss nor warning, and when Sylvia had found her the following morning, she had her rosary beads in one hand and the faintest of smiles on her face.

They buried her on the hill beside Tomasz, up high, away from the beach. She always did hate the sand.

And though Ciocia Nelka, herself now comfortably into her nineties, missed her older sister terribly, the family had gone to great lengths to keep her occupied. At some point, by way of distraction, Hanna had taught her to text, and now everyone in the family randomly received the most delightfully weird messages from her. Luke in particular was a great fan of Nelka's messages, and would always chuckle with delight when they came through, his low vibration of a laugh that Eva felt deep in her chest.

She could hear the rumble now from over the other side of the stage. When she looked up, there he was, leaning lightly against a box of props as he watched the sheep sketch draw to a close and laughing with his whole heart. The heart that was hers now.

The sheep sketch was followed by a tap dance, and then a surprisingly good gymnastics display which was met by gasps from the audience, and one solitary shriek of joy. Eva followed the shriek to see Fran right there in the audience, bouncing her ten-month-old daughter on her lap. And beside her, her husband of two years: Justin the accountant.

They'd met quite by chance, some six months after Eva's date with him, and fallen madly and almost immediately in love. Eva had been thrilled. They made a beautiful family.

The gymnastics display ended with a bang, and then Neeta was on the stage, a vision in plum silk and rose gold. She was giving her standard speech, about how hard the children had worked, how proud they had made the school, how the whole community wished them well on the next stage of their educational life.

She spoke about the staff, their unending commitment, the many different roles they played in a day, and how proud she was of each and every one of them.

'My particular thanks', Neeta was saying, 'go to Mr and Mrs Mallory, for the incredible work they have put into this production, and into all the productions we have in school. They make a great team.' She held a hand out to each of them and they joined her on the stage. And as the children began to sing their final song, Eva's eyes went to her husband while her fingers grasped the pendant hanging on a chain around her neck: a habit.

It was exactly one half of Tomasz's wedding ring.

Sylvia gave Eva the ring soon after she and Luke got together, but Eva had never quite made her peace with giving it to Luke, however much she'd wanted to marry him. It had never seemed quite fair to her that they would have that last piece of her father all to themselves. So instead, she'd found a jeweller who was able to melt it down and recast it into two tiny heart pendants, one for each of the twins.

It felt a million miles from the old cursed ring now, more like her own good-luck charm, the gold bright, burnished by a thousand touches of her fingers. It was a little piece of her father which was always with her.

So he was right there when she came round from her operation, pressed into her palm as her eyes fluttered open. He was right there when Luke dropped to one knee on the icy ground below the Christmas Ferris wheel, two years to the day after the flying sky monster had stolen Eva's glove. He was there right now, listening to the children butcher the farewell song so completely that half of the audience were crying with pride and the other half with laughter.

Now that she no longer felt guilty for her father's death, Eva was able to get on with the quieter business of missing him, plus of course the important task of making him proud.

And she honestly believed that he would be proud. After all, she'd come a long way.

Did she break the curse? Not in the way that she'd imagined she would. Instead she had slowly learned to look for the good, just as Irenka had told her she should. She was just as unlucky as she ever had been in real terms, but she had tried her hardest to let those things slide, to give no weight to them, to laugh in the face of disaster.

She'd learned to count her blessings, and it had turned out that her blessings were many: her family, crazy as they were, her friends, her job, her husband, particularly when he was being Music Luke which was still her very favourite thing in the world.

And most of all, her life, just exactly as it was, exactly as it had *always* been: the good and the bad coming together to make her *her*.

Eva Mallory.

The luckiest unlucky woman in the world.

Acknowledgments

Thank you so much for reading Eva's journey.

It was inspired by my own luck — the Dyson curse — which has been a running joke in our family for a long time. While it's true that I do encounter more than the average amount of minor inconveniences, on the whole I have learned to look for the good, and I know that I have a lot to be grateful for.

After all, I get to share my books with the world. And these are the people who helped make that happen, and who I would particularly like to thank:

Everyone at One More Chapter, particularly my lovely editor, Jennie. It takes a village to create a book and you're the best village around. Thank you for believing in my ideas and bringing them to life in such an amazing way. I still can't quite get over the fact that my stories have been turned into actual real books that people can read and it's all because of you. Thanks also to Dawn Cooper for the cover illustration of dreams.

Amanda, my absolute legend of an agent. I'd thought that by my second book I might know a bit more about publishing. Long story short, I still don't, but *you* do, and I'm forever grateful for that. Thank you for guiding me through the ups and downs, for the overexcited brainstorming sessions, and for occasional showing me your dog on video calls.

Charlotte and Clare, my friends and education consultants. You know about all the bits of school that I don't, and your input was vital for writing beyond phonics and snotty noses. Thank you for helping me make Burton Lane School come to life, and beyond that, for everything, always.

My colleagues and friends in school for making my day job a constant source of inspiration and humour. There aren't many jobs where you'll hear lines like 'Lobsters are NOT weapons' or 'Put. The. Banana. DOWN' on a daily basis, but honestly it gives me life. Thank you for being your brilliant, ridiculous selves. These characters weren't based on any of you, but I won't say anything if you tell people that they are.

The children I support at school who helped to inspire the character of Juniper. You have main character energy, honestly, but it wasn't that kind of book.

My writing clan on Twitter. It can be quite a lonely journey writing a book, but I know I always have somewhere to go to vent frustrations, or to celebrate wins, or to trade Backstreet Boys gifs. I am grateful for all of you, every day.

My real-life friends, neighbours and extended family. Thank you for asking how the writing's going, for shouting about my books, for recommending them to your book clubs and for passing them on to your friends/sisters/children/office mates/yoga instructors. It matters.

Carey, for buying a bazillion copies of my books for everyone you've ever known.

Laura and Rog, for the Thai takeaways and games nights. Essential to the writing process.

Amy, for everything. I promise I'll make you a baddie in the next one.

My parents, for your unwavering support and unbridled optimism. When I tell you I've got good news it's never going to be that someone's making a film of my books but I love that you always believe it could be.

And finally, Paul, and Phoebe, and Finn. For all the things. For not giving me too much hassle when I wrote most of this book on holiday, and generally, always, for being you.

Read on for an extract from Lily Bennett's Bucket List

What would Lily Bennett do?

This is the question Lydia Grey finds herself repeatedly asking ever since she discovers Lily's bucket list at the bottom of her shopping trolley. Lily clearly knows how to live life and it's about time Lydia started to live hers. And what better start than to tick off all Lily's life-long dreams . . .

Available now in ebook, paperback and audio

Chapter One

Lydia Grey had become so accustomed to bad dates that she didn't even flinch at the unexpected warmth of someone else's tongue in her mouth.

The man smelt nice enough, fresh and masculine, and he kissed with a vigour which she was sure came from a place of passion, but something about the rhythm of his movement and the firm grip of his hand on her shoulder left her cold. His name was Matt, or maybe it was Mark – she wasn't sure. He'd introduced himself, of course, but Lydia had been so distracted that she'd only half heard him.

Because Matt-or-Mark had a strange quirk in one of his eyebrows, and from the very beginning Lydia had not been able to take her eyes off it.

The hairs seemed to change direction somewhere in the middle, growing straight upwards right at the apex of the arch before falling back into a taper as would be expected. It gave him a strange expression: one of perpetual intrigue, perhaps with an underlying note of something more sinister. And, quite unfortunately, that one unruly eyebrow seemed to be the only thing about him in which Lydia had any interest at all.

He'd talked almost solidly about himself for somewhere close to an hour, but Lydia had zoned out after a minute or two, making sure to nod at what felt like the appropriate times, and occasionally muttering, 'Absolutely,' followed by a small sound. Something like *Merp*, or *Mart* maybe. Something she hoped was vague enough to fall anywhere between *Matt* and *Mark*, as she'd forced her expression into a smile and tried to ignore the shrink of her shoulders away from the casual arm he'd wrapped about them.

Lydia probably should have asked him to repeat his name when she didn't hear it the first time, but she hadn't. She'd been much too distracted by his jaunty eyebrow.

And when he'd leaned in to kiss her a few minutes ago, that damn eyebrow was all she could think about.

This was the way it always happened for Lydia.

Every date.

Every man.

They were fine, until they weren't, the slight curl of her lip away from her teeth almost imperceptible as she noticed things about them. Small things, usually. Small, sometimes tiny details which all added up to mean one crucial thing: that Matt-or-Mark was *not* the man Lydia really wanted to be kissing.

He pulled away from her at that point, his eyes opening slowly as the hint of a smile pulled at his lips. 'Wow,' he said, roughly. 'What are you doing to me?'

She couldn't begin to say. She wasn't sure she'd been doing anything at all.

But she plastered a smile on her face that she hoped looked genuine and shrugged. He seemed to take her silence as contentment, and she forced herself to relax as he leaned back into her. She tried to go with the flow, tried to mentally will herself into feeling something, and when very little feeling arose in return, a small sigh escaped into Matt-or-Mark's open mouth before she could hold it back.

His lips tightened then, into the whisper of a smile, and she felt his free hand move to the curve of her hips and tighten, his grip possessive in a way she wasn't sure she liked at all. Because Lydia Grey had already promised her life to a man, in the presence of God and both of their families, and she was not a woman who easily went back on a promise.

She didn't like the word *divorce*, but she couldn't deny that it had become easier to say over the passing months.

The first time had been like a knife twisting up into her gut.

'So you want a *divorce*?' she'd gritted out, the swell of her tears cutting off the word before the final syllable.

And all it had taken was a single nod to undo her completely.

Adam Grey had been her first love, her soulmate, her best friend for more than half their lives, and with one small nod he'd burned two decades of their shared history to the ground.

But that was a year and a half ago now, and though Lydia had promised their daughter that she would move on, there was no doubt in her mind that she was still absolutely and completely in love with her husband.

Ex-husband.

Urgh.

Lydia had ugly-cried in the departure lounge with her daughter only a few weeks previously, wiping tears from her cheeks with the cuff of her lambswool cardigan as she clung to her daughter with her spare arm.

'It's only six months, Mum,' Ollie had said, sliding her overstuffed rucksack to the ground as she wrapped lean arms tightly around Lydia. 'I'll be back before you know it.'

And with that, Lydia's arms had tightened too. 'I'll miss you, Ol.'

'I know.' Ollie's lips had tugged into a smile. 'But do you know what would distract you?'

'Olivia, no.'

'Come on, it's been over a *year*.' She'd emphasised that last word, as if a year were a long time. It had passed in a heartbeat.

Lydia had taken a sharp breath in. 'I love him.'

'I know,' Ollie had said, pulling back from the embrace and setting both hands firmly on her mother's shoulders. 'But he's moved on. You should too.'

Lydia's voice had strained through the stranglehold of her grief. 'I'm not ready.'

'Try,' Ollie had said simply. 'For me?'

And Lydia had nodded her agreement, although in reality she couldn't think of a single thing worse than dating a man, any man at all, who wasn't Adam.

And yet here she was, currently on a date with a man who definitely was not Adam.

Matt-or-Mark pulled away then, planting one last kiss on her lips before dragging his up the side of her neck and whispering hoarsely into her ear.

'I'll be right back.'

Lydia watched as he headed off down the small corridor

that led to the toilets, the hitch of his swagger making his stride dip now and again. He was tall, maybe even taller than Adam, and the shirt he was wearing pulled here and there as it navigated the swell of a muscle. He definitely looked like a man who took care of himself.

He would have been very appealing indeed, had it not been for that one quirky little eyebrow.

She pulled her phone from her bag, hoping to see a message from her daughter as she unlocked the screen, even though she knew full well that it was the middle of the night where Ollie was now.

She thought about escaping while she could. She'd done that on a date before, though she hadn't been particularly proud of herself. But she'd promised Ollie that she would try, and she'd meant it. And, if she thought about it objectively, Matt-or-Mark wasn't the worst man she'd dated in the last few weeks. In fact, he was probably the best.

Better than the first man, whose name Lydia hadn't even caught, so distracted had she been by his inexplicable scent of garlic sausage.

Better than the second, who'd been Ollie's age, *if that*, and who had talked about cougars in a manner that had somehow been simultaneously childlike *and* predatory.

The third hadn't even bothered to take his wedding ring off. He didn't deserve a place in the rankings.

And all of them were infinitely better than John, the man she'd escaped from, who sent her overly emotional text messages on the hour, every hour, for six full days after their single incredibly brief date. He'd had something about him, a strange vibe that had sent a chill down Lydia's spine, and she'd seized the first opportunity she could to get the hell out of there.

In fact, Lydia thought, comparatively speaking, Matt-or-Mark was not that bad a prospect at all. Her mother might even like him.

As much as Agata Pearson ever liked anyone, of course.

Lydia loved her parents, but she loved them much more when she didn't have to live with them. She was a woman within spitting distance of forty, with one failed marriage under her belt, and her mother *never* let her forget it.

She shuddered, thinking back to her last birthday, when Aga had hit the vodka hard and let slip her intricate plans to marry Lydia off to Andrzej – the unbearable son of one of Aga's old friends, and, Lydia had once worked out, possibly her distant relative.

'If we are here on your fortieth birthday,' Aga had boomed, 'and you don't have a half-decent man in your life, Andrzej will take you on a date.'

Just like that. As if she had no choice in the matter. Because even without taking the likelihood of their shared bloodline into account, Lydia very much did not want to go on a date with Andrzej. He made Garlic Sausage Man look good.

Still, the threat of it loomed heavy over her dating life, and she was acutely aware that months had already passed since that day, and nothing much had changed since. She was still a single thirty-nine-year-old who lived with her parents.

Not exactly a catch.

She necked the rest of her wine in one and sighed to herself. Could someone in her position reasonably write off this not-completely-repellent man? She wasn't sure she could. As far as she could see, she had two choices: she could keep drinking until she felt attracted to Matt-or-Mark, or she could go home to her mother.

She chose the first option.

She ordered another glass of wine and had half finished it by the time Matt-or-Mark slid back into the seat next to her, one side of his mouth hitched into a cocky smirk. She smiled back, trying her absolute hardest not to overthink it.

By the time she heard Matt-or-Mark's husky, 'Let's get out of here,' almost an hour later, Lydia was what she would describe as comfortably drunk, and actually having a much better time. She found herself nodding almost enthusiastically at the proposition.

'I'll pay, babe,' he muttered, and Lydia couldn't help the *urgh* which escaped her, but if he heard, he didn't seem to mind.

He tapped his credit card to the reader, allowing a clear view of his name embossed in bold silver across it:

MR MARK DUNN

YES!

Now she thought about it, he did seem more of a Mark than a Matt.

And with that, Lydia downed the rest of her wine in one long gulp, and it gave her just enough of a buzz to look over at Mr Mark Dunn and feel kind of aroused. What was she thinking before? He was a good-looking guy. And he smelt nice. And he paid for drinks, amongst possibly several other qualities that she was not currently able to identify.

What more do I need? she wondered to herself, hopping off

the barstool with rather less dignity than when she had got on it. *He's a good catch.*

And she smiled to herself as she followed him out into the night.

Her mother was going to love him.

Chapter Two

Lydia had rarely moved with such precision as she did in the half-dozen steps it took her to get from Mark Dunn's bed to his bedroom door. She made the whole manoeuvre in one breath, fearing even the slightest exhale might wake him, and even when she was safely through the door she made sure to breathe slowly and carefully, just in case.

In fact, she didn't dare completely fill her lungs until she was a quarter of a mile down the road, trotting precariously on black patent heels which had seemed like such a good idea the previous night, but were now cutting into her swollen feet in all the wrong places. And speaking of places, she wasn't even completely sure where she was.

It all came back to her in flashes, an increasingly blurry montage underscored by the light thumping in her temples: the bar; the taxi ride home; the press of unfamiliar fingers on her hips as they walked through the front door; Mark's perfectly adequate performance in bed; and then that bloody eyebrow staring her in the face as the glare of morning sun woke her up.

She was being dramatic about the eyebrow, she realised that. In truth, she'd quite enjoyed her romp with Mark while it was happening, but she hadn't been able to stop imagining she was with Adam. Not even for a moment.

But Adam was gone, and Lydia was alone.

Alone and lost on the streets of Leeds.

She harrumphed to herself and pulled out her phone, pleasantly surprised that her battery still had life in it. She opened her map app and waited until it had found her location, smiling with relief to find she was far enough out of her way that she was unlikely to accidentally run into Mark again, but close enough that one bus would take her home. She walked the few hundred yards to the stop and plopped down on the bench, sighing at the sudden relief for her feet.

The bus timetable had been graffitied with the most realistic drawing of a penis she'd ever seen, but the column that Lydia was straining to see fell right in the centre of the shaft. She laughed out loud when she noticed.

Every 15 minutes.

Perfect.

The red notification tag on her dating app was the first thing she noticed when she pulled out her phone again, and she suddenly remembered ignoring it in the bar. She thought back to the look on Ollie's face at the airport.

Just try, Mum. For me?

Urgh.

She swiped to open and was confronted with a picture of a man's crotch, clad in the tightest gym shorts she had ever seen and the message – *msg back for no strings fun* – followed by a winking face and an aubergine emoji.

Lydia grimaced. She'd promised Ollie that she would try, and she *was*, but every message she got made her feel more and more disillusioned by the already very underwhelming world of internet dating.

She blew out a long breath and was just about to slip her phone back into her bag when it rang, triggering the last remnants of her panic reflex and making her involuntarily fling the damn thing skyward. By some minor miracle she caught it in two fingers mere seconds before it hit the ground, still muttering swear words as she swiped to answer.

'Lyds!' the voice on the other end exclaimed, completely ignoring the barrage of obscenity coming out of her mouth. 'Where the bloody hell are you?'

Antoni Zielinski had been born in the same ward of the same hospital as Lydia, only twenty-three days later – a fact he brought up often. Their mothers had been best friends as far back as either woman could remember, and so it was perhaps an inevitability that they would end up in each other's lives. Tosiek to some, Tosh to most, he was Lydia's oldest and dearest friend, and a near-constant pain in her arse.

Like right now.

'I'm at a bus stop in Oakwood, actually,' Lydia said, her hangover slipping a note of annoyance into the tone.

Tosh snorted. 'I wasn't actually asking *where* you are. I was asking why you aren't here.'

'Where are you?'

'At your house.'

Lydia's face crumpled in confusion. 'Why are you at my house?

'Why aren't *you* at your house?' He clucked his tongue in disapproval, a habit he'd got from her mother. Lydia made a mental note to tease him about it later. 'You've forgotten, haven't you?'

Lydia's long breath out was almost a laugh. 'I think we've both realised by now that the answer to that is yes. I don't even know what it is that I've forgotten.'

'Your dad's birthday?'

Shit.

His seventieth.

She'd known about it, of course, and somewhere in her mind she vaguely registered Aga's voice telling her not to be back too late as she'd walked out of the door the previous night.

Because of the party.

Shit.

'Don't panic,' Tosh continued on the other end of the line, 'the party isn't actually starting until one, but Ags wanted me to make sure you weren't dead in a ditch somewhere.'

Lydia huffed out a little laugh. Tosh was the only person on the planet that Agata Pearson would allow to call her Ags.

'Anyway,' he said breezily, 'now I've found you, you can make it up to us by picking up a few bits for the party on your way.'

'Which "us" am I making it up to?' Lydia asked, one hand trying to rub the pounding out of her temple.

'It's the royal "us", actually.' He chuckled, and Lydia could clearly see his face in her mind at that moment. She could almost hear the smirk in his voice. 'Just me. Had a bad night with the wee one and forgot my shopping list.' His tone turned apologetic. 'Tried to wing it, but we both know how good I am at winging stuff.'

'Not good.'

His laugh was genuine that time. 'Not good at all.'

'Fine,' Lydia blew out. 'Text me the bloody list.'

'You're an angel! I'll smooth things over with Ags.'

'I'm a grown woman!' Lydia said, indignation creeping into her voice. 'I'm allowed to stay out past—'

But Tosh had already gone.

Lydia sighed to herself and stretched her legs out in front of her as if taking the weight off her feet might magically heal the rubbed-raw parts. She pulled her pocket mirror out of her handbag, wincing when she took in her reflection, all smeared eyeliner and knotty brown hair. She'd always made a big effort to look good, and seeing herself like this in the harsh light of day made her stomach grip into a tight knot of shame.

She wanted to cry, but she didn't. That wouldn't have done anything at all for the eyeliner situation. Instead she found a tissue in the bottom of her bag, mercifully unused, and neatened herself up as best she could, pulling a set of false lashes from where they'd migrated to her hairline and sighing again, this time much more dramatically.

She was too old for this.

Her eyes found the stop for Sainsbury's on the bus timetable, as she was rolling them, and Lydia decided on a whim that she would shop there, rather than the murky haunt of a mini-market that she usually frequented. It would mean getting on another bus afterwards, but it was her dad's birthday, after all, not to mention that every extra minute she spent on her journey was a minute she wasn't being harassed by her mother.

She still had her legs out in front of her when the bus pulled up to the stop, and the moment she finally put her feet back on the ground and stood up, the slice of leather on her toes made her want to cry again.

And maybe she would have if it weren't for the growing queue eyeing her. There was zero chance she would allow herself to get emotional in front of other people. She pushed her tongue up against the roof of her mouth in the way Aga had taught her, staving off the shudder of tears, and plopped down onto the first free bus seat with a small squeak of relief that she couldn't have held in if she'd tried.

The supermarket was mercifully quiet for a Saturday morning, and Lydia kept her head down as she made her way meticulously down the list that Tosh had sent, wondering as she went if he'd actually bought anything at all for this party.

Even thinking the word *party* made her cringe. Her thumping temples had eased back into a milder but more general ache, gripping the top of her skull and the back of her neck. She couldn't think of anything she'd like to do less than spend her Saturday being interrogated by her nearest and dearest.

But she pushed through it, buying sliced meat from the deli counter rather than the cheaper pre-packaged kind, and rooting through assorted packs of bagels to find the poppyseed ones that her father liked.

Her dad would appreciate it. At least, she assumed he would. Not least a hazard of being married to Aga, Steve Pearson had not spoken a full sentence in twenty years.

Lydia had got as far as the pickles and preserves aisle when she heard a sound that made her blood run hot and cold all at once. It was a laugh – quiet at first – that grew in volume with each snicker until she could be in no doubt at all.

Her husband was walking towards her.

Ex-husband.

Urgh.

She tried her best to focus all her attention on the two jars of gherkins she was considering, pulling her chin back so that her hair would obscure the view of her face. Traditional whole gherkins with dill, and the small cocktail-size variety which she secretly preferred but would never have dared admit as much to her mother.

Modern nonsense, Aga had said on the matter once. *Why on earth would I want my ogórki to be smaller?*

Aga had been born in Yorkshire, but English wasn't her first language, and even now there were certain words she would refuse to translate. Lydia hadn't known the English word for gherkin until she was seven. But she was making up for it now, repeating the word over and over in her mind while she froze in place and waited for Adam to pass her by.

Adam was a big believer in keeping up appearances. He couldn't see her like this.

She was acutely aware of his proximity as he got closer and closer and just at the point where he was so near that she could smell his aftershave, she took a deep breath, the familiar scent nipping at her eyes and making her stomach churn and tighten.

And then, from nowhere, she heard a woman's voice reply to him, and her heart dropped like a stone. She'd heard that he'd been dating – Ollie had told her that much – but she hadn't wanted to believe it was true.

Lydia couldn't concentrate on the words the woman was saying, just her bright tone and the smooth drawl of an accent – Spanish perhaps? Something warm and sexy anyway, with a quality that made Lydia want to see the person it came from despite the pull of jealousy at her throat.

Except, just as she thought about turning slightly to try and catch a glimpse of the woman, that accented voice spoke again, just two simple words, but two words that picked Lydia's stone heart from the ground and smashed it into a million pieces.

'Ok, baby.'

And then Adam's reply: 'Thanks, baby.'

Lydia's tongue went to the roof of her mouth again. Adam had never called her baby. Not once in the twenty years they'd been together, and it wasn't even something she'd missed. Not something she'd thought she wanted, but somehow hearing him say it to somebody else made her stomach flip with jealousy.

The love of her life was calling another woman *baby*, and here she was, standing alone in the pickles and preserves aisle trying as hard as she could not to cry.

She held a jar in each hand, her eyes fixed on the curve of one of the lids as she heard Adam and his mystery woman pass directly behind her. She didn't move a muscle, holding her breath until she'd heard them go by.

Except that didn't happen. Instead, their footsteps came to a complete stop.

And then she heard him speak.

'Lyds?'

She took the deepest breath she could manage before turning, her fingers tightening impossibly around the pickle jars as she did. But even then, when she met his eyes, it was all she could do not to drop them.

His hair was cropped shorter than when they'd been together and it made him look younger than he was. Younger and more handsome in a way that made her feel as if she couldn't breathe. As if her heart was physically trying to clamber out of her chest and into his.

But he just smiled amiably, like they were casual acquaintances. As if he hadn't ripped her heart clean out of her chest right around a year and a half ago.

'Oh hey, it *is* you!' His smile didn't seem to crinkle his eyes as much as it used to. 'I almost didn't recognise you in those shoes.'

Lydia forced a laugh, but it came out so loudly, so awkwardly, that she immediately wanted to grab the sound and shove it back in.

'Yeah, I was out last night, so—' She cringed, unable to finish her sentence, and absolutely mortified at the way she must have looked. She'd imagined accidentally running into Adam a hundred times over the last couple of years, but she had always imagined that, when she did, she would look her absolute best. She had never considered that she might encounter him while she was on a full-scale walk of shame.

She felt sick.

'God, sorry, I'm being so rude.' Adam smiled again and held up one hand, his fingers intertwined with the tanned, slender digits of the woman Lydia still couldn't bear to look at. 'This is my girlfriend, Aurora. Aurora, *this*,' he emphasised the word heavily, as if the name itself were an explanation, 'is Lydia.'

Girlfriend.

The word hit Lydia in the stomach like a fist, knocking the wind clean out of her. She didn't say anything for what felt like a long time, and she didn't look up at the woman either, not at first. Not until she heard her speak, and then she couldn't look away.

'*Lee-dyah,*' that velvety voice said, drawing out the first syllable. 'I have heard very much about you. I am so happy to meet you.'

And there was no other word Lydia could find to describe the woman she saw then, but *stunning.*

Absolutely bloody stunning.

She was young, but not awkwardly so, with glossy brown hair which fell forwards over one shoulder almost to her waist, and legs that went on for miles. And, worst of all, from the look of her, not a single scrap of makeup on.

'Nice to meet you,' Lydia muttered, trying her hardest to keep resentment out of her voice as she forced herself to smile at the vision of effortless beauty in front of her. Lydia felt like an ogre in comparison.

But if Adam noticed her tone he didn't react, and when he looked down at Aurora it was with so much adoration in his eyes that it just about tore Lydia's heart in two. He looked different from the man she had known so well, something in his eyes or in his face which she couldn't quite place.

'We're just picking up some snacks and supplies for a hike.' He beamed. 'Aurora's taking me up Scafell Pike tomorrow.'

Lydia couldn't stop the huff of a laugh bursting out of her, but she covered it with a cough. Her husband Adam hadn't even liked climbing the stairs.

'Aurora runs ultramarathons, so it'll be a walk in the park for her,' he continued, Lydia's interjection barely registering with him. 'She's so *adventurous* I sometimes struggle to keep up.'

He laughed then, and Aurora giggled too. Lydia faked a laugh to join in, but inside she was screaming. Who was this man? He certainly wasn't the man she'd married. Had he levelled up somehow, by leaving her? He'd said that the excitement had gone from their marriage, but she hadn't thought he meant *that* kind of excitement.

Had he actually meant that she wasn't adventurous enough for him?

'Anyway, we'd best dash.' His smile was genuine, without even a flicker of regret. 'It was good to see you.'

Lydia nodded, forcing down the churn of emotion in her chest. 'Yeah, same. See you around.'

'Nice to meet you, *Lee-dyah*,' Aurora said with a dazzling smile, and then the two of them were off hand in hand, down the preserves aisle and across into nuts and snacks.

Lydia turned her attention back to the gherkins she was still holding, putting the cocktail-sized ones in her trolley and abandoning the others to the mess of the mid-morning shelves. She needed a win, and if that had to come from lying to her mother so she could eat her preferred style of small pickled cucumber, then so be it.

Insecurity gnawed at her. She'd never considered herself a particularly boring person, but perhaps that was because she wasn't looking closely enough. She was cautious, that much was true, but that had never seemed to be a problem for Adam when they were together. Had he been thinking it the whole time, and just never voiced it? The way he'd dragged out the word *adventurous*...

Urgh.

She'd never forget it.

She swallowed past the lump in her throat and carried on picking up items from Tosh's list, half holding her breath in case she accidentally had her heart shattered again while comparing produce too casually.

But the rest of the shop proceeded without incident, and by the time she reached the checkout, the tightness of her chest had eased down into a low hum behind her breastbone. Nothing more than the background longing that she had grown accustomed to since Adam had left.

She was still thinking about the knot of Adam's fingers around another woman's hand as she loaded her items onto the checkout belt. But then, as she picked the bag of bagels out, she saw something right at the bottom of the trolley that she hadn't even noticed before she'd put them in.

It was a folded sheet of light-purple writing paper, the quality noticeably better than the scraps of envelope or lined paper that were usually left in trolleys. And there was a single line of writing visible at the opening of the fold, a single line that compelled Lydia to pick up the folded paper and slide it neatly into the front pocket of her handbag.

A single line that read:

Lily Bennett's Bucket List

The author and One More Chapter would like to thank everyone who contributed to the publication of this story...

Analytics
Emma Harvey
Maria Osa

Contracts
Georgina Hoffman
Florence Shepherd

Design
Lucy Bennett
Fiona Greenway
Holly Macdonald
Liane Payne
Dean Russell

Digital Sales
Laura Daley
Michael Davies
Georgina Ugen

Editorial
Charlotte Ledger
Federica Leonardis
Laura McCallen
Jennie Rothwell
Kimberley Young

Marketing & Publicity
Chloe Cummings
Emma Petfield

Operations
Melissa Okusanya
Hannah Stamp

Production
Emily Chan
Denis Manson
Francesca Tuzzeo

Rights
Lana Beckwith
Rachel McCarron
Agnes Rigou
Hany Sheikh
Mohamed
Zoe Shine
Aisling Smyth

The HarperCollins Distribution Team

The HarperCollins Finance & Royalties Team

The HarperCollins Legal Team

The HarperCollins Technology Team

Trade Marketing
Ben Hurd

UK Sales
Yazmeen Akhtar
Laura Carpenter
Isabel Coburn
Jay Cochrane
Alice Gomer
Gemma Rayner
Erin White
Harriet Williams
Leah Woods

And every other essential link in the chain from delivery drivers to booksellers to librarians and beyond!